Lakeside Cottage

**Center Point
Large Print**

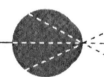

**This Large Print Book carries the
Seal of Approval of N.A.V.H.**

Lakeside Cottage

SUSAN WIGGS

CENTER POINT PUBLISHING
THORNDIKE, MAINE

This Center Point Large Print edition
is published in the year 2005 by arrangement with
Harlequin Books S.A.

The text of this Large Print edition is unabridged. In other
aspects, this book may vary from the original edition. Printed in
Thailand. Set in 16-point Times New Roman type.

ISBN 1-58547-669-2

Cataloging-in-Publication data is available from the Library of Congress.

PART ONE

". . . as you all are aware, the President looks forward to visiting some of our brave troops at Walter Reed on Christmas Eve. It's an opportunity for the President to thank those in our military who have served and sacrificed to make the world a safer place, and make America more secure. He will also give remarks to the medical personnel at Walter Reed and thank them for the outstanding job they do. However, because of the space limitations, it will be an expanded pool. So it will probably just be one camera, and then the correspondents will be able to attend it. . . ."
—The White House, Office of the Press Secretary

"Everybody loves a hero. People line up for them, cheer them, scream their names. And years later tell how they stood for hours in the cold rain just to catch a glimpse of the one who taught them to hold on a second longer. I believe there's a hero in all of us who keeps us honest, gives us strength, makes us noble, and finally allows us to die with pride, even though sometimes we have to be steady, and give up the thing we want the most. Even our dreams."
—Spider-Man 2

One

The ambulance backing into the bay of Building One looked like any other rig. It appeared to be returning from a routine transport run, perhaps moving a patient to the stepdown unit, or a stabilized trauma victim to Lowery Wing for surgery. The rig had its customary clearance tags for getting through security with a minimum of hassle, and the crew wore the usual crisply creased navy trousers and regulation parkas, ID tags dangling from their pockets. Even the patient looked ordinary in every respect, in standard-issue hospital draping, thermal blankets and an O_2 mask.

Special Forces Medical Sergeant Jordan Donovan Harris wouldn't have given the crew a second glance, except that he was bored and had wandered over to Shaw Wing, to the glassed-in observation deck on the mezzanine level. From there, he could view the ambulance bays and beyond that, Rock Creek Park and Georgia Avenue. The trees were bare and stark black against a blanket of snow, ink drawings on white paper. Traffic trundled along streets that led to the gleaming domes and spires of the nation's capital. A fresh dusting of powder over the 147-acre compound gave the Georgian brick buildings of the Walter Reed

Army Medical Center a timeless, frozen, Christmas-card look. Only the activity at the intake bays hinted that the campus housed the military's highest level of patient care.

Although there was no one around, Harris knew he was being watched. There were more security cameras here than in a Las Vegas casino. It didn't matter to him, though. He had nothing to hide.

Boredom was desirable in the life of a paramedic. The fact that he was idle meant nothing had gone wrong, no one's world had been shattered by a motor-vehicle accident, an unfortunate fall, a spiking fever, an enraged lover with a gun. For the time being, no one needed saving. Yet for a medic, whose job was to save people, that meant there was nothing to do.

He shifted his stance, grimacing a little. His dress shoes pinched. All personnel present wore dress uniform today because the President was on the premises to visit ailing soldiers and spread holiday cheer. Of course, only a lucky few actually saw the Commander-in-Chief when he visited. His rounds were carefully orchestrated by the powers that be, and his entourage of Secret Service agents and the official press corps kept him walled off from ordinary people.

So Harris was a bit startled when he saw a large cluster of black suits and military brass exiting the main elevator below the mezzanine. Odd. The usual route for official visits encompassed Ward 57, where so many wounded veterans lay. Today it seemed the tour would include the in-processing unit, which had recently undergone renovations courtesy of a generous party donor.

The visitors flowed along a spotless corridor. Instinctively, Harris stiffened his spine and prepared to snap to, not that anyone would notice whether or not he did. Old habits died hard.

He let himself relax a little. From his glassed-in vantage point, he craned his neck for a glimpse of the world leader but saw only the press and bustle of the entourage, led by the sergeant major of the army. A moment later, a civilian administrator greeted everyone with a wide smile. She looked as gracious and welcoming as a Georgetown hostess. Apparently, her domain was on the itinerary and she appeared eager to point out its excellence.

Harris knew that her name was Darnelle Jefferson and that she had worked here for a quarter of a century. She was fond of telling that to anyone who would listen. Looking at her, you'd never guess what the regulars here knew—that like many civilian administrators, she tended to spend her entire day being a pain in the ass to all personnel and creating a mountain of paperwork to justify her own existence. Still, she looked cheerful and efficient in a Christmas-red dress with the requisite yellow ribbon pinned to her bosom, and the wattage of her smile increased as the impossible occurred. The President separated from the pack and stepped forward for a photo op.

Then, even more surprisingly, Mrs. Jefferson took charge of the tour, leading the group along the wide, gleaming corridor. Two cameramen trolled along beside them, the big lenses of their cameras capturing every movement and nuance for the nightly news. The party stopped off at the first intake room, where a wounded soldier had arrived from another facility. Harris knew that the official photos and film would portray the President with the soldier and his family in an intimate circle around the hospital bed. The pictures wouldn't show the vigilant Secret Service, or the booms and mikes hovering just out of sight.

That's showbiz, thought Harris. He didn't understand how anyone could put up with public life. To have everyone's scrutiny on you was a peculiar sort of torture, as far as he was concerned.

The entourage was on the move again, down the scrubbed hallway toward the Talbot Lounge, one of the newly renovated waiting areas, where a twelve-foot noble fir stood, decked in splendor by one of D.C.'s finest florists. They stopped for more photos. Harris could see flashes going off, but he'd lost sight of the President.

Elsewhere in the same wing, the recently delivered patient lay in an intake room flanked on two sides by wire-embedded glass walls. The transport crew had gone to the main desk to fill out their report, and no hospital personnel had arrived yet to in-process the newcomer. The staff members on duty were probably just like Harris, slacking off as they tried to get a look at the President. The patient lay alone, no family member or friend standing by to comfort him in this strange new world. Some people just didn't have anybody. Harris himself might be a prime example of that, if not for Schroeder. He and Sam Schroeder had been best friends for years, since meeting in a battle zone in Konar Province, Afghanistan. Sam and his family made up all that was important to Harris, and he told himself it was enough.

He took the stairs down to the main level, hoping to get a look at the President's face. He didn't know why. Maybe it was the fact that he'd spent a decade serving this country and another four years at the hospital, keeping people from dying. He sure as hell ought to be able to catch a glimpse of the President up close. A memo had advised that there would be a reception later at the hospital rec center—with the Gatlin Brothers performing—but that was sure to be a mob scene.

A pair of marines in dress blues stood sentinel at the double doors to the unit. Harris gestured with his clipboard and flashed his ID, projecting an air of brisk efficiency. Once inside the unit, he had to act busy or they'd know he was loitering in order to see the President, a practice that was frowned upon.

Harris stopped outside the admittance room where the new arrival lay. He took a chart from the U-shaped holder on the door, flipped up the metal cover and pretended to be studying it.

The sound of footsteps and voices grew louder as the presidential party approached.

". . . new Cardiothoracic Stepdown Unit is equipped

with state-of-the-art monitoring equipment," Mrs. Jefferson explained in broad, grave tones. "It's now our country's leading center of clinical care, research and evaluation . . ." She droned on as though reading from a prepared script, and Harris tuned her out.

The party drew closer. Finally Harris caught a glimpse of the Commander-in-Chief. His expression was set in his trademark look of compassion, one that had endeared him to the nation for two terms. The President and the hospital administrator separated from the group. Darnelle Jefferson led the way toward the in-processing unit where the new arrival lay.

Damn, thought Harris, time to disappear. Quickly—but not too quickly—he slipped into an admit room, connected to the unit by a set of green swinging doors. By looking through the round portals, he could see straight through to the next two rooms. He focused on the new patient through the glass, expecting him to be lying there quiet and alone, probably scared shitless, unaware that the President of the United States was just a few steps away.

Except that the guy wasn't quiet. For a cardiac patient, he seemed awfully busy, sitting up on the gurney, tearing away his mask.

Harris studied the chart he'd grabbed from the rack outside the door. Terence Lee Muldoon. He was a combat vet, a transferee from a U.S. military hospital in Landstuhl, Germany. The chart listed him as twenty-five years old—damn young for heart trouble.

In his time, Harris had seen thousands of cardiac

12

patients. The condition was always characterized by a grayish pallor and palpable look of fatigue.

Not this character. Even from a distance and through two sets of doors, Harris could see that his face was a healthy pink, his movements economical and assured.

At that moment, the entourage stopped in the corridor and the President and Mrs. Jefferson entered Muldoon's room. The glassed-in cubicle was too small to accommodate more visitors, and the bodyguards hovered outside, craning their necks, their gazes constantly on the move, their lips murmuring into their hidden radios. A pair of photographers pressed their camera lenses against the glass. The President greeted Muldoon with a handshake, then moved behind the gurney for the requisite photo op.

There was never a specific moment when Harris decided something was wrong. He never saw a maniacal gleam in the impostor's eyes or heard some sort of evil cackle like in the movies. Real evil didn't work that way. It was all quite . . . ordinary.

Sweet baby Moses, thought Harris.

There was also never a particular moment when Harris decided to take action. Making a decision implied a thought process that simply didn't happen. Harris—and the unsuspecting President—had no time for that. Flipping the silent alert signal on his shoulder-mounted radio, he slipped through the double doors into the next in processing room, adjacent to where the President was. He knew the security cameras were recording his movements, but the stranger next door didn't appear to have noticed him.

Harris refrained from shouting or making any sudden movements. The patient was not yet aware of him, and he didn't want to draw attention to himself. He had to move fast, though, because his movements were going to look highly suspicious to the security cameras. Those watching him were going to think he was a nutcase or worse—a bad guy.

The flow of events unfolded with a peculiar inevitability. Later—much, much later—Harris would watch the videos made by both the security monitors and the press corps, but he would remember none of it.

Seconds before the personnel in the hallway responded to the alert, the patient swept aside the thermal blanket. With his free hand, he yanked away the gown to reveal rows of dynamite duct taped to a body-hugging vest.

"Anybody takes me out," he screamed at the glass wall, "and I go up like the Fourth of July. And I take this whole wing of the building with me." He leaped to the floor and glared at the horrified crowd on the other side of the glass. His fist closed around the igniter, ready to detonate the explosives.

The President stood stock-still. Darnelle Jefferson gave a hiccuping gasp of sheer terror. Harris froze, too experienced to let fear get in the way. He recognized the shield tattooed on Muldoon's forearm. It was the iron falcon and sword of a Special Forces unit.

So they were dealing with a rogue from Special

Forces, as highly trained as Harris himself, a disciplined killer gone awry. The assassin hadn't seen him yet. He was strutting in front of the wire-embedded glass while a dozen firearms were aimed at him.

Harris studied the homemade explosive vest and wondered how the hell the transport crew had failed to notice it. The explosives appeared to be plastic ordnance with an igniter operated by a toggle mechanism secured with more duct tape and connected to wires that would activate the explosives. It would have to be detonated manually, unless there was a secondary trigger he wasn't seeing.

Outside the cubicle, bodyguards and marines broke into action. Honed by countless drills, procedure would be followed to the letter. There would be an immediate lockdown, all units would come to full alert and alarms would shriek across the vast, snowy campus of Walter Reed. Even now, a security squadron was probably surrounding the building.

Mrs. Jefferson made a tiny sound for such a big woman and fainted dead away, taking a Lifepak monitor along with her. It crashed to the floor, startling Muldoon, and Harris was sure he'd spook and ignite the explosives. His left hand, which had been gripping the manual trigger, let go momentarily as he regrouped.

Darnelle had given Harris a seconds-long window of opportunity. Knowing he had a chance was all he needed. It was only one chance, though. If he blew it, they were all toast. Or confetti, more accurately.

15

He burst through the double doors, everything focused on the assailant's trigger hand. His entire body launched itself at the assassin in a single-move tactic, one he'd been trained for but had never used until now.

Muldoon went down, screaming as Harris crushed the man's left wrist to disable his hand. They hit the floor together. Muldoon was shocky from the crushed wrist. That was something.

There was a sound like a rifle shot. Harris felt something hit him like a cannonball. Jesus, had the son of a bitch detonated the explosives?

No, the igniter, Harris realized. The impact had triggered it, but it had misfired. That was the good news. The bad news was, the failed explosion was killing him. His limbs went immediately ice cold as if everything had been sucked out of him. He was aware of movement all around, the President taking cover, the frenzy of highly trained Secret Service men jolted into action. Alarms bayed and someone was screaming. A furious ringing sound blared in his ears. The reek of chemicals seared his throat.

The world dissolved into double images as Harris's consciousness seeped away like the blood on the floor. Sounds stretched out with an eerie echo, as though shouted down a well. "Freeze . . . *freeze, freeze. . . .*" The barked order reverberated through Harris's head. "Nobody move! *oove, oove. . . .*"

Harris's pulse was thready. Lying in a widening pool of blood, he imagined each system shutting down, one by one, a theater's lights going dim after a final performance. He felt himself quiver, or maybe it was the assassin struggling against him. To die like this, he thought, at the President's feet. That just sucked. Offended his sense of propriety. Sure, it wouldn't matter to him after he was gone. It shouldn't matter at all, but somehow it did.

Harris could see his own reflection in the dome of the 360-degree security camera mounted in the ceiling. Blood spreading out like an inky carpet. It always looks worse than it is, he told himself. He said that to his patients all the time.

The swarm descended, a pandemonium of black suits and dress uniforms as the Secret Service came forward to apprehend the crazy and secure the chief executive.

Harris was cold and headed somewhere dark. He could feel himself slipping, falling into a black well.

"Make way," a loud voice barked, the words echoing, then fading. "Somebody get this man some help."

PART TWO

"The best way to escape from a problem is to solve it."
　　　　　—Alan Saporta, American musician

Two

Port Angeles, Washington
Summer

"It is a truth universally acknowledged, that a single woman in possession of a half-grown boy must be in want of a husband." Squinting through her vintage cat's-eye glasses, Mable Claire Newman defied Kate Livingston to contradict her.

"Very funny," Kate said. "You tell me this every year."

"Because every summer, you come back here, still single."

"Maybe I like being single," Kate told her.

Mable Claire aimed a look out the window of the property management office at the half-grown boy and his full-grown beagle, playing tug-of-war with a sock in Kate's Jeep. "Are you at least dating someone?"

"Dating I can manage. It's getting them to come back that seems to be the problem." Kate offered a self-deprecating grin, an almost jaunty grin, just wide enough to hide behind. Men were often startled to discover she was a mother; she'd had Aaron at twenty and had always looked young for her age. And when they saw what a handful her boy was, they tended to head straight for the door.

"They're nuts, then. You just haven't run into the right fellow." Mable Claire winked. "There's a guy staying at the Schroeder place you ought to meet."

Kate gave an exaggerated shudder. "I don't think so."

"Wait until you see him. You'll change your mind." She opened a cupboard with an array of tagged house keys and found the one marked with Kate's name. "I didn't expect you until tomorrow."

"We decided to come up a day early," Kate said, hoping there would be no further questions. Though Mable Claire had known Kate through all the summers of her life, she wasn't ready yet to talk about what had happened. "I hope that's okay."

"Nothing wrong with starting the summer a day early. The housekeeping and yard crew have already been to your place. School out already?" she asked, tilting her head for a better view of Kate's boy through the window. "I thought the kids had another week."

"Nope. The final bell rang at three-fifteen yesterday, and third grade is just a bad memory for Aaron now." Kate dug through her purse, looking for her key chain. Her bag was littered with small notes to herself because she never trusted her own memory. Besides, this made her feel organized and in control, whether or not she actually was. She had a number of projects lined up for the summer. She needed to regrout the downstairs bathroom tile at the cottage. Paint the exterior trim. Not to mention renewing the bond with her son, reinventing her career and finding herself.

In that order of importance? She had to wonder at her priorities.

"So are you going to be all right," Mable Claire asked, "just the two of you in that big old house?"

"We'll be fine," Kate said, though it felt strange to be the only one in the family headed for the lake house this summer. Every year, all the Livingstons made their annual pilgrimage to the old place on Lake Crescent, but recently everything had changed. Kate's brother, Phil, his wife and four kids had relocated to the East Coast. Their mother, five years widowed, had remarried on Valentine's Day and moved to Florida. That left Kate and Aaron in their house in West Seattle, on their own a continent away. Sometimes it felt as though an unseen force had taken her close-knit family and unraveled it.

This summer it would be just the two of them—Kate and her son—sharing the six-bedroom cottage.

Quit wallowing, she warned herself, and smiled at Mable Claire. "How have you been?" she asked.

"Good, all things considered." Mable Claire had lost her husband two years before. "Some days—most days—I still feel married, like Wilbur never really left me. Other times, he seems as distant as the stars. I'm all right, though. My grandson Luke is spending the summer with me. Thanks for asking."

On the form to activate trash pickup, Kate filled in the dates. The summer loomed before her, deliciously long, a golden string of empty days to fill however she wished. A whole summer, all to herself. She could take the entire time to figure out her life, her son, her future.

Mable Claire peered at her. "You're looking a little peaked."

"Just frazzled, I think."

"Nothing a summer at the lake won't cure."

Kate summoned up a smile. "Exactly." But suddenly, one summer didn't seem like enough time.

" 'In want of a husband,' my eye," Kate muttered as she locked the Jeep at the Shop and Save, leaving the window cracked to give Bandit some fresh air. Aaron was already scurrying toward the entrance. Heck, thought Kate, watching a guy cross the parking lot, at this point I'd settle for a one-night stand.

He was a prime specimen in typical local garb—plaid shirt, Carhartts, work boots, a John Deere cap. Tall and broad-shouldered, he walked with a commanding, almost military stride. Longish hair and Strike King shades. But was that a mullet under the green-and-yellow cap? From a distance, she couldn't tell. Ick, a mullet. It was only hair, she conceded. Nothing a quick snip of the scissors couldn't fix.

"Mom? *Mom.*" A voice pierced her fantasy. Aaron rattled the cart he'd found in the parking lot.

"You're acting like an impatient city dweller," she said.

21

"I *am* an impatient city dweller," he replied.

They passed beneath the sign of the giant laughing pink pig, which had stood sentinel over the grocery store for as long as Kate could remember. The marquee held a sign that advertised, Maple Sweet Bacon—$.99/lb.

What are you so happy about? Kate wondered, looking at the pig. She and Aaron went inside together to stock up on supplies, for the lake house had sat empty since last year. Something in Kate loved this process. It was like starting from scratch, with everything new. And this time, all the choices were hers to make. Without her mother or older brother around, Kate was the adult in charge. What a concept.

"Mom? *Mom.*" Aaron scowled at her. "You're not even listening."

"Oh. Sorry, buddy." She selected some plums and put them in the cart. "I'm a bit preoccupied."

"Tell me about it. So did you get fired or were you laid off?" he asked, hitching a ride on the grocery cart as she steered toward the next aisle. He regarded her implacably over the pile of cereal boxes and produce bags.

She looked right back at her nine-year-old son. His curiously adult-sounding question caught her off guard. "Maybe I quit," she said. "Ever think of that?"

"Naw, you'd never quit." He snagged a sack of Jolly Ranchers from a passing shelf and tossed them into the cart.

Kate put the candy back. Jolly Ranchers had yanked

out more dental work than a bad dentist. "Why do you say I'd never quit?" she asked, taken aback. As he grew older, turning more and more into his own person, her son often said things that startled her.

"Because it's true," he said. "The only way you'd ever quit on your own is if something better came along, and I know for a fact that it hasn't. It never does."

Kate drummed her fingers on the handle of the shopping cart, the clear plastic scratched with age. She turned down the canned-goods aisle. "Oh, yeah?" she asked. "What makes you so darned sure?"

"Because you're freaking out," he informed her.

"I am not freaking out," said Kate.

Oh, but she was. She absolutely was. At night, she walked the floors and stared out the window, often staying up so late she could see the lights of Seattle's ferry terminals go out after the last boat came into the dock. That was the time she felt most alone and most frightened. That was when Kate the eternal optimist gave way to Kate in the pit of despair. If she had any interest in drinking, this would be the time to reach for a bottle. *L'heure bleue,* the French called it, the deep-blue hour between dark and dawn. That was when her relentlessly cheerful façade fell away and she engaged in something she hated—wallowing. This was her time to reflect on where she'd been and where she was going. This was when her lonely struggle to raise Aaron felt almost too hard to carry on. By the time the sun came up each morning, she snapped herself out of it and faced the day, ready to soldier on.

"We should get stuff marked with the WIC sticker," Aaron advised, pointing out a green-and-black tag under a display of canned tuna.

She put back the can of albacore as though it had bitten her. "Why on earth would you say that?"

"Chandler told me his mother gets tons of stuff with WIC. Women, Infants and Children," he explained. "It's a feld . . . fed . . . Some kind of program for poor people."

"We are not poor people," Kate snapped.

She didn't realize how loudly she'd spoken until a man at the end of the aisle turned to look at her. It was the same one she'd stared at in the parking lot, only he was much closer now. Beneath a five-o'clock shadow, she could make out a strong, clean jawline. He had traded the shades for a pair of horn-rimmed glasses, one side repaired with duct tape. In the split second that she met his gaze, she observed that his eyes had the depth and color of aged whiskey. But duct tape? Was he a loser? A nerd?

She whipped around to hide her flaming cheeks and shoved the cart fast in the other direction.

"See?" Aaron said. "This is how I know you would never quit your job. You get too embarrassed about being poor."

"We are not—" Kate forced herself to stop. She took in a deep, calming breath. "Listen, bud. We are fine. Better than fine. I wasn't getting anywhere at the paper, and it was time to move on, anyway."

"So are we poor or not?"

She wished he would lower his voice. "Not," she assured him.

In reality, her salary at the paper was barely a living wage, and the majority of her income came from the Seattle rental properties left to her by her father. Still, the job had defined her. She was a writer, and now that she'd been let go, she felt as though the rug had been ripped out from under her. "This means we get to spend the whole summer together, just the two of us." She studied Aaron's expression, spoke up before he turned too forlorn. "You got a problem with that?"

"Yeah," he said with a twinkle of mischief in his eye. "Maybe I do."

"Smart aleck." She tugged the bill of his Seattle Mariners baseball cap down over his eyes and pushed onward. Lord, she thought, before she knew it, her little red-haired, freckle-faced boy would be as tall as she was.

The storm of his mood struck as it always did, without warning and no specific trigger. "This is stupid," he snapped, his eyes narrowing, the color draining from his face. "It's going to be a stupid, boring summer and I don't even know why I bothered to come."

"Aaron, don't start—"

"I'm not starting." He ripped off his hat and hurled it to the floor in the middle of the aisle.

"Good," she said, trying to keep her voice emotionless, "because I have shopping to do. The quicker we finish, the quicker we get to the lake."

"I hate the lake."

Hoping they hadn't attracted any more attention, she steered the cart around him and fumbled through the rest of the shopping without letting on how shaken she was. She refused to allow his inability to control his behavior control *her*. When would it end? She had consulted doctors and psychologists, had read hundreds of books on the topic, but not one could ever give her the solution to Aaron's temper and his pain. So far, the most effective solution appeared to be time. The minutes seemed endless as she worked her way up and down the aisles, ignoring him the whole time. Sometimes she wished she could get into his head, find the source of his pain and make it better. But there was no Band-Aid or salve for the invisible wounds he carried. Well-meaning people claimed he needed a father. Well, *duh*, thought Kate.

"Mom," said a quiet, contrite voice behind her. "I'm sorry, Mom. I'll try harder not to get all mad and loud."

"I hope so," she said, her heart quietly breaking, as it always did when they struggled. "It's hurtful and embarrassing when you lose your temper and yell like that."

"I know. I'm sorry," he said again.

She knew a dozen strategies, maybe more, for where to go with this teachable moment. But they'd just driven three hours from Seattle, and she was anxious to get to the cottage. "We need stuff for s'mores," she said.

Relief softened his face and he was himself again,

eager-to-please Aaron, the one the teachers at his school saw so rarely. His storms were intense but quickly over, with no lingering bitterness.

"I'll go," he said, and headed off on the hunt.

Some practices at the lake house were steeped in tradition and ancient, mystical lore. Certain things always had to be done in certain ways. S'mores were just one of them. They always had to be made with honey grahams, not cinnamon, and the gooey marshmallow had to be rolled in miniature M&Ms. Nothing else would do. Whenever there was a s'mores night, they also had to play charades on the beach. She made a mental list of the other required activities, wondering if she'd remember to honor them all. Supper had to be announced each evening with the ringing of an old brass ship's bell suspended from a beam on the porch. Come July, they had to buy fireworks from the Makah tribe's weather-beaten roadside stand, and set them off to celebrate the Fourth. To mark the summer solstice, they would haul out and de-cobweb the croquet set and play until the sun set at ten o'clock at night, competing as though life itself depended on the outcome. When it rained, the Scrabble board had to come out for games of vicious competition. This summer, Aaron was old enough to learn Hearts and Whist, though with just the two of them, she wasn't sure how they'd manage some of the games.

All the lakeside-cottage traditions had been invented before Kate was born, and were passed down through generations with the solemnity of ancient ritual. She noticed that Aaron and his cousins—her brother Phil's brood—embraced the traditions and adhered to them fiercely, just as she and Phil had done before them.

Aaron came back with the crackers, miniature M&Ms and marshmallows.

"Thanks," she said, adding them to the cart. "I think that's about it." As she trolled through the last aisle, she noticed the guy in the John Deere cap again, studying a display of fishing lures. This time Aaron spotted him, too. For a moment, the boy's face was stripped of everything except a pained combination of curiosity and yearning as he sidled closer. The guy hooked his thumb into the rear pocket of his pants, and Aaron did the same. The older he got, the more Aaron identified with men, even strangers in the grocery store, it seemed.

Then she caught herself furtively studying the object of Aaron's attention, too. The stranger had the oddest combination of raw masculine appeal and backwoods roughness. She wondered how much he'd overheard earlier.

Snap out of it, she thought, moving the cart to the checkout line. She didn't give a hoot about what this Carhartt-wearing, mullet-sporting local yokel thought of her. He looked like the kind of guy who didn't have a birth certificate.

"Aaron," she said, "time to go." She turned away to avoid eye contact with the stranger, and pretended to browse the magazine racks. This was pretty much the extent of her involvement with the news media. It was shameful, really, as she considered herself a journalist.

She didn't watch TV, didn't read the papers, didn't act like the thing she said she was. This was yet another personal failing. Thanks to her late unlamented job, her work had consisted of nothing more challenging than observing Seattle's fashion scene.

People magazine touted a retrospective: "Reality TV Stars—Where Are They Now?"

"A burning issue in my life, for sure," Kate murmured.

"Let's get this one about the two-headed baby." Aaron indicated one of the tabloids. Kate shook her head, although her eye was caught by a small inset photo of a guy with chiseled cheeks and piercing eyes, a military-style haircut and dashing mustache. American Hero Captured by Terrorist Cult, proclaimed the headline.

"Let's get a *TV Guide*," Aaron suggested.

"We don't have a TV."

"So I can see what I'm missing. Wait, look, Mom." He snatched a newspaper from the rack. "Your paper." He handed it over.

Kate's hands felt suddenly and unaccountably cold, nerveless. She hated the pounding in her throat, hated the tremor of her fingers as she took it from him. It was just a stupid paper, she told herself. It was the *Seattle News*, a dumb little weekly crammed with items about local bands and poetry slams, film reviews and fluffy culture articles. In addition to production and layout, her specialty for the past five years had been fashion. She had generated miles of ink about Seattleites' tendency to wear socks with Birkenstocks, or the relative merits of body piercing versus tattooing as a fashion statement.

Apparently not quite enough miles, according to Sylvia, her editor. Instead of a five-year pin for distinguished service, Kate had received a pink slip.

The paper rattled as she turned to page B1 above the fold. There, where her column had been since its debut, was a stranger's face, grinning smugly out over the shout line. "Style Grrl," the byline called her, the self-important trendiness of it setting Kate's teeth on edge. Style Grrl, who called herself Wendy Norwich, was really Elsie Crump, who had only recently moved up from the mail room. Today's topic was an urgent rundown of local spray-on tanning salons.

At the very bottom of the page, in tiny italic print, was the reminder, *"Kate's Fashion Statement is on hiatus."*

That was it. Her entire professional life summed up in six little words.

"What's on hiya-tus mean?" Aaron asked.

"Kind of like on vacation," she said, hating the thick lump she felt in her throat. She stuffed the paper back in the rack. *Only I'm never coming back.*

"Can I have this gum?" Aaron asked, clearly unaware of her inner turmoil. "It's sugar free." He showed her a flat package containing more baseball cards than bubble gum.

"Sure, bud," she said, bending to unload her groceries onto the conveyor belt.

An older couple got in line behind her. It took no

more than a glance for Kate to surmise that they'd been together forever. They had the sort of ease that came from years of familiarity and caring, that special bond that let them communicate with a look or gesture.

A terrible yearning rose up in Kate. She was twenty-nine years old and she felt as though one of the most essential joys of life was passing her by. She had never heard a man declare he loved her and mean what he said. She had no idea what it felt like to have a true partner, a best friend, someone to stay by her side no matter what. Yes, she had a son she adored and a supportive extended family. She was grateful for those things and almost ashamed to catch herself craving more, wishing things could be different.

Still, sometimes when she saw a happy couple together, embracing and lost in each other, she felt a deep pang of emptiness. Being in love looked so simple. Yet it had never happened to her.

Long ago, she'd believed with all her heart that she and Nathan had been in love. Too late, she found out that what she thought she had with him had no solid foundation, and when tested by the reality of her pregnancy, their relationship had broken apart, the pieces drifting away like sections of an ice floe.

As she unloaded the cart, Kate felt the John Deere guy watching her. She was sure of it, could sense those shifty eyes behind the glasses. He was two lanes over and his back was turned, but she knew darned well he'd been staring just a second ago. He was probably checking to see if she used food stamps.

None of your business, she thought. And you do too have a mullet. She glared at the broad, plaid shirt–covered shoulders.

She finished checking out, marveling at the amount of the bill. Ah, well. Starting over took a little capital up front. She swiped her debit card through the machine and got an error message. Great, she thought, and swiped it again. "Please wait for cashier," the machine flashed.

"I don't think my card's working," Kate said, handing it to her.

The cashier took it and put in the numbers manually. "I'm sorry, ma'am. The card's been declined."

Declined. Kate's stomach dropped, but she fumbled for a smile. "I'll write you a check," she said, taking out her checkbook.

"We can only accept local checks," the cashier said apologetically.

Kate glanced at the couple behind her. "I'll pay in cash, then," she muttered. "You do accept cash, right?"

"Have you got enough?" Aaron asked. His piping voice carried, and she knew the lumberjack guy could hear.

She pursed her lips and counted out four twenties, a ten and two ones, and thirty-three cents change. It was all the cash she had on hand. She looked at the amount on the cashier's display. "Check your pockets, Aaron," she said. "I'm two dollars and nine cents short."

I hate this, she thought while Aaron dug in his Levi's. I hate this.

She kept a bland smile in place, though her teeth were clenched, and she avoided eye contact with the cashier or with the couple behind her.

"I got a quarter and a penny," Aaron said, "and that's it." He handed it over.

"I'll have to put something back." Kate wished she could just slink away. "I'm sorry," she said to the older couple. She reached for the bag of Cheetos, their favorite guilty pleasure.

"Not the Cheetos. Anything but the Cheetos," Aaron whispered through clenched teeth.

"Don't do that," said a deep, quiet voice behind her. "It's covered."

Even before Kate turned to look at him, she knew it was the guy. The mullet man, rescuing her.

She took a deep breath and turned. Go away, she wanted to tell him. I don't need you. Instead, she said, "That's not necessary—"

"Not a problem." He handed two dollars to the cashier and headed out the door with his sack of groceries.

"Hey, thanks," said Aaron.

The man didn't turn, but touched the bill of his cap as he went outside.

Thoroughly flustered, Kate helped sack the groceries and load them into the cart. She hurried outside, hoping to catch the guy before he left. She spotted him in a green pickup truck, leaving the parking lot.

"That was real nice of him, huh?" said Aaron.

"Yep."

"You forgot to tell him thank-you."

"I didn't forget. I was . . . startled, and then he took off before I could say anything."

"You weren't startled," he said. "You were embarrassed."

She opened her mouth to object. Then she let her shoulders slump. "Totally humiliated." For Aaron's sake, she summoned a smile. "I shouldn't have said that. I should remind you that the kindness of strangers is a rare and wonderful thing."

"A rare and wonderful and humiliating thing," he said.

"Help me load these groceries, smart aleck. Let's see if we can get to the lake before the Popsicles melt."

Three

Kate's Jeep Cherokee had seen better days, but it was the perfect vehicle for the lake, rugged enough to take on the unpaved roads and byways that wound through the mountains and rain forests of the Olympic Peninsula. Bandit greeted them as though they'd been gone a year, sneezing and slapping the seat with his tail.

"Now to the lake," Kate said brightly. "We've got the house all to ourselves, how about that?"

Aaron buckled his seat belt in desultory fashion, barely reacting to Bandit's sloppy kisses, and she realized she'd said the wrong thing.

"It's going to be a great summer," she assured him.

"Right," he replied without enthusiasm.

She could hear the apprehension in his voice. Though she wouldn't say so aloud, she felt as apprehensive as Aaron.

He regarded her with disconcerting insight. "They fired you because of me, didn't they?"

"No, I got fired because Sylvia is an inflexible stick of a woman who never appreciated real talent anyway. Deadlines and the bottom line, that's all she cares about." Kate made herself stop. No point venting to Aaron; he already knew she was angry. The fact that Kate had been let go by Sylvia Latham, the managing editor, stung particularly. Like Kate, Sylvia was a single mother. Unlike Kate, she was a perfect single mother with two perfect kids, and because of this, she assumed everyone else could and should juggle career and family with the same finesse she did.

Kate ducked her head, hiding her expression. Aaron was clued in to much more than people expected of him. He knew as well as any other boy that one of the most basic realities of modern life was that a single mom missed work to take care of her kid. Why didn't Sylvia get it? Because she had a perfect nanny to look after her perfect children. Until this past year, Aaron's grandmother and sometimes his aunt watched him when he missed school. Now that they'd moved away, Kate tried to juggle everything on her own. And she'd failed. Miserably and unequivocally.

"I have to call the bank, figure out what's the matter

with my debit card," she said, taking out her cell phone. "We don't get reception at the lake."

"Boooring," Aaron proclaimed and slumped down in his seat.

"I'm with you, bud." She dialed the number on the back of her card. After listening to all the options—"because our menu has recently changed," cooed the voice recording—she had to press an absurd combination of numbers only to learn that the bank, on East Coast time, was already closed. She leaned her head against the headrest and took a deep, cleansing breath. "It's nothing," she assured Aaron. "I'll sort it out later."

"I need to call Georgie next," she said apologetically.

All five grandkids—Phil and Barbara's four, plus Aaron—called her mother Georgie and sometimes even Georgie Girl.

"Don't talk long," Aaron said. *"Please."*

Kate punched in the unfamiliar new number and waited for it to connect. A male voice answered.

"This is Clinton Dow." Georgie's new husband always answered with courteous formality.

"And this is Katherine Elise Livingston," she said, teasing a little.

"Kate." His voice smoothed out with a smile she could hear. "How are you?"

"Excellent. We're in Port Angeles, just about to head to the lake."

"Sounds like a big adventure," he said as jovially as could be. You'd never know that only last spring, he was urging her mother to sell the summer place. It was a white elephant, he'd declared, a big empty tax liability that had outlived its use to the family. With that one pronouncement, he had nearly lost the affections of his two newly acquired stepchildren. The lakeside cottage had been in the Livingston family since the 1920s, far longer than a once-widowed, once-divorced retired CPA.

"We're never selling the lake house," Phil had said. "Ever. End of discussion." It didn't matter to Phil that he had moved cross-country, all the way to New York, and that his visits would be few and far between. For him and Kate and their kids, the lakeside retreat held all that was special and magical about summer, and selling it would be sacrilege.

"I'll get your mother," Clint said. "It's great to hear from you."

While she waited, Kate pulled the Jeep around to the far edge of the parking lot so she could look out over the harbor. She had stood in this spot, regarding this view hundreds of times in her life. She never got tired of it. Port Angeles was a strange city, an eclectic jumble of cheap sportsman's motels and diners, quaint bed-and-breakfast getaways, strip malls with peeling paint and buckled asphalt parking lots, waterfront restaurants and shops. A few times a day, the Coho ferry churned its crammed, exhausted hull across the Strait of Juan de Fuca to Victoria, British Columbia, in all its gleaming splendor, and vehicles waited for hours for a coveted berth on board.

"So you're headed off into the wilderness," her

mother said cheerfully into the phone.

"Just the two of us," Kate said.

"I wish you'd decided to bring Aaron here for the summer," Georgina said. "We're an hour's drive from Walt Disney World, for heaven's sake."

"Which is precisely why I didn't want to bring him," Kate said. "I'm just not a Disney sort of gal."

"And Aaron?"

"He'd love it," she confessed. "He would love to see you, too." She watched her son rifling through the groceries in search of something to eat. He found the sack of golden Rainier cherries and dived in, seeing how far he could spit each pit out the window. Bandit, who was remarkably polite when his humans were eating, watched with restrained but intense concentration. "We want to be here this summer," she reminded her mother. "It's exactly where we need to be."

"If you say so." Georgina had never loved the lakeside cottage the way the rest of the Livingstons did, though in deference to her late husband and children, she'd always been a good sport about spending every summer there. Now that she'd finally remarried, however, she was more than happy to stay in Florida.

"I say so," Kate told her mother. "I can finally spend quality time with my boy, and figure out what I want to be when I grow up."

"You'll both go stir-crazy," Georgina warned.

Kate thought about her mother's new home, a luxury condo on a golf course in Florida. Now *that* would make a person stir-crazy.

She let Aaron say hello to his grandmother, and then she called Phil, but got his voice mail and left a brief message. "There," she said. "I've checked in with everybody who matters."

"That's not very many."

"It's not the number of people. It's how much they matter," she explained. It made Kate wistful, thinking about how much she would miss her brother and his family this summer. She didn't let it show, though. She wanted Aaron to believe this would be the summer of a lifetime. Sometimes she thought she'd give anything for a shoulder to cry on, but she wouldn't allow her son to play that role. She'd seen other single moms leaning on their kids for emotional support, and she didn't think it was fair. That was not what kids were for.

Last year, she'd consulted a "life coach," who'd counseled her to be her own partner in parenting and life, encouraging her to have long, searching conversations with herself. It hadn't helped, but at least she found herself talking to someone she liked.

"Ready?" she said to Aaron, putting away the phone. She eased the Jeep out of the parking lot and merged onto Highway 101, heading west. The forests of Douglas fir and cedar thickened as they penetrated deeper into the Olympic Peninsula. Soaring to heights of two hundred feet or more, the moss-draped trees arched over the two-lane highway, creating a mystical cathedral effect that never failed to enchant her. The filtered afternoon sunlight glowed with layers of green and gold, dappling the road with shifting patterns.

There was a sense, as they traveled away from the port city, of entering another world entirely. This was a place apart, where the silences were as vast and deep as the primal forests surrounding the lake. Thanks to the vigilance of the parks department, the character of the land never changed. Aaron was experiencing every-thing just as she and Phil had as children, and their father and grandparents before them. She remembered sitting in the back seat of their father's old station wagon with the window rolled down, feeling the cool rush of the wind in her face and inhaling the fecund scent of moss and cedar. Four years her senior, Phil had a special gift for annoying her until she wept, though she had long since forgiven him for all the childhood torments. Somehow, seemingly by magic, her brother had turned into her best friend over the years.

Five miles from the lake, they passed the final hill where cell-phone reception was possible, in the parking lot of Grammy's Café, which served the best marion-berry pie known to man.

At the side of the road, she spotted a green pickup truck pulled off to the side. She slowed down as she passed, and saw that the driver was bent over the front passenger side, changing a tire, perhaps.

It was the John Deere guy. The one who had bailed her out at the grocery store.

She applied the brake, then put the car in Reverse and pulled off to the shoulder. She had no idea how to change a tire and he probably didn't want or need her help. But she stopped just the same, because like it or not, she owed him one.

"What're you doing?" Aaron asked.

"Stay put," she said. "Don't let Bandit out." She got out and walked toward the truck.

Here, surrounded by the extravagant lushness of the fern-carpeted forest, he looked even more interesting than he had in the grocery shop, a man in his element. Suddenly she felt vulnerable. This was a lonely stretch of road, and if he decided to come on to her, she'd be in trouble. Her brother often accused her of being too naive and trusting, yet she didn't know how else to be. She did trust people, and they seldom let her down.

"Keep away," he called to her without looking up from what he was doing. "I've got a wounded animal here."

Definitely not a come-on.

She saw a half-grown raccoon lying on its side, struggling and making a terrible noise. Wearing a pair of logging gloves, the guy was trying to bag the hissing, scratching creature in a canvas sack, but the raccoon was having none of it.

Ignoring orders, Aaron jumped out. Bandit whined from the Jeep.

Kate grabbed Aaron's shoulder and held him next to her. "What can we do to help?"

"That's— Damn." The guy jumped back, examining his gloved hand.

"Did it bite you?" she asked.

"Tried to."

"Did you hit it?" Aaron asked. His chin trembled. He

41

absolutely hated it when an animal was injured.

"Nope. Found it like this," the man said. For the first time, he took his eyes off the raccoon and turned to look at them. The sunglasses masked his reaction, but she could tell he recognized her from the grocery store. Something—a subtle tensing in his big, lean body—reacted to her.

"Is it going to die?" Aaron asked.

"Hope not. There's a wildlife rehab station back in Port Angeles. If I can get it there, I'm pretty sure it can be saved."

"How can he fight like that?" Kate said. "He's half-dead."

"Not even close. And the survival instinct is strong when something feels threatened."

"Hey," Aaron said, diving into the back of the Jeep. "You can use the Igloo."

Kate helped him empty the forty-five-gallon cooler, which had plenty of room for a half-grown raccoon. Together, they pulled the cooler out and dragged it over, easing it over the raccoon. It scrabbled around, but the stranger managed to get the lid under it. Slowly and gently, the three of them tilted the cooler until it was upright, then pressed the lid in place.

"Will he smother?" asked Aaron.

Kate opened the drain plug. "He should be all right for a while."

The man loaded the cooler into his truck. The back was littered with tools, cans of marine varnish and a chain saw. Behind the driver's seat was a gun rack, which held fishing poles and a coffee mug instead of guns. When he turned back, she got a good look at his face. Even with those glasses, he had the kind of rough masculinity that made her go weak in the knees—strong features, a chiseled mouth, a five-o'clock shadow. Oh, Kate, she thought, you're pathetic.

"Thanks," he said.

Aaron's chest inflated in that unconscious way he had of puffing up around another male. Kate ruffled his hair. "We're glad to help."

"Do you live around here?" the stranger asked. "Can I bring the cooler to you when I'm done?"

Kate felt a prickle of hesitation. It was never a good idea to tell a stranger where you lived, especially if you lived in a secluded lakeside cottage where no one could hear you scream.

"I'm staying at the Schroeder place," he said as if reading her thoughts. "It's on Lake Crescent."

The Schroeder place. She used to play with Sammy and Sally Schroeder when she was little. Mable Claire Newman had even mentioned this guy, only half teasing: *Wait till you see him.* And the guy was a rescuer of raccoons, Kate reflected. How bad could he be?

"We're a quarter of a mile down the road from you," she told him. "The driveway is marked with a sign that says The Livingstons. I'm Kate Livingston, and this is Aaron."

"Nice to meet you. I'd shake hands, but I've been handling wildlife."

For some reason, that struck Kate as funny and she

giggled. Ridiculously, like a schoolgirl. She stopped herself with an effort. "So, are you one of the Schroeders?" she asked.

"A friend, actually," he said. "JD Harris."

"JD?" Aaron echoed.

"Mr. Harris to you," Kate told him.

"Everyone calls me JD, Aaron included," the man insisted.

Aaron stood even straighter and squared his shoulders. Kate kept staring at JD Harris. There was something . . . it was crazy, but she was sure that behind the dark glasses, he was checking her out, and maybe even liking what he saw. And instead of being offended, she felt a flush of mutual interest.

"I'd better get this thing transported," he said, turning away. "I'll bring your cooler over later."

So, thought Kate as she put the Jeep in gear and pulled out onto the road, maybe I read him wrong. Still his image lingered in her mind as she headed west. He intrigued her, even with two days' growth of beard. Even the sunglasses gave him an unexpected sexiness, reminiscent of that guiltiest of pleasures, Johnny Depp.

Snap out of it, Kate, she told herself. He probably had a wife and kids with him. That would be good, actually. That would be great. Kids for Aaron to play with.

Her son was turned around in the seat, watching the green truck heading back toward town. "You really think that raccoon will live?"

"It was acting pretty lively," she said.

Around the east end of the lake, the road narrowed.

Like Brigadoon, the lake community was locked in the past. Decades ago, President Roosevelt had declared Lake Crescent and its surroundings a national treasure, and designated it a national park. Only those few already in residence were permitted to retain their property. No more tracts could ever be sold or developed, and improvements were restricted. The hand-built cabins and cottages and the occasional dock tucked along the shore seemed frozen in time, and an air of exclusivity served to underscore the specialness of the summer place.

The families of the lake were a diverse group who generally kept to themselves. Mable Claire Newman's property management company looked after the vacation homes, including the Livingston place.

Kate pulled off the narrow road and turned between two enormous Sitka spruce trees. Aaron jumped out to unhook the chain across the driveway. Bandit leaped after him, ecstatic to finally be here.

Even this small act was the stuff of family ritual. The opening of the driveway chain had the ponderous significance of a ribbon-cutting ceremony. It was always done by the eldest child in the first car to arrive. He would already have the dull, worn key in one hand and a can of WD–40 in the other, because the padlock inevitably rusted over the damp, dark winter. Aaron freed the lock and let the thick iron chain drop across the gravel driveway. He stood aside, holding out his arm in an old-fashioned flourish.

Kate gave a thumbs-up sign and eased ahead. Summer was officially open for business.

· · ·

With the dog at his heels, Aaron ran ahead down the driveway. It was littered with pinecones and the occasional bough blown down by the winter storms. Kate felt a familiar childlike sense of anticipation as the property came into view. A grove of ferns, some the size of Volkswagens, filled the forest floor bordering the driveway. Speared through by sunlight, it had the look of a magical bower. In fact, Kate's grandma Charla used to tell her that fairies lived here, and Kate believed her.

She still did, a little, she thought, watching her son and the dog do a little dance of glee.

The driveway widened and lightened as the trees thinned. Ahead, like a jewel upon a pillow of emerald silk, sat the lake house.

She loved the way the lake property revealed itself to her, bit by bit. Its charms were cumulative, from the gardening shed with moss growing on the rooftop to the boathouse that not only housed a boat, but a homemade still left over from Prohibition days. As always, the lake water had a certain mesmerizing clarity, and indeed the drinking water had always been drawn from it.

The lawn had been mowed prior to their arrival. The house looked as though it was just waking up, the window shades at half mast. Over the eyebrow window were the numbers 1921, to commemorate the year the place was built. Godfrey James Livingston, an immigrant who had made a fortune cutting timber, had commissioned the lake house. The family, with somewhat willful naïveté, always referred to the place as a cottage because old Great-Grandfather Godfrey liked to be reminded of the Lake District of his boyhood in England.

Yet the term "cottage" was an irony when applied to this place. Its timber and river-stone facade spanned the spectacular shoreline, curving slightly as if to embrace the singular view of the long lake with the mountains rising straight up from its depths. The house was designed in the Arts and Crafts style, with thick timbers and multi-paned dormer windows on the upper story and a broad porch that took full advantage of the setting.

Godfrey's son—named Walden, with inadvertent prescience—was Kate's own grandfather. He was a gentle soul who in one generation had allowed the family fortune to dwindle, mainly because he had the distinction of being a devout conservationist in an era when such a thing was all but unheard of. His passion for preserving the virgin forests of the Northwest had been spoken of in whispers, like an aberrant behavior. "He loves trees" had the same hushed scandal as "he loves boys." Back in the 1930s when Grandfather was growing up, he had fought to protect the forests. Later, during World War II, he'd served as a medic, winning a bronze star at Bastogne. Having gained a hero's credibility, he later appeared before Congress to urge limits on clear-cutting federal lands. In the 1950s, his enemies denounced him as a Communist.

A decade later, Grandfather came into his own. The

flower children of the 1960s embraced him. He and his wife, Charla, an extremely minor Hollywood actress who had once played a bit part in a Marlon Brando movie, protested the destruction of the environment alongside hippies and anarchists. To the acute embarrassment of their grown children, they attended Woodstock and smoked pot. Walden became a folk hero, and he wrote a book about his experiences.

When Kate was a small girl, he was widowed and moved in with her family. She had loved the old man without reservation, spending hours at his side, chattering on in the way of a child, certain her listener hung on her every word.

With a patience that could only be described as saintly, he would listen to her describe the entire plot of *Charlotte's Web* or every exhibit in the school science fair. Later, when she was a teenager, it was Grandfather Walden who heard all her Monday-morning quarterbacking about the weekend football games, parties, dates. Her grandfather was the keeper of all her secrets and dreams. It was to him that she first explained her ambition to become a famous international news correspondent. He was the first one she told when she was accepted in the honors program at the University of Washington. And it was to him that she had confessed the event that had changed the course of her future. "I'm pregnant, and Nathan wants me to get rid of the baby."

"To hell with Nathan." The old man, wheelchairbound by then, still managed a lively gesture with his hand. "What do *you* want?"

Her hands had crept down over her still-flat belly. "I want this baby."

A gleam of emotion lit his eyes behind the bifocals. "I love you, Katie. I'll help you in any way I can."

He'd given her the most critical element of all—his wholehearted, nonjudgmental approval. It meant the world to her. Her parents were supportive, of course. It was the role they felt compelled to play. But every once in a while, Kate sensed their frustration. *We raised you for something more than single motherhood.*

Only Grandfather knew the truth, that there was no career or calling more thrilling, demanding or rewarding than raising a child.

She loved her grandfather for his great heart and open mind, for his passion and honesty. She loved him for accepting her exactly as she was, flaws and all. Over the years, he gave her plenty of advice. The bit that stuck in her mind consisted of two simple words: *Don't settle.*

She wished she'd done a better job following that advice, but she hadn't, in her career, anyway. She had settled for a popular but uninfluential newspaper that required little from her, only a clever turn of phrase, a canny eye for fashion and the ability to produce eighteen hundred publishable words on a regular basis.

This was it, then, she decided, parking near the back door. This summer was her chance to find something she could be passionate about. She would do it for her own sake, in honor of her grandfather.

Grabbing the nearest grocery sack, she got out of the Jeep and unlocked the back door. At least, she thought she unlocked it. As she turned the key, she didn't feel the bolt slide.

That's odd, she thought, opening the door and stepping inside. The cleaners must have forgotten to lock up after themselves. They'd left the radio on, too, and an old Drifters tune was floating from the speakers. She would have to mention it to Mable Claire Newman. Crime wasn't a problem around here, but that was no excuse for carelessness.

Other than leaving the door unlocked, the cleaners had done an excellent job. The pine-plank floors gleamed, and all the wooden paneling and fixtures glowed with a deep, oiled sheen. The shutters had been opened to dazzling sunlight striking the water.

Kate inhaled the scent of lemon oil and Windex and went to the front window. Everyone who came here rediscovered the old place in his or her own way. Kate always started with the inside of the house, checking to see that the cupboards and drawers were in order, that the clocks were set, the range and oven working, the bed linens aired, the hot water heater turned on. Only after that would she venture outside to touch each plank of the dock, to admire the lawn, and to feel the water, shivering with delight at its glacial temperature.

Aaron headed straight outside, the dog at his heels. He ran along the boundaries of the property, from the blackberry bramble on one end to the growth of cattails on the other. Bandit raced behind him in hot pursuit.

When they pounded out to the end of the dock, Kate bit her tongue to keep from calling out a warning. It would only annoy Aaron. Besides, she didn't need to caution him to stay out of the water. He would do that on his own, because the fact was, Aaron refused to learn to swim.

She didn't know why. He'd never had an accident either boating or swimming. He didn't mind a boat ride or even wading in the shallows. But he would not go in over his head no matter what.

Kate felt badly for him. As he got older, he suffered the stigma of his phobia. Whenever one of the boys at school celebrated a birthday at the community pool, Aaron always begged off with a stomachache. When invited to try out for the swim team, he managed to lose the forms sent home from school. Last summer, he spent hours sitting on the end of the dock while his cousins—even Isaac and Muriel, who were younger than him—flung themselves off the dock and played endless games of water tag and keep-away with the faded yellow water polo ball. Aaron had watched with wistfulness, but the yearning to join them was never enough to motivate him to give swimming a try. She could tell he wanted to in the worst way. He just couldn't make himself do it. He had to be content standing on the dock or paddling around in the kayak.

Don't settle, she wanted to tell him. If she did nothing else this summer, she would help Aaron learn to swim. She suspected, with a mother's gut-deep instinct, that learning to overcome fear would open him up to a world of possibility. She wanted him to know he shouldn't make do with less than his dreams.

There. The thought had pushed its way to the surface. Aaron had "problems." According to his teachers, the school counselor and his pediatrician, he showed signs of inadequate anger management and impulse control. A battery of tests from a diagnostician had not revealed any sort of attention or learning disorders. This had not surprised Kate. She knew what Aaron wanted—a man. A father figure. It was no secret. He told her so all the time, never knowing that each time he mentioned the subject, it was a soft blow to her heart. "You have your uncle Phil," she always told him. Now that Phil had moved away, Aaron's behavior in school had worsened. She'd missed one too many deadlines, attending one too many parent-teacher conferences, and Sylvia had shown her the door.

Her throat felt full and tight with unshed tears. Really, she thought, she ought to feel grateful that her son was healthy, that he loved his family and most of the time was a great kid. But those other times . . . she didn't always know how to deal with him.

Maybe that was why parents were supposed to come in pairs. When one reached her limit, the other could pick up and carry on.

Or so she thought. She didn't know for certain because she'd never had a partner in parenting Aaron. She'd had a partner in making him, of course, but Nathan had disappeared faster than the Little Red Hen's friends in the old bedtime story.

Kate went outside and grabbed another sack of groceries. "How about a hand here?" she called to Aaron.

He turned to her and applauded.

"Very funny," she said. "I'm letting your Popsicles melt."

He sped across the lawn, his face flushed. Already he smelled like new leaves and fresh air. "All right already," he said.

Kate set the sack on the scrubbed pine counter. In the sink was a tumbler half-full of water. She dumped it into the drain. The cleaners had probably left it. She put things into the freezer, then opened the fridge and found a covered disposable container with a plastic fork.

"What the . . . ?" Kate murmured. She removed the container and put it straight in the trash. Lord knew how long it had been there.

"What's that?" Aaron asked.

"Nothing. The cleaners left a few things behind. I'll have to speak to Mrs. Newman about it." She finished putting away the perishables and let Aaron go outside again to toss a stick for Bandit.

Then she grabbed two suitcases, heading upstairs. Since it was just her and Aaron this summer, she decided to take the master bedroom. It faced the lake with a central dormer window projecting outward like the prow of a ship. She'd never occupied this room before. She'd never been the senior adult at the lake. This room was for couples. Her grandparents. Then her parents, then Phil and Barbara. Well, she'd have it all to herself, all summer long, she thought with a touch of defiance.

Juggling the suitcases, she pushed open the door. Another thing the maids had forgotten—to open the drapes in here. The room was dim and close, haunted by gloom.

With a frown of exasperation, Kate set down the luggage. Her eyes hadn't yet adjusted to the dimness. When she straightened up, she saw a shadow stir.

The shadow resolved itself into human form and surged toward her.

A single thought filled Kate's mind: *Aaron.*

With that, she bolted down the stairs.

Four

JD felt the woman's eyes on him. His pulse sped up as he sensed her gaze lingering a few seconds too long.

"Is that all the information you need from me?" he asked, pushing the form across the counter to her.

"That'll do." She offered a smile he couldn't quite figure out. These days he was suspicious of every look, every smile. "Thanks, Mr. . . ." She glanced down at the form. "Harris."

She was young, he observed. Pretty in a fresh-faced, college-girl way, probably volunteering at the wildlife rehab station for the summer. Darla T.—Volunteer, read the tag on her pocket.

He hoped like hell she wouldn't volunteer any information about him to her friends. Even out here, in the farthest corner of the country, he was paranoid. Sam had assured him that in Port Angeles he could escape all the hoopla that had disrupted his life since the incident last Christmas, particularly if he changed his appearance and kept a low profile.

After being accosted in every possible way—and in ways he hadn't even imagined—he was wary. When a tabloid photographer had popped out of his apartment complex Dumpster to get a shot of him in his pajama bottoms taking out the garbage, JD knew his life would never be the same. The notion was underscored by a woman so obsessed with him that she injured herself just to get him to rescue her. The day he'd received an important classified delivery containing a toy company's prototype of the Jordan Donovan Harris Action Figure, garbed in battle-dress uniform and hefting a Special Forces weapon the real Harris had never even seen before, was the day he'd filed for a discharge. Then, on a rainy night in April, a call came in, a reporter asking him about his mother.

JD had ripped the phone from the wall that night. It was bad enough they hounded him. When they turned like a pack of wolves on his mother, something in JD had snapped, too.

Enough.

If he had to put up with any more attention, he'd end up as loony as the guy whose bomb he'd stopped.

JD needed to disappear for a while, let the furor die down. Once he fell off the public radar, he could slip quietly back into private life. Sam had offered his family's summer cabin and wanted nothing in return. That was just the kind of friend he was.

So far, JD's retreat seemed to be working. His mother, Janet, was getting the help she needed, and here in this remote spot, three thousand miles from D.C., no one seemed to recognize him. Though confident that he bore no resemblance to the clean-cut military man he'd once been, he had his moments of doubt. Like now, when a pretty girl batted her eyes at him. He no longer trusted a stranger's smile. Maybe there used to be a time when a girl smiled because she liked him, but that seemed like another person's life. Now every friendly greeting, every kind gesture or invitation was suspect. People no longer cared who he was, only that he'd stopped a suicide bomber in the presence of the President.

The media and security cameras at the hospital had recorded the entire incident. The drama lasted only minutes, but when it was over, so was life as he knew it. TV stations around the world ran and reran the footage, and it could still be seen in streaming video on the Internet. The press had instantly dubbed him "America's Hero," and to his mortification, it stuck.

"It's you I should be thanking," he said to Darla, picking up the ice chest. "Good to know there's a place like this in the area."

She nodded. "We can't save them all, but we do our best." She handed him a printed flyer. "We can always use volunteers, ages eight to eighty. Keep us in mind."

Carrying the now-empty cooler, he went out to his

truck. Sam's truck. Everything had been borrowed from Sam—his truck, his vacation cabin, his privacy. JD glanced again at the volunteer form and stuffed it in his back pocket. Then he headed for the car wash. Best to clean out the woman's cooler before giving it back.

As he was pulling out of the parking lot, he heard the quick *yip* of a siren and looked down the road. An ambulance rig glided past at a purposeful speed, heading for the county hospital. The cars that had pulled out of its way slipped back into the stream of traffic again, ordinary people, going about their ordinary lives. Anonymity was such a simple thing, taken for granted until it was taken away.

JD felt a thrum of familiarity as the vehicle passed. That was what he was supposed to be doing. Helping. Not hiding out like a fugitive, rescuing raccoons.

Of course, once his face was splashed on the front page of newspapers and magazines across the globe, he wasn't much good on emergency calls. Sometimes he'd attract more rubberneckers and media than a five-car pileup, just for being on the scene.

There had been no time to adjust to having all his privacy stripped away. He'd awakened from a medically induced coma to discover that a) he was going to survive his injuries and b) everything had changed. Right after the incident, his image had been inflated to ten times larger than life on a lighted billboard in Times Square. While that was happening, JD had been mercifully unconscious. "Fighting for his life" was the way many media reports put it, though of course he had done no fighting at all. He'd just lain there like a heap of roadkill while the docs did their thing.

If he'd known what was going on, he probably would have stayed asleep for decades like Rip Van Winkle, hoping the world would have forgotten him when he woke up.

No such luck. Jordan Donovan Harris: The Nation Sits Vigil awakened to Jordan Donovan Harris: The Nation's New Hero. It was insane, a feeding frenzy. The press always referred to him by all three names, the way they did mass murderers—John Wayne Gacy, Coral Eugene Watts, John Wilkes Booth—or JD's own personal assassin, Terence Lee Muldoon.

No one had seen the attack coming. No one could have, which was why Muldoon had almost succeeded. A member of both the Blue Light Commando and Black Ops, he'd been decorated for bravery in battle during the first strike of Operation Iraqi Freedom. He had the perfect record of a career soldier. "He was a quiet, unassuming man who kept to himself . . ." Wasn't that what was always said about loonies and mass murderers? No one ever said, "He was crazier than a shithouse rat, and you couldn't trust him any farther than you could throw him."

No. Like most crazies, he was always described as "a hard worker" and "model citizen . . ." The scariest part was, when Muldoon had hatched his plan, there had been no one to stop him. Except JD, who had literally blundered into the situation.

It was all behind him now, he thought, finishing up at

the car wash. He didn't exactly have his life back since he'd had to go underground, but at least he had some privacy. Some breathing room. Don't blow it, he cautioned himself, thinking of Kate Livingston and her kid. They couldn't know it, but today's encounter was the longest conversation he'd had with anyone since moving into the Schroeders' cabin.

For those few minutes, at the side of the road in the middle of nowhere, he'd felt easy and natural, almost like himself again. Just a guy staying at the lake, taking some time off work, chatting with a woman who had red hair, sexy legs and a friendly kid. A woman who made him miss the things he'd never had.

Sam's wife, Penny, a hopeless romantic, was constantly urging him to find someone who made him feel special, to settle down and start a family. Since Christmas, he'd learned that he didn't want to feel special. He wanted to feel like himself.

At the time of the incident at Walter Reed, he'd had a woman in his life. Tina, a congressional aide, said she adored him. That was all well and good until he stumbled into fame. Then she went on national television and said she adored him. She repeated it in magazine interviews and on talk radio, and that wasn't all. She didn't hesitate to reveal some of the most private aspects of their relationship, including the first time he'd told her he loved her, the first gift he'd given her, his fondness for Chesapeake blue crab and his preference in sexual positions. Somehow, she had parlayed her professed adoration into a stupid self-help book called *How to Date a Real Man.*

He still remembered the feeling of lying helpless, propped in his hospital bed, hearing his girlfriend, dewy-eyed with sincerity, describe the intimate details of their life. The sense of betrayal was a dull reverberation that shuddered through him, awakening memories of other occasions, other betrayals.

Why was he surprised? he wondered. This was what people did. They took what they wanted from him and then they left.

After the shooting, even Janet had crawled out of the woodwork and had begun calling herself his mother again. She had wept at his hospital bedside. News photographs showed her, Madonna-like, praying for his recovery.

The irony was, he no longer needed this woman to love him and pray for him. He had needed that when he was a kid in school, desperate for affection and approval. He'd needed that when he was a teenager, crying out for reassurance and control. She hadn't been there for him then, and when he turned eighteen he had mortgaged his future to get his mother into rehab. Everything he'd saved for college and—yes, he did dream big—medical school, he'd spent on the rehab clinic. The miracle was, his investment paid off. After ninety days at Serenity House in Silver Spring, Maryland, Janet Harris had emerged clean and sober, sincerely grateful to the son who had saved her from the overdose that would have made him an orphan.

She was a changed person. JD had seen that immediately and Janet was the first to admit it. "I need to make a fresh start," she'd said. "I can't be around anything—anyone—who was a part of my life when I was an addict."

It took JD a little time to figure out that she meant him as well as all the dealers and pimps she'd run with while JD was growing up.

Her desertion that summer had been a gift, or so he told himself. Her sobriety had cost him his meager savings, but it had given him insight into what his future held. He was on his own, and that was fine with him.

Then, fame had happened to him, and suddenly Janet was back in his life, the ideal mother of an American hero. She should have known better. She should have understood that the reporters surrounding her were not her friends. They'd turned on her, of course, and the revelations they brought to light turned her back into the person she'd been all through JD's childhood—an addict. Fortunately for Janet, he now had every resource at his disposal, and just before disappearing, he'd arranged for her to go to the best rehab facility in southern California. He hoped like hell they'd do their job—and that Janet would do hers, and get better. Years of sobriety shattered by a handful of press reports. God, he hated the media.

Growing up, JD always thought he wanted to be a family physician, caring for people from cradle to grave.

But he'd been wrong. His true calling was to be an EMT, like the men and women who had brought his mother back from that final overdose. JD had never learned their names, had never seen them again. And that seemed somehow appropriate. To JD, it was the ideal job—saving people and then setting them free. That was the best of both worlds. As an emergency-aid worker, he could savor the rush of satisfaction of keeping them from dying, yet he wouldn't have to think about where they'd be the next day or the next month or even the next decade. An EMT spent an average of 13.5 minutes in the life of a victim, and in that blink of time, he made all the difference.

Works for me, JD had said to the army recruiter. After his mother had cleaned herself up, cleaned out the rest of JD's savings and then ditched him for a better life in California, he'd enlisted in the U.S. Army. They promised him a great job, a steady income, a life of travel and adventure and money for his education.

Sometimes JD wished he had read the fine print better. Still, he'd gone through the toughest training the army offered and, after eighteen months of unbelievable hell, he was certified as a Special Forces Medic, the most qualified and elite trauma specialist in the military.

In Port Angeles, far from the rest of the world, he turned down First Street and found a parking spot. He went to the marine-supply store for a long list of supplies—tar and seam filler, varnish, epoxy, marine plywood, fiberglass glue. When Sam had offered the lakeside cabin for the summer, he had urged JD to use the cosine wherry, a wooden rowboat hand built by his late father. He'd gone on and on about the hours he and his dad had spent in the boat when Sam was a boy. He probably pictured it as something perfect from his boyhood. Well, it wasn't perfect. Not even close. JD had found the boathouse draped in spiderwebs, the boat stored hull up and half-rotted. Some sort of rodent—maybe chipmunks or raccoons—had made a nest under it. Though he didn't know the first thing about boatbuilding, JD had immediately decided to make the boat his project. He would restore the wherry so that when Sam brought his family to the lake at summer's end, the boat would be ready for him.

After loading the supplies into the truck, he decided to check his post office box. Sam was diligent about forwarding his mail from D.C. Sam had carte blanche to open and throw away anything that looked weird, which was pretty much all of his mail these days. People came out of the woodwork to send him everything from invitations to prayer chains to unsolicited marriage proposals. He was flooded with photographs of women and the occasional man wanting to meet him, the images sometimes pathetic, sometimes lewd, sometimes downright scary. Early on during the ordeal, he had made a serious error in judgment, signing an agreement with Maurice Williams, LLD. The media agent had promised to represent and protect JD's interests, to guide him through the quagmire of public life. Instead, he kept trying to persuade JD to agree to be a consultant for a feature film about his life and what had come to be called "the incident." According to Sam, Williams was beside himself over JD's absence. He'd even threatened to bring suit, which Sam and JD thought was hilarious.

As he walked along the tired-looking main street of Port Angeles, he contemplated crossing the road to avoid venturing too close to the Armed Forces recruiting office. He resisted the urge. Penny and Sam said he needed to have confidence that he wouldn't be recognized. Still, it was weird and surreal to see his face plastered on brochures and recruiting posters. Without his permission—because the army didn't need it—he had become one of this year's model soldiers. In the shopfront window was a placard three feet high with his service portrait and the caption Real Heroes for the Real World.

Yeah, that was JD, all right. He was so real there was an unauthorized movie coming out about him, so real he kept getting offers to endorse a line of camping gear or sunglasses, even prophylactics. According to the unauthorized biography that had appeared just weeks after the attack, he was "America's most appealing brand of hero—one who was 'just doing his job.'"

Tina had cooperated with the publisher of the instant book. So had Janet. Jessica Lynch had gotten a Pulitzer Prize–winning coauthor, but not JD. His biographer was Ned Flagg, a failed journalist with a flair for invention and a fast Internet connection. The book was heavily promoted and just sensational enough to rocket briefly onto the bestseller list.

Feeling almost defiant, JD paused in front of the

recruiting office. Through the open door he could see a round-cheeked boy talking to an earnest recruiter who was no doubt promising him the same action and adventure JD had been promised years ago.

He moved directly in front of the recruiting poster, studying it while the plate-glass window reflected his true image back at him.

The strange thing was, he hadn't really gone to elaborate measures with some complicated disguise. Coached by Sam and Penny, JD had grown out his hair and was as surprised as the Schroeders when it came in a glossy dark blond. He'd worn it in a military-style buzz cut for so long he'd lost track of the color. He had shaved off his mustache, traded his contact lenses for an ancient pair of glasses and cultivated a beard stubble. "Backwoods chic" Penny Schroeder called his new look. "They'll never guess America's hero is under that." With the John Deere cap to complete the outfit, he looked more like Elmer Fudd than Captain America.

"I could mess up your dental work," Sam had offered. "Get rid of that toothpaste-ad smile."

"I'll take my chances," JD said. "I just won't smile." That promise had been remarkably easy to keep. Until today. Until Kate Livingston and her boy. He didn't recall actually smiling at them, but he might have. A little.

Two teenage girls wandered past, popping gum and window shopping. They slowed down to admire the poster.

"God, he is so hot," one of them murmured. For a

moment, JD felt her eyes flicker over him. Shit, he thought. He'd gotten cocky about his disguise and now he was busted.

"Excuse me," the girl said and brushed past him.

JD let out the breath he'd been holding and headed the other direction. It was crazy, completely crazy. People projected all their yearning onto an oversize poster while looking through the actual person as if he wasn't there.

Shaking his head, he headed into the post office and checked his box. Sam had sent on a batch of bills and notices. At the bottom of the stack was an item that had not been forwarded by Sam. JD had requested it on his own, with unsteady hands and a heart full of trepidation. It came in a flat white envelope, weighty and substantial in his hands.

He couldn't believe how intimidating this felt. It was insane. After all he'd been through, nothing should intimidate him. But this was something he'd always wanted. Always.

He opened the envelope and took out a glossy booklet the size of a small-town phone directory.

He smoothed his hand over the logo: The David Geffen School of Medicine @ UCLA.

JD told himself that he still hadn't decided whether or not to send in his MCAT scores and begin the application process to enroll the following year. But he sure as hell might. He had the entire summer to think about it.

For the time being, he turned his thoughts to other matters. On the drive to the lake, he felt an unaccustomed ripple of anticipation. For the time being, his mother was all right, and he was finally starting to feel human again.

Five

Kate slammed the bedroom door behind her just in time, because the intruder was lunging for her.

"Aaron," she screamed, clattering down the wooden steps and out the back door. "Aaron! Get in the car! Now!"

He was outside, tossing a stick for Bandit. Instead of responding to her panic, he scowled at her. "Huh?"

"In the car, darn it, there's an intruder in the house," she said, whipping out her harshest epithet. "Bring Bandit. I mean it, Aaron."

It felt as if their escape took hours, but it was probably only seconds. Aaron and the dog got in back as she leaped into the driver's seat.

She reached for the ignition.

Oh, God.

"No keys," she said in a panicked whisper. "Where are the keys?"

It was a nightmare, worse than the scariest horror movie ever made, the kind in which a character named Julie (it was always Julie, no last name) fumbled in the car, desperate to escape, but the car wouldn't start and the next thing you knew, old Julie was chopped liver.

"I blew it," Kate said, sinking back against the head-rest as she remembered leaving her keys on the kitchen counter.

A hulking dark shape loomed at the driver's-side window. Bandit went into a barking frenzy, baying at the glass.

"Don't hurt us," Kate babbled. "Please, I beg you, don't—"

"Mom." Aaron spoke up from the back seat. He quieted the dog.

"Hush," she said. "I have to negotiate with—oh."

The monster, she saw, was holding out the car keys. "Looking for these?" the monster asked.

Except it wasn't a monster, Kate observed as the red haze of terror faded from her vision. It was . . . a girl. Cringing at the sight of the dog.

"For heaven's sake," Kate said, rolling down the window. Bandit inserted his muzzle into the gap, and the stranger moved back a few more steps. "What in the world is going on?"

The girl looked as embarrassed as Kate felt. Her face turned red and she stared down at her dirty bare feet. Her messy hair fell forward. "I didn't mean to scare you."

"Well, you did." Kate's adrenaline had nowhere to go, so it crystallized into outrage. "What were you doing in my house?"

The girl straightened her shoulders, shook back her hair. "I was, um, like, cleaning the place. I've been working with Yolanda for Mrs. Newman, cleaning summerhouses."

Judging by the sleep creases on one side of her face, the kid was cleaning the way Goldilocks had for the Three Bears. In fact, she even looked a bit like Goldilocks with her coils of yellow hair. She was older, though. Pudgier. She'd clearly helped herself to a bellyful of porridge.

But like Goldilocks, the girl appeared to be quite harmless and full of remorse. Kate felt her anger drain away. "What's your name?"

"California Evans. Callie for short. Am I in trouble?" The girl snuffled and wiped her nose. She had bad skin and carried herself awkwardly.

Studying her, Kate felt a wave of compassion, though she tempered it with caution. "I haven't decided yet."

"Can we get out now?" Aaron asked.

Kate still felt a bit apprehensive. The cottage didn't have phone service and her cell didn't work here. Yet the girl truly seemed remorseful and embarrassed by the whole incident. Kate's customary impulse to trust took over, and she nodded. "Okay."

Callie gasped as Aaron and Bandit jumped out. When the dog wagged his tail and sneezed a greeting, she wrapped her arms around her middle and backed away. Her face changed from red to stark white. "I'm scared of dogs," she said.

"Bandit won't hurt you, honest," Aaron said.

"Hold him anyway," Kate advised, recognizing the terror in the girl's face. "I'm Kate Livingston and this is my son, Aaron. And Bandit."

"He's mostly beagle," Aaron said. "We call him

Bandit because of the black mask on his eyes." He pointed out the dog's unusual markings but the girl withdrew even more.

"What are you doing here?" Aaron asked bluntly.

Callie looked a bit queasy. Beads of sweat formed on her forehead and upper lip.

Oh, heavens, thought Kate. Was she sick? An addict? This was not good.

On the other hand, she reflected, the situation was terribly interesting. Kate reminded herself that she was now a freelance journalist. She thought she'd have to go looking for stories. Maybe a story had come to her.

"Let's go inside," she suggested. "Bandit can stay out." He had a bed on the porch, one of those overpriced orthopedic sling beds from a catalog. Spoiled thing. Callie regarded Kate through narrowed eyes, but she went along readily enough. In the kitchen, her eyes widened as she took in the wealth of groceries on the counter.

Kate poured glasses of ice water for everyone and put out a bowl of Rainier cherries, summer's most fleeting delicacy.

"Have a seat," she said. "Tell me about yourself, Callie. How long have you worked for Mrs. Newman?"

"A few months." The girl eyed the cherries with yearning.

Kate pushed them closer to her. She noticed that the old pine table, one of the original pieces in the house, had been scrubbed shades lighter than she remembered, and then waxed until it shone. Similarly, the floor and all the fixtures gleamed and not a single cobweb lingered in the corners of the windows. If this was Callie's doing, it was impressive, though she needed to increase her understanding of boundaries.

"Um, are you going to tell her?" Callie asked.

"I should," Kate said.

"Mom." Aaron's voice rose in protest. He hated it when people got in trouble, probably because that's where he found himself so often.

Unjustly fired only a week ago, Kate was quick to sympathize. "I won't," she reassured her, "but I'd like an explanation."

The girl sipped her water. "I, um, I've been staying in the houses I cleaned, the ones that are empty," she confessed. "I never bothered anybody and I always cleaned up after myself, a hundred percent. I didn't know you'd be coming today, I swear. I had you down for tomorrow."

"We decided to come up early." Kate studied the girl's troubled eyes, the pinched and worried forehead. "Where's your family, Callie?"

"I don't have a family," she said flatly.

"That needs a little more explanation."

"My mom's away and I've never known my dad." She shook back her hair, acting as though it didn't matter to her.

"So are you homeless?" Aaron asked.

Callie plucked a cherry and ate it. "I'm supposed to be in a foster home, but I had to leave the last one. I couldn't stay there."

71

"Why not?" Aaron asked.

Callie's eyes, as gray and turbulent as the lake during storm season, expressed a truth Kate knew she would not utter in front of Aaron.

"I didn't really get along with the family," the girl said.

"You can stay with us," Aaron said.

Kate nearly choked on a cherry.

Fortunately, Callie anticipated her reaction. "I wouldn't do that to you and your mom, kid," she said, pushing back from the table. "Totally time to clip. I'll go up and get my stuff and then I'll be out of your hair." She headed for the stairs.

As Kate watched her go, something about Callie touched a chord in her. The girl moved awkwardly within an oversize gray sweat suit, and she kept her head partially ducked as though anticipating a blow. Yet despite the ugly sweats and dirty bare feet, there was a touch of teenage vanity. Her fingernails and toenails were painted a beautiful shade of pink.

Aaron eyed Kate reproachfully.

"Don't even say it," Kate warned, getting up. "I'll go talk to her."

"I knew it," he said, shooting out of his seat and punching the air.

"You can go play with Bandit while I sort this out."

In the big bedroom, Callie had opened the drapes to let in a flood of afternoon sunlight. A large backpack was propped by the door, and Callie was busy putting the sheets on the bed.

"I used my sleeping bag, honest," she said. "I didn't use your linens." She tucked the fitted sheet around one corner of the mattress.

Kate tucked the opposite corner. "I'm not worried about the linens," she said. "I'm worried about you. How old are you, Callie?"

"I'll be, um, eighteen in July," she said, her gaze shifting nervously. "That'll be good because I'll be a legal adult and I can do whatever I want."

Kate wondered what she wanted but decided to start with a different set of questions. Callie didn't look as though she was nearly eighteen. There was a subtle softness and roundness in her face and a haunted, lost look in her eyes that made her seem younger. "Talk to me, Callie," she said. "I'm not going to turn you over to the authorities. Where are you from?"

Callie opened the top sheet with a snap. The motion stirred a golden flurry of dust motes as though the house was waking up. The air was filled with the sunny smell of clean laundry.

"California," she said.

"That narrows it down," Kate commented. "Do you mind telling me why you were in foster care?"

"Because my mother belonged to this creepy commune," she said, giving up the information without resistance. "It was near Big Sur, and it was supposed to be this incredible self-sufficient utopia." Callie must have noticed Kate's surprised glance. "They homeschooled us, and some of us actually got a decent education. Brother Timothy—he was the founder—has a

73

Ph.D. in cultural anthropology from Berkeley." She opened the cedar chest at the end of the bed. "Is this quilt okay?"

Kate nodded and helped unfold the quilt, a sturdy, colorful family heirloom stitched by one of the Livingston women a couple of generations back.

"So, this Brother Timothy?" she prompted, sensing Callie's dislike.

"He's not anybody's brother and I'm sure by now Berkeley's ashamed to claim him. He's doing time for child molestation."

Kate's skin crawled. "Are you one of his victims?" she asked.

Callie worked with brisk agitation, creating perfect hospital corners. "When I was a kid, I had fun living there. We ran around and swam in the ocean and actually had a couple of good teachers. But once we hit puberty, *pow.* We didn't get to be kids anymore. Brother Timothy called us—the younger girls—his angels."

Kate abandoned making the bed. She sat on the side of the bed and motioned for Callie to do the same. "Didn't your mother . . ." She hesitated, knowing she ought to choose her words carefully. "Do you think the adults in the commune were aware of this?"

Callie snorted and nodded her head. "None of the mothers lifted a finger to stop him. They were all, like, under his spell or something. He convinced them that we were their gifts to him. Even if a girl got hysterical and fought back, the mothers made her go to Brother Timothy. They did everything they were told, like they

74

were Stepford hippies, you know?"

"That's a nightmare," Kate said.

"You're telling me."

Kate noticed that Callie hadn't answered her question about whether or not she was one of Brother Timothy's victims. "So is this commune . . . still around?"

"Nope. This girl named Gemma O'Donnell, like, three years ago, she saved us all." Callie studied the floor. "Gemma kept trying to tell someone what was going on, and every once in a while, somebody from social services or the school district would come up and take a look around but they never found anything. To an outsider, it looked like utopia—vegetable gardens, a flower farm, our own milk cows, everybody reading William Carlos Williams. Nobody listened to Gemma until she finally found a way to make them listen." Callie paused, took a gulp of air. "She went to the Big Sur Family Services Agency and threatened to kill herself if they didn't believe her." Callie's voice lowered to a shaky whisper. "She was pregnant by Brother Timothy. They took him away, and I never saw Gemma again. I don't know what ever happened to her or the baby."

Kate put her hand on the girl's shoulder. The girl flinched and Kate removed it. "I'm sorry. I hope things got better for you after that."

"They did for some of us," she said. "For me, for a while. But in the last home I was placed in, well, that was bad so I had to leave."

"Callie, where's your mother?"

75

Callie dropped her gaze. She picked at her nails. "I haven't seen her in over a year."

"Do you think she might be worried about you?"

"She should have worried about me when we were all living with that pervert," Callie snapped. Then she lowered her voice. "You going to call social services?"

"Not if you've been straight with me."

"You can check out my story on the Internet," Callie said. "Millennium Commune, look it up."

"I don't have Internet service here. If I need to go online, I have to drive to the library in Port Angeles."

"Whatever. I've been straight with you." She looked out the window as she spoke.

There were still secrets concealed within Callie, Kate was sure of it. She studied Callie's profile. The girl was quite pretty, though that wasn't immediately apparent thanks to the acne and some dark patches on her skin where she'd probably forgotten to wash. Her hair needed a trim, and the shapeless sweatpants and old Big Sur Folk Festival T-shirt didn't flatter her heavyset figure. Yet when the sunlight from the windows outlined the tender curve of her cheek, Kate saw a different person sitting there, a girl who was still a child no matter what the calendar said.

The protective instinct rose inside Kate, stronger now, urging her toward a leap of faith. She knew she had to give this girl a chance.

"Would you like to stay in the guest suite?" she heard herself saying. Back in the early days of the lakeside cottage, the first Livingstons had traveled with a housekeeper and cook, who had occupied the small bedroom and washroom off the main floor. Later generations used it to accommodate visitors, giving them more privacy than the upstairs rooms.

Callie narrowed her eyes. "What's the catch?"

"There's no catch. You need a place to stay, I have tons of room here, so—"

"I'd better not." She stared at the braided rug on the floor.

"You're going to run out of options," Kate pointed out. "In the off-season, plenty of houses are vacant, but now that summer's here, everything will change."

"I've got camping gear."

"I've got a six-bedroom house."

"Why?" Callie asked. "There's got to be a catch."

"No catch, like I promised. You said you've been straight with me. You've had a rough time of it. Why not stay here where you're safe?"

She snorted softly, a sound of bitter mirth.

"Is something funny?" asked Kate.

Callie shook her head. "I'll stay tonight. After that, we'll see."

Don't do me any favors, Kate thought. She reminded herself that if this girl's story was even partially true, she'd lived a nightmare. She didn't take Callie's reluctance personally, though. Giving her a room here was the right thing to do. "I'll call Mrs. Newman and let her know you'll be staying with us."

The girl looked amazed, her expression that of a starvation victim facing her first plate of food.

"It'll be all right," Kate said softly. "You'll see."

Callie sat very quiet and still for a few moments, and Kate suspected that gestures like this were rare in her life.

"You expecting someone?" Callie got up and went to the window.

Kate heard the crackle of tires over gravel, then the sound of a car door slamming. Bandit bugled his usual greeting.

"Who is it?" she asked.

"A really hot guy. He your boyfriend?"

For some reason, the suggestion brought a flush to Kate's cheeks as she joined Callie at the window. "The guy who lives down the road. Come and meet him."

Six

When Kate and Callie went out into the yard, Aaron was running circles around JD, talking a mile a minute. JD looked a bit discomfited by the boy's enthusiasm. Possibly he was already regretting having stopped by.

Seeing Aaron's efforts to get the man's attention, Kate felt a familiar pang. Aaron wanted a father in the worst way. He always had. As a toddler, he sometimes tried to wander off in the mall or at a baseball game, and she'd catch him trying to follow random men around, imprinted like a duck.

The way he emulated the stranger suggested just a hint of hero worship. As far as Kate could tell, JD was Aaron's ideal in faded work pants and Wolverine boots. He had a pickup truck and a chain saw. What more could a boy want?

She caught herself staring at his shoulders. They were broad without being bulky, and he moved with a certain athletic ease, suggesting a natural fitness rather than some kind of intensive training. There was something about JD. She couldn't quite put her finger on it. His careless choice of clothes suggested a lack of vanity, yet he bore himself with a curious dignity.

"Hello," she called, motioning for Callie to join her. "How is the victim?"

JD turned to her, and her heart flipped over. It was crazy, he wasn't her type at all, but she couldn't take her eyes off him. Okay, she thought, studying his hair, so it wasn't a mullet. Just long hair, and like Brad Pitt's in his best movies.

"The volunteers at the wildlife rehab place think he'll make a recovery." He indicated his truck. "I washed out your cooler."

"Thanks. JD, this is Callie Evans. She's going to be staying with us."

Aaron's eyebrows lifted almost comically, but he made no comment.

"Nice to meet you," he said.

Callie blushed and looked bashful. Kate wondered if, given her background, the girl had issues with men.

"JD, you want to check out the dock?" Aaron had a

fascination with the dock and the water. "You, too, Callie."

"Sure," she said. "Is it deep enough to dive off the end?"

"Yep. My cousins used to dive off it all the time."

"What about you?"

"Nope." Aaron's cheeks reddened, but he didn't explain further. Kate suspected he couldn't. He didn't have the vocabulary to put his emotions into words. Maybe, she thought, just maybe this would be the summer he'd finally swim.

Callie gave the dog a wide berth. "A kayak," she said, lifting the tarp that covered a long, narrow boat. "You ever go out in it?"

"All the time," Aaron said, clearly loving the attention. "It's a two-man, see?"

Despite his refusal to learn to swim, he loved boats and always had. The ferries of Puget Sound, a Zodiac raft, anything that would float appealed to him, bringing him close to the thing he dreaded.

"Maybe we could take it out," Aaron suggested.

"Of course we'll take it out," Kate assured him. She was determined for this to be a fun summer for him even though his cousins wouldn't be around.

Aaron showed off the kayak, which had been around since powerboats had been banned from the lake years before. Kate stood back and watched him, this boy whose teachers said he was a poor student with poor skills of self-control, as he effortlessly went through the attributes of the boat.

They had never met two strangers in one day, Kate reflected. And certainly they'd never encountered a teenage runaway and a quiet but unexpectedly interesting guy. Now she watched him next to her son, and he was patient and respectful in a way that appealed to her deeply.

Most men she met lost interest as soon as they discovered she had a child, or as soon as they discovered Aaron's rambunctious nature. So far, this one seemed to be all right with her son's constant chattering. He seemed to be sensitive to Callie, too, Kate noticed. He gave the girl plenty of space, didn't ask her a lot of questions.

A sensitive diamond in the rough. Right here on the shores of Lake Crescent. Who knew?

You're getting ahead of yourself, Kate, she thought. All he did was borrow your ice chest.

Aaron, on the other hand, seemed to have no reservations. "So you want to go kayaking right now, or after dinner?" he asked.

"Maybe another time."

He was diplomatic, thought Kate. He seemed to sense that you didn't just paddle out onto a remote glacial lake with a child you'd only just met.

A look of disappointment clouded Aaron's face. Then Bandit came back from some inexplicable dog's errand. He was flecked with twigs and sticker burrs and panting hard. Callie scooted away from him again, though she tried to be discreet about it.

"Well," said Kate. "I need to finish putting things away . . ."

JD seemed to catch her tone. "I should get going, too."

"Aw, come on," Aaron said. "Stick around a while."

"I'll see you around the lake," JD assured him. "Thanks again, Kate. See you, Callie. Take care of yourself."

She frowned at him suspiciously. "Sure."

Aaron walked with JD to his truck, bouncing along beside him as if he were a ball and JD was dribbling him. "Hey, guess what? When I was six, I walked the whole Spruce Railroad Trail all by myself."

"You don't say."

"Yep. There are mountain bikes in the shed. Five of them. Want to go mountain biking?" He didn't wait for an answer. "This is a really cool truck," Aaron said, speeding ahead, scrambling up over the tailgate. "Is this the Schroeders' truck?"

"Uh-huh. I'm borrowing it for the summer. The Schroeders live on the East Coast now."

"Hey, my cousins moved to the East Coast." Aaron started bouncing again. "All four of them. That's all I have. Four cousins. No brothers or sisters. You got kids?"

Way to go, Aaron, thought Kate, holding her breath as she waited for his answer.

"Nope," JD said easily, taking his keys out of his pocket.

"You married?"

"Nope."

"Seeing anybody special?"

82

"Aaron." Kate couldn't take it anymore.

"I was just trying to figure out all the stuff you'd want to know anyway," Aaron said, then turned again to JD. "If we were in the city, she would Google you on the Internet, but there's no Internet here."

"All right, buddy," she said. "Why don't you go make yourself useful and stop embarrassing me in front of company."

He saluted her and sped off, waving to JD.

"Sorry about that," she said as he got into his truck.

"Don't worry about it." He propped his elbow on the window frame. He looked as though he wanted to say something else, but he stayed silent for a few beats, staring out across the lake. His arm still rested easily on the edge of the window as though he was in no hurry to leave. "Do you really do that, look people up on the Internet?"

"Of course. Don't you?"

"I figure if I need to know something about a person, I just ask."

"What a concept."

"Like what about Aaron's father?"

"I beg your pardon?" She'd heard him perfectly well, but she needed to stall and reel in her thoughts.

"How does he fit into the picture?"

Oh, gosh, she thought. This is Date Talk.

"He doesn't," she replied. "Never has." Then, because she couldn't help herself, she added, "Why do you ask?"

"Why do you think I asked?" He still hadn't smiled at

her, but she caught a glint of humor in his eyes. At least, she thought it was humor.

When he looked at her like that, she felt a tug of . . . she couldn't quite put her finger on it. Recognition? How could that be? They'd never met before. Had they?

She narrowed her eyes and studied his face. What was it about him? Besides the fact that underneath the scruffy exterior, he had definite potential.

"I think you asked because you're interested in me," she said. "Am I right?"

"Lady, a guy would have to be comatose not to be interested in you," he said, sounding annoyed. Then he started up the truck. The radio station—KXYZ out of Seattle, the only one that came in reliably at the lake— blared news at the top of the hour. He shut it off, gave her a wave and drove away.

She stood looking after him for a long moment. "Then why don't you look happier about meeting me?" she asked no one in particular.

Seven

Each year after she got to the lake, it always took Kate a few days to decompress. She still tended to wake up and spring out of bed, already making a mental to-do list. Back in the city, it was likely to be a lengthy one: her deadlines at work and any number of errands, appointments and notes to herself about Aaron. Looking after her son meant checking his schoolwork, making his lunch and organizing his backpack, driving carpool. After school, the schedule was packed with karate, Cub Scouts, homework and playdates.

Playdates. Now there was a concept, she thought. Sadly, Aaron's dating life was more successful than her own. Other kids liked him even if their mothers thought he was a terror.

On their third morning at the lake, she got up and put the kettle on for tea. No coffee here. Coffee meant rush hour and work and stress. Tea meant serenity.

She was determined not to rush or to allow herself to get frantic about being jobless. She had a decent income from the Seattle properties. Her father had left her a wonderful legacy. If she was careful, she could get by for a long while without her salary from the paper. What she missed, though, was her identity. Writing defined who she was. She wanted to feel like herself again, producing copy, getting it published.

Stop, she told herself. You've got the whole summer to figure this out. Taking a deep breath, she looked out at the lake. Just the sight of it calmed her. Clear and flat as a mirror, the surface of the water reflected the surrounding mountains covered in evergreens, some with tiny veins of snow hiding in the topmost crevices. She checked the temperature—51 degrees at 7:30 a.m. Perfect. Maybe she'd take Aaron and Bandit for a hike later.

As they had so often over the past few days, her

thoughts drifted to JD Harris. Thinking about him was probably a bad idea, yet that was exactly where her undisciplined mind went. At the ripe old age of twenty-nine, she was still softhearted and romantic, capable of imagining what it was like to have a love affair or even a full-blown relationship, to plan a future with someone. While her friends at college had partied, falling in and out of love with the seasons, Kate had gestated. After Aaron was born, she'd lactated. She'd been much more productive than her friends. But she had never flung herself into an affair. As a single mom, she didn't have time for that.

Still, a girl could dream, and Kate did. She wondered what was going on with JD Harris—who he was, how he had come to be here at the lake. She had definitely sensed a spark of interest between them. He'd said so, though she couldn't be sure whether he was joking or not.

Though he'd made no promises, she'd half expected him to come calling.

But when in her life had she not been disappointed by a man?

The kettle rattled on the burner, and she turned off the flame before the whistle blew. A few minutes later she settled down with her tea and opened her laptop at the old-fashioned desk in the corner. Yesterday she'd composed a note to an old friend. Tanya Blair was a friend from college, a resounding success story from the UW's School of Communications. She worked as an editor at *Smithsonian Magazine*, and she was Kate's first and best prospect. It was quite a leap from local weekly to a national magazine, but Kate decided to think big. In the past, she'd tried thinking small, aiming low, and look where that had landed her.

She read over the note, and when she was satisfied with it, she printed out the letter, folded it and put it in an envelope. She felt a vague sense of dissatisfaction. Though she'd told Tanya her pen was for hire, she had no material to offer. Not yet, anyway. She needed to write, that was true, but she wasn't sure *what* to write.

A few minutes later, Callie came shuffling out, dressed for the day in her customary sweats. Her face was puffy from sleep. "Morning," she said, stifling a yawn.

"Hi," said Kate. "Tea?"

"I think I'll go straight for breakfast," Callie said, helping herself to a bowl of Total. She held out the box to Kate, who shook her head.

"I'll wait for Aaron," Kate said.

Callie indicated the window. "He's been waiting for you." On the lawn, he and Bandit were playing tug-of-war with what she hoped was an old towel.

"I didn't even hear him get up." Kate shook her head. "So what's on your agenda for today?"

"Yolanda is picking me up. We've got three houses to do on Lake Sutherland." She grimaced. "I *so* don't feel like working."

She looked a bit peaked, Kate observed, though there was nothing wrong with her appetite. Teenagers, Kate thought. They stayed up too late, no matter what time they had to get going in the morning. Kate had no complaints about the girl, though. She helped around the house, Aaron adored her and she seemed to be behaving herself.

She poured a second helping of Total and noticed Kate watching her. "I shouldn't," she said. "I'm getting fat as a pig." But she added milk and sugar anyway. "What about you? Do you have plans today?"

"I might take Aaron hiking up to Marymere Falls. Have you seen it?"

"No. I've heard it's pretty up there. Maybe I could go on my day off."

"I should also get some work done," Kate said, glancing at the silent black rectangle of the laptop.

"Have you figured out what you're going to write yet?"

"I've got a few ideas."

"I still think you should do Walden Livingston," Callie said. "He's like, this totally famous cult guy."

"I know. He still gets mail from some of his fans," Kate said. "Just a few, every year."

"He's the reason I picked this house to stay in, you know," Callie said. "When I saw the Annie Leibovitz photo of him and figured out that this was his place, I was totally blown away. His books are, like, sacred to people who care about the earth."

Kate never failed to be startled by this girl. She was a combination of streetwise runaway and naive idealist, incredibly well read in some areas and completely ignorant in others. "Not many young people are aware of Walden Livingston. How did you hear of him?"

"I was placed with a couple who made environmentalism, like, their whole life, and old Walden was their number one man. They had a signed copy of the book he wrote and a book of his collected quotations. You know, 'Leave no trail for a future traveler, let him find his own way' and all that. Did he really talk like that?"

Kate rested her chin in her hand and studied the Leibovitz portrait, which hung on the wall by the door. The picture captured the twinkle in his eye, the dramatic sweep of his snowy hair, which he'd told her was once as red as her own. His face had a geography as distinctive as the land itself, and Leibovitz's eye brought that out. I miss you, she thought, then turned to Callie. "I'm not even sure he said all those things."

"Did he seem, like, completely different from other people, in real life?"

"Good question." Kate smiled, remembering. "Maybe he did. To me, he was just Grandpa. That's about as special as it gets for a kid."

"I've only met my grandparents one time."

"Do you think you'd like to visit them again one day?"

Callie took a big bite of cereal and regarded Kate with wariness.

"I don't mean to pry," Kate said.

"Then why did you ask?"

"I'm curious, I admit it. I want to know about your life."

Callie considered this for a moment. She set down her

spoon and pushed the bowl away. "Here's what I know about my grandparents, the ones on my mother's side. They never did find my dad, so his parents were out of the question. When Brother Timothy got busted and the commune broke up, my mom and I came to Washington. She was so broke, she went to her folks in Tacoma and just ditched me there. Didn't even say goodbye or say where she was going."

Kate ached for her. "I'm sorry, Callie."

The girl shrugged. "No big deal. I'm totally over it. Anyway, they called CPS—Child Protective Services. They said they couldn't take me. I bet your grandfather wasn't like that."

"No," Kate said. "He was . . . magical. I feel so lucky to have known him."

"Did you know he was different?"

"I don't think I really concerned myself with his life's work. I know he had a lot of demands on his time. He traveled pretty much all during the school year." She went to the bookcase and got a leather-bound album, the one devoted to her grandfather's career.

Together, she and Callie perused the photographs, magazine clippings and newspaper articles. There was an entire page devoted to pictures of Walden posing or shaking hands with U.S. presidents, from Lyndon Johnson through Ronald Reagan. He had managed to get each one to sign some sort of legislation to help the environment.

"Man," said Callie, "I wonder what it would be like to do something so big, so important with your life."

"I don't think he could imagine doing it any other way." Although Walden had always been beloved by activists concerned with saving the earth, he had disappointed his parents by failing to take up the reins of the family business. When the family business was timber, and the eldest son's passion was conservation, it must have made for some unhappy times, especially when he spent most of the family fortune on his cause, but all that had happened before Kate's time. She studied Callie, whose coloring looked better now that she'd eaten. There was a question beneath Callie's question about Walden—Am I anybody? Do I matter?

"Callie, what's your mother like?" Kate knew it was risky to broach the subject, but she sensed that it was at the heart of the girl's troubles. "That is, if you don't mind me asking."

"It's fine. I don't have much to say, though. She's a loser and I don't miss her one bit." A car horn sounded, and Callie jumped up. "Gotta bounce," she said. "I'll be back by seven."

"Don't forget your lunch." At the door, Kate handed her a paper sack.

Callie gave her a stark look of gratitude, then headed for the door.

Kate knew the girl didn't have much kindness in her life. Even the smallest act of thoughtfulness came as a surprise to her. Kate found herself wishing that someone had loved Callie as a little girl, had fixed a sack lunch for her and told her goodbye in the morning. She was convinced that if everyone could have that in their life, the world would be a better place. The thought made her glance at the computer. No, she thought. No. One crusader in the family is enough. She needed to get her own act together before saving the world.

She closed the album, and used a soft cloth to clean the old leather covers and the edges of the pages. Her grandfather had led an important life. She was supposed to do the same, with her big plans for a big career. Things had worked out differently for her.

Just then, Aaron came bursting into the house, dancing around at the boot tray to kick off his shoes. "Mom!" he yelled. "Hey, Mom!"

"I'm right here," she said. "You don't have to shout."

"Okay. I found a fossil." He hurried over and showed her a stone imprinted with some beetlelike shell.

"You sure did, buddy," Kate said. "Where did you find it?"

"In the woods." He held it out to her. "You can keep it if you want," he said. "For a present."

"Hey, thanks," she said, putting away the album. She *was* doing something important with her life, she reflected, taking the offering from her son. What was more important than this?

Eight

"Kate Livingston," JD said into his cell phone as soon as Sam answered. "What can you tell me about her?"

He had driven into town to buy some fly-fishing sup-plies and check his mail. Having nothing to do all day, every day, was keeping him extremely busy.

"Katie Livingston in the big house down the road?" Sam gave a low whistle. "I haven't thought about her in years. You've met her?"

"Yeah. So what do you know?"

There was a muffled sound as Sam moved on his end, perhaps to get out of earshot of his wife or kids. "That I used to be in love with her," he said in a strained whisper.

"How's that?" JD grinned and shook his head. Sam was big-hearted and completely unafraid of his emo-tions. Since JD had known him, he'd fallen in and out of love a half-dozen times, soaring to the height of joy and plummeting to the depths of despair with reckless abandon. Finally, a few years back, he'd fallen for Penny, a civilian contractor, and announced to JD that he'd found his final soul mate. He'd kept his promise, too, lavishing her and their kids with adoration and rev-eling in both the struggles and pleasures of family life.

"Seventh grade," he confessed. "She was a year younger. I had a giant crush on her. When I was a hor-monal twelve-year-old, the sight of her in a bikini could put me in a coma. God, she was cute. Red hair and freckles. Later, when we were in high school . . ." He gave a low whistle.

"That doesn't exactly answer my question." Now thoughts of an adult Kate in a bikini crowded into his head.

"Damn. Little Katie Livingston. I was nuts for her, every summer. She still incredibly hot?"

Oh, yeah, he thought. "You're a married man."

"Who intends to stay that way. So . . . is she?"

"She's . . ." JD looked out his truck window. The Strait of Juan de Fuca was a flat, glossy blue, dotted by freighters heading for open water. He tried to think of a word for Kate Livingston. *Down, Simba.* "Smoking hot still works for her."

Another whistle. "Man. I haven't thought about her in years."

"I borrowed her ice chest. Long story. She's got a kid. Looks to be around ten years old or so."

"Husband?"

"I didn't meet one."

"If she goes by the name Livingston, she's probably single. Comes from an old, old lake family. The Livingston place is legendary. Huge. It's been there for almost a century. The family fortune was made during Prohibition. Timber and Canadian whiskey. Not very politically correct but it put them on the map—for a while, at least. I think subsequent generations managed to spend it all, but they kept that lake house. I lost track of Katie, though. I went into the service and I heard she went to college. She was some kind of genius and we all thought she'd do something big with her life."

"Is the whole family there?" Sam asked.

"No, but she had a kid," JD pointed out. "That's big."

"Hard to believe she never married."

"Why is it hard?"

"You met her. You tell me. What's she like now?"

Beautiful, thought JD. Kind and funny and a little bit vulnerable. Completely wrong for him in every way he could think of. The whole world was wrong for him, he reflected. That was the thing about what he'd done. He didn't regret it for a moment, but now he was a misfit wherever he went.

To Sam, he said, "She seems like . . . a nice person."

"A nice person. Oh, that tells me a lot."

"Like I said, I just ran into her one day."

"You could do worse than her for a neighbor, my friend."

JD said nothing, though he nodded his head. Sam was right. Judging by their first meeting, she was exactly the kind of woman any guy would fantasize about, a combination of girl-next-door and pole-dancer. "I believe I'll spend the summer minding my own business," he said.

"Bull. I can hear it in your voice. You're into this woman. I can't help you out, though. It's been too long since I've seen her. You'll have to do the work yourself."

JD knew a challenge when he heard one. "I'll pass. That's not why I'm here. Besides, my track record is . . . hell, it's scary."

"Aw, come on. Don't dismiss the entire female race over a few stalkers and loonies."

"That's the only kind I attract. How's my number one fan, anyway?" JD braced himself.

"She's still on that extended vacation, courtesy of the

District of Columbia. No word, so I assume the recuperation's going well."

JD eased a breath of relief from his chest. Ever since the incident, events and circumstances had been shoving him toward the moment of decision, when he'd finally shattered and begged Sam to help him disappear. A young woman named Shirlene Ludlow had cut herself on purpose and nearly bled to death, just so she could call 911 and get Jordan Donovan Harris to come to her house. Not long after, the call came from California. His mother was using again. That night, he'd realized that not only had his privacy been stripped away from him; he was actually a danger to people like his mother and Shirlene Ludlow.

"So your cover's still working?" Sam asked.

"As far as I can tell."

"I knew it would. Maybe Katie Livingston will make your exile less lonely."

Or more apparent, thought JD. At least she didn't seem like the type to slit her wrists to get a guy's attention. "Not likely," he said.

"Where's the fun in that?" Sam asked.

"This is not supposed to be fun," JD said. "This is supposed to be a way to get my life back, or am I stupid to think that's even possible?"

"Once you've been named one of *People* magazine's 50 Most Beautiful People, it's kind of hard to return to obscurity."

"Not funny, Sam."

"Listen, I don't blame you for being snake bit after

what happened with Tina." Sam had been with JD through the entire ordeal at Walter Reed. He had been the only one contacted after the incident. JD had no next of kin to speak of, none he would ever contact, not even in the worst emergency. "But something tells me Kate is nothing like Tina."

JD knew damn well he wasn't ready for a new relationship, but there was something about Kate that drew him, almost against his will. Something about who she was, her whole world, tantalized and tugged at him. He didn't even know her, but it was remarkable how much he'd projected onto meeting her that one time. "She's got some teenager staying with her," he told Sam. "You know anything about a Callie Evans?"

"Name doesn't ring a bell." Sam paused to tell one of his preschool-age boys to get his hand out of the fish tank. "Ever heard of Walden Livingston?"

"No."

"Kate's grandfather. He was some kind of activist who became a cult icon in the sixties."

"Yeah," said JD. "So?"

"So she knows a celebrity puts on his pants one leg at a time just like any other poor slob."

"I'm not telling her," JD said. Just the thought gave him flashbacks. After weeks of recuperation and physical therapy, he had looked forward to being discharged—both from the service and from the hospital. He planned a new life for himself—medical school, an old dream that had been resurrected by his brush with death. Becoming a doctor was something he always thought he'd do . . . someday. The incident with Muldoon was a stark reminder that it was a bad idea to put off "someday." But once he was discharged, his troubles were far from over. In fact, they had only begun.

"You can't stay underground forever."

"Let's hope I don't need to." JD got out of his truck and paced the parking lot. A family of four crossed in front of him, oblivious to his presence. The woman pushed a stroller while the man carried a small boy on his shoulders. They were laughing, and the boy was clapping his hands.

JD had seen families do terrible things to each other, and he knew love could turn to a poison as lethal as anthrax. Even so, there was a diehard inside him that could not stop wishing, hoping, yearning to be part of something bigger than himself—a family.

"You won't need to stay away that long," Sam assured him. "Your fifteen minutes of fame are nearly over."

"Good."

"You'll start finding discontinued Jordan Donovan Harris action figures for sale on eBay."

"Okay, now you're starting to tick me off."

Sam laughed. "Listen, enjoy the summer. Do you need anything?"

"No, I'm good. In my dreams, I never imagined a place like this existed."

"It's something else, isn't it?" Sam said. "Listen, quit worrying about the future. Everything's going to be fine."

His change in tone was so subtle that only JD, who knew Sam like a brother, detected it. "All right," he said, pacing in front of his truck. "What's going on?"

"You, um, remember Private Glaser?"

"Hell, yes." Glaser was the first casualty he and Sam had treated together in the field. "Why would you . . ." He stopped pacing and shuffled through his mail, fury snagging in his chest when he opened a large manila envelope and found himself staring at a gossip magazine with a photograph of himself as a young Green Beret medic, years ago in Afghanistan. "What the fuck is this?" he demanded.

"Ah," said Sam, "I see you found the latest sleaze-fest."

The black-and-white photograph depicted three young men—JD, a marine he'd dragged in from battle and Sam. "God, Sam," he asked, his voice grating with disbelief.

"I figured I should send it. Most of the stuff they publish is pure fiction, but that one you might want to take a look at."

Sweat trickled down his temples as he flipped open the issue and scanned the article. The article was illustrated with more photographs and a bunch of hyperbolic pull-out quotes. "This is Glaser's story, isn't it?" He scowled at the pictures of Max Glaser, the marine in the front-page photo. The man whose life Sam and JD had saved, long ago in the mountains of Konar Province in Afghanistan. They'd never seen him again after that incident, but apparently being rescued by

Jordan Donovan Harris was enough to warrant a lead story.

"Yo," said Sam, "you still with me?"

"I'm here." JD shook off the memory and set down the magazine. He felt like wiping his hand on his pant leg, shampooing his brain. Taking a deep breath, he focused on the whipped-cream peaks of the mountains visible beyond the Straits. "I thought you just said my fifteen minutes were nearly over."

"You know what I think? I think you're looking at this all wrong. Use it to make things happen, get what you want."

Like a mother in rehab? he wondered.

"Instead of getting freaked out by all the attention, make it work for you," Sam continued.

"Now you sound like Maurice Williams," JD said, scowling as he spotted something from the West Hollywood agent amid the stack of mail. Taking Maurice's advice had already gotten him more than he'd bargained for. He had signed with him because he'd been promised control over a feature film based on his life and the incident at Walter Reed. Naively, he thought this meant he'd be given discretion over whether or not the film was made. He'd nixed the project, only to discover the production company was going forward anyway.

"He's got a point," Sam said. "Because of what you did, you can make anything happen. Have you seen the bottom line on your foundation?"

"It's not 'my' foundation." It was a nonprofit foundation set up in response to unsolicited donations that had inexplicably come pouring in following the incident. One of the positive by-products of his fame had been that the American people, for reasons that often went unstated, felt compelled to send him money. Checks, and even cash, arrived with no explanation, no return address or perhaps a scribbled note: "For basic decency." "In appreciation." There was a certain level of discomfort in being given money for doing what anyone would have done under the circumstances. He'd tried sending everything back, but there were too many, a number without any return information. He quickly became overwhelmed by the flood of mail.

A nonprofit administrator took over, setting up the foundation. That way, JD didn't have to deal with the money. It didn't belong to him. He wanted it to be given to paramedics injured in the line of duty, and to help disadvantaged kids pay for college.

"You'll find some new statements in the mail I sent you," Sam said. "You've got some decisions to make. You can do anything you dream about. So what do you want?"

Oh, there was so much. And so little. He wanted for this all to go away and to be his own person once again. He wanted the past to be different, for his father to be around and his mother to be a mother. He wanted the American dream of living a normal, ordinary life. He wanted Janet to get better.

He'd had to go to war in order to fund his education. His foundation offered a different option to kids like he was. Thanks to the American people and their unpredictable generosity, a good number of kids were getting their education paid for.

And all it was costing JD was life as he knew it.

In front of the Port Angeles library, Kate turned off her cell phone and grinned at Callie, who sat next to her on the bench. "It's a go," she said.

Callie grinned back. "Really?"

"Yep. My friend Tanya loves the idea of running a retrospective about my grandfather. She pitched the project to her editorial board, and they gave it the green light. So it looks like I've got a lot of work to do." She felt a soaring sense of elation. She'd started the summer in defeat, but now her fortunes were improving. "I have you to thank," she told Callie. "You gave me the idea."

Callie flushed and looked away. She tended to shy from praise.

Kate didn't push. "Let's go inside," she said. "I need to get going on my research."

Aaron was already in the children's room for a Friday morning program on making paper airplanes. Kate couldn't stop herself from checking to see that he was behaving himself. For the moment, he seemed to be engrossed in paper folding. She released a small sigh of relief and headed for the computers.

There, she spent a pleasant half hour seeking out archived articles and images of her grandfather, a few of which she'd never seen before. Then, thinking about Callie, she searched for Millennium Commune and

Timothy Stone. Within minutes, she was engrossed in all the shocking, lurid details of the commune. Everything Callie had told her was true. And there were even some things Callie had not shared, like the fact that when Brother Timothy elected to rape a girl as a coming-of-age gesture, it was the girl's mother who procured the child for him, bathing and dressing her like a miniature bride.

Kate found the name and likeness of Sonja Evans, Callie's mother. Callie said she hadn't seen her in over a year. Maybe . . . Kate clicked through link after link and eventually found her way to another likeness, a mug shot from the sheriff's department of Pierce County, Washington. Even in the mug shot, the woman scarcely resembled a hard-faced criminal. In fact, she looked remarkably pretty, soft and vulnerable.

Kate felt a little queasy. Sonja Evans had been arrested for theft and was serving time at the Washington State Correctional Center for Women in Purdy. I'm so glad they locked you up, she thought. You don't deserve to be called anyone's mother.

She put her things away and went to find Callie. The girl was seated at a table, paging through an oversize book. "Find anything interesting?" Kate asked.

"A book about Cake—that's my favorite group. I'll put it back on the shelf."

"You can check it out if you want."

"I don't have a library card."

"No problem. We'll get you one right now."

A short time later, when they left the building, Callie

held a temporary card in her hand, cradling it as though it was fragile. When she saw Kate looking at her, she gave a fleeting smile. "I've never had a library card before."

Kate had a powerful urge to hug her, but held back. Callie didn't seem comfortable with hugging. They went outside into the sunshine. Kids were testing their paper airplanes on the lawn, and they stood watching while Aaron flew his again and again.

"I looked up Millennium Commune," Kate said. "In there, on the Internet. I hope you don't mind. I was . . . curious."

"It's not like it was a secret or anything. It was in the papers in California."

"It's awful, Callie. If there's anything I can do, if you just want to talk—"

"I had counseling and all that crud," she said with a dismissive shrug.

Kate gently touched her on the shoulder. "You didn't tell me about your mother."

"Oh, gee, sorry," she said sarcastically. "That's usually the first thing I tell people, that my mom's in the slammer."

"Are you allowed to visit her?" Kate asked.

"Sure. Not that I do or anything."

"I could take you there," Kate suggested. "If you wanted to, that is."

"Nope."

Kate dropped her hand. "Sorry. What I'm really sorry about is that you didn't do anything to deserve this."

"What makes you so sure of that?"

"Because you deserve better, Callie. You're young and incredibly smart, and you deserve the best life has to offer."

She regarded Kate with incredulity. "God, are you for real?"

"Do you have a problem with me wanting the best for you?"

"Just seems kind of pointless," Callie muttered.

"I disagree. What if I had decided there's no point in thinking I could write an article for a national magazine?" Kate persisted. "What if I hadn't even bothered to try? Then I'd still be rattling around at the cottage, convinced I had no future as a writer. It's not a bad thing, wanting something and thinking you deserve it. So what do you want?"

"A different life," Callie blurted out. "To be a different person, not some fat loser with zits." Callie stared at the ground. "I can't believe I said that."

It wasn't quite what Kate had in mind. Teenagers, she thought, glancing over at Aaron and the other kids playing on the lawn. "I don't want you to be a different person, and I bet you don't, either. Not really."

"Yeah, everything's just peachy."

Kate refused to get annoyed. "For what it's worth, I thought I was a loser when I was your age. Dated the same guy all through college because I thought Nathan was as good as I could ever get. He wasn't such a great catch, but I thought, hang on to him, Kate. If he dumps you, you'll have nobody. And of course, he dumped me. Never even saw Aaron."

"What a jerk."

"Took me years to figure that out." Kate caught Aaron's eye, waved to tell him it was time to go. She felt nonplussed, having forgotten the point she was trying to make. "That's the guy in my life now," she said, watching her son tell the library volunteer goodbye.

"What, you don't date because of one bad experience? Don't you think you deserve better?" She managed to imitate Kate's tone exactly.

"I didn't say that. I do go on dates. I just . . . haven't had much luck in that department."

"What about that guy?"

Kate's heart sped up. "What guy?"

"Right. You know who."

Kate turned and headed toward the Jeep. She did know. She did indeed.

Nine

As Kate walked down the driveway to the Schroeder place, she reflected that this was quite possibly going to seem like the most lame, transparent ploy a desperate woman had ever committed. He was going to see through it immediately. And the hell of it was, she hadn't managed to talk herself out of it. Her conversation with Callie had haunted her, and ultimately, she'd had to concede that the girl, young and confused as she was, had made a point. Here she was, urging Callie to set goals and take chances, yet she herself held back, acting as though everything was fine.

Well, everything wasn't fine. Here she was, twenty-nine years old, and some nights she was so lonely that she feared she might shatter, and all the little pieces would melt into the atmosphere, rendering her invisible. All right, so that was fanciful. But she wasn't fine and it was time she stopped pretending she was. Time to try something new.

She wanted to get to know her neighbor at the lake better, and she wasn't going to accomplish that by waiting for him to make the first move. She would proceed with caution, though. She'd checked with Mable Claire Newman who assured her that, according to the Schroeders, JD Harris was the best sort of guy, taking the summer off after being discharged—honorably— from military service. That sounded promising to Kate. She'd never known anyone from the military. The fact that he'd served his country made him seem reliable and brave.

The Schroeder place was decidedly rustic. Nestled amid soaring Douglas firs, it consisted of a main house with sleeping quarters for a small army in a loft, a boathouse and shed. Like the majority of homes on the lake, there was no cable TV or cell phone reception. Most people preferred it that way. It was one of the few places left where it was possible to unplug and retreat for a while. That was what this whole magical place was about—relaxing. Recharging. Rewinding your life to a simpler place.

Through the screen door, she could see him working at the kitchen table, bent over some project with total absorption, like a surgeon in an operating room. For the first time, she was seeing him without the John Deere cap. His long hair was touched by sunlight. In profile, he had a clean, square-jawed handsomeness she had failed to appreciate at first glance. His hands worked with surprising delicacy, wielding a tiny pair of needle-nose pliers. She thought about those big hands and their delicate movements, and her imagination took flight.

Get a grip, Kate.

The portable CD player was turned up loud, playing a Ben Harper tune, soulful and true, an unexpected choice for a man who looked as if he preferred honky-tonk music. Making quick, inaccurate judgments about people was Kate's specialty. She needed to watch that.

"Hello," she called, simultaneously knocking on the screen door.

He shot up from the table, the bench scraping the pine-plank floor. Tiny feathers scattered in the air around him.

"Jesus," he said, turning down the volume.

"I didn't mean to startle you." Without being invited, she stepped inside. "Sorry about that. I—oh, my word, look at your hand."

"My—damn." He held up his left thumb. A fishhook was embedded in the pad. Blood dripped on the floor.

"This is my fault," she said, bustling forward. "I am

so sorry. Sit down, and I'll help you."

"There's no need." His eyes, behind the thick lenses, narrowed in suspicion.

"Sit down," she repeated, giving his shoulder a nudge. Under her hand, he felt bulky and muscular. It had been a long time since she'd touched a man, and the sensation was surprising. Once he sat down, she went over to the sink and wet a paper towel. Then she put a pan of water on the propane cookstove, lit the burner and returned to the table.

"Let's see," she said.

"I can get it," he said, but gamely turned the thumb toward her.

"It's bad," she said, feeling herself go a little green around the gills. "The barb is buried all the way into your thumb." She took his hand and turned it. Even under the circumstances, the gesture felt strangely intimate. "Do you think I should drive you into town? There's an urgent-care clinic in P.A.—"

"No. I said I've got this, Kate."

She pretended not to hear the sharpness in his voice. "At least let me help. Is it a single- or double-barb hook?"

"Single. Doubles are illegal."

"I know that, but most fishermen cheat."

"Cheating a Beardsley trout. That's pretty pathetic."

He was definitely not pathetic, she thought, studying the broad shoulders, the square jaw. That jaw, she couldn't help noticing, was now tightening with a tic of annoyance. "I shouldn't have come," she said, her heart sinking. "You were having a perfectly good time tying flies, and I came by and ruined it."

"Yep."

She frowned. "You're supposed to deny that."

He propped his elbow on the table. "All right, look. If you want to help, I'll push the barb through and you can cut off the end so I can slide it out."

"You can't do that," Kate said, aghast. "It'll hurt like—oh."

As she was speaking, he gave the hook a quick jerk, grimacing and uttering a word that made Kate wince. More blood squeezed from the wound as the bloody tip pushed through his flesh.

"Get the shears from the aid bag over the sink," he ordered.

"Aid bag." She felt stupid.

"First-aid kit," he said. "Then I need you to snip the barb off the end of the hook. I'd do it myself, but I'm left-handed."

"When I snip this, it's going to move and hurt you."

"Just do it, Kate."

"I don't want to hurt you."

"Be quick and I'll survive."

"I want you to know, I feel terrible about this." She went to the cabinet and rummaged for the first-aid kit.

"It was an accident," he said.

"Which I caused." She found the first-aid kit, which was indeed a bag, a surprisingly big one filled with a bewildering array of paraphernalia. "Are you a doctor?" she asked.

"Nope." He didn't offer anything further.

"A paranoid survivalist?" she ventured.

"Yeah, that's me." He directed her to a zipper compartment, which contained some weirdly shaped shears in a sterile pack. Trauma shears, he called them. She opened the packet, took a deep breath, then snipped off the barb, cringing as she did so. He made no sound other than a quick intake of breath. Her hand shook as she set down the cutters.

With a motion of his hand so swift she nearly missed it, he removed the hook. Then he went over to the sink and ran water over the thumb. Working one-handed, he disinfected and dressed the wound with assured, professional efficiency.

"So are you . . . what, a veterinarian?" she asked him, thinking of the raccoon.

For some reason, her questions embarrassed him. Even from across the room she could see his ears redden.

"No," he said.

"Then . . . what do you do?"

"I thought I'd try fly-fishing, but it's not going well."

"I mean, when you're not here at the lake."

"I decided to give myself the summer off."

Well. He was really opening up to her, wasn't he? Maybe she was getting just what she deserved for barging in uninvited. "Time off from what?" she asked.

"Everything." He grinned, though she sensed he was being serious. "I think I picked the right place to do that."

"Mrs. Newman said you were in the military." Kate flushed again. "I asked."

He looked none too pleased about that. "Then why the Twenty Questions?"

He made her feel slightly ridiculous, but she held her ground. "They're getting-to-know-you questions. The kind people ask when they first meet and they want to know more about each other."

"Okay," he said, not smiling, though she detected a gleam in his eye. "Don't get so defensive. I asked about you, too. I asked my friend Sam Schroeder."

She didn't know what to say to that. "Should I be flattered?" she asked. *Or are you a weirdo?*

"You should definitely be flattered. Especially given the things he said."

"What things?"

"He was in love with you. And you broke his heart."

Kate remembered Sam as a stocky, athletic boy with a general sense of irreverence and an absolute fearlessness when it came to physical danger. As far as she knew, he still held the record for diving off the highest rock ledge into the Devil's Punch Bowl, the lake's natural deepwater swimming hole surrounded on three sides by limestone cliffs.

"He's lying," she said. "I never did a thing to Sam Schroeder."

"That's why he was brokenhearted."

"Very funny." Against her will, she recalled some steamy-windowed nights at the local drive-in theater, but they'd been in high school. Ancient history.

"What's he up to these days?"

"He's married and has two kids."

Of course he was married. Of course he had kids. Didn't everybody? Kate never regretted her choice to raise Aaron alone, but she often found herself wondering what it would be like to have a spouse, a partner, a best friend and lover, someone who cared about her ·and Aaron the way a loving husband would care.

Restless, she got up from the table and studied the pictures in rustic frames on the walls. Some were a good twenty years old. At least one looked familiar, and she pointed it out to JD, a snapshot of a group of kids in their bathing suits, standing at the edge of the lake, feeding the ducks. "This is me, right here in the green swimsuit. Freckles, skinny legs, knock-knees and braces."

"To a twelve-year-old boy, you were a wet dream."

"That's an obnoxious thing to say, especially to someone who just saved your thumb."

He didn't apologize. Instead, he regarded her with an impenetrable look. "I'd say you got over the skinny, knock-kneed, braces phase."

"Is that a compliment?"

"You're blushing, aren't you?"

Discomfited, she sat back down at the table. "I used to call him Sammy," she confessed. "Sammy Schroeder. So what else did he tell you besides the lie about his broken heart?"

"That he hasn't seen you since high school. He asked about your folks. Sounded like he thought a lot of them."

She nodded. "I think he did. Everyone likes them. My dad passed away and my mom remarried and moved to Florida." She waited for the usual awkward sympathy but didn't hear it. "So you and Sam were in the service together?" she ventured.

"That's right." He didn't volunteer anything more. When the silence became awkward, she racked her brain, trying to think of something else to say.

He beat her to it. "Is Callie still with you?" he asked.

"Yes. As far as I know, she'll be staying indefinitely."

"So is she a friend?" he asked. "Relative? Babysitter?"

"By now, she's a friend *and* a babysitter," she said. "She's great with Aaron. To be honest, I was a little apprehensive at first, offering her a place to stay." She didn't add that Callie had scared a good seven years off her life that first day. "She's going through a rough patch, so I told her she could stay. I've got tons of room at my place. Usually we've got a full house all summer, but this year it's just Aaron and me. Do you think I'm crazy, offering her a room?"

"Jesus, Kate. Yeah, I do. How much has she told you about herself?"

"Enough," Kate said. "More than you've told me about you."

"But I'm not moving into your place," he pointed out.

"I know everything I need to know about Callie for now." The fact was, Kate felt herself growing closer to her with each passing day. The girl opened up a little more every day, offering glimpses of the pain and uncertainty of a life of being shuffled around, never quite feeling safe. More than anything, Kate wanted to give her a feeling of safety and security, and gradually, little signs of trust were emerging, like when she no longer seemed taken aback when Kate made her a sack lunch for work, or when she shyly asked if they could go to the drugstore and get something for her skin. Maybe it was Kate's imagination, but her whole outlook seemed to be improving.

"She's feeling all right?"

There was something in the way he asked that made her frown at him. "Well, she's fine. In so many ways, she's a typical kid—passionate about music, curious. She and Aaron have been taking the kayak out every day." At first, Kate had made them stay in sight of the house, but as she trusted Callie more and more she let them explore farther. The girl was a hard worker, up early every day, and she'd grown comfortable with Kate and Aaron. And Aaron adored her, tagging along wherever she went. She still didn't like Bandit, though, and shrank from the dog whenever he came near.

"That's good," JD said.

"Is there something about her that I'm missing?"

"Doubt it. I just wanted to make sure things were going okay for you."

"Things are fine," she repeated. "Thanks for asking." Ill at ease, she got up again and went to the window, tucking her hands in her back pockets as she gazed out at the lake.

"What are you doing here, Kate?"

She turned to face him. His intense stare ruffled her. "I was curious about you, so I was going to pretend I needed to borrow a tire pump." Her cheeks stung. "I'm not very good at this."

"At what?" He shifted a little closer to her.

She could feel the nearness of his body. Even though they weren't touching, there was a flare of heat like a struck match.

"At . . . this," she replied lamely, fumbling the explanation. "At getting to know someone new."

"What can I do to make it easier?" His voice was both soft and rough at the same time.

She moved away, unable to think clearly with him standing so close. "And anyway," she said, "as it happens, I do need a tire pump. Mine has a blown hose, and the tires on a couple of our bikes are flat as pancakes."

"I'll see if I can find one," JD said, but he made no move toward the shed. He just stood there, watching her.

"Thanks," she said a bit uncertainly. She couldn't decide where to look—at his face? His chest? Did he know how distracting those glasses were? Her lips felt dry, and she ran her tongue over them. Then, realizing how that must look to him, she said, "I'm curious about something else. Why did you bail me out that day at the grocery store?"

He almost smiled then. She could sense it, a gleam in his eye, the upward slant of his mouth, just for a moment. "Why do you think, Kate?"

She had no idea what to say. Was he flirting? Was it a

rhetorical question, or was she supposed to reply?

Just when the tension grew palpable, he said, "I'll go find the pump."

"Thank you." She cringed inwardly. How many times could she thank him?

He stepped outside, and she stood alone in the small cabin. She spied a minimum of personal things lying around. A copy of the *Olympic National Park Trail Guide*, with certain pages marked. Next to the wood-framed sofa was a Coleman lantern, an extra pair of glasses and a well-thumbed paperback-thriller novel.

Under that was a glossy magazine of some sort. Knowing she shouldn't, but unable to stop herself, Kate sauntered over to the table and moved the book aside.

It wasn't a magazine but a catalog. "Applicant Information—The David Geffen School of Medicine at UCLA." She picked it up and flipped it open. There were notes on the inside cover in swift, ballpoint strokes.

"What are you doing?" JD demanded loudly from the door.

Startled, Kate let the catalog slip from her fingers. "Snooping?" she said tentatively.

"I can see that." He strode across the room to her.

"Are you a medical student?" she asked, even though he clearly wasn't in the mood to talk about it.

"Nope."

"Thinking about applying?"

"I'm past the age of going to school. Given where I have to start, it'd be a seven-year commitment, minimum. By the time I finished, I'd be nearly forty."

"How old will you be in seven years if you don't go?" she asked.

"I don't want to discuss this with you."

"Because I'm right and you have no argument."

"Because it's none of your business."

She felt cornered. "Look, I—"

"Here's your tire pump." He thrust it at her. "Keep it as long as you want."

She took it from him and refused to flinch despite his irritation. "Thank you," she said yet again, her voice holding a crisp dismissal this time, as though ending the conversation had been her idea.

He stood aside to let her pass and she did so with her chin slightly elevated. Coming here had been a mistake, of course. Pretty much everything she did when it came to dating and men turned out to be a mistake. She didn't know why she had expected this one to be different. Or why his rejection stung worse than usual. Maybe it was because the attraction she'd felt was so intense. She couldn't help it. He was strange and attractive, maybe even a little dangerous. And maybe it was because much as she loved being with Aaron and Callie, there were things she wished she could share with another adult, preferably male—a glass of wine on the porch at sunset, a conversation about her work on the *Smithsonian* article. It was one of her personal failings that she craved validation. She ought to figure out how to be happy with the way things were.

And how stupid to let herself get excited over a guy.

She was experienced. She ought to know better. It had been ages since she'd dated someone exciting. Of course, in her life, excitement always led to trouble. She ought to know that by now.

Ten

"You're afraid of water, aren't you, kid?" Callie asked Aaron as they paddled the kayak in tandem toward the footbridge and the Devil's Punch Bowl, the most popular swimming hole on the lake. The Punch Bowl was surrounded by steep rock faces that plunged all the way down to the bottom of the lake.

Aaron was glad he sat in front of her in the kayak so he could look straight ahead and not have to face her. They were getting good at paddling the kayak together. They'd been out nearly every day, exploring the rocky, forested edge of the lake for hours each afternoon. At first, his mom made them stay within sight of the house and then gradually, as she saw they knew how to be safe, she let them go anywhere they wanted. "It's not the water," he admitted. "I just don't like getting in over my head."

"In my book, that means you're afraid of water."

"So what if I am?" he said.

"So I tell you to snap out of it," she said easily. "Believe me, there are worse things in the world than water."

"What, like beagles?" Aaron couldn't help getting in a dig.

"There's a reason I'm afraid of dogs," she said.

"What's the reason?"

The kayak rocked as she shifted in her seat.

Aaron almost dropped his paddle as he clutched at the sides. "Hey," he said. "Take it easy."

"Don't have a cow," she said. "I'm not going to tip us over. I'm trying to show you something. Check this out."

Aaron adjusted his grip on the paddle. With an effort, he swiveled around. The thick life vest restricted his movements, but he managed to wedge himself backward to look at her.

Callie had her leg up on the hull of the kayak. She had rolled up her sweatpants to expose her knee. "This will tell you why dogs scare me."

Aaron felt a little seasick as he looked at the thick, shiny red damage. Frankenstein scars tracked across her knee, twisting in all different directions like mountain roads. There were deep dimples on either side of the kneecap.

"A dog bit you," he said.

"Mauled." She slowly folded down her sweatpants. "The word is mauled. A dog mauled me."

Aaron had never heard the term before. *Malled.* It sounded evil and painful, like shoe shopping with his mother.

"How did it happen?"

"I stupidly trusted a dog just because he looked

friendly and was wagging his tail. I should've kept walking, but no. I had to pet the dumb thing because I thought he was cute. Two seconds later, he practically took my leg off."

Aaron didn't know what to say. He made a picture in his mind of a cute dog latched onto Callie, growling like a monster. "Must've hurt."

"Like nothing I ever felt before. I needed like a hundred stitches, and then they treated me for toxic shock. So anyway, that's my reason," she concluded. "Whenever I see a dog, any dog, I remember that one."

"Oh," he said. "Bandit's not just any dog. He's real gentle. He'd never bite anybody."

"Tell you what, kid," she said. "I'll make friends with Bandit if you'll swim with me in the lake."

His teeth chattered at the very thought of getting in over his head, the water closing over his mouth and nose, his eyeballs. "I can't."

"Fine. I can't make friends with Bandit, then."

He worked the pedals of the kayak, steering it toward the Punch Bowl.

"Come on, Callie," he said. "Bandit's great. He's my best friend. He'd never hurt a flea."

"The lake water doesn't hurt anything, either, as long as you respect it and learn to be a strong swimmer."

"I can't do it," he said again.

"Bummer," she replied easily, dipping in her paddle. "It would have been fun swimming with you in the lake."

"But—"

"A deal's a deal," she said.

Aaron gritted his teeth. She didn't understand. No one did. He really really wanted to swim and play in the water like any other kid. He had forced himself to wade out into the shallows clear past his knees. Some nights, he even dreamed about swimming, plunging in, coming up for air, diving back down. In his dreams, he was the best swimmer in the world. And this was the best place in the world to do it.

"It's cool of your mom to let us take the kayak out," Callie said.

Cool? His mom? Aaron had never thought of her as cool before. "She likes you," he said. "She trusts you."

"Amazing," Callie murmured.

On weekends, the swimming hole would be crowded with college kids and teenagers from town, but today was a weekday and they were the only ones out here. The kayak glided silently under the narrow arch of the bridge, the only man-made structure on the whole lake. He leaned back, pressing into his life vest.

The rock walls rose in steep stair steps, most of them big enough to stand on. Those who were brave would jump off into the cold, crystal water. Aaron tried to imagine it, free-falling and landing in the water, getting sucked down into mystery. He leaned over the edge of the kayak. Seeing the blue depths of the lake gave him a dizzy, shivery feeling.

"There's supposed to be a ghost that haunts this place," he told Callie. "It's the ghost of a boy who dived off and drowned here."

"Yeah, right."

"They say he was a Makah Indian. He thought if he dived deep enough, he would turn into a fish and live forever. But he didn't turn into a fish. He became a ghost, and every evening he climbs up the rocks and dives into the water, over and over again."

"Really?" she asked in a fake-sounding voice.

"Really."

"Well, guess what, kid? My bullshit detector is going off."

Aaron grinned. He liked it when Callie talked like that. It made him feel grown up. "It's true," he insisted. "My grandfather said so, and my uncle saw the ghost when he was a boy."

"With all due respect to your grandpa, kid, he's full of shit."

"Is not."

"Is so. Is that why you're scared of water? Because you think there's a ghost in it?" Callie snorted.

Aaron hesitated, seriously considering her question. Unfortunately, he was afraid of all water, haunted or not, swimming pools, the lake or the ocean. "There's no reason for me not to like water. I just don't. Like a cat."

"You crack me up, you really do."

"It's not funny. The kid jumped off that high ledge right there." Aaron pointed it out. "He dived off, only instead of swimming to the surface, he just kept going, straight to the bottom. He never came up, ever. And now, every once in a while, people see his ghost, still jumping off the ledge, year in and year out."

Callie chuckled in an annoying way. It was annoying, because he could tell she didn't believe a word of his story.

"Kid," she said, "you've seen one too many reruns of *Unsolved Mysteries*."

"Have not," he said, twisting around in the kayak to glower at her. "I never get to watch TV. I don't even have a TV or cable."

"Not at the lake house," she conceded. "I'm talking about the city."

"Not there, either. My mom thinks it's bad for me." Usually Aaron was sheepish about admitting he was forced to live in a TV-free zone, as his mom liked to declare their house. Now that it proved his point, he didn't mind.

"Bull. Everybody has a TV."

"We don't. Ask my mom. My friends all think it's weird, but she refuses to have a TV in the house. Do you think it's weird, too?"

"We didn't have TV either, where I grew up," Callie said, her voice soft and kind of far away, like she wasn't even talking to him.

She never said much about that, not to Aaron. He knew that for some reason they took her away from her mom and made her live with different families. Foster families, they were called.

Aaron was curious about Foster families, and now he decided it was time to ask her. They paddled around in small circles in the middle of the Punch Bowl. The sunlight shot like lasers straight through the water in wide golden slants, and he could see so far down that it made him woozy with awe. He didn't look at her when he asked his question.

"So when you went to live with the Fosters, then did you watch TV?"

She snorted again, the way she did to show she was feeling sarcastic.

Aaron was sorry he asked, but it was too late. The words were out, hanging there between them.

"They're not named Foster," she said. "They're foster families. These are people who take care of kids who can't live with their real parents."

Aaron waited. He sensed she would keep talking if he kept his mouth shut. It was really hard, but he stayed quiet.

Sure enough, she told him more: "A few years ago, they decided I was in an unhealthy living situation and my mom was a loser who tried to ditch me, and I went to live with my first foster family. They were okay, I guess. The state gives them money to keep foster kids and they took in a bunch of us. And you talk about TV." She gave a low whistle. "There was a TV on in every room. I watched about a hundred years' worth of TV when I lived at that house."

Aaron tried to decide if that was a fair trade, giving up your own mother in exchange for a hundred years' worth of TV. No, he decided, even though *Nickelodeon* was just about the best thing ever. He watched it at his friends' houses every chance he got.

"I had to move every year," Callie explained. "I'd just

get used to a place and then they'd move me."

"Why?"

"That's the way it works. They never explained it to me. Just told me to pack up my stuff. The last place, I left on my own."

"Why?"

"I didn't . . . get along with the family. I decided to try living on my own. I thought I'd check out Canada, but I couldn't go there without picture ID and a birth certificate, so I ended up in Port Angeles, and Mrs. Newman gave me a job."

"And then you met us," Aaron filled in for her.

"That's right."

"Are we your family now?"

She fell silent, but he didn't turn to look at her. Then she lightly punched his shoulder, teasing a little. "Yeah, kid," she said. "You're my family now."

That was cool, he thought. Callie wasn't as much fun as his cousins, but she was still somebody to paddle around with, and—

"What was that?" she asked suddenly, in a snake's hiss. Her tone of voice made his skin itch.

"What?" Aaron asked.

"I saw something, up in the woods." She pointed at the cliffs, which were shadowed by giant evergreen trees.

"I didn't see anything." Aaron's skin itched some more.

"Look again. It's—oh my God."

That was when Aaron saw it, too. Saw *him*. The ghost

boy. He gave a war cry as he burst through the trees and hurled himself off the ledge, arms pinwheeling as he plunged headfirst toward the water. It all happened in a splash of blinding sunlight that quickly disappeared into the cold shadows of the lake.

Aaron tried to cry out, but his voice was gone. Then he saw, to his horror, that he had let go of his paddle. It was floating an arm's length away from the kayak. For a second, he just looked at it, regretting that he hadn't used the nylon line and Velcro wristband to secure it to his arm. In a complete panic, he lunged for the oar, coming half out of his seat.

"Kid, sit still," Callie yelled at him. "You're going to dump us—"

It was too late. The kayak rolled over, taking them both into the water.

Aaron's face hit the surface and he knew he was lost. If they were better at kayaking, they'd keep rolling and turn upright again, but that didn't happen. The lake dragged at his arms and legs, icy cold, inescapable. He was heading down, down, and maybe he would turn into a fish if he managed to go deep enough. Or a ghost boy. He was going to become a ghost just like the Indian boy.

He screamed, but the water sucked away his voice. He was drowning, with the cold water filling his mouth and nose. Terror closed around him, pressing in, squeezing the life out of him. Someone—something— dragged at the collar of his life vest, and he didn't sink at all. The life vest, which his mom said was the best money could buy, buoyed him up and he floated, his legs dangling above the eternal depths. The terror thrilled through him again and he peed a little, but since he was in the water, no one could tell.

Callie, also floating in her vest, whipped the hair out of her face and spat out a mouthful of lake water. "I swear, kid," she said, gasping. "You are such an idiot." She glided over to the kayak, which lay with its underside toward the sky. "Help me get this thing turned over."

"I can't swim." Aaron's teeth clacked like train wheels on a track.

"That's why you're wearing a vest, genius." She didn't even try to save him and haul him out of the water to the safety of the shore. She was just going to let him stay in the water, scared out of his mind.

Just then, the ghost swam over. Aaron was too horrified to scream. He could only shiver and stare. There was nothing under his feet. Nothing but hundreds of feet of deadly water.

"Need some help with your kayak?" asked the ghost.

And of course, Aaron realized, it wasn't a ghost at all, but a kid. A big kid with tanned shoulders and a tattoo on one arm.

"Yeah," said Callie, sounding tough. "You scared the crap out of us."

"That's what I was trying to do." The kid swam over to the kayak. Working together, he and Callie rolled it upright. Water sloshed in the hull, causing it to ride low.

"It worked," she admitted, looking at him all soft-eyed. "You shouldn't swim alone."

The boy grinned. Maybe even winked at her. "I'm not alone now. Your brother looks like he needs some help," the boy added.

"He's not my brother. And he can make it. Come on, Aaron, kick."

Aaron didn't know what else to do. He could barely think, he was panicking so bad. He fluttered his feet and waved his arms. He wondered if the motion would attract the monsters of the deep, and that made him want to hurry, and he fluttered faster.

With surprising speed, he made it to the kayak. By that time, Callie and the boy were facing each other, two floating heads, talking like old friends. The boy said his name was Luke Newman. He'd just finished high school and was spending the summer with his grandmother, who was Mrs. Newman.

Aaron's fast, wheezing breathing made him light-headed, and he started to gasp, hoping Callie would notice and drag him to safety. Instead, she scowled. "Chill out. This is not going to kill you. Just pretend you're on *Fear Factor.*"

"I've never seen *Fear Factor.*"

"It's pretty much like this, only you win a million bucks at the end. Nobody gets hurt, just scared a lot."

He wanted to scream at her in a rage. This was all her stupid fault, and he was so scared, he knew he was going to die any second. But he was too afraid to spend any of his energy screaming, so he forced himself to slow down his breathing. He kept kicking and scooping his arms toward dry land.

"We need to bail out the water from this thing," said Luke, pulling the kayak to the rocky shore. "Give me a hand, will you, Aaron?"

No. I'm too scared. Aaron thought the words but he didn't say them. His teeth were chattering too hard. There was nothing else to do but help. His feet kicked something rough and hard, and he pressed against it.

"Hey," he said, wobbling a little. "Hey, I'm standing up." Relief and amazement gave him back his voice.

"Good job, genius." Callie stayed in the water, her teeth chattering from the cold. With her hair all wet and smooth, and her eyelashes spiky, she looked different. Or maybe it was the way she was staring at Luke Newman.

"You forgot something," Luke told him, pointing.

Aaron turned, filling up with dread as he saw. "My paddle." It was floating away, hovering over calm blue water. He turned a pleading look at Callie. "Will you—"

"You dropped it, you fetch it."

Just that, and nothing more. No sweet-talking, like his mom did: *Come on, baby, the water won't hurt you,* his mom said whenever she tried to get him to go in over his head. *I'll be right here for you.* Callie acted as if she didn't give a hoot.

"Fine," he snapped. "I'll get it." And then, leaving no time to talk himself out of it, he stepped off the rocks and plunged into the lake again—on purpose. Because of the life vest, he didn't go under very far before he bobbed right to the surface and struck out toward the paddle.

Callie didn't clap or praise him the way his mom would have. When he came back with the paddle, she simply said, "You need to help Luke now."

Aaron and Luke turned the kayak and tipped out the water; then Luke said to Callie, "I didn't mean to scare you all the way into the lake."

"It's all right. I love swimming."

What about me? Aaron wondered. Where's my apology?

It was lost, he realized, in the you're-*sooo*-cute eye contact between Callie and Luke. "Hold the boat still," he said loudly, "so I can get in."

Luke braced his arms on the hull. "Maybe I'll see you around this summer," he said.

Aaron knew he was talking to Callie.

"Just don't sneak up on us anymore," she said.

"I can't promise you that."

Aaron looked back to see that Callie's face was as red as a tomato. Teenagers, he thought. They were always falling in love with each other. It didn't look like much fun at all. It looked painful, embarrassing. He wondered why it always seemed to happen. His oldest cousin, Brent, fell in love with a different girl every other week. Sick, thought Aaron.

"So there's your ghost," Callie murmured later as they paddled back toward the dock.

Bandit had already spotted them and was trotting back and forth on the bank, baying at them.

"I didn't say he was the ghost," Aaron said. His skin and hair felt cooler and fresher than ever, like there was something magical in the lake water. His fingernails were completely clean for a change.

"There is no ghost," Callie assured him.

He thought about the shadows on the lake and the submerged rocks and logs. He thought about his grandfather and Uncle Phil, who were big storytellers.

Bullshit artists, Callie would call them, but Aaron wasn't allowed to say bullshit.

So maybe there wasn't a ghost after all. He felt a little saddened by the thought. In a way it was fun, believing in ghosts. Now he truly had nothing to fear.

"That the first time you went swimming in the lake?" Callie asked.

"I wasn't swimming. I fell in."

"That's your own fault. And you were too swimming. You swam like a snail darter."

In spite of everything, Aaron felt a grin spread across his face. The afternoon sun warmed his skin and took away the shivers. "Maybe we'll do it again."

"As soon as we get to the dock," Callie suggested. "You can show me how your cousins jump off."

"On one condition," Aaron said, feeling strong, but at the same time strangely light, like the fear was a load of rocks and he'd just dumped them overboard.

"Yeah? What's that, kid?"

"You'd better make friends with my dog."

Eleven

Kate looked up from the screen of her laptop computer. She heard Bandit barking and a playful yell from Aaron. He and Callie must be back from their daily kayak trip. She smiled a little, even though the screen was blank and had been for the past forty minutes. The sound of her son at play always lifted her heart. And Callie's presence was an unasked-for blessing. Though sometimes difficult and troubled, she showed remarkable patience and understanding when it came to Aaron. And instead of brooding about the fact that his cousins weren't around, he was learning to be content with his own company, or with Callie's, unlikely as that seemed. The girl would reach legal adulthood soon, but she had a childlike, playful side to her that Aaron adored. They squabbled like siblings, yet it seemed so . . . normal.

Though tempted to go outside and join in whatever adventures they had concocted this time, Kate resisted. Her long piece on Walden Livingston was not going to be published as filler or an afterthought. It would run as a feature with plenty of photographs, some from the Smithsonian archives, others that she would provide. The unique slant, which Tanya urged her to play up, was the personal angle. In terms of the natural environment, his life had mattered greatly. His legacy was intact. However, the article was more about his personal qualities—the exuberance and commitment he gave to both his cause and to the people he cared about. Kate wanted the world to know how he had accomplished that.

She supposed.

Oh, Kate, she thought. Don't start doubting yourself now. This is your shot. To motivate herself, she paged through the e-mail letters she had printed out at the library. Three other magazine editors found her profile impressive and her topics intriguing. She didn't lack for interest. When she finished with Walden, there would be a number of options to choose from. If she didn't watch out, she might actually make a decent living from this.

"So finish, already," she muttered. The trouble was, she had finished the article repeatedly. Then she'd done it over. And over. Organizing her fingers on the keyboard, she rewrote the beginning for the umpteenth time: "He grew up in the pristine beauty of a primeval rain forest, never knowing his life of privilege was funded by the destruction of the wilderness he loved."

Kate discovered that she could highlight a sentence with three clicks and delete it with one stroke. *Poof.*

This lacked the drama of crumpling up a sheet of typing paper and lobbing it into the wastebasket, but at least it saved trees. Old Walden would've approved.

She thought about other writers she knew who had found success in their freelance careers. They talked about their passion for their topic. Their inability to leave the piece alone until it was done. Their sense of urgency to get it finished.

Why wasn't she feeling that now?

She clicked to a game of computer solitaire, which she won without thinking.

All right, she told herself. Back to work. She forced herself to concentrate on her grandfather. He'd been so vibrant, so inspiring to her. Why couldn't she bring him to life for a national readership? What was the matter with her that she couldn't write about a man who was a real American hero?

Studying the photograph she had propped on the desk to motivate herself, she closed the solitaire game. The picture was a yellowing Kodacolor print, circa 1979. It showed Kate standing on a deadfall log at least five feet in diameter. The log had become a nursery for ferns and moss, even other trees that wrapped their roots around its girth. On the ground next to her were Walden and Charla, the one who had been in a Marlon Brando movie. She still had that star quality, even in a casual snapshot. Her smile was genuine, her stance almost unposed. The picture was dominated by Walden himself, as all pictures seemed to be. Even standing left of center and looking at Kate rather than at the camera, he was a commanding presence, radiating vigor and energy. Kate herself—carrottop Kate, he used to call her—looked as plainly happy and carefree as any kid spending a summer at the lake.

She knew then why she couldn't capture that for the article. She already owned it and didn't have to go seeking the essence of her grandfather. There was no mystery to him, not for Kate.

Restless, she got up and wandered outside. There had to be something wrong with her that she couldn't write here in this quiet place, with no phone, TV or Internet to distract her. She was distracted anyway. She replayed her last meeting with JD Harris over and over in her mind, knowing it was probably not a healthy thing to do but unable to stop herself. Now, *there* was an intriguing mystery. He'd been amenable enough to letting her extract a fishhook from his thumb. They'd even exchanged a bit of idle conversation with personal information. But when she had guessed at his interest in medical school, he had all but shown her the door. Why? she wondered. Was he a commitment-phobe? Or was he hiding something she might not like?

Mulling over the possibilities, she began taking down the laundry Callie had pegged out earlier in the day to dry in the sunshine. Callie—now there was yet another intriguing mystery. Her background was incredible. This summer, it seemed Kate was surrounded by people who were more interesting than she was. Maybe that could be a good thing for a freelance writer.

She moved along the clothesline, folding the clean clothes and linens one by one and putting them in the basket. As each item was plucked from the line, a broader view was revealed. The highest peak was called Mount Storm King—for good reason. In the winter, the peak was the scene of violent, blinding storms producing snows so deep that remnants lingered even in the summer, thin veins of white tucked into the shadowy folds of the mountaintop.

Callie had so little, Kate thought, folding one of the girl's T-shirts, size XL, with the Incubus logo on the front. All Callie seemed to own were a few pairs of jeans and sweatpants, T-shirts and sweatshirts and two nightgowns, all extra large.

Kate was tempted to do something, more than she already had. Callie tolerated her help sometimes. At the drugstore in town, they had stocked up on hair and skin products. Styling gel and acne lotion would not repair the damage done to Callie's childhood, but anything that boosted her self-esteem, even a tiny bit, seemed worth it to Kate.

Her brother, Phil, had reminded her to proceed with caution. "She's a runaway, Kate," he said during their last phone conversation after her visit to the library. "It's what she does, and she'll do it again if you spook her."

While at the library, Kate had also toyed with the idea of doing an Internet search for JD Harris, just as Aaron had predicted she would. She couldn't do it, though. It felt dishonest, somehow. Besides, she rationalized, the name was so common she'd probably wind up with about 14,000 matches, most of them having to do with genealogy.

Phil had some advice for that as well. "Quit sneaking around and ask the guy."

"What if I spook him, too?"

"If a guy gets spooked by a beautiful woman asking questions, then he's not worth having."

She thought about his reaction to her snooping in his

house. No way would she be asking him nosy questions anytime soon.

She plucked the last item from the line, a crisply clean bedsheet. As she was folding it, she heard another bark from Bandit. The dog was small but had a voice like a pack of hounds on the hunt. Then she heard a splash and another bark, and glanced in the direction of the dock.

The clean sheet, half folded, slipped from her fingers. She barely felt it underfoot as she raced down the bank toward the lake.

Aaron had fallen into the water. Her Aaron, deathly afraid to go in over his head, unable to swim.

"I'm coming, baby," Kate shouted, pounding along the dock. She could see him in the water a few yards from the end. She jumped, fully clothed, into the lake.

The shockingly cold water stole her breath, but she was already swimming strongly toward him as she broke the surface. Fortunately, his state-of-the-art life jacket had a handle on the back of the collar for dragging him out.

"Mom," said Aaron. "Mom."

"I've got you, baby. You're all right now." Kate swam like a pro. She was filled with the adrenaline of a mother's panic for a child. It was the most powerful performance-enhancing drug there was. Under its influence, a mother could walk on water, lift a crashed car, scale a skyscraper in order to save her child.

"Mom. You can let go now," Aaron said. "I can swim on my own."

Kate's numb fingers kept hold of his life vest. "What?"

"Callie's teaching me to swim," he said with a curiously adult-sounding patience.

Kate twisted around to look at Callie, calmly treading water in her life vest. Then she looked back at her son.

"It's all right," he said. "You can let go."

Kate opened her hand and he drifted away from her. She resisted the urge to snatch him back.

"It's not really swimming on account of I'm wearing a vast," Aaron explained. "But I went in, didn't I, Callie?"

"Underwater and everything. Just for a second," she hastened to tell Kate.

"Watch me jump off the dock, Mom," he said. "Just watch."

"I'm watching." There was no getting used to the glacial water of the lake. Pretty soon, they would all succumb to hypothermia. A few more minutes, she thought.

Aaron swam clumsily to the dock ladder. Like a turtle with an oversize shell, he climbed up and out. Callie was busy tying the kayak to a cleat on the dock. Bandit paced back and forth, and then pounced with joy as Aaron got out. He stepped back a few paces, then ran for it.

Kate couldn't believe her eyes. Her son, skinny arms and legs splayed like a starfish against the blue summer sky, was flinging himself into the water.

He landed with a splash, going under for a fraction of

a second before the buoyancy of the vest brought him to the surface.

"Way to go, Aaron," Kate said, beaming at him. "I'm so proud of you." She turned to ask Callie what she had done to get Aaron in the water, but Callie was already headed toward the house.

"I'll get us some towels," she said over her shoulder, and hurried to the clothesline. The wet clothes were plastered against the girl's body, and self-consciousness seemed to roll off her.

Body-image issues. All teenage girls suffered from that. For Kate, it had been an excruciating embarrassment about her stick legs and flat chest. For Callie, it was a palpable sense of shame and defeat that she was so heavy and had bad skin. Kate ached for her. She wanted to assure Callie that she was attractive and smart, that how she felt inside was more important than how she thought she appeared to the world.

Kate watched Aaron jump in a few more times. Callie returned with the towels from the clothesline and sat down. Wrapped in a striped towel, she dangled her bare feet in the water. Bandit sat beside her, and she shot him a look of distrust but then gave the dog a tentative pat on the head. He licked her face, which made her cringe, but she stayed where she was and endured the licking.

"How did you get him in the water?" Kate asked Callie.

"I went in by accident," Aaron explained, paddling to the ladder.

"Oh, God . . ." A chill crawled over Kate's skin.

"I was right there with him," Callie said hastily. "Once I was in, I just stayed in. Simple."

"I should have dumped you in the lake long ago, then," said Kate.

"I said I'd swim if she would make friends with Bandit," Aaron said.

"That's a very sophisticated agreement," she said, "but there's something you need to know about swimming in this lake. If you stay in too long, you get hypothermia."

Over his protests, she made him get out. He agreed only when she promised to let him swim every day for the rest of the summer.

"One of these days I'm going to go in without the life vest," he announced, peeling it off and dropping it on the dock.

"Only if someone's watching you," she said, overriding her protective instincts to forbid him. Every child had to learn to swim. There was no getting around it.

"Of course," he said expansively.

Kate caught Callie's eye, and Callie nodded. "I'd never let anything happen to him," she said. "I swear."

"We saw the ghost," Aaron said, jumping up and holding the towel around his neck like a superhero's cape. "We saw the ghost of the drowned boy."

Callie rolled her eyes. "It was a guy named Luke Newman. He's Mrs. Newman's grandson." The girl's face changed when she spoke of him. Her eyes became unfocused and her features dreamy, and the towel she held tightly around her slipped a little. She quickly wrapped herself back up.

It was one of the rare occasions Kate had seen her acting like a typical teenager. It broke Kate's heart that it took so little.

"I haven't seen Luke in years," she said. "I bet he was younger than Aaron last time I saw him."

"He graduated this month and came to spend the summer with his grandmother." Callie's voice held a note of wonderment. It was, perhaps, hard for her to fathom the concept of spending the summer with a relative.

"It's fine if you want to invite him here whenever you like," Kate said. "I don't mind if you have friends over."

"I don't have any friends." Callie stood abruptly, pulled the towel firmly under her arms and headed toward the house.

"I'm your friend," Aaron said, trotting along behind her. "Hey! Callie! Wait up. I'm your friend. And Bandit, too." The dog trotted at their heels.

Callie reached out and gently cuffed him on the head. "Whatever you say, kid."

Bemused, Kate went to make sure the kayak was secure and the life vests hung up to dry. The image of Aaron plunging into the lake with joyous abandon lingered in her mind.

Leaving a great fear behind was such a liberating thing. She wondered if Callie knew what a gift she'd given Aaron.

In the zipper pocket of Aaron's life vest, she found

some treasures he had collected—two fossils and an agate. She set them down on the picnic table, then turned when she heard a car coming down the driveway.

A green pickup truck nosed its way toward the house. What do you know? Kate thought. JD Harris had returned.

She straightened her shoulders but resisted the urge to reach up and neaten her hair. She would primp for no man. But still, she was dying. In a waterlogged Corry's Slug Death shirt—no bra—and cutoffs, she looked like a white trash wet T-shirt contestant. Note to self, she thought. Don't dress like such a slob every day. You never know who might come calling. She was exasperated with herself for caring but couldn't help it.

"Hey," she said, casually greeting JD as he parked behind the house.

He got out of the truck, and Kate maintained her casual air even though her heart tripped into overdrive at the sight of him. There was something about a guy in faded Levi's, and he definitely had that something.

It had simply been too long since she'd had a man in her life, she thought. She definitely needed to get out more. The monklike existence of a single mom made her too vulnerable to attacks of unbridled lust. Besides, he'd been rude to her last time they were together, all but showing her the door just because she'd been nosy.

He held out a plastic creel. "I brought you some trout."

It was all she could do to keep her stare above the belt. "I'm sorry . . . What?"

"Trout," he said, a grin tugging at the corner of his mouth. He was doing a little staring of his own. He seemed intrigued by the Corry's logo. She resisted the urge to cover up. "I caught them about an hour ago and thought you might like them for supper. As a thank-you for the first aid." He showed her his bandaged thumb.

"Did you know you're supposed to catch and release in this lake?"

"These aren't from the lake," he said easily. "I went to the Elwha River down the road."

Apparently, it was too much to expect an apology for his rudeness, if he even realized he'd been rude. Of course he did. Didn't he? She kept looking for something wrong with this guy, some flaw that would contradict her attraction to him. The reason, she supposed, was that when it came to men, there was always a catch. In her experience, anyway.

Catch and release, she thought.

She wondered what the catch would be in JD's case. She wondered if it was something that could hurt her.

"Thank you," she said, peering into the creel. "You already cleaned them."

"It wouldn't be much of an offering if you had to do the cleaning."

"True. But I'll accept this on one condition." Before she could talk herself out of it, she went on. "Stay and have dinner with us."

He said nothing. Kate instantly felt like a fool but covered it up with a bright smile. "There's fresh trout on the menu."

"Sure," he said. "Thanks. I wasn't trying to finagle an invitation."

"I'd love to have you." As soon as the words were out of her mouth, Kate realized the double meaning. "Uh, I mean we. Aaron especially. He's celebrating a little something today."

"His birthday?"

She shook her head. "I'll let him tell you."

He indicated the outdoor spigot. "Mind if I get cleaned up?"

"Not at all," she said. "I'll be in the kitchen."

She lied. She went straight to her room and put on dry clothes, exchanged her wet things for a pale blue V-neck top and jeans, ran a comb and some styling gel through her damp hair, then put on lipstick—just a touch. She didn't want the primping to be obvious. She could hear Aaron talking to himself in the shower and smiled. He was probably reliving his adventures of the day. She could hear the downstairs shower running, too. Callie seemed to love endless showers.

Then she hurried down to organize dinner. On the landing, she glanced out the window to check on her visitor.

Oh, boy, she thought, suddenly riveted to the spot. He had taken off his shirt to wash up. Water from the outside faucet sprayed like diamonds in the sun, surrounding a body that was the stuff of dreams. He was not a hunk but a work of art, with perfectly muscled pecs and shoulders and abs, brawny arms. Kate leaned so close to the window that her breath steamed up the glass, but he was too far away to see in greater detail. Everything she was dying to know, like the pattern of his chest hair and if he had any scars or tattoos, eluded her. She couldn't figure out how to get closer without being too obvious. Flushed, she stepped back.

Snap out of it, Kate, she thought. Easier said than done. This man awakened wild yearnings inside her, reminded her of unfulfilled dreams and all the endless lonely nights she had spent trying to convince herself that everything was fine.

When he came into the kitchen, his hair damp and finger-combed, his T-shirt molding itself to his chest, she pretended not to notice. His massive size dwarfed everything in the kitchen, his broad shadow falling across the floor. Even so, he looked at ease here, as if he belonged. He was looking around the place, his expression unreadable.

A person's surroundings said a lot about her; Kate knew that. The lakeside cottage was a repository for generations of family history, from her grandfather's prized photographs of both Teddy and Franklin Roosevelt to last year's photo collage, which Phil's wife had made of their kids.

"My world and welcome to it," she said. "I'll just start dinner."

"What can I do?" he asked.

And just like that, she had a partner. Some people were lost and awkward in the kitchen. Not JD. He seemed perfectly at ease preparing ears of corn for roasting, slicing tomatoes onto a platter and carving a watermelon. It felt utterly natural to work alongside him, and reminded her of other times here, when preparing supper was a family affair. The kitchen was designed to make meal preparation a group activity, with a center island and plenty of room to maneuver.

"This is quite a feast," he said.

"I hit a roadside stand on the way from doing errands in town." She emptied the creel into the sink and turned on the water. He'd done a professional job filleting the fish with almost surgical precision.

Music from the radio drifted from Callie's room, and Kate hummed along with a tune by the Libertines while brushing melted butter on the fillets. "That girl is obsessed with music," she said to JD. "Smart about it, too. I brought a collection of CDs from home, but I know she thinks they're hopelessly uncool."

He finished peeling off the last strands of silk from the ears of corn. "Does she have any kind of plan? For the end of summer, I mean."

"Callie? I haven't pressed her for one." Kate seasoned the fresh trout with lemon, salt and pepper. JD held the door for her while she headed outside to fire up the grill. "I have a feeling she wants to keep a low profile until she officially turns eighteen. She's probably worried they'll stick her in another foster home she doesn't like." She considered telling him what she'd learned about Sonja Evans but immediately talked herself out of it. She was tempted, though. For some strange reason, it felt perfectly natural to discuss the kids with him. She needed to snap out of it. He wasn't her partner in this. He wasn't her anything.

While the fish and corn were grilling, they set the outdoor table. She wondered if it was her or if this whole scenario felt incredibly domestic, like something they had been doing together for a decade instead of ten minutes.

"I was going to ask you something about Callie," he said, distributing the old speckled enamel plates. "Do you think she'd like to earn some extra money at the Schroeder place? Off the books," he added. "I'd pay her cash for maybe a few hours' cleaning each week."

Kate couldn't help herself as a huge smile unfurled on her face. Her heart felt different. Fuller, warmer. She knew he didn't need a weekly cleaning service at his place. He just wanted to help Callie out. She was starting to get a read on this guy. He was like her favorite kind of candy, a hard outer shell and a sweet mushy center. "All right," she said. "You're busted."

"Busted?" Even with sunglasses on, she could tell he was scowling.

"I knew you'd been hiding something, but your secret is out now," she said.

He dropped a fork to the table. "Look, Kate, I—"

"You don't have to explain yourself," she said. "It's nothing to be ashamed of." She decided then to go for broke. "I'm glad I found out the truth about you."

He picked up the fork. "You are?"

"Of course. You don't have to pretend around me. But I'll keep your secret, I promise."

"You will?"

"Sure. Although why you'd want to hide this is beyond me. I think a guy with a heart of gold is incredibly attractive. Why would you pretend otherwise?"

She could see him let out a long, slow breath as he went back to setting the table. "Good to know," he said.

"I just said I think you're incredibly attractive," she reminded him. "Did that make any impression on you?"

"You said a guy with a heart of gold is attractive. I didn't assume you meant me."

At least he was a good listener. "Well, you do have a heart of gold."

"Yeah, that's me. Twenty-four-karat gold. Don't make assumptions about me, Kate."

"Then tell me about yourself and I'll know."

"Nothing to tell. I'm taking some time off, considering my options."

"Like medical school."

"That's right."

"You were so touchy about that."

"Didn't mean to be. So, about Callie . . . ?"

He was shutting down now. Kate sensed that she'd pushed hard enough—for now. "I bet she'd jump at the chance to earn some extra money," she said.

"I'll ask her tonight."

"JD!" Aaron leaped out onto the porch and ran down to the yard.

"Hey, Aaron." JD shook hands with him.

For a moment, Kate could only blink at her son. Finally, she had to ask. "What did you do to your hair?"

149

"Callie did it." He touched the spiky bristles that crested his head. "It's called a faux-hawk."

"That's great, buddy." Kate turned quickly to the grill, hiding the look on her face.

"I've been jumping in the lake all day," Aaron informed JD.

"Sounds like fun." JD handed him a sack of corn husks. "Take that out to the trash can, will you?"

Kate watched her son willingly do the simple chore. A simple chore that would have taken her a half hour of nagging to make him do. JD could have no idea that it was actually a big deal to get Aaron to do chores. She found herself wondering what pretense JD was practicing, if any. Perhaps none. Perhaps this was who he was.

She turned off the propane grill and saw that JD had put out glasses of ice water. She was momentarily rattled, accustomed to going it alone.

Aaron returned from taking out the trash and rang the brass ship's bell on the porch, signaling dinner. JD sent him to wash his hands. Callie made an appearance, seeming a bit bashful as JD greeted her.

"We're having fresh trout from the Elwha," Kate said, transferring the fish from grill to plates.

"Is it safe?" Callie asked, then blushed. "I mean, I've heard certain fish have a high mercury content . . ."

"You're right," JD said. "Not freshwater trout, though. Scout's honor."

"Cool. I'm starved. What can I do to help?"

"It's all done," Kate said. "Have a seat."

Callie looked momentarily nonplussed, then sat down at the picnic table. Aaron went for a spot next to JD. Kate noticed JD giving him a discreet, wordless warning to wait until she sat down. Only then did JD give Aaron the nod to proceed. As she murmured a quick, simple blessing over the food, Kate privately thanked JD for knowing what manners were.

Dinner was a feast, topped off with bowls of salmonberries gathered from the bushes along the driveway. Aaron chattered on about swimming in the lake, Luke the ghost boy, skipping stones and kayaking. In between stories, he managed to eat everything on his plate, a rare occurrence for her usually restless son.

"When it's my birthday," Aaron said, "I get to say what's for supper."

"So what do you pick?" asked Callie.

"Pepperoni pizza and white cake with chocolate frosting. Every year. What about you?"

"I don't get to pick."

"Why not?"

"You want to know something weird?" she said.

He perked right up. "Of course."

"I've never had a birthday party."

"No way." Aaron's eyes bugged out.

"Way."

"That sucks." Aaron glanced at Kate. "I mean, that stinks. It really does."

Callie shrugged. "I wouldn't know. Where I grew up, we were told that being born was a natural, everyday process that doesn't need to be validated by artificial means."

Kate couldn't help herself. "That's just absurd."

"It's the way things were." Callie ate the last of her watermelon. "When I found out the day I was born, I always had a secret celebration for myself. It wasn't the same as a birthday party but I did it anyway."

"Good for you, Callie. You matter in this world. Every person matters," Kate said, privately cursing Callie's mother. "I'm glad you're with us now."

She flashed a bashful smile.

"When's your birthday?" Aaron demanded.

"The fifteenth of July."

"You're going to have the best birthday this year," he vowed.

"Whatever."

Callie didn't have much more to say, but she had plenty to eat and insisted that she and Aaron clean up after dinner. Once again, he helped without complaint. As they sat outside watching the sun touch the mountaintops at the west end of the lake, Kate could hear the two of them inside, talking and teasing.

"They're like old friends," she murmured to JD. Almost, she thought, like brother and sister, but she didn't say so aloud.

Callie had turned up the radio and was offering a detailed critique of Velvet Revolver's "Sucker Train Blues."

"She's very savvy about music," Kate observed. "I think she's incredibly smart, but she hasn't had much of an education."

"It's not too late for that," JD pointed out.

Their silence was companionable. Kate considered opening a bottle of wine but rejected the idea. That was getting a little too . . . romantic. Not yet, she thought. But maybe someday. She was cautious when it came to men and romance, but she had her reasons. The biggest one was Aaron. He tended to form an early, intense connection with men she dated, and when a guy stopped coming around, it was harder on Aaron than it was on her. She smiled a little, shook her head.

"Something funny?" JD asked.

"I tend to overthink things," she admitted.

"Like what?"

"Like us." She laughed aloud at the expression on his face. "It appears you aren't even aware that there's an 'us.'" She waited for him to respond, but he didn't. Unlike her, he seemed perfectly content to sit in silence. Too bad, she thought. She had questions. "When you were in the military, what did you do?"

"I was a medic."

"And you worked with Sam?"

"Sometimes. We started off in different units but crossed paths a lot."

A medic, she thought. So he already had a medical background. His interest in medical school made more sense than ever.

"Dishes are done," Aaron yelled through the screen door. "Can I have dessert?"

They had ice cream with caramel syrup, and afterward, Kate noticed Aaron rooting around in a cupboard for board games.

"You should escape while you can," she murmured to JD. "Otherwise you'll get roped into Chutes and Ladders."

Despite the music from the radio, Aaron overheard. "No way," he said. "We'll play Scrabble."

"What's Scrabble?" asked Callie.

Aaron rolled his eyes. "Duh." He set up the board for three players—Kate, JD, and for himself and Callie as a team. "She's new and I'm a kid," he explained, "so we get to work together."

"You don't have to stay," Kate said to JD.

"I'll stay," he replied.

Covering an inner thrill at that, Kate started with "gamble," not exactly inspired, but at least it used her three best letters. After a whispered consultation, Callie and Aaron attached "gas" to that. In a stunning move, JD added "adenoma" to that. "Time to open a can of whup-ass on the Scrabble board," he said, very nearly smiling.

"Whup-ass," Aaron said under his breath.

"Adenoma," Kate said, frowning. "I've never heard of it. Are you sure it's a word?"

He narrowed his eyes at her. "It's a word. And give me my thirty-nine points."

"Thirty," said Kate.

"Look again. The M gets a triple-letter score."

He was right. One of his tiles occupied the coveted square.

154

Kate refused to give up without a fight. "I'm looking it up." She grabbed the old yellowed paperback dictionary and flipped through the well-thumbed pages. "A noncancerous tumor," she conceded. "I didn't know that."

"Thirty-nine points," he reminded her.

It was only the beginning of her humiliation. For someone who made a living with words, she should have done better. The tiles were cruel, though. She drew a Q, but no U. She even had the sought-after X, though the board offered no place to attach it. She took so long deliberating over each move that both Callie and Aaron started yawning, their eyelids drooping. They both seemed relieved when the tiles ran out and the game ended. The final tally added up to victory for JD.

"I'd better get going," he said. "Quit while I'm ahead."

"JD, wait," Aaron said, sounding a little desperate. "How are you at fixing things?"

"What things? Like raccoons?"

"Bikes. We got the tires all pumped up, but the chain on mine keeps falling off."

"I'll help you fix it," Kate said, mortified by her son's obvious ploy.

"Nope. I want JD."

Me, too, she thought.

"I don't mind," JD said. "I'll have a look at it one of these days."

Kate walked outside with him. "You don't have to, you know," she said. "I know how to fix a bike."

"Then that makes one of us."

"Aaron . . . um, he does this. He looks for father figures in guys we meet."

"Is that a problem?"

"It is when he gets his heart broken." Kate bit her lip. She'd said too much. He probably knew perfectly well that Aaron wasn't the only one who got his heart broken. "Look, I didn't mean—"

"Don't worry about it, Kate."

And just like that, she didn't. He had a weirdly soothing way about him. Most men had the opposite effect on her, bothering and unsettling her.

The sun was gone at last, though its light would linger in the sky until well past ten o'clock. This was the most beautiful time of day at the lake. The water, a vast flat mirror, reflected the mountains. Along the shore, a few lights and campfires flickered like a necklace of gold. Crickets and frogs sang from their hiding places in the shadows.

This truly was a world apart, Kate conceded. That was the magic of summer at the lake, she thought. This place was a world apart, and you could be anyone you wanted to be out here.

She couldn't fathom why it worked that way and why it always had. An exhausted single mother could be Susie Homemaker. A boy who struggled in school could be Tom Sawyer, skipping stones, running barefoot through the grass and learning to swim. A homeless girl could have a family.

"Overthinking again?" JD asked her.

She realized she'd let her silence go on too long. "Just . . . thinking. I love it at the lake. I can be a different person here."

"Why would you want that?"

"Doesn't everybody? When I was a kid in Seattle, I was always being teased about having red hair and freckles, and for knowing all the answers in class. Each summer, I'd come to the lake and metamorphose into an Indian princess, a pirate queen, an Olympic swimmer, a legendary mermaid. Anything but my true self."

"I'm glad you got over that phase," he murmured.

When she grew older, she used to let Sammy Schroeder steal kisses behind the boathouse. Later on, when they were in high school, he used to take her to the drive-in movie in Port Angeles, and there would be more kissing in the musty-smelling cab of his El Camino.

She wondered if Sam remembered those times. She wondered if he had mentioned them to JD. She could ask him, certainly, but she didn't. That would seem presumptuous, as if she was sure of his interest. They weren't yet at the point of discussing their friends of the past or future in any detail. They only existed right now, in this moment. Both seemed to understand that going beyond that would be a mistake. At the moment. There was plenty of summer left for getting to know him.

"Thanks for having me," he said, apparently not interested in pursuing the conversation.

"It was no trouble at all."

"I didn't mean to make you invite me, but I'm glad you did."

"Me, too," she said. "I'm glad you stayed."

"Maybe we'll do it again sometime."

"Maybe."

"Thanks, Kate." He lingered. The last light of day burnished his hair, the squared-off jaw and big shoulders, the sculpted lips.

"You're welcome," she said softly, and took a step forward. This was the lake, after all. She was allowed to be different here, bolder, romantic. It had been so long since she'd had a summer romance—or any romance for that matter—that she was amazed to find that the flirting came so naturally. She focused on his lips. Brushed her hand against his arm accidentally-on-purpose.

He leaned down, his lips nearly touching hers, so close she could almost feel him, taste him.

"See you around, Kate," he said softly, his breath warm in her ear.

She realized then that he was reaching for the handle of the car, not putting his arm around her. He got in the truck and drove away, leaving her bemused and frustrated on the driveway.

She shouldn't have let him get away. She should have made him either kiss her good-night or flat out reject her. As things stood, she didn't know what sort of goodbye that was.

She went into the house. The Scrabble board lay as they had left it on the kitchen table. Before putting it away, she studied JD's words: target, bivouac, gamer, pet, adenoma. Did the words a person spelled in Scrabble give any insight into his state of mind? Probably not. He was just going for the big score, every time. Her own words—gamble, elate, not, nip, lonesome—said nothing about her, gave no hint as to what made her tick.

Except for "lonesome." That was a little too revealing, but she couldn't help herself. It was a chance to land on a double-word-score square.

She picked up both sides of the board and poured the tiles into the old blue Crown Royal bag, a convenience provided by her father years ago. As she put the game away, she reflected that this evening had been a good one, maybe too good to be true. They were like the family in that old television show, *The Waltons*. Except this family was made up of an unemployed single mother, a runaway teenager, a nine-year-old boy and a mysterious mountain man.

Other than that, they were just like the Waltons.

Twelve

JD was supposed to be dealing with an unavoidable stack of mail this morning, but thoughts of Kate made him restless. He constantly reminded himself that he'd come here for the isolation, the solitude, the chance to get his life back. The last thing he needed was to fall for

June Cleaver and little Beaver. But against all common sense, he felt drawn to her simple human decency. Her world-class tits.

Keep your distance, he cautioned himself. Yet a woman like Kate made it hard for him to follow his own advice. He had brought her an offering of food, a gesture as telling and transparent as the first caveman bringing home the hunt.

He had almost kissed her. He had leaned down so close he could smell her hair. He had felt a tug of recognition, and all his instincts had urged him to press closer and explore.

Thanks to what had happened to him last Christmas, he could not allow himself to do this. Not now, not for a very long time, maybe never. He doggedly barred the door to further thoughts of Kate Livingston and tried to concentrate on the mail he had brought from the post-office box in town. Sam was adept at filtering out the flood of letters and packages from the loonies of America. Who knew the Land of the Free was Home of the Brave as well as Home of the Crazies? And dozens of them seemed compelled to send him things, week in and week out.

Thanks to Sam, JD received only the legitimate bills and normal correspondence.

If getting a large, flat envelope from a Hollywood agent could be considered normal.

JD stared at the envelope. He drummed his fingers on it. He wished he had never heard of Maurice Williams, LLC. "Taking control at this stage is for your own protection," Williams had assured him. "Nobody needs your permission to do the film. An unauthorized version can pop up any minute, like that god-awful book. Is that what you want?" Williams had handed him the contract. "This is your chance to be in charge. You'll thank me, Jordan. I swear you will."

JD hadn't thanked him. Taking control meant agreeing to be a consultant on the biopic. It meant agreeing to promote the film. It even meant attending its premiere at the end of it all.

In exchange, JD would be paid a fortune, all of it going to benefit the foundation. That was his only consolation. All he really wanted was a normal life again, to go and buy a bag of Fritos or a three-pack of Jockey shorts without being stalked by paparazzi, accosted by loonies or asked for his autograph. To have an uninterrupted meal in a restaurant or, God willing, to have sex with a woman, any woman, who wouldn't turn around and sell the whole story to the tabloids. It didn't seem like so much to ask, yet it seemed impossible from where he was now.

Along with the mailing from Williams, Sam had sent a copy of *Shout* magazine, quite possibly JD's least favorite of the celebrity rags. On a Post-it note, Sam had scrawled, "Ha ha. You and Anna Nicole." The tabloids certainly gave him a more interesting life than he'd ever actually had. People he'd never met before came out of the woodwork to describe encounters they'd had with him, all fictional. The cover of the magazine featured an old photograph of JD as a Green Beret medic in combat gear. The headline read TV's Next Reality Star?

Apparently there was speculation that JD's disappearance was due to the fact that he was off taping some sort of bachelor or makeover show.

The idea made his gut churn. This was saying a lot, because he had a stomach of iron. In his everyday work, he saw people filleted like brook trout, burned, bruised and battered beyond recognition, shot and stabbed. He had removed week-old corpses from overheated apartments, having to pour them into a body bag. He had seen maggots at work in places most people dared not imagine.

These things did not make him feel like puking.

Seeing himself in a gossip magazine—that made him feel like puking.

A footstep on the porch outside startled him. Callie.

He stuffed the magazine into the wood-burning stove. There was no fire going because the summer nights were warm, but he knew he'd be lighting one tonight.

"Hey, Callie," he said, holding open the door. "Thanks for coming."

"I don't mind a bit. I can always use the extra money."

He knew she had her pride. She also had secrets, and he hoped, in time, she might open up about that. He couldn't put his finger on it, but something was not right. He suspected the two of them had a few things in common. "How are you feeling?" he asked.

"How . . . what?" She tucked her hair behind her ear

and eyed him in confusion.

"I mean, how are you doing?" he amended.

"Fine," she said. "Great. Ready to get started."

He wondered if it was a mistake to have Callie working at his place. In all honesty, it wasn't that hard to clean the cabin, especially for someone programmed by the army to keep things neat. Yet he felt compelled to help her. She didn't seem like a normal, healthy teenager. She was lethargic today, and he wondered if the shadowy patches on her skin might be acanthosis nigricans. He didn't want to scare her off by prying, though. If he dug too deep, she might bolt. Still, maybe she would open up to him, though he doubted it. If she hadn't come clean with Kate, it was unlikely she'd do so with him.

He showed her where everything was, including snacks and drinks. He also invited her to take a break whenever she wished.

She tilted her head a little to one side. "Are you, like, this big worrywart or something?"

"Or something," he said.

"Do you mind if I listen to the radio?" she asked, folding a stick of gum into her mouth.

"Not at all. There's a CD collection."

She leaped right on that. "Anything good?"

"Depends on what you like." He gestured at a shelf.

"*The Best of the Eagles.* Not too promising."

"Keep looking."

"Oh! The Mothers of Invention." She pulled out the disc. "That's a little more like it." She rejected Elton

John, the Grateful Dead and Queen, but happily gathered in Eric Clapton, the Cars and the Talking Heads.

"You have interesting taste in music," said JD.

"I've loved it all my life, and I almost never forget a song. My dream job is to be a disc jockey who's allowed to play pretty much anything."

"Ever thought about going for the dream job?" JD couldn't help himself. Her comment caused his attention to flick to the shelf above the writing table. The medical-school application was still there. Still untouched.

"Sure," she said, taking a bottle of Windex from under the sink. "It's a long shot, though. I'm lacking in a few areas, such as an education. A permanent address. A birth certificate, for that matter."

"Have you thought about what you'll do once . . . when summer's over?"

"Sure. I'll get a place of my own. Find work somewhere. I might not have a diploma but I'm not stupid."

"What about the dream job?"

She popped her gum. "It's a dream, you know? It's not real. That's why it's called a dream."

"I don't think that it's that far-fetched, you being a disc jockey."

"Maybe."

"Definitely. Anyway, I'll be out in the workshop if you need anything."

She gave him a dismissive nod.

She was an okay kid, all things considered. Kate had expressed surprise that someone with Callie's background had turned out relatively normal. JD understood, though. When a kid's home life was a nightmare, being normal was a willful act of survival.

He ought to know. By the time he was a first-grader, standing in the unwelcome spotlight of show-and-tell, he had learned it was best to make up a family of his own, just so people wouldn't ask why his mother never attended school plays or PTA meetings. His father was in the foreign service, he told his teacher and classmates, and his mother worked during the day and also went to night school, studying to be a linguist. At six, he had no idea what a linguist or the foreign service were. He'd heard about them from the only constant source of information in his life—the TV.

With the diligence of an anthropologist, he studied other families on TV and modeled his life on them. The family in JD's imagination cared for each other like the Huxtables. They had the cleverness of the people on *Family Ties*, and the sense of humor of the *Growing Pains* family. Those endless programs taught him things that had never crossed his mother's mind or heart—the value of affection and compassion. The healing power of a child's imagination was one of the most potent tools in his arsenal. That, and the EMS substation down the block from his apartment.

Some kids grew up with one father or stepfather. JD grew up with a firehouse full of men who helped raise him. He never asked them to do this. But soon after he discovered the nearby station and started hanging around it, the personnel there took an interest in him.

He ate more meals there than at home, found more acceptance and guidance with the EMTs than he ever had with his mother.

Now that he was a paramedic, he understood. In this profession, you developed a sense about people, the way he had about Callie Evans. Under Kate Livingston's roof this summer, the girl was probably experiencing more stability and compassion than she had her whole life.

That was Kate. He barely knew her, but she seemed genuine, as warm and devoted as the mothers he had observed on TV, as loving and generous as the one he had fabricated for show-and-tell when he was a boy. And even in an old T-shirt and cutoffs, she looked like a lingerie model.

He headed out to work on Sam's wooden boat. JD had heard about the wooden cosine wherry for years. It was part of the mythology of the lake. Sam had told stories, shown pictures of his father's handmade rowboat, had practically begged JD to take it out on the water.

Clearly, it had been a long time since Sam had seen the boat. The wood was dry and brittle, its finish gone. The hull resembled a mound of kindling with broken ribs and rotted-out planking, its epoxy finish turning to dust. Since JD didn't know much about boats, he was armed with books, manuals, sketches and plans and most of all, the determination to restore this one. The Schroeders had a good selection of tools and supplies, and he'd bought more in town. Boat-building was a craft requiring surgical precision and strict adherence to rules. He liked that. No iron nails could be used; wooden pegs of persimmon or black cherry were required. Waterproof sealant had to line every lap and groove. For some reason, JD felt driven to do this— repair the broken parts and smooth away the scars, make the craft seaworthy again. It was a measurable project, the results concrete. Something that wasn't a life-or-death matter. This wasn't a patient screaming at him or puking on him. It wasn't going to die on him. Yeah, that was the appeal. Even if he screwed up, the thing would never die on him.

He positioned the hull bottom up on a pair of sawhorses. Time to get busy sanding, filling the cracks, sealing the wood, bringing the craft back to life. He used more clamps than a trauma surgeon. The nearby trash can filled up with wood scraps and sawdust, the air with the smells of cedar and spruce. Music drifted from the house. Callie had found an album by Jethro Tull. Every once in a while, he could see her through the window, working away.

He lost any sense of time, though the sun tracked its slow progress over the lake, flickering and glinting on the surface. A flock of mallards lifted, trailing drops of water as they arrowed to the sky. "Thick as a Brick" played on the stereo. Sweating behind a protective face mask, arms and hands flocked by sawdust, JD felt something unexpected stirring inside him. A shift, a weird buoyancy. It took him a moment to recognize the feeling. Then he realized that for the first time since Christmas Eve, he was happy. Not in general but in this moment. Doing simple work with his hands, listening to music, feeling the sun on his back—they gave him something he hadn't felt in a long, long while.

This was going to be a thing of beauty, he swore it.

The music changed to Eric Clapton singing "Layla," and that made him think about Kate again. Having dinner with her had meant far too much to him. For her, it had been a simple meal. Something routine that happened all the time. She had no way of knowing that for him, sitting down as a family around the supper table was an alien concept. The undeniable pleasure of sharing a meal had been deep and sweet, painful in its intensity, yet not the sort of pain he wanted to avoid. Instead, he craved it. Her, he craved her, red hair and freckles, curves his hands wanted to outline, green eyes that fascinated him with facets that changed like the surface of the lake in the sun.

He went down on one knee to face the hull head-on and judge its symmetry, comparing it to the original published plans. The sides flared out in graceful curves that, amazingly, appeared to match. Today, he was a reconstructive surgeon.

Now "Change the World" was on the stereo. JD straightened up, stepped back to determine what the next step would be. He whistled between his teeth, matching the melody on the stereo. He didn't hear Callie coming toward him but saw her from the corner of his eye and turned. She walked with an oddly purposeful stride, and even in the golden light of late afternoon, her skin looked pale. She had smudges of dirt and ash on her hands and face, evidence of her hard work.

"You look like Cinderella," he said with a grin.

"Yeah, that's me, Cinder-fucking-rella," she said, and he noticed a blaze of anger in her eyes. She held something clutched against her chest.

When JD realized what it was, his heart sank like a cold stone. Very slowly, he put down the sander he'd been using. Then he took off the protective mask and hung it from the end of the sawhorse. He said nothing. He stood frozen, waiting. "Worried Life Blues" in the background sounded distant and tinny.

"You're him," she stated, slapping the magazine down on the end of the sawhorse. "You're that guy."

Tiny flakes of ash flew from the pages.

Damn it, he thought. He should have been more careful. Shouldn't have let himself get so comfortable with his anonymity. "Do you make a habit of snooping in people's woodstoves?"

"I was going to clean out the ashes. I found this and took a break, just like you told me to, and I started reading. I saw the note someone stuck to it. At first, I was confused, but it didn't take me long to put two and two together."

"Listen, I never meant—"

"So were you ever going to tell us the truth, Sergeant Jordan Donovan Harris, or just make fools of us?"

JD swallowed, tasting sawdust. He considered denying that he was the man in the magazine, wondering if he could lie his way out of this. Looking at her face, her dark, accusing eyes, he knew better. This was a girl who, in one way or other, had been lied to all her life. She knew what a lie sounded like.

He didn't speak for a moment. He wanted a few more seconds to be anonymous, a guy spending summer at the lake, nobody in particular.

"I didn't want to make a fool of anyone, and I sure as hell didn't mean to hurt anyone," he said at last. "Sorry if your nose is out of joint."

"Why wouldn't you just own up to who you are?" she asked.

He gestured at the magazine. "That's why."

She picked it up, flipped it open to the now-familiar image of him attacking the Walter Reed bomber. "This is not something to hide from your friends. This guy—Jordan Donovan Harris—he's a hero. He's, like, the biggest hero in the country."

JD shook his head. "He's a guy with some good training who happened to be in the right place at the right time. The last thing I wanted was this." He took the magazine, closed it, set it aside. "Don't be ticked off at me. I'm trying to get away from all the attention, be normal."

"I don't get it. You're famous. You can do anything you want. Go anywhere, hang out with Paris Hilton."

He wiped his hands on his jeans. "I rest my case. You're a smart girl. Think about it. When people know who I am, I can't even buy toothpaste without being followed."

"Is it true about that woman who cut herself and called 911 just so you'd rescue her?"

Shirlene Ludlow. She just wouldn't go away. "That woman," he told Callie, "is a real person who put herself in real danger. Knowing there are people like her out there makes it kind of hard for me to stay on the job."

"It's not your fault she's a loony."

"Maybe not, but would she have sliced herself up otherwise?" He shook his head. "No telling, but I couldn't take that chance."

"So you gave up your job because of a crazy woman? That's not fair."

He almost laughed. Fair wasn't in his vocabulary, not any longer. "That's part of the reason. Because of what happened, I wasn't effective in my job anymore, so I had to leave. I'm out here trying to get my life back. So far, it's been working." He waited. Other than the Schroeders, he had not encountered anyone who was capable of keeping his secrets. It was too irresistible. It was human nature for people to say, "I met him, shook his hand, spotted him in VIP seating at a ball game, saw him putting gas in his car at the Georgia Avenue Texaco."

For his unauthorized biography, the author had dug out comments from a waitress who had served him coffee at the neighborhood diner ("As I recall, he took both cream *and* sugar."), his high school football coach ("He always knew how to make an end run when it counts."). Even the laundry where he took his uniforms to be cleaned offered some comment, and he hadn't even known they could speak English.

Now here was Callie, a lonely teenage runaway with secrets of her own. Would she try to parlay this into something for herself, or would she respect his privacy?

She leaned against the sawhorse and reopened the magazine to the article. "So how much of this is true?" she asked.

"Does it look like I'm filming a dating show here?"

"I'm glad you're not. Those shows creep me out."

"All the articles sound the same. In a lot of them, the only thing they get right is the spelling of my name."

"So what do people really call you? Jordan?"

"Nope. That's something the press started. JD has always been it. Harris in the army."

She turned the page, looked from the service portrait showing him as a Green Beret to him now—unshaven, long hair, glasses. "I can't believe how different you look."

"People see what they want to see." He waited some more. He had no idea what this girl was going to do, but if she decided to rat him out, his summer underground would come to an abrupt end. He didn't want to ask her about her intentions, to put ideas into her head. She stayed quiet, scanning the article.

Finally he decided to say what was on his mind. He did not mean to threaten her or to point the finger. He was simply speaking the truth. "Everyone has secrets. They have things they keep to themselves. They have their reasons. You of all people should know that."

She took a step back, studied the ground. "Yeah," she said quietly. "So?"

172

"I don't want anyone to figure out who I am."

"I figured it out, and I'm no genius," she said.

"Clearly, I'll need to be more careful."

"Is this stuff about your mother true?" She indicated a shaded inset in the article.

He hadn't read it. He didn't have to. He knew without going over the text that it was filled with Janet's sudden rise to fame, and then her plummeting fall from grace. After ignoring him for years, she'd burst back into his life, claiming that her wise and attentive parenting had shaped his character, molding him into the type of man who would sacrifice himself for others. At first, the media had gobbled up the story of the courageous, hardworking single mom, making Janet a role model for women across the nation.

Then, inevitably, some nosy reporter had scratched beneath the surface of Janet's story and discovered the truth.

To Callie, he said, "There might be a little grain of truth, but it's always distorted to make whatever point the reporter's aiming for."

Callie was quiet for a long time. The CD changed to Green Day. He saw her lips move, but couldn't hear what she was saying.

"What's that?" he asked.

"I said, my mom's in prison." There was a world of pain in her eyes. It spoke to his own pain, and she must have known that because she watched him expectantly.

Oh, he knew her. It was like looking into a mirror to the past. He recognized her pain because he'd seen that in his own mirror, long ago. Don't do it, he cautioned himself. But he couldn't ignore what he saw in Callie. Whether they liked it or not, they were kindred spirits.

He thought he'd left his adolescence behind, but she was a reminder that he could never do that. She wasn't the first, of course. On the job, he'd seen that look too many times to count. Kids whose parents walked away from their wrecked lives and left them to fend for themselves. Kids who had no idea what the next day would bring. Kids like he'd been.

"Why don't you put that magazine down and have a seat," he said to Callie. "I'll tell you the real truth." He sensed that being straight with her might be a way to get her to open up. He was nervous about it, though. He'd never explained about his mother to anyone. "Before all this happened to me," he said, "my mother and I hadn't spoken in twelve years."

"I don't get it. Why not?"

He hadn't planned to sacrifice his relationship with his mother. That had been her idea. He grabbed a work rag and wiped the sweat and sawdust off his face. "She didn't want to have anything to do with things from her past. From her days as an addict. I was one of those things."

Callie nodded. Clearly she understood that some women were capable of such a thing.

"Anyway, she moved to L.A. and never contacted me again."

"Until you became the star of the evening news," Callie filled in, laying the magazine atop a sawhorse.

"It says she's got a talk-radio show in Orange County."

"That part's true."

"I bet being your mother is the reason for that."

"You'd win the bet."

She was catching on fast. After the incident, like the rest of the world, his mother had wanted a piece of the action. After a tearful reunion (her tears, not his), she sold her version of the story to anyone who would pay, along with the few grainy, often crooked photographs she'd kept of him as a skinny, grinning boy with his laughing single mom.

He studied the photographs reprinted in the magazine and realized he didn't recognize these people. In the pictures—taken at the Maryland shore, or a city park or school picnic—the two of them looked happy together. The future hero and the mother who raised him to be a man of courage and honor, to hear her tell it. They looked happy together in the pictures, but that was a false memory that didn't exist outside the photographs.

Cameras did this to people. Nobody wanted to show their true face to a probing, unblinking lens, not if that face was shadowed by misery. No matter who you might be, how high you were or how broke, no matter who you had to screw in order to get your next fix, you always summoned a smile for the camera.

Whenever he saw a photograph of his mother, JD was always struck by how beautiful she was. He didn't remember that about her. Beauty was not what he thought of when he thought of his mother.

Still, when she'd come bursting back into his life, he

hadn't tried to stop her. Stupidly, he'd failed to assess the risks. Instead, he let her parlay his fame into her own talk radio show and articles in national magazines. She published a pamphlet: *How to Raise a Real Hero.*

Step one, he thought: Sell your body for drugs and stay high all the time.

Step two: Sleep all day and ignore the kid so he goes wandering the streets. Hope that the firefighters and EMTs at the station down the block will take him under their wing.

Step three: Use all the money the kid saved up in order to get sober. Then walk away from him, explaining that you can't see him anymore because he's part of the past you need to escape.

"So then she blew it, right?" Callie said. "She got her own radio show and things should have been fine but she screwed it all up."

He gestured at the magazine. "She had some help. At first, she was fine with all the attention. Everybody bought her made-up past. You can't hide things, though, not in this day and age, not for long." It was true. Within weeks of Janet coming forward, reports of her addiction and criminal record surfaced. Then came the invitations she couldn't refuse, to wild Hollywood parties and exclusive clubs. "She dived into her relapse headfirst," he explained. "By the time I figured out what was going on, it was almost too late. She's in rehab now, down in Southern California. She'll be there until the fall. It's supposed to be one of the best programs in the country." He broke a wooden dowel in his hands and looked down in surprise. He didn't remember picking it up.

"I bet you're paying for it," Callie said.

"You win again."

"So are you like really rich now?" she asked, indicating the address for donations given in the article. "Because of this foundation?"

"I didn't ask for anything, but . . . people are basically kind and decent," he said. "Donations started coming in for no particular reason."

"Oh, only that you saved the leader of the free world."

He waved away the comment. "Nobody throws himself on a bomber for money. It just happened. The upside is, I put the money in a nonprofit foundation. People can apply for aid." He studied her for a moment. "You could request a college scholarship," he suggested, hoping she wouldn't think it was an attempt at bribery.

"Yeah, college. What a laugh."

"I'm not laughing."

"You never do," she pointed out. "Jeez, here you are, America's hero, and you can't even enjoy it."

"I don't want to enjoy it. I'm trying to get my life back."

"So when are you going to tell Kate?" Callie asked, the blunt question prodding at him.

"I'm not telling her or anybody else. I hope you'll respect that, Callie."

"What's the big deal? She already likes you. She'll just like you more."

Women all across America claimed they loved him because of what he'd done. It felt false to him, and it was a wall between him and other people once they found out. "I just explained this to you. I can't risk things happening to people like Shirlene Ludlow and my mother because of who I am. I'd just prefer to stay anonymous," he said. "I can't explain it any better than that."

"Well, I totally don't get it. She might be a little put out with you at first, like I was. But then—"

"I'm asking you not to say anything, Callie." His voice was sharp. Urgent.

She rolled the magazine into a tube. "That's asking a lot."

She wasn't stupid. He knew that. She understood that there was a certain potential, perhaps even a profit in this for her if she went about exploiting it in the right way.

"I know it's asking a lot," he conceded. He thought about bribing her. He could afford to do that, for sure. He couldn't take that step, though. Couldn't say to her, "I'll give you five hundred bucks to keep quiet about this." Not only was it undignified; it was like a single droplet of contamination, radiating outward, spreading God knew where. "In fact," he added, "I could really use your help in keeping this under wraps."

"I think it sucks that you didn't tell us," she said. "I don't know why you're acting like it's so hard to be famous."

"Ordinary people aren't cut out for all the attention," he said. "I can't really explain it. It's just . . . true." He knew it for a fact, because he'd found some case studies. The rescue worker who had pulled baby Jessica McClure out of a well in West Texas committed suicide. The guy who jumped off the George Washington Bridge to save plane crash victims from the icy Potomac became a recluse. The man who'd stopped Squeaky Fromme's assassination attempt later killed himself, too. All their troubles could be traced to an unplanned act of heroism.

"You'll deal," Callie assured him. As she spoke, she tossed the magazine in the trash can, stirring up a flurry of wood chips and sawdust. "By the way, I finished cleaning for the day."

"Thanks."

He pulled out his wallet and paid her in crisp bills.

She folded the cash without looking at it.

"Don't you want to count it?" he asked.

"Nope. I trust you." The Rolling Stones came on the stereo, singing "Paint It Black." She smiled. "I like this one."

"So do I."

"When you were an army guy, did you listen to music a lot?"

"All the time."

"What do you think of 'Quiet Day'?"

He shouldn't be surprised that she knew of that one. Billy Shattuck, a country-and-western star, had written a song about the Walter Reed incident, spreading awareness of JD even further. "Not my cup of tea," he said.

"Mine, either. Don't you want to have a look around?" she asked, gesturing back at the cottage. "Make sure I did a good job?"

"Nope," he said, pulling the safety mask down over his face. "I trust you."

PART THREE

"As memory may be a paradise from which we cannot be driven, it may also be a hell from which we cannot escape."

—John Lancaster Spalding,
Aphorisms and Reflections

Thirteen

Kate awakened slowly, thinking about lingerie. She didn't normally have much excitement in her life. That was perhaps why she had, over the years, developed a taste for spectacular lingerie. She slept in teddies or scandalous baby dolls, though for Aaron's sake she kept her obsession private, preserving modesty beneath a nondescript bathrobe. Underneath, she might be wearing a petal-pink pushup bra, black lace panties so skimpy she forgot she was wearing any, even a garter belt if the mood struck her.

The lingerie thing had started years ago with the debut of her column. As the city's fashion writer, she was the recipient of any number of design samples, preview pieces, sometimes even outright bribes.

A new boutique called Ooh-La-La had gone overboard, sending her beautiful parcels filled with samples of what they called "Dreamwear." Since that time, Kate had become the boutique's best customer and good friends with its owner, Frenchy LaBorde.

There was no obvious reason to wear fancy lingerie. Or perhaps there was. Maybe she dressed like this underneath to remind herself that she was still a sexual being. It had been an eternity since she had dated anyone long enough or seriously enough to try impressing him with her taste in lingerie.

The elephant seal had more sex than she did. At least it mated once a year.

A swift version of all these thoughts and rationalizations whirled through Kate's mind when she realized she had overslept. It was past nine o'clock. And someone was breaking into the house.

She sat up straight in bed. Maybe she had dreamed it.

But no. There was a rhythmic tinkering sound that sent chills through her.

Aaron.

She moved like a fluid shadow, coming up out of the bed while simultaneously pulling a bathrobe over her Chantilly lace baby dolls, skimming silent and barefoot down the hall to his room.

His door was ajar, the bed empty.

Aaron.

Driven by panic, she rushed down the stairs and burst out onto the porch, prepared to scream. Then she saw them.

Aaron and JD were working together on the lawn, putting a chain on a bicycle.

"Hey, Mom," Aaron called out, barely looking at her. "Me and JD are fixing this bike."

Barefoot and wearing Spider-Man pajamas, Aaron kept working. JD stood up, removing his hat in gentlemanly fashion. "Morning, Kate," he said. She heard a curious note in his voice. She saw an odd, almost pained look shadow his face.

Then it dawned on her what he was staring at. Her bathrobe was gaping open, showing off the skimpy baby dolls.

With a firm tug, she closed the gap and tied on the belt. But she was not quick enough to discount an undeniable reaction. Though he stood clear across the yard, she could feel his gaze like a burning caress. Everywhere his stare touched her, she was lit on fire.

She could feel the heat in her cheeks and wished she didn't blush so easily. She hoped her voice sounded casual and perhaps even dismissive when she said, "We don't usually entertain company first thing in the morning."

"You're doing a good job, though," he said mildly. "Of entertaining."

Her attention flickered to Aaron. If he picked up on the innuendo, she was going to kill JD. To her relief, Aaron remained absorbed by the dark, greasy chain.

She took a deep, flustered breath. "I'm going to make coffee."

He nodded, almost but not quite a dismissal.

She all but fled into the kitchen and made a huge racket putting together the old percolator with the glass lid. So much for her vow to stick to tea all summer. This morning, she definitely needed a jolt. She didn't worry about Callie waking up. On her day off, the girl slept like the dead.

Once she had the coffee on, she rushed to the bathroom and stood at the sink, staring into the mirror. She looked exactly like what she was, a woman who had just tumbled out of bed. Hair loose, no makeup, and that soft, unguarded look of someone stirred from sleep.

"Too sexy for your robe," she muttered, grabbing her toothbrush. Now, once again, she was faced with the dilemma of how much to primp for him. Did she comb her hair, wash her face? What about makeup?

"Oh, come on," she grumbled, spitting toothpaste. "Grow up."

She ought to put on the Slug Death T-shirt. Then she worried that it would remind him of the last time he'd seen her in it, soaking wet, no bra. She considered cropped pants and a short white top. No, that revealed her midriff, which was a perfectly fine midriff but she didn't want to show him any skin. Frustrated, she simply belted the robe more securely, washed her face, combed her hair and grabbed a pair of flip-flops. That was the image she wanted to project—modest, casual and utterly uninterested in impressing him.

All right, so maybe she brushed her hair until it shone and put on lip gloss. That was simply good grooming, after all.

She took her time heading down to the kitchen. No need to give him the notion that she was in a hurry. She hadn't seen him since dinner the previous week. Each day, she spent far too much time thinking up ways to encounter him again. She'd already used the bicycle-pump excuse, but there were many others—the faulty porch light, a hedge that needed pruning, even the old kite-stuck-in-the-tree ploy. Never mind that the kite had been there since 1998; she actually considered asking him to get it down.

Aaron didn't need any excuses, and didn't know how to be coy about his liking for JD.

When Kate came downstairs, her robe firmly belted, the house was empty. In the kitchen, the coffee had per-colated and the burner was turned off. Neither JD nor Aaron was in sight. Bandit sat in misery at the door, looking forlornly through the screen.

Kate poured herself a cup of coffee, opened the door and followed the dog outside. Aaron and JD were using Gojo to get the grease off their hands.

"Mom," Aaron said, "we're going on a bike ride, okay? Is it okay, Mom? I ate breakfast already and I've got my helmet."

"Sure," she said. "Go upstairs and get dressed. Long pants and sneakers. I'm not letting you go barefoot."

"So this is all right with you?" JD asked.

"It had better be, or I'll have one unhappy camper on my hands." She offered her first smile of the day. "This means the world to him," she assured JD.

"We'll stay on the road in sight of the house." They stood watching the water. Rings formed here and there, fish rising to feed.

"If he pesters you," Kate said, "just bring him right home."

"He doesn't pester me. He's a good kid. You must be proud, Kate."

He's a good kid. The words meant more to her than he could know. "I am," she said, then bit her lip. She considered warning him about Aaron's temper but decided against it. Sooner or later, he'd discover it on his own.

"So his father—"

"Like I said, not in the picture." She wasn't eager to discuss Nathan, but she wanted JD to understand. "He never has been, never will be. We get nothing from him and more importantly, we *want* nothing from him." That was almost true. In fact, Aaron was desperate for a father.

"His loss," JD said simply.

All right, that's twice, Kate thought, feeling a rush of pleasurable heat. Twice today that he'd said exactly the right thing, and it wasn't even ten in the morning. She grew flustered under his scrutiny and sought to change the subject. "I've been meaning to ask you. How did it work out with Callie?"

"She did a good job for me."

"She's a good worker."

"Did she say anything?"

Kate raised her eyebrows. She was having flashbacks to junior high. "About what?"

"Nothing. Just making sure she didn't have any complaints about working for me."

On the contrary, Callie had been in a wonderful mood

after finishing up at his place. "He's *awesome,*" she'd practically sung. Kate decided he didn't need to hear that from her. "No complaints," she said.

He hooked his thumbs into his back pockets and watched the lake some more. Their silences, Kate reflected, were not awkward. Not even with her standing here in her robe.

"Have dinner with me, Kate." The invitation came out of the blue, startling her.

"I promised Aaron hot dogs tonight." Her reply was swift and automatic.

"Callie can fix them. I want to take you to dinner, just the two of us."

"Why?"

"I could say it's to thank you for supper the other night."

"You could say that."

"I could also say I'm attracted to you and I'd love to take you out."

That was probably it, Kate reflected crazily. There was always a moment when you knew you were going to sleep with a man, and she knew that moment had arrived. It was embarrassing how little it took. *I'm attracted to you and I'd love to take you out.* Oh, Kate, she thought. "All right. Not tonight, though." Best not to seem too eager and available, she reminded herself.

"Friday, then," he said.

"Friday's perfect if Callie's willing to watch Aaron." She saw the way he was looking at her. "Is it the lingerie?" she asked before she could stop herself.

187

He turned, a grin spreading slowly across his face. "I was attracted to you before I saw what you sleep in."

"Really?"

"Yeah. Of course, I'm glad . . ." With one finger, he gently parted the robe at the top, and she was too stunned to stop him. "Glad about this."

"Why?"

"Gives me something to think about. For the rest of the summer, I'll never be bored."

Fourteen

On Friday, Callie had only one cleaning job, which she finished at lunchtime. Kate loaded up a cooler and a bag of towels, threw the lawn chairs in the Jeep and drove them to the small public beach at the east end of the lake. Eager to be in the water, Aaron went to join a group of kids playing in the shallows, and Kate and Callie sat down to relax with their lunch.

"I have a favor to ask you," Kate said.

"Sure."

"Can you watch Aaron tonight?"

Callie didn't answer right away. She studied Kate, then said, "Oh, my God. You're red as a beet. You're going out with JD."

"Do you think it's a bad idea?"

"Let me see. He's totally into you. He likes Aaron.

He's a . . . cool guy. And you're worried it might be a bad idea?"

Kate rubbed her cheeks, wishing she could make the red go away. "I have my insecurities when it comes to dating."

"I'll watch him," Callie said. "I've got nothing else to do." She seemed a little too nonchalant. "How is the article coming?" she asked, sipping lemonade from a can.

Kate smiled distractedly. It was nice having someone to talk to, even a sometimes-moody teenager. "It's done. And I have both good news and bad news. The good news is, it'll be published next February. The bad news is, my editor is leaving. That means the person who was my contact and a fan of my work there won't be around anymore."

"So what're you going to do?"

"Well, that's the very weird part of all this. My editor is going to work for a much bigger magazine, and she wants to stay in touch." She paused, hardly daring to say it. "Ever heard of *Vanity Fair*?"

"Are you kidding? I love that magazine. The photos are crazy. Is that where your editor's going? And she wants to publish your articles?"

"That's where she's going. And she said she wants to stay in touch. But trust me, she doesn't want me to write her articles about guys who died a long time ago. If I'm going to impress her, I'll need to find something more contemporary and relevant. Something that illuminates someone's life right now."

"Like what? Doesn't that magazine specialize in sports gods and celebrities?"

"I think you're right. Too bad I don't know any celebrities."

"You sure about that?"

"A hundred percent."

Callie looked pained, as though she wanted to argue. Then she blew out a breath in exasperation. "I guess you'd better think up another angle."

"I'm working on it. But not today." She leaned back in her lawn chair and folded her arms behind her head.

Callie put on a pair of cheap sunglasses and gazed at the people on the beach. "I always wonder, when I see strangers, who they are, what their lives are like."

"When I was your age, I was looking at cute boys."

"I look at cute boys," Callie protested. "There's one." She indicated a guy in trunks and a muscle shirt playing volleyball.

"Hmm," Kate said, following her gaze. "Late teens and he's already got the beginnings of a beer gut. Heavens, my mouth," she said, instantly apologetic.

"Don't worry, you're right. Just because I'm over-weight doesn't mean I think it's attractive."

"It was a dumb thing to say. He's probably a perfectly nice person—"

"Fat kids always are." Callie waved away her apology and pointed at another guy.

Though Callie was forgiving, Kate wasn't. She wanted to kick herself. Dealing with a teenager—and a girl at that—was much different than dealing with a little boy. There were land mines everywhere.

"Now, *there's* a great body," Callie murmured.

Kate studied the new specimen. Sculpted, smoothed, tanned and glistening, the square-jawed young man looked as though he'd been dipped in caramel. "Nice," she agreed, "but that's a gym body."

"What's that?"

"He spends hours at the gym getting into that shape. Probably spent a fortune on the best club in town, maybe personal trainer, too. Oh, and all the body shaving and oil is expensive. It's fine for a guy to take pride in his appearance, but when he spends so much time doing it, where does that leave his girlfriend?"

"Waiting outside the locker room?"

"You're a quick study. How about this one?" Kate nodded toward a dark-haired, slender boy in cutoffs and a bandanna around his head.

"How about him?" Callie said softly, and smiled.

Kate glanced over at her, then did a double take. It was true that she believed Callie was a very pretty girl despite her troubles with self-esteem. But when she saw the way Callie was gazing at the lanky boy, she revised her opinion. When her eyes shone and she smiled that way, she was downright beautiful.

Callie waved her arm, and when she caught his attention, he veered toward them.

"You know him?" Kate asked.

"Luke Newman."

"Well, what do you know," Kate said. "I never would have recognized him."

Callie composed herself in time to greet him with an offhand "Hey, Luke."

"Hey." The boy seemed nervous, looking over his shoulder.

"This is Kate Livingston, the one I'm staying with," Callie said. "Aaron's mom."

"Nice to meet you."

"We met years and years ago," Kate told him. "I'm a friend of your grandmother's. So you're spending the summer with her?"

"Yes, ma'am. That's right." Luke glanced around almost furtively. Kate sensed he might not want to be seen with her, but she gave him the benefit of the doubt and offered him a lemonade. He hunkered down in the sand beside Callie's chair. "So you're off work this afternoon?"

Kate decided to give them a little privacy. She got up, saying, "I was just going to take Aaron for a swim." She headed down to the water. So Callie had made a friend, she thought, encouraged by the development. And one who looked like a homecoming king, at that. Luke seemed a bit awkward, even secretive in his manner, but perhaps in time they'd get past that phase. It was always a critical time in any relationship, seeing if you could get past that fumbling stage and discover more about each other.

There was much to discover about Callie, and Kate was pleased to observe that the boy called Luke seemed to appreciate that.

Good, she thought. It was time somebody did.

• • •

It was so insane, getting nervous about a date. Kate had dated before. She was used to this. In fact, one reason she dated so much was that she failed so often.

Most men stopped calling after they learned she had a half-grown son. That was what Kate told herself, anyway.

Now she studied her reflection in the mirror, and doubts crept in. What if I'm the problem? she wondered. What if I'm the one they don't like?

She sat down on the bed and stared at the floor. She often told herself men didn't want to get involved because she had a child. Deep down, she knew it was a lie. It was her, Kate, all along, driving people away, and maybe it was time she faced up to that.

She shivered, not because she was cold but because the notion was something she had never even begun to deal with. She looked longingly at the cell phone, so useless here at the cottage. What she wouldn't give to call her mother right now and—

And what? Ask her if men dumped her because of her or because of Aaron? It wasn't fair to ask her mother that. Her question would be better posed to the men who had dumped her.

"Brilliant, Kate," she muttered. "Just brilliant. It's every man's dream to hear from an ex-girlfriend wanting the truth about why he stopped seeing her."

She leaned toward the mirror and put on Peach Melba lipstick. All right, she conceded, blotting her lips, bad idea. There was probably a statute of limitations on calling ex-boyfriends to sift through the aftermath of a failed romance.

From now on, she thought, putting a few things into a small, sleek handbag, I'll ask the guy up front. When JD dumps me, I'll make him explain exactly why.

"Oh, good attitude, Kate," she said, still talking to herself, as she slid her feet into black satin sandals. "That's the power of positive thinking, for sure."

She sprayed on a little perfume, grabbed her bag and hurried downstairs to sit with the kids until JD came to pick her up. It was funny how easily she slipped into thinking of Callie as one of the kids, as though she had always belonged to Kate.

Stepping out onto the porch, she saw that they had laid out the ancient croquet set and were locked in a hot competition. Bandit slept in a patch of sunlight on the doormat.

"Mom," yelled Aaron. "Hey, Mom."

"I hear you, buddy," Kate said.

"You don't need to yell," Callie said, "she's right there."

"I know that," Aaron said. "Hey, Mom, look where I am." He pointed to a blue-striped ball. "Two wickets ahead."

"We'll see about that." Callie took aim with her yellow ball and gave it a firm whack. It tumbled through the wicket she was aiming for, giving her another shot. She made this one, too, catching up with Aaron.

He hopped from one foot to the other in agitation.

Callie scowled. "Do you need to use the bathroom or something?"

He scowled back.

"Stand still. You're messing up my aim."

He fidgeted even more, his jaw set in defiance.

Kate resisted the urge to intervene. She was not supposed to manage every moment of his life, especially not a flare-up over a game of croquet.

Callie turned her back on him and hit, not only getting through the next wicket but landing her ball right up against his.

"Hate to do this, kid," she said, bracing her foot on top of her ball as she prepared to knock his out of bounds.

"Then don't do it," Aaron yelled, a panicky note in his voice.

Kate recognized that tone. He was about to lose it. She used all her willpower to avoid mediating. She'd learned long ago that it didn't work.

"I hate losing worse," Callie explained and whacked his ball a good ten yards away.

"Mom!" Aaron howled.

Callie ignored him as she took her next shot. Then she said, "Your turn."

"I was almost to the post," Aaron hollered. "You ruined it."

"Tough break, kid."

"I'm putting my ball back where it was." He marched over to where it lay in some tall grass.

Callie beat him to it. "If you touch that ball, you're

disqualified and you automatically lose."

"Mom!" Aaron howled again, his face bright red.

Kate stayed seated. If she stepped in to mediate, it would weaken Callie's control over him. And then Callie wouldn't want to watch him tonight while Kate was out, and then Kate wouldn't be able to go out at all, and once again, a man she was interested in would dismiss her the way all his predecessors had.

Of course, Callie was not familiar with the pattern. Nor was she at all rattled or intimidated by his fury. "Whatever," she said in exasperation. "If you're not going to play by the rules, we might as well not play at all." She turned her back and walked away, calmly and deliberately.

Aaron exploded. He let out a yell, raising his mallet high overhead and bringing it down as hard as he could, gouging divots in the grass. "Mom!" he hollered. "Make her play fair. Make her—"

"Not my job," Kate said, but he didn't hear. He was lost in a world of anger, a place he went all by himself, and sometimes seemed unable to find his way back. With wooden mallets and balls everywhere, she worried he might hurt himself—or someone else. She was on the brink of going to him, trying to calm him down, when Callie intervened.

"Jeez, kid," she said, acting unimpressed. "You're a real drag when you blow a gasket like this." She turned away and bent to pick up her ball.

"Wait," said Aaron. His voice was taut but controlled. "It's . . . it's my shot."

Because her back was to him, Aaron didn't see Callie's look of relief. But Kate did. The girl was a wonder. She had been onto Aaron all along.

Kate beamed at Callie, who acted nonchalant as she turned back to Aaron. He was breathing hard and his face was still red, but he had conquered his temper. Progress, thought Kate. A year ago, he would have had to spend an hour in time-out, making everyone miserable.

"Whatever," Callie said, and stepped back. "Go for it."

Aaron visibly shook off the episode and bent over to aim his ball. One stroke put him back in the game, aligned to get through the double wickets to the stake.

"Nice hit, kid," Callie said.

Kate hoped her antiperspirant was still working. She had been unbelievably tense during the game, and the relief spreading through her now made her feel limp and boneless.

Callie said, "You look good in that dress."

Kate picked up her purse. "You think?"

"Totally."

"Thanks."

They went back to their game as though Aaron's outburst had never happened. Callie's compliment boosted Kate's self-confidence. The girl possessed a surprisingly sophisticated fashion sense. Surprising, because Callie herself always dressed in oversize clothes. She never even wore a swimsuit, preferring to swim in cutoffs and a black Corona T-shirt, size extra-large. Kate wished she could erase the things that had happened to Callie in the past, things the girl only hinted at but never fully explained. She knew better, though. She knew perfectly well that the past couldn't be changed. So the key, then, was for Callie to come to terms with it. Kate still hadn't figured out what it would take to do that.

Callie and Aaron took a break from their game, and she gave them instructions for the evening.

"Make sure you turn the propane off after you grill the hamburgers. And Aaron, you go to bed when Callie says. No monkeyshines, got it?"

"Callie said I can stay up as late as I want," he said, standing up straighter.

Kate's heart sank. She had explained to Callie that Aaron's control tended to slip when he was tired or over-stimulated. Apparently Callie had not listened.

"Tell her the rest, smart aleck," Callie said, elbowing him.

"If I stay up, I have to be lying down flat in my bed, reading a book." He flicked a glance at Callie. "A chapter book, not a comic book."

Kate kissed him on the head. "Sounds good to me. Brilliant, in fact." She beamed at Callie.

Just then, JD arrived. Kate felt a flutter of nervousness.

He got out of the truck and came toward her, and the flutter escalated to a storm. He looked . . . Golden, that was the word that came to mind. He shone. In khaki slacks that fit his slim hips, a golf shirt and navy blazer, he had an unexpected air of grace. He wasn't smiling;

he almost never did, but she suspected that behind the dark glasses, his eyes were shining.

Unlike him, she couldn't keep from grinning as he approached her.

"You're slaying me, Kate," he said. "That dress is a lethal weapon."

"You don't look so bad yourself," she said, grabbing a light wrap and draping it over her arm. "I almost didn't recognize you."

He said hello to the kids. Then, as she told them goodbye, Kate struggled against the impulse to go down the list of admonishments yet again. Callie had more than proven herself to be equal to Aaron's behavior. Kate had to trust that they would be all right.

"You're too quiet," JD said as they drove away.

She focused on a small St. Christopher medal swinging from the rearview mirror of the truck. "Thinking about everything that could go wrong. They've got no phone, no way to get in touch with me."

"The park ranger station is a few hundred yards away," he reminded her. "Quit worrying and relax."

"When you have a child, worrying is second nature."

"Only if you let it take you over."

"I don't know any other way to be."

"Then you have a lot to learn. Like, if you spend the evening worrying, we'll both have a bad time."

She knew then why her dates never worked out. Her worrying—not the fact that she had a child—made them miserable. She pressed back against the seat and vowed it would not happen tonight. She'd relax, enjoy the evening. Lord knew, this man was worth the effort.

He took her to C'est Si Bon, an unlikely restaurant with an even more unlikely name. In a town like Port Angeles, diners and roadhouses were the norm. Yet for years, the French restaurant had flourished at the side of the highway, a gastronomic oasis with a fantastic garden and interior décor of pink and gold, which had not been changed in decades.

"Have you been here before?" Kate asked him.

"No, but Sam made me promise I wouldn't miss it."

"He's right," she said. "You've never been anywhere quite like this."

The small, energetic woman who greeted them at the entrance lit up when she recognized Kate. *"Oh, la belle,"* she exclaimed. *"Et vous êtes retournée enfin."*

Kate barely spoke a word of French, but the effusive greeting needed no translation.

"Bienvenu, monsieur, je suis enchantée," said the hostess.

"Merci pour nous avoir ce soir," he said in what Kate suspected was perfect French. So much for thinking he was an uneducated bumpkin.

Even the hostess looked startled and impressed. *"Alors,"* she said, picking up menus and the wine list. *"Á table."*

The waiter lit a candle at one of Kate's favorite white linen-draped tables, a private one tucked in a glass-enclosed alcove. A jar of dahlias and settings of Limoges china created a palpable air of romance.

"You speak French," Kate observed.

"I get by." He put on his glasses, flipped open the wine list and his menu.

"Where did you study French?" she asked, even though he seemed preoccupied with reading the selections.

"I was friends with a Haitian kid, growing up," he said. "Later I took classes in French and Spanish."

"Was that part of your military training?"

"Uh-huh." He didn't elaborate.

"I never would have pegged you for a guy who speaks French," she said.

"Why not?"

"Must have been the work boots and plaid shirt."

"Maybe I'm French-Canadian."

"Are you?"

"You're a snob," he observed.

"I am, aren't I?"

He turned the wine list over to her. "I'm not so good at wine," he said. "You pick something."

The waiter arrived to take their bar order. Kate suspected JD was desperate for a beer, so she suggested a Kronenbourg from the Alsace-Lorraine region of France. She also ordered a bottle of Vouvray to go with dinner.

For dinner, they ordered coquilles St. Jacques with pommes Anna, followed by a salad of fresh greens with walnuts and Roquefort cheese. Kate had a funny feeling, not about JD but about other patrons of the restaurant. She noticed people staring at them a time or two, though they were always looking the other way when she tried to make eye contact. JD drew his shoulders forward and lowered his head, and Kate started to think the attention from strangers was a figment of her imagination. He was a hunk, she reminded herself, and she was wearing a tight designer dress, one of the perks of her former job. It struck her that tonight they looked like one of those couples she often regarded with envy—young and attractive, gazing at each other longingly.

"You look happy about something," he said.

"I am happy. I like going out. Never had the chance when Aaron was little, so this is a treat for me." Nice segue, she thought, beaming at him. "What about you? Do you date much?"

"No."

She realized he wasn't going to elaborate. "Well, then," she said when the first course was served, "should I start the round of Twenty Questions or will you do the honors?"

"What questions?"

"The getting-to-know-you questions."

"I don't have any of those," he said. "I know all I need to know about you."

"That's impossible."

He took a sip of beer. "It's true."

His certainty struck a chord in her. A highly resonant chord.

"All right," she said, "what do you know about me?"

"Fishing for compliments?" he asked.

"Huh. Challenging you to put your money where your mouth is."

"Fine. Here's what I know about you. You're smart and you brought enough novels with you to read one every day of the summer. Although you're not athletic, you pretend to be in order to encourage Aaron. He's the number one priority in your life. You're missing your family a lot this summer, even more than you thought you would. How am I doing?"

"Remarkably well." She shifted a little in her seat, startled by his observations.

"You look surprised."

"I am. Most men I've gone out with tend to focus the conversation on themselves," she admitted. "They hardly notice the color of my hair, or if they did, it's only to ask if I'm a natural redhead—nudge, nudge, wink, wink." Her cheeks flushed. "I can't believe I said that."

"I won't ask, then," JD assured her, then added, "I'll find out on my own. Nudge, nudge, wink, wink."

She held out her wineglass. "I need a refill."

He managed to pour without taking his eyes off her. "You haven't been seeing the right guys," he said.

"Not at all."

"Then I have good news for you."

"What's that?"

"Your luck is about to change."

She felt warm and shivery all at once, a sensation she had not felt in ages, maybe never. "You sound awfully sure of yourself," she said.

"I am sure."

"I don't even know you."

"I know how to read a menu in French, I suck at fly-fishing but I can fillet a trout. I'm handy with tools. Kids and dogs like me."

"I figured all that out on my own," she said.

"Favorite color, blue. Favorite song, 'Radio America' by the Libertines, but that changes weekly. I don't like TV sports, heights or crowds. I do like pickup trucks, quiet places and loyal friends. And you. I like you. What more do you need to know?"

Her head was reeling—in a good way—from his list.

"What does JD stand for?"

"Juris Doctorate, for one thing."

"Very funny. Does that mean you're a lawyer?"

"No. Pulling your leg."

"So what does it stand for? Really?"

"Just dandy? John Deere?"

"Oh, I get it. You were named after J. D. Salinger." She glared at him. "Maybe Aaron is right. Maybe I do need to Google you on the Internet."

"You mean you haven't already? I Googled you."

"What?" She felt her color fade, probably leaving nothing but freckles behind.

"You're either a professor of semiotics at Cooper Union, or the star of an Internet porno site."

"Guilty as charged," she said, feeling her face fill up with color again.

"Of which one?"

"Maybe both," she said.

His grin faded. "I didn't really look you up, Kate."

She felt such ease when she looked into his eyes. "I

didn't look you up, either. Search engines are overrated when it comes to getting to know someone." She paused. "John David."

He looked at her. "What?"

"I bet your initials stand for John and David."

He put his hand on top of hers, and she caught her breath. She could not believe the way that simple gesture set off a chain of such complicated reactions.

It was the first time he had deliberately touched her. His first physical acknowledgment of the attraction she had felt toward him from the very first time she'd seen him. She studied their joined hands. Was there anything sexier than this man's hand, cradling hers as though it was something precious and fragile?

"Are you all right?" he asked.

She cleared her throat, tried to drop the silly smile as she held up her glass of wine. "We are very agreeable this evening," she observed.

"Then my plan is working," he said.

"You have a plan?"

He didn't reply to that, but showed great appreciation for the cuisine—luscious scallops in buttery sauce, more wine and a good deal more flirting. Kate felt relaxed and natural with him.

His gaze traveled over her, lingering here and there.

Just as she started to squirm, the waiter approached the table. "Will there be anything else?"

JD didn't take his eyes off her. "Uh, yeah." Then he blinked, struggling so visibly to snap out of it that Kate laughed. "Check, please."

At the door, JD held out her wrap for her, his hands cupping her shoulders and lingering there as the restaurant owner came to say goodbye.

"Dinner was delicious," Kate told him.

"All the more so when consumed in pleasant company."

"Of course."

"Bonsoir, les amis." He winked at JD. *"C'est un bon soir pour sauter la femme."*

"What did he say to you?" she asked as JD held the door for her.

"He told us to have a good evening." His ears were bright red, hinting at a different translation.

"Liar. I can see right through you."

"What?" He looked perfectly innocent as he pulled open the passenger door of the truck.

Kate refused to have a seat. She stared challengingly up at him. "Tell me what he said."

"It was very . . . French."

"French as in rude?"

"French as in frank."

She touched his cheek. "My God. You're blushing."

"I don't blush."

"Yes, apparently you do. It's so cute that you're blushing."

"I don't blush and I'm not cute."

"Now I have to know." Kate braced her arm on the truck door. "I'm not going to budge until you tell me what that man said."

JD took a deep breath. He placed one hand on either

side of her, leaning close. Humor glinted in his eyes. "He said—" JD bent and whispered the rest in her ear, his breath warm and tantalizing, the suggestion he whispered, scorching hot.

"Oh, God," said Kate.

He grinned at her and stepped even closer, his hips brushing hers. "Who's blushing now?"

Fifteen

"Come on, kid," said Callie. "You promised if I read to you, you'd go to sleep by nine."

"Wrong," said Aaron, wide awake in his quilt-covered bed. "I said I'd go to bed by nine. Sleeping's a different story."

Sleep sounded delicious to Callie. She was tired. Lately, she felt tired all the time, and it wasn't just the hard work that caused it. Sometimes she felt low and draggy even on her days off. At least she had a great place to stay, she reminded herself. She couldn't get over what a good feeling it was to come home to Kate's house at the end of a long day and find a place all straightened up, dinner on the table. Kate and Aaron always waited for her to get home so they could all eat together. They said a blessing before the meal. To Callie, they were remarkable and rare, even though they didn't see anything unusual about themselves.

It was driving her crazy to keep quiet about JD, even

though she knew she would honor the promise she'd made him. But talk about unusual. He was the guy. The one who had been all over the news, who was still in the celebrity mags and on the TV gossip shows. She thought he was totally nuts to be hiding away instead of living like a celebrity. Cars, boats, houses, travel, parties . . . why would he shy away from that? These were the things most people dreamed about, and he could have them if he played his cards right. The weird thing was, he seemed perfectly content hanging out at the lake where nobody knew him.

Takes all kinds, she thought. And lately, there was a strong incentive for him to stay put, right here at the lake. Whenever he came around, Callie could see the chemistry between him and Kate getting stronger. And the weird thing was, Kate didn't know. She liked him as plain old JD, without even realizing he was Captain America, pride of the U.S. Army, winner of the Presidential Medal of Honor.

She had found some information about the medal in an ancient set of encyclopedias that Kate said had been in the family for years. It was an extremely rare honor, the highest military decoration in the United States of America. It was awarded "for conspicuous gallantry and intrepidity at the risk of life, above and beyond the call of duty."

No shit, Sherlock, she thought, flashing on horrific images that had played on the TV news, over and over again last Christmas. She totally couldn't believe no one had figured out he was Jordan Donovan Harris.

She'd been just as fooled, though, she reminded herself. What was it JD had said? People saw what they expected to see. That sure as hell was true in her case.

Take Luke Newman, for example. Luke of the dark hair and dreamy eyes. What did he see when he looked at her? A fat chick or a girl just trying to get by? A friend or something else, something romantic?

"Yo, earth to Callie," Aaron said. "Let's read some more."

"I already read you two chapters of *Soup and Me*."

"Fine. Pick something else."

She took in a deep breath, for patience. "One more," she told him. "One more, and you're reading it to me."

"Aw, Callie." He squirmed restlessly in bed.

"Nope, that's the deal. Take it or leave it." She knew he had trouble with his reading. Kate had explained that he had trouble with pretty much everything having to do with school. Browsing a painted bookcase, she looked for something short and simple so as not to put him on the spot. "I'll go easy on you and pick something short.

"You've got quite a collection here," she said.

"It's not mine. It belongs to the lake house."

Everything here belonged, Callie thought. She would never admit it to anyone, but sometimes she pretended she belonged here, too, part of a family that handed quilts and picture albums down through generations, and upheld traditions that made everyone feel happy and included. It was a lame fantasy, but sometimes she couldn't help wondering what it would really be like.

The bookcase held everything from Peter Pan to Nancy Drew to Harry Potter, but she didn't want to make him struggle with a novel. "This one," she said, selecting a glossy picture book. "*The Little Red Hen.*" It featured a drawing of a plump, happy-looking chicken dressed like a housewife in an apron and kerchief.

"You've got to be kidding. That's a baby book."

"Then you'll get through it quick. Or would you rather read something longer?" She showed him the Harry Potter tome.

"Forget that." He pushed it away, and she handed him *The Little Red Hen.*

"It's a dumb story," he said.

"Why not let me be the judge of that?" She flipped open the book.

He gaped at her. "You don't know the story?"

"Nope." As a kid, she had missed out on all of Mother Goose because Brother Timothy had found talking animals and wish-fulfillment stories objectionable. Pedophilia, he had no problem with, but Old Mother Hubbard was a deviant. "Go ahead," she said to Aaron. "Humor me."

"Fine," he said in a long-suffering tone. He scooted up in bed and began reading. The story turned out to be a good choice for him, with simple words and repeated phrases: "Who will help me?" the Little Red Hen kept asking everyone in sight.

And the answer was always the same: "Not I. Not I. Not I."

Callie could totally relate. When the commune finally

got busted, the caseworkers tried to place her with relatives, but they all took one look at Callie—overweight, with bad skin and a worse attitude—and said, "Not I," until she had to go into foster care.

She thought about Kate, and what an unexpected gift she was, like an angel. Asking only very few questions, Kate had let her stay, treating her first like a guest and then like a friend, or maybe even a niece or something. Kate was the first person Callie had ever met who had refused to say, "Not I." She did just the opposite, saying "I will. I'll help," and actually meaning it.

And Callie tried to repay her by being a good houseguest, but there was no denying that she was a big fat phony.

She found herself actually getting tense as the Little Red Hen was forced to do everything all by herself—cutting the wheat, threshing it (whatever that was), grinding it into flour, making the dough, baking the bread. It was work, work, work, all day every day and her loser friends didn't lift a finger—or a hoof—to help.

And as if she didn't have enough to do, the Little Red Hen had some eggs to hatch. She wound up with six babies and, not surprisingly, no rooster in sight to help with all those mouths to feed.

The hen wasn't daunted, though. She soldiered on, making the bread, hatching the eggs, facing the world with bold defiance. Callie was delighted when the bread turned out perfect. Drawn by its fragrance, the barnyard animals gathered around, now eager for a taste, of course.

The Little Red Hen's triumph was sweet when she turned them all away, letting them know in no uncertain terms that since they weren't there for her when she had so much work to do, she wouldn't share the finished product with them. There she was, a single mother doing all the work, and no one would give her a break when she needed help. She showed them.

". . . aaand she did," Aaron concluded, reading the last line with a dramatic flourish.

"Cool," said Callie. "I like that story."

Aaron made a face. "You do?"

"Sure. It's a story of personal triumph over adversity, don't you think? She did everything her way, and by the end, she made it on her own. Good for her."

"She lost all her friends." Aaron shut the book and handed it over. "What's good about that?"

"They weren't friends. They were users," said Callie. Even though it was a fairy tale, she felt the truth of it in her bones. "Her babies sure did like her, though."

Sixteen

On the drive back to the lake, Kate could not get her mind to form a coherent thought. Raging, unrequited lust tended to do that to a person. She stumbled through some sort of conversation with JD but it must have been inane, practically meaningless. Maybe his conversation was idiotic, too; she couldn't judge. Her hormone-crazed, infatuated self hung on his every word as though he was telling her every secret of the universe.

Like the surface temperature of Venus. It didn't matter. She'd lost all power to judge. She felt a burning inside, and sensed her pulse speeding up. This all felt new to her. After all these years, she had finally met a man who surprised her and defied all her expectations. In addition to turning her on, he confused and challenged her. There seemed to be so much about him to discover. Turning slightly sideways on the seat of the truck, she drew up one knee, knowing her pose was provocative.

And clearly not lost on him. In the very faint glow of the panel light, she caught a glint in his eye. "What are you thinking?" he asked her.

"Hmm. About a matrioshka doll."

"What's that?"

"You know, one of those painted Russian dolls that comes apart, and inside there's a smaller one, and inside that a smaller one, and so on. You keep opening them until you get to the prize in the middle."

"And the point of that is . . . ?"

"Human nature. How can you not keep opening them up until you get to the middle? The final doll is pretty anticlimactic, though."

"I can't say I've ever given that much thought." He turned on to East Beach Road. Though it was nearly ten o'clock at night, the sky still glowed with the deepest colors of twilight—pink and orange layered across stripes of amber, beautifully reflected by the glassy surface of the lake.

"And here," he said, slowing the truck down to a crawl, "is where I ask you if you'd like to come to my place for coffee or a nightcap."

She bit her lip. *Easy, girl.* Did he really want the evening to go on, or was he just being polite?

He looked completely relaxed except for one telltale sign. He had one arm draped easily across the back of the seat. With his other hand, he gripped the steering wheel so hard that the skin stretched taut across his knuckles.

Somehow it gratified her that he appeared so nervous.

In just a few hundred yards, they would pass the driveway to his place. A quarter-mile after that, they would reach hers. She had only a few seconds to make up her mind.

"Whenever a man offers coffee or a nightcap, it never actually means coffee or a nightcap," she commented.

"You sound like an authority."

"*Not.* I'm a single mother. Invitations like this don't come along every day."

"That's hard to believe." He turned into his driveway. The headlamps washed over the snug cabin and outbuildings, the placid surface of the water.

She felt a flutter of alarm in her chest. "I didn't say I'd come over," she protested.

"Executive decision." He parked and got out, came around to her side of the truck. He opened the door and shocked her by reaching across her lap, unbuckling her seat belt. The way his hand brushed her hip was unsettling in the extreme, both briskly professional and knowingly sexy.

"You're like an expert at this," she said.

"At what?"

"I'm not sure what it's called. Extraction and seduction?"

"You could say that." He took her hand and drew her to her feet. Then he held her pinned between him and the truck, and she felt such a surge of need that she couldn't speak, could not even move.

He touched her hair, a tender and intimate brush of his hand. Then he cupped her cheek, his thumb tracing the outline of her cheekbone, her jaw.

She needed his kiss with an urgency that burned. Now, she thought. Please, now.

As though he knew exactly what she was thinking, he smiled a little bit and stepped back. "I want to show you something," he said.

"Don't tell me. You have a collection of etchings."

"Even better." He helped her down the bank, lighting the way with a flashlight he'd taken from the truck.

She spotted a strange silhouette and realized it was the hull of a boat, upended on sawhorses. The smell of fresh-cut lumber and varnish hung in the air.

"It's a project I started," he said. "I'm restoring Sam's boat."

Kate wasn't sure why this moved her—the careful layout of the tools, sketches covered in hand-written notes, the lovingly crafted repairs. She reached out and put her hand on the smooth mahogany hull. "I remember this boat. Sam and I used to take it out when we were little."

"Which makes me insanely jealous of Sam."

"Because he had a boat?"

He slipped his arms around her from behind and drew her close to his body, bending down to inhale the scent of her hair. "Because he had you."

She sank back against him. Surrendering. Good heavens, could he be any more sexy? "Did Sam tell you that?" she asked. "Did he say we were boyfriend and girlfriend?"

"He said he wanted to be, but you had other ideas. True or false?"

"True. I was such an idiot." She remembered Sam so well, as loyal and strong as a Saint Bernard. She'd fooled around with him, probably led him on, but never crossed the line into a serious relationship. "When I was a kid, I always seemed to be dreaming of someone different, someone who didn't exist except in my imagination, like Spider-Man or . . . some superhero." She felt him tense with restraint. "Don't laugh. I was sixteen years old. Every girl that age wants a superhero."

"And now . . . ?"

She laughed and turned in his arms. "Now my standards have relaxed. Sometimes I think I'd settle for someone who was breathing."

"You're one tough cookie."

She looked up at him. *Let's get this show on the road.* "Honestly, I'm happy simply to go out on a date."

"Like we just did?"

"Exactly."

"We're still doing it."

"Doing what?"

"The date. It's not over yet. I haven't taken you home and kissed you good-night."

"You haven't kissed me at all."

"I'm painfully aware of that."

And still he didn't. Kate gritted her teeth against a moan of frustration as he stepped back. Keeping his arm around her, he walked her to the cabin. They stopped on the porch, turning to look at the lake. In high summer, the darkness took its time. The lake mirrored the purple color of the sky and the pinpoint stars, so thick and numerous they misted the surface of the water.

Oh, she wanted him. She wanted his mouth on hers, his bare skin next to hers, his hands in places that had been lonely for far too long. A soft sound slipped out of her before she could catch herself.

"You okay?" he asked. His arm felt lazily comfortable, yet unsettling at the same time.

"I'm not staying," she whispered.

"Beg pardon?"

"Here. With you, tonight. I . . . can't stay." She knew she was blowing it with this guy, but she didn't know what else to tell him.

A half smile curved his mouth. "You can't stay."

"That's right. See, I'm a responsible mother. I can't . . . I would never . . ."

"Then don't," he said easily, rescuing her from the fumbling explanation.

She nodded, feeling foolish and far more frustrated than relieved.

From one end of the porch, she could just make out the lights of her place. Only a couple of windows glowed—Callie's room and the back porch.

"Checking on Aaron," JD observed.

"Always."

"He's fine."

"I know." She hesitated and then decided to explain. "Aaron has . . . issues. Ninety-nine percent of the time, he's an angel."

"And the other one percent?"

"That's where the issues come in. He's impulsive, sometimes loses his temper. It makes him quite a challenge to raise."

"Have you ever heard of a kid being easy to raise?"

"I have no basis for comparison, but according to teachers and counselors and doctors, Aaron's needs are definitely special. According to men I've dated, he's much too special for them."

"Forget those guys, Kate, forget anybody who takes that attitude. Aaron's a gift from God. Anyone who doesn't see that isn't looking. All these things they claim are wrong with him don't add up to who he is."

She leaned back against the porch railing, held on for support. "I can't believe you just said that."

"Why not?"

"It makes you too good to be true. And I don't want

that. I want you to be true."

"Your boy is a blessing. Believe it. I bet you wish you had ten Aarons."

"Well, maybe not ten . . ."

"But you do want more kids."

Oh, dear. Now what? "I don't know . . . Aaron wasn't planned. He just happened."

"Like a gift."

Like you, she thought, smiling up at him.

Seventeen

"Go ahead and say I told you so," Kate offered Mable Claire Newman as they sat over coffee at the First Street Haven Café.

"Refresh my memory. What did I tell you?"

"I'm seeing someone. He was your idea. The guy who is staying at the Schroeder place."

Mable Claire beamed at her. "Good for you, Kate. He seems like a perfectly nice fellow. Not to mention he's a hunk."

"I noticed that right away." Kate couldn't suppress a smile. She had all the classic symptoms of pure infatuation. The light-headed moments of disorientation. The pounding heart and quickened breathing at the mere thought of him. The constant sense of hovering between laughter and tears. The heightened sensitivity to anything and everything, from the smell of coffee to the warmth of the sun on her skin. There was no denying it. Kate was in the staring-out-the-window, smiling-at-nothing stage of this relationship.

"So keep talking," Mable Claire said. "Old widowed lady like me, I need all the romance I can get."

"I don't really know how to explain this. Our first date was dinner at C'est Si Bon. After that, we started spending most evenings together, sometimes with the kids, sometimes by ourselves. There's this rhythm that we've started and it's . . . I don't know. Special." Kate speared a piece of watermelon from the fruit plate she'd ordered. Another symptom—wild swings of appetite from voracious to nonexistent. "Isn't that awful? Here I am, calling myself a writer and I can't even find the words for—"

"Oh, stop," Mable Claire said. "Of course you can't. But the good news is, every person who's ever been in love or even dreamed of it knows exactly what you're talking about."

"I'm not—" Kate nearly choked on her watermelon.

"You are, too. You're moving in that direction, anyway. Let yourself, Kate. You deserve to fall in love."

The words struck to the heart of Kate's uncertainty. *You deserve to fall in love.* Did she? Why had she never allowed it to happen?

"There's a huge gap between dating for the summer and falling in love."

"So what? Let your heart go and see what happens."

"That would be fine if I had only myself to think about, but there's Aaron. He's absolutely crazy about

JD, and it will crush him when we go our separate ways."

"Not when. If."

Kate felt a welling of tears, yet another symptom of this bittersweet affliction. She wept at the drop of a hat. At the sound of a heart-tugging song on the radio or the sight of an old married couple holding hands in church. For Kate, falling in love was like being terminally ill. Painful to go through, with a predictably bad outcome.

"He's not going to stay with us," Kate said. "Why would he?"

"Oh, let me think. You're a warm, wonderful, beautiful young woman with an adorable son. Whatever could a man see in you?" Mable Claire buttered a marionberry scone. "You're already planning to let him go before you've explored all the possibilities."

"I'm trying to be practical and keep Aaron from getting his hopes up," Kate insisted. "These things never work out for me."

"Just because ninety-nine percent of soufflés fall when taken out of the oven doesn't mean you shouldn't ever bake a soufflé."

"I'll make a note of that." She offered a grudging smile. "We have this unspoken agreement that we don't talk about the end of summer. He's from the East Coast, and he's looking at going to UCLA for medical school. There's no way I can leave Seattle, so—"

"Quit thinking about how this is going to end. Try thinking about how things are right now."

"Things are amazing right now," Kate admitted with

a dreamy smile. JD seemed to be growing more and more at home in her company. With good-natured cooperation, he participated in some of the most ancient Livingston family rituals—bike rides, cannonballs off the dock, hiking expeditions, games of lawn darts and badminton, ghost stories and marshmallow roasts around a lakeside bonfire. She had not told him so, but he was stepping into the breach left by her brother, bringing strength and laughter and that ineffably male jocularity to the family, the one thing she couldn't replicate.

"All right," she said, giving herself a mental shake. She indicated the folder on the table. "I'm returning your photographs. They've been converted into digital files for the article on my grandfather. I made you a copy on a CD."

"He was a lovely man, your grandfather," she said. "Aaron takes after him, doesn't he?"

Same red hair and twinkling eyes, thought Kate. But Walden had been a leader, some would say a visionary. She wondered if Aaron could possibly have those gifts. Your son is a gift, JD had told her. Believe it.

"Anyway, the article is being published next February."

"Kate, that's exciting." Mable Claire beamed at her. "I'm so proud of you."

"Thanks." Mable Claire made her miss her mother. "I was at such a low spot at the beginning of summer."

"But you kept your chin up, and look at you now."

"I wanted to talk to you about Callie. Her birthday is coming up and I'm planning a surprise party for her.

Can you and Luke join us Saturday night?"

"Sure, I'd love to come. Luke, too, probably. He was so bored at the beginning of summer. Fortunately, he found a group of other teenagers to pal around with."

"He's always by himself when he visits Callie. Maybe he could invite the others, too."

"I'll ask him. This is awfully nice of you, Kate."

"I like doing things for Callie. Aaron's in on the surprise. He's beside himself."

"It sounds like fun. She doesn't seem to be a girl who's had a lot of birthday parties."

"I agree. That's about to change."

The evening before the party, Kate left Callie to watch Aaron while she and JD went out—on a date, they said. Beforehand, they had some stops to make, choosing gifts for Callie's birthday. Music, of course—a Jimi Hendrix collection and some new electronica that JD swore she loved, even though it made Kate cringe. She selected four new colors of nail polish, something she knew Callie liked, and then she lingered over the displays at the clothing store. "She only ever wears jeans, sweats and T-shirts," she told JD. "I don't want her to think I disapprove of that." In the end, she settled on a gift card. It was uninspired but practical, she decided. Finally, at the stationery shop, she found a stock of notebooks and creamy writing paper, faintly lined, and pens in beautiful colors.

"She's starting to matter so much to me," Kate told JD.

"Lucky girl," he said.

"You think so?"

"I know so. Let's go get dinner."

The plan was to catch a new movie at the local cinema, but halfway through the peach pie à la mode, Kate noticed him staring at her with unmistakable intensity. She fancied she could feel actual heat from his gaze.

"Something wrong?" she asked.

"I'm not in the mood for a movie." Simple words, but they were spoken in a tone that was taut with an undercurrent she recognized, because she felt it, too.

"Me neither. What would you like to do?" she asked.

"Let's go to my place."

Hardly a radical suggestion. But it was different now; and they both knew that. "All right," she said.

They didn't speak much on the ride to the lake. A soft, slow love song drifted from the radio speakers. He helped her out of the truck and they walked together to the front porch. "You're quiet," he said, taking out his keys.

She took a deep breath and decided to say it. "You haven't kissed me yet and I want to know why. What have you got against it?"

He fell still, his features shrouded in darkness. "Kissing in general or kissing you?"

"You're opposed to kissing me?"

"Those are your words, not mine."

She wanted to scream in frustration. "Look, maybe I should go—"

"Kate," he whispered, taking her arm and pulling her around to face him. "You . . ." He was like an actor who had forgotten his lines, yet there was nothing gradual or tentative about his kiss. He pulled her against him and kissed her without further preamble or ceremony, his mouth open and searching. Her nerves hummed with a fine edge of desire, and she sank against him, wanting and fearing, knowing she was ready and refusing, for now, to let herself worry about tomorrow.

He was new and exciting, yet she fit perfectly into his arms, into his kiss. The dizzily romantic thought struck her that she had been waiting for him all her life.

"Better?" he asked, his mouth hovering over hers.

"You get an A+." She took in a deep, shuddering breath. "But maybe we shouldn't . . . I can't . . ."

"Come on, Kate. I know you're a responsible mother, like you once told me. But you're also responsible for your own happiness."

"And you think . . ." She paused, tried to organize her thoughts. "You think making love with you would make me happy."

"I don't think that. I *know* it." He grinned. "I promise."

And then he picked her up as though she weighed nothing and pushed open the door with his shoulder. When he set her down, she felt the edge of the bed pressing against the backs of her legs.

He still didn't stop kissing her, not until he stepped back to turn her, gently lifting her hair away from the nape of her neck. He unzipped her dress, skimming it from her shoulders. Drowning in sensation, Kate kept her eyes shut, though she tried to picture what she'd worn tonight for underwear, because she had some real doozies from Ooh-La-La. It was all right, she recalled. Basic tasteful cherry red was always appropriate. Even if it was a thong.

She was on fire when she opened her eyes to face him, and she was gratified by the speed with which he shed his jacket and shirt. The only light in the room came from the moon, a clear pale glow highlighting a physique that, she strongly suspected, would cause women's jaws to drop.

Deep shadows dappled his chest, and with a shock, she realized he was scarred—and not just a little. Thick, shiny tissue scored his chest and lower rib cage. "What happened to you?" she asked.

"I was in the service."

"What, last week?"

"I signed up right out of high school, and stayed in until last spring."

"And you were a medic," she said, "like Sam."

"That's right."

She gently traced a scar with her finger. "I thought medics *helped* the wounded."

"Sometimes you put yourself in harm's way to do that."

"You act like it's such a simple thing, putting yourself in harm's way."

"In the service, that's your job, whether you're a truck

226

driver, a cafeteria worker or a sniper. It's not simple. It's the job."

"Where were you in harm's way?"

"Konar Province in Afghanistan. That's where I first met Sam."

"I'm waiting for you to elaborate."

"Honey, you're standing there in a thong. The only thing I want to elaborate on is what I'm going to do to you."

His words melted her resolve to take this slowly. Yet, while a part of her was ready to jump into bed with him, another part held on to caution. With an almost painful reluctance, she pulled her dress back up.

He groaned as though she'd wounded him.

"I told myself I need to get to know you," she explained, though she felt his pain.

"You know me, Kate," he said. "You know what's important."

"You never talk about your life. Your family. Your past—"

"I have a crappy apartment in D.C. and I'm a paramedic. Growing up, I just had my mother. Closest thing I have to family is Sam."

"What were you doing in Afghanistan?"

His jaw tightened with a slight tic, but she held her ground. Finally, he gave a sigh of resignation. "We were medics in two different units. There was a sort of rough brotherhood made up of Northern Alliance Uzbeks and Tajiks, and a handful of U.S. Special Forces soldiers. They sent us down one night into a valley where a recon unit had been ambushed. Our job was to evacuate the wounded."

It sounded surreal to her, particularly rendered in his matter-of-fact tone. "I have a feeling you're making this sound easier than it was," she said.

"I never said it was easy. That night, we hit the UXO jackpot."

"UXO . . ."

"Unexploded ordnance. There was a world of it littering the field."

"Is that how you got those scars?" she asked, feeling a bit queasy.

"No, but it sure as hell made things interesting. And I met my best friend that night, so it wasn't a total loss. And now . . ." He slid the dress off her shoulder, bent to kiss her there. "About that thong . . ."

She considered struggling, but his mouth on her just felt too good. "Finish the story," she said weakly.

"It's over. Tell me about you." He bared the other shoulder and kissed her there, too.

"Oh, right. Like I can top yours. I wish I'd done something more with my life."

"You've done plenty."

She rested her forehead against his chest. Having a nine-year-old made her feel so ancient compared to her childless girlfriends. "It's a conundrum. Nathan was a huge mistake, but if I hadn't met him, I wouldn't have Aaron."

He touched her hair. "Did you love him?"

"I wouldn't have slept with him if I didn't love him."

"Does that mean you don't sleep with anyone unless you love him?"

"Are you trying to get me to say I love you?"

"Only if you mean it."

Oh, she was close. He had no idea how close she was to letting the dam burst. "I know what love is," she said. "And what it isn't." She smiled up at him but remembered the old Kate, pregnant and abandoned by a boy she had adored and trusted. "These things happen in their own time."

He nodded, and very deliberately reached around and unhooked her bra. She reveled in the fire of his touch, all her reservations receding to a far corner.

"This is going to change everything," she whispered in a voice she didn't recognize.

"I sure as hell hope so."

"You do?"

He traced his finger around the band of the thong. "Hell, yes."

She was mesmerized by the movement of his finger. "What was wrong with the way things were before?"

"Nothing, but . . . we weren't like this."

She caught her breath at the way he touched her. "That's true," she whispered. Then, because she knew in a few moments she would not be able to speak at all, she spoke the truth. "I'm afraid."

He pulled her closer, threaded his fingers into her hair. "Afraid of what?"

"Of losing you as a friend." She tilted back her head to look up at him and was struck by a wave of dizziness.

Good Lord, he was incredible. "That's what will happen, you know. Once we sleep together, we won't be friends anymore."

"No," he said softly, whispering against her mouth. "We'll be closer."

Eighteen

On her birthday, Callie felt like an old woman with an aching back and bad knees. She had spent a rotten afternoon cleaning up a party house on Lake Sutherland after the vacationers had gone back to the city. The place was designed to sleep six, but clearly, they'd had twice that many drinking, eating junk food, using every dish and utensil in sight, littering the decks with cans, bottles, wrappers and spent fireworks.

To top it off, Yolanda had bugged out early, leaving Callie to finish up and walk the half mile back to the Livingstons' house. Actually, Callie didn't mind the walk and she knew she could use the exercise. It was the best part of a crappy day.

The road was empty of cars as usual, dappled by shifting patterns of sunshine and shadow. Through the trees, she glimpsed the lake, not Sutherland with its buzzing Jet Skis and pounding ski boats, but Lake Crescent, pristine and protected, home to only a privileged few. It was kind of amazing that she had wound up here, as if it was meant to be. Sometimes she imagined the lake was part of an enchanted world, protected by an invisible bubble. When she was there, with the Livingstons, she belonged in that world, safe and protected.

The lake itself was the center of the world. She loved the water. She always had. She loved holding her breath and sinking under, into the darkened silence. In that silence, she could forget about her own screwed-up life for whole minutes at a time.

She turned up the volume on her Discman and let the cool music of The Visitors fill her up, until she was drowning in the smooth notes and lyrical poetry about someone else's hurt, which somehow made her own fade away, just for a few blessed minutes. That was why she loved music. She wished she could disappear into the sea of notes, sink underneath them and never come up for air, never again break the surface and see what a mess she had made of her life.

She wasn't stupid enough to believe she could actually do that. She was stupid, though. This was something she had to quit hiding from herself, because she couldn't any longer. Her mistakes were part of her and she couldn't get away from them. She tried running, but here was the problem. You couldn't run away if the thing you were trying to escape was your own self. She would forever be California Sequoia Evans, raised on a loony farm, then shuffled from house to house by folks who saw foster kids as an extra check from the state every month.

Not all of them, though. She had to be fair. The first

family she'd been placed with as a scared, surly misfit had been kind enough. The Clines. She still remembered the wonder she'd felt at the simplest things—a mother helping with homework, Saturday-morning cartoons. The relief of feeling normal had been strictly temporary, though. Just when she was learning to like her life again, she had been reassigned to a different family, this one tense and restrictive, and when she broke too many of their bullshit rules, she'd wound up with the Coldwells, a well-to-do family made up of a bitter, suspicious mother, a critical, demanding father and their nineteen-year-old son, still living at home.

And now here she was with Kate and Aaron at their house at the lake. She'd never known anybody like them. Kate was kind and funny and caring, and Aaron was a doll. A little freaky sometimes, but what kid wasn't? Callie shouldn't let herself get too involved. Summer would end and they'd go back to their lives in the city. Knowing Kate, she'd probably try to help Callie out, but Callie wouldn't take advantage of her anymore. She'd figure out . . . something. She had no idea what.

She rotated her shoulders as she walked, trying to ease the cramping there. Yolanda was always advising Callie to try yoga, which was a nice way of urging her to do something about being so fat, like yoga would actually help at this point. Shaking her head, Callie rubbed the small of her back. Nothing would help. She had read somewhere that time heals all wounds, but by now she knew that was a crock of shit.

She was having depressing thoughts on her birthday. Big deal. This was a depressing birthday. Here she was, marking the day she was born, and all she could do was think about how much her life sucked.

"Snap out of it," she muttered, stopping to take a bottle of water out of her tote bag. Kate fixed her a sack lunch every day and always included a chilled bottle of water. Callie took a long drink and sprinkled the last drops from the bottle onto her overheated face. She was sick and tired of dragging herself around every day, tired of wearing fat-girl clothes and acting all normal.

Honestly, she didn't want anything for her birthday. She wanted something for her *life.* To be normal. To laugh and have fun and not worry about the future. To have a best friend. A boyfriend.

"Yeah, sure," she muttered, but even in the middle of nowhere, she automatically straightened her shoulders and strutted like a beauty queen down the middle of the road. Just the thought of Luke Newman did that to her, made her want to stand up straight and face the world with a smile.

It was the freakiest thing. He liked her. He didn't seem to mind her looks or the fact that she hadn't been to school since before Christmas or that she dressed like a bag lady. He didn't judge her. It was so weird that she had met him now, right after meeting Kate and Aaron. Just when she didn't think she could get any further down on her luck, she'd lucked into all these people here at the lake. After a lifetime of having no one, she suddenly found herself with people who actually gave a hoot about her.

Which made her feel lousy about lying to them, but she didn't quite know what to do about it at this point. Except to keep lying.

She felt an echo of the dizziness that had been bothering her all day, and stumbled in the road.

Easy now, she told herself. Take it easy. Must be the heat. She felt a raging thirst and wished she hadn't emptied that water bottle.

Ah, well. She was nearly home now. Maybe she'd take Aaron for a swim in the lake. That always made her feel better, plunging in and sinking down, disappearing for a while. She never wore a bathing suit, not the way she looked, fat as a pig and with those weird dark patches on her skin here and there. When they'd first appeared at the base of her neck, she had thought it was dirt and tried to scrub it off. To her horror, she realized the dark patches were a part of her. It was totally creepy. Some sort of punishment for being a liar and a fraud?

Or just bad luck. It was the only kind she ever had.

She forced herself to put one foot in front of the other and focused on the lake. Yes, she should go swimming. And for Chrissake, rinse her mouth out. Her breath had a weird, fruity taste. She wanted to drink up all the water in the lake to ease the burning inside. And if she still couldn't shake the dizziness, maybe she'd just close her eyes, lie back in the water and let it take over, spinning endlessly. Maybe she would float forever, out through the channel at the end of the lake, down the river and out to sea.

The driveway came into view. Home at last, she thought with an ironic smile. It was quiet around here today. Maybe Kate and Aaron had taken the dog for a walk, because normally Bandit came yapping up the driveway to greet her. If someone had told her she would make friends with a dog, she would have thought they were nuts, but she actually liked Bandit. He was proof that not all dogs were dangerous just because one bit her.

Maybe they had gone to see Sergeant Harris, because these days, Kate and Harris were quite an item together, even though they tried to be discreet about it. Except nobody but Callie knew he was a sergeant. That he was *the* sergeant as in Sergeant Jordan Donovan Harris, whose heroic act had been all over the news since Christmas.

Callie had to hand it to the guy. He had truly gone underground, erasing who he was and becoming a different person entirely. Maybe she should ask him for pointers.

The moment she'd figured out his secret, she'd been royally ticked off. She'd felt duped, somehow, and it was totally off base but she couldn't help herself. She understood, though, that hiding something, even for the best of reasons like JD did, was always going to get you in trouble. After he'd explained all about his rotten mother and all the weird stuff that happened because of his fame, she had forgiven him. And then a sizzle of possibility had shot through her. Just knowing him made her special. One phone call and she could have the crew of *Extra* here, interviewing them all. There was probably a way to make money off selling his secret, a lot of money. She could trade him for a secure future for herself.

The only trouble was, she'd given her word that she wouldn't say anything. And she liked him too much to do that to him.

She caught a faint whiff of smoke from the barbecue, and her stomach cramped in anticipation. Lately she ate like a pig; she couldn't seem to stop herself. Too bad. Today was her stupid birthday. Just for today, she wasn't going to worry about anything.

She let herself in the back door. It wasn't locked, which meant they hadn't gone far.

"Hello," she called out. The house was empty and quiet, but in a friendly, waiting way. A box fan in the window blew a gentle breath of fresh air through the downstairs.

"Anybody home?" she called, dropping off her backpack and Walkman in her room.

No answer. She went to the sink to get a drink and splash water on her face. In those old Georgette Heyer books she'd found in one of the crammed bookcases in the family room, women were always bathing their wrists when they were upset. Bathing their wrists, as though that was supposed to help anything.

Callie let cool tap water run over her wrists but it didn't make her feel any better.

She headed for the door, intending to sit on the porch

facing the lake and wait for everyone to come home. Happy birthday to me, she thought.

She opened the door to the porch, and the world exploded.

"Happy birthday!" shouted a chorus of voices. "Surprise!"

Callie stood in the doorway, frozen with shock. For a moment, she couldn't make sense of anything, not the smiling faces or the crepe-paper streamers, not even the picnic table with the giant three-tiered cake or the stack of brightly wrapped gifts on the lawn.

"Today Is Your Birthday" blasted from the stereo.

"Callie," Aaron yelled, jumping up and down. "Were you surprised, Callie? Were you?"

She forced herself to close her mouth and nod in mute assent. It was just like on TV, with all the good wishes, the music playing, people clapping.

Except there was one big difference. On TV, the birthday girl looked lovely, flushed with pleasure and gratitude. Callie was not able to act like that, not at all. She tried, she nearly succeeded in forcing herself to smile and say thank you, but all she could manage to do was burst into tears.

Right there in front of everyone, she broke down and sobbed. It was totally humiliating, but she couldn't help herself. She cried with happiness that someone had finally cared enough to give her a birthday party, and with sadness that it had taken all the years of her life. She cried for joy that she'd found friends so true they felt like family, and cried with misery that it would all end with the summer.

"Hey, now," said Luke, somehow looking both awkward and gallant as he patted her on the shoulder. "Are you okay?"

"You're supposed to be glad," Aaron said, sounding so put out that she had to smile. "This is a party, in case you hadn't noticed, *genius.*"

"I noticed." Callie gratefully took a paper napkin from Kate and wiped her face. "And I'm glad." She looked at the small group gathered on the lawn—Kate and Aaron and JD, Mrs. Newman, Yolanda and her boyfriend, Richie. And of course, Luke, by her side.

There were silly games and way too much food. Aaron taught everyone the official Livingston method of making s'mores, otherwise known as s'mores for dummies. You had to roast the marshmallow until it flamed, slip the black char off it, then roll the sticky marshmallow in miniature M&Ms and squish the whole mess between graham crackers. Luke made and ate four of them at least, and Callie envied his ability to eat anything he wanted and not get fat. She refused to worry about her weight tonight, though, and ate her own share. The s'mores and cake made her incredibly thirsty, but even sucking down a liter bottle of water didn't seem to help.

The dizziness swept up and over her again, but she closed her eyes and went with it, riding it like a surfer catching a wave.

"Thank you," she whispered, knowing they couldn't hear but well aware that they would never realize that they had made this the happiest day of her life.

Nineteen

"I think it was a smashing success," Mable Claire said hours later as they all sat on the beach watching the moon rise over the lake. "We surprised the heck out of her and everyone had a great time."

"It was perfect," Kate said. Around the campfire, the others were playing charades, though she and Mable Claire were sitting this round out. "I've never given anyone a surprise party before."

"Me neither," Mable Claire said. "I guess when you're Callie, everything good that comes your way is a surprise."

Kate leaned back against the huge log that had lain there for generations. Phil had carved his initials in it and the date: 7–4–84 to commemorate a long-ago night of fireworks. She looped her hands around one drawn-up knee. It was Richie's turn, and he was desperately trying to get them to say the name of some sort of horned animal.

"Bull," Aaron shouted.

"Caribou, moose, water buffalo!"

"Yak," JD suggested, causing Richie to sink to his knees in gratitude, nodding approval.

"Yakety Yak! (Don't Talk Back)" was the solution, and it came from Callie, of course, who knew every song ever written.

"My turn," Mable Claire said, joining the group as

Callie selected a clue from the hat.

Tiny orange sparks danced in the air. The firelight gilded the group in its kindly glow, and the sight of everyone, relaxed and playing together, caused Kate to feel a tug of nostalgia. The image took her back to other times, summers from long ago, nights filled with fun and laughter.

Aaron was wandering away from the game, unable to stay focused on it. Before Kate could call him back, JD snatched the kid up, swinging him around until Aaron shrieked with laughter and rejoined the group. Kate felt herself grinning like an idiot as she watched the festivities. She had anticipated this being the loneliest summer of her life. Who knew she would find happiness here?

A few minutes later, JD eased himself down beside her. "You look pleased with yourself."

"The party turned out great."

"Yep." He reached across her for the sack of marshmallows and speared two of them on a sharpened stick.

She felt a thrill at his easy familiarity. Frankly, she acknowledged, everything about him was thrilling. She loved feeling like a couple with him. "You know, I came here this year with very low expectations. I thought Aaron and I would be miserable without the rest of the family."

He meticulously toasted the marshmallows, concentrating on browning them evenly and slowly. "And now?"

"And now that doesn't matter. We're having a wonderful summer." She gestured at the charades game, which was getting rowdier by the minute. "This feels like family to me. Nobody's related to anybody, but it all just works."

Still watching the marshmallows, he turned the stick slowly in his hands.

"Callie seems so happy," Kate said, watching her grabbing onto Luke's arm as he teased her about something. "I hope that boy is good to her."

"He's awfully young," JD said.

A subtle note in his voice caught her attention. "He's Mable Claire's grandson and according to her, he can do no wrong. Do you think he's bad news?"

"I think he's awfully young, that's all I'm saying."

"So is she," Kate pointed out.

He held the perfectly toasted marshmallows in front of her. "For you, madame," he said, formal as a French waiter.

"How do you do that? Get them all brown without setting them on fire?"

"I'm a professional. Trust me." He hovered the warm marshmallow in front of her, and she took it from him. It was meltingly sweet as it slid into her mouth, and she made him eat the other one.

"This is making me have wicked thoughts about you," she said, watching him.

"Those are the best kind." He glanced at the others to make sure they weren't watching, and then leaned forward to place a brief but scorching kiss on her mouth.

She nearly melted like a marshmallow, but forced herself to shift away from him on the blanket. "Whoa," she said. "There are youngsters present." She stuck two more marshmallows on the stick.

"Which is why I haven't jumped your bones right here and now," he said. "Quit worrying, Kate. Everyone knows. I don't think it does Aaron any harm to see that somebody's crazy about his mother."

Her breath caught, and she fought to keep her expression neutral. That was as close as he had ever come to declaring his feelings for her. She could hardly believe her ears.

"Define crazy," she said. "Do you mean crazy like you're lusting after me or—" She stopped, not wanting to say the rest or let him see how much she needed to hear it.

"Nope," he said. "I mean, I do lust for you constantly, that's a given. What I meant was the other kind of crazy."

Kate felt the stick slip from her fingers. The marshmallows turned blue with flame and then blistered black, disappearing into the coals. Deep inside Kate, a voice whispered, *Don't throw this away. Don't . . .* "I'm sorry," she said. "I don't think I heard right. Did you just say—"

"Kate." Mable Claire's sharp summons cut through the night, severing the tension of the moment. "Kate and JD both, we need you. Something's the matter with Callie. She fainted."

Even before Kate could assimilate the words, JD had shot up and rushed to Callie's side. She lay limply on the beach, with the others gathered around, all laughter gone now.

JD broke into action, checking her over, yelling her name and shaking her. "Someone go to my truck and get the aid bag," he ordered with an authority she had never heard before. "It's in the toolbox." Richie sped off to get it.

"Thank God somebody knows what he's doing," said Mable Claire.

JD took over. He moved in, the soul of competence, and went to work, using gear of surprising substance from the bag Richie brought from the truck. He kept calling her name, jiggling her, checking her vital signs. Yolanda took charge of Aaron, reassuring him and keeping him quiet. For once, this was not difficult. He seemed to understand the gravity of the situation.

As JD checked Callie's breathing and pulse, Kate went for her handbag and keys.

By the time she returned, JD had scooped Callie up in his arms. She lay limp and unresponsive.

Kate gave Aaron a quick hug. "We have to get Callie to a doctor. You stay with Mrs. Newman and Luke, and I'll be back as soon as I can."

"I'm scared," he said.

"I know. She's going to be all right. I have to go now, buddy." She squeezed him one more time and then ran to the Jeep. Richie and JD were getting Callie into the back seat. Luke stood by, looking as pale and scared as Aaron had been.

Kate expected him to insist on riding along, but he didn't. "She's going to be all right," she said, just as she'd told Aaron.

He nodded and stepped back, his hands stuck into his pockets.

She and JD worked as a team. She drove while he stayed in the back with Callie. He grabbed a flashlight, stethoscope and blood-pressure cuff from his aid bag and kept talking to her, trying to get her attention.

As Kate drove off into the night, Callie came around, offering weak protests but giving vague answers to the usual questions about what year it was or the name of the president. She didn't want to go to the hospital. That was clear enough. JD brooked no argument, which was equally clear.

The second they got into cell phone range, he made the call. Kate understood maybe half of the technical jargon he dictated into the phone, giving the information with precision and clear competence. "Caucasian female, eighteen years of age . . . Syncopal episode . . . BP's 102 over 66," he stated. "Pulse 160, respiration 22 and shallow. Patient's shaky, skin's damp, she's obviously dizzy. She's muscularly toned. . . ." There was something incredibly comforting about his manner. He seemed so professional and confident. He also seemed like a different person, someone she didn't know.

"ETA's ten more minutes," he said.

Kate didn't hear the rest. Her hands shook but she forced herself to keep a firm grip on the steering wheel. She bit her lip to keep from interrupting his report to the dispatcher.

Kate wanted to believe Callie was safe in his care. Yet a seemingly healthy girl didn't simply collapse.

PART FOUR

"We cannot change anything until we accept it.
Condemnation does not liberate, it oppresses."
—Carl Gustav Jung, *Psychological Reflections*

Twenty

"I'm not staying here." Trapped like a thief in the stark glare of fluorescent lights, Callie felt a cold fist of panic knocking in her chest. "You can't make me stay," she said to the doctor or nurse or whoever the woman in blue scrubs was. Despite her insistence on escaping from the narrow, scary room and eluding the strangers poking and prodding her, Callie didn't really know what her rights were. Would she be classified as a runaway? Turned over to authorities? Sent up to juvy? There were no good options for her, none, except to run . . . again.

"We're going to take good care of you," the woman said.

"You can't make me stay. I'm eighteen years old."

"No, you're not." The woman spoke quietly but distinctly.

Callie felt icy dread prickling over her scalp. At first she couldn't speak. She felt trapped. She wanted to scream that she was, too, eighteen. Old enough to vote. Old enough to pluck the clear plastic clips off her fingertips, pull out the IV and walk away from the noise and light of this strange, intimidating place.

But somehow, the woman in the scrubs had figured out her secret.

"What do you mean?" Callie said. "I know how old I am."

"So do I."

She narrowed her eyes in resentment. "How do you know?"

"I'm a doctor. It's my job to know. My name is Dr. Randall, ER doc and total wizard when it comes to accessing patient records."

Callie shuddered. She needed to get out of here, *now.* Yet truthfully, she was terrified to pull out the IV. It was ironic, given everything she'd survived in the past, but she couldn't bring herself to rip out the white tapes, the tube and the needle buried deep in her arm. She'd endured pain others inflicted on her, but had a deep and probably healthy reluctance to hurt herself. She'd seen IVs torn out in movies with a brave, dramatic flourish. Now, confronted with actually doing it, she balked. What if it hurt? What if the hole in her arm spewed blood? And even if she did manage to free herself from the IV, then what? She couldn't just walk away; she was wearing a blue paper smock. She had no idea what they'd done with her clothes. Oh, man. They took her clothes. How humiliating was that?

Luke, she thought. Luke would rescue her. Yet she

realized she didn't want him to. If he saw her now, he'd run screaming to the next town, probably.

She tried a different tack with Dr. Randall. "I don't have any money. I won't be able to pay my hospital bill."

"That's been taken care of."

"By Mr. Harris?" She didn't even have to think about it.

"I don't know. That's not my department."

Callie knew. It had to be JD. Of course it was him. She was grateful to know he was taking care of her to be sure, but frustrated, too. She didn't want to be treated like some kind of charity case, even though that's exactly what she was. And whether he liked it or not, JD was Daddy Warbucks. But he didn't owe her a thing and there was no reason for him to take care of her except that he was a good guy. Well, she didn't need any freaking hero. She just needed to get the hell out of here.

"Undo me," she said to the woman, indicating the tubes. "And give me back my clothes. I'm leaving."

"Before you make any decision, you need to understand your condition." The woman spoke so calmly it was annoying. She offered a quick, I'm-a-professional smile. "You were brought in because you collapsed. That's worrisome in and of itself, even more so because of your condition."

"My condition?" Callie eyed her with suspicion. Her condition was obvious—she was a fat, homeless loser, but staying in the hospital wasn't going to fix that. "Oh,

God . . ." Her teeth started to chatter. She tried to remember the last time she had her period. "Oh, God," she said again.

"When was the last time you saw a doctor?"

"What makes you think I've ever seen one?" Callie tried to sound tough, uncaring. Never having seen a doctor was a badge of honor, really. Her caseworkers made sure she had a record of immunization, but no one had ever taken her for a checkup or anything.

Dr. Randall's response was a simple nod. It was kind of a relief that she didn't act all indignant or self-righteous. The first family Callie had been placed with had had that reaction. The mother was all like, *How dare they neglect this poor child, it's abuse, I tell you, pure and simple. . . .*

"Callie? Can I call you Callie?" The doctor broke in on her thoughts.

She stared up at the ceiling tiles. "So I guess you think I need a doctor now."

"Depends. We'll need to do a number of tests."

"What kind of tests?" She shuddered, wondering if they were going to make her tell who she'd done it with, and how often, and if she'd used protection. Oh, God.

"You've had a blood glucose reading of fifty, which confirms a condition known as hypoglycemia. That's why you're getting intravenous feedings."

"Great, thanks." Callie frowned, too cautious to feel relief just yet. She watched the long, slow drip of the IV apparatus. "I can use the calories."

The doctor didn't think that was funny. "What are your eating habits like?"

She looked in disgust at her pudgy hand. "Isn't that obvious?"

"I need for you to be more specific. Are your eating habits irregular? Have you been skipping meals? Maybe fasting and then eating a lot?"

"Yeah. So?" Didn't the doctor get it? Callie wondered. Before she moved in with Kate, she'd had little choice about where, when and what to eat. When you didn't know where your next meal was coming from, you learned to stock up. "Not so much since I've been staying with . . . friends at the lake."

"But you've still been skipping meals, sometimes overeating and fasting."

"Big deal. It's not like I'm some weirdo—"

"No one said that. In fact, your eating habits are probably typical of any teenager. However, in your case, it's led to a dangerous condition." She scribbled something down on the chart.

Callie felt a dark thrill of fear. "What kind of dangerous condition?"

"You're going to need a full workup, but preliminary observations indicate insulin resistance. For you, that's good news and bad news."

"Give me the bad first."

"This is likely to develop into type 2 diabetes. Do you know what that is?"

"Kind of. Like you can OD on sugar or something."

"There's a lot more to it, but we'll take it one step at

a time. After the tests show what we're dealing with, you're going to get a crash course in this disease."

Disease, thought Callie. I have a disease. It wasn't bad enough that she was fat. She had to have a disease on top of everything else. "Didn't you say you had some good news for me?"

"If you manage to get this condition under control and keep it there, you'll live a long and healthy life."

"And if I don't?"

"The health risks of ignoring this are enormous. Trust me, you want to take care of this now. You'll learn all about it in class."

"What class?"

"Several, actually. You'll be joining a support group, a diabetes-awareness group, a lifestyle-management class—"

The idea of classes and support groups made her skin crawl. "Who says?"

"You just heard me say it, didn't you?"

Callie expected to feel mutinous. Instead, the doctor's bossiness was weirdly gratifying. No one had ever bothered to lay down the law for her. Still, some devil of impulse compelled her to push back. "So who put you in charge?" she asked.

"No one. I simply took charge. There's only so much I can do, though. Taking care of your health is going to be up to you. I can't force you to cooperate. But you owe it to yourself to obtain a full and detailed diagnosis and learn exactly what you're dealing with."

"Isn't there like a shot or something you can give me

to make it go away?"

"Insulin resistance doesn't work like that. The goal is to control this without medication for as long as possible."

"Excuse me," Callie snapped. "The goal is to get rid of it."

"Once we have a diagnosis of diabetes, there's no cure. It's a chronic disease that will require lifelong management. But it does go away with weight loss, exercise and diet control."

"You can't cure it but I can make it go away?"

"If it turns out to be insulin resistance, you're at high risk for developing diabetes. But this is a disease you don't have to develop if you change your life now." She glanced down at her clipboard. "Here's a rundown on your condition." She started explaining things slowly and clearly, showing Callie a brochure with simple diagrams.

Callie tuned the lecture out. *Chronic disease.* The words stabbed at her like an ice-cold knife—frightening, damaging, numbing. *Lifelong management.* She refused to let herself cry. Crying had never helped, and it sure as heck wouldn't now. "And if I don't see a doctor and do the classes and stuff?" she demanded, interrupting the lecture.

"Then you're taking your chances. It's your choice."

I don't want any choices. Tell me what to do. I'm just a kid.

"Your friends are outside," the doctor said. "I know they're anxious to see you."

No. She tried to say it but her head nodded against the pillow: *Yes.*

A few minutes later Kate and JD stood next to her bed. She looked at them both and her heart recognized the emotions emanating from them. She had never felt this before and there was no reason she should be able to identify the sentiment, but there it was. Kate and JD were not here out of duty or guilt or because the state sent them a check every month. They were here out of love and compassion, and the truth of it broke over her like the rising sun.

Once again, Callie told herself not to cry. She repeated the instructions like a mantra in her head: *Don't cry. Don't cry. Don't cry.* There was no point. Yesterday, she couldn't help herself when she saw what they'd done for her. A birthday party. A real party, with games and gifts picked out just for her. A celebration, just because she had been born. No wonder she broke down and cried.

You'd think one day of bawling was enough, but now it happened again. Tormented by the kindness and concern on their faces, she lost it even worse than before.

Kate's arms went around her and she stroked Callie's hair, and somehow that tender, affectionate touch made things worse. Callie cried because she was scared and her life was a mess, because she didn't know how to save herself. She cried because she had made terrible mistakes and there was no way to fix them. She sobbed until she was wrung out like a dishrag that had seen better days. She barely had the strength to look up at

Kate. Then when she did, she was shocked to see that Kate was crying, too.

"I'm sorry," Callie managed to choke out. It hurts, she thought. Love hurts. Can that be right?

"There's nothing to be sorry about."

JD offered a box of Kleenex and they both took some and wiped their faces. He seemed remarkably calm. Probably in his other life he saw stuff like this all the time—people falling apart, looking for somebody to lean on, hoping for support from their family, freaking out when they figured out they were on their own. He had a terrible job, Callie thought, struggling to get a grip. And she was so freaking lucky he'd been around when she collapsed last night.

"I wish you'd told me you weren't feeling well," Kate said.

"I wanted to say something but I was afraid. And . . . I guess confused. I knew something wasn't right, but I didn't want to complain, or worry you."

"Oh, honey, that's what I'm here for."

Callie felt drained, as though she'd run out of tears. "I'm supposed to get all these tests done. That doctor—Randall—says after a complete workup, I have to do all this other stuff. Classes and tests and checkups."

"We want to do everything possible to help." She glanced at JD. "I do, anyway."

"We both want to help," he said.

"There's something I need to tell you," Callie said. She knew she sounded like an idiot, but it was safe to sound like an idiot around them now, considering everything that happened and all they knew about her. Still, she was terrified. There was one more thing, a major thing, she hadn't told them. "Both of you."

Kate touched her hand. "We're listening."

She didn't know where to begin. "Remember that first day we met?" she asked Kate. "After I scared the crap out of you and you invited me to stay?"

"Sure," Kate said.

"Remember you told me I was safe with you, and I kind of laughed? Well, I wasn't laughing at you. It was because you had no idea what you were inviting into your house."

"I certainly did." Kate smoothed out the woven blanket that covered Callie. "And I don't regret it for a single second."

"You can't be safe from something inside yourself," Callie said, her voice breaking.

"I don't understand," Kate said.

Callie glanced at JD, who looked really patient but not confused, like Kate. Why would he be? Like Dr. Randall, he was in the business, and she now realized she hadn't fooled him for a single minute.

"Go ahead, sweetie. What is it you wanted to tell us?" Kate gave her hand a gentle squeeze.

Callie nearly choked, trying to bring up the words. "I lied about my age," she said, her voice shaking. "I won't blame you if you want me to hit the road."

She heard Kate catch her breath. "No way," she said. "What do you mean, you lied."

Trying to numb herself to feeling, she made herself

continue. "I wanted to be on my own and so I lied. Yesterday wasn't my eighteenth birthday."

Kate smiled. "We don't care about getting the day right," she said.

"No, you don't understand," Callie said. "That's not what I lied about. I'm not eighteen yet." She stared down at her swollen hands, the absurdly clothespinned fingertips. "I just turned fifteen."

Twenty-One

Kate phoned Mable Claire Newman to check on Aaron and Bandit and let her and Luke know what was going on. "Diabetes," Mable Claire said, her voice soft with sympathy. "That poor girl."

"According to the doctor, she's luckier than most, because it's insulin resistance, which isn't full-blown diabetes." She paused, knowing Mable Claire would have to be told about Callie's age. The implications were still unclear, and Kate needed time to study the situation. "We're going to be here for a while."

"Say no more. I've got Aaron and Bandit for as long as they need to stay. And I'll explain this to Luke."

Mable Claire's grandson was seventeen and had graduated high school. There was more to explain than she thought. When Kate believed Callie was eighteen, his age hadn't mattered. She'd let Callie go out driving with him, giving her liberties she never would have afforded a fourteen-year-old. This was all getting complicated, and the sleepless night was dragging at her like a riptide.

"You'll also need to tell him that Callie is just fifteen."

Mable Claire was quiet for a moment. "Oh, dear."

Oh, dear was right. They had to shift their thinking from the assumption that Callie was a couple of months older than Luke to a couple of years younger. At their age, the gap was significant. "Long story," Kate said. "I'll tell you more when I come to pick up Aaron. Is he awake?" Tired as she was, Kate felt a bittersweet pang of love and fear. She had a powerful urge to see Aaron, to hold him close, to make sure he knew she loved him with every bit of her heart. Callie's ordeal was a stark reminder of how precious life was—and how tenuous.

"Still sound asleep. When he wakes up, I'll give him your love."

When Kate got off the phone, she turned to find JD holding out a cup of coffee. "Bless you," she said.

He gestured at an upholstered Naugahyde bench. "Have a seat. The exams and testing are going to take time."

She sank down next to him, feeling at ease in a way she never had before. Last night put everything into perspective. In a crisis, they had come together and now somehow she sensed that everything mattered more. They weren't just fooling around here and having a summer fling; they were developing a relationship, sharing common concerns and goals. Perhaps even looking toward the future. "Callie was so lucky you knew what to do," she told him.

"I was in the right place at the right time."

"And you knew what to do," she insisted. "That's a compliment, okay? Don't knock it."

He sipped his coffee. "I'm not knocking it."

She felt heavy with fatigue. There was much to talk about with him, but now was not the time. They needed to focus on helping Callie get better. "I still can't believe she's so much younger than she said she was." She massaged the small of her back, feeling every moment of the sleepless night. "It's just not something I was looking for, so I didn't see it."

JD went to the window, which framed a view of the Straits, the calm water and distant Canadian peaks painted orange by the rising sun. "You never can tell with kids. I've seen twelve-year-olds who look like adults, and people in their twenties who could pass for high-school kids."

"Do you know very much about diabetes?"

"Some symptoms, emergency measures." He hooked one thumb into his back pocket. His posture was tense.

"What's going to happen, do you know?"

"Typically, they'll need to get a fasting glucose level and an oral glucose tolerance test. She'll need a hemoglobin test and a full workup—body mass, thyroid check, probably a lot of other stuff. The doc is pretty confident they'll find insulin resistance."

Kate couldn't help but be impressed. He wanted to be a doctor, and she hoped he made it. She already knew he'd be a good one. "And insulin resistance is bad."

"It's not a death sentence. The objective is to control her blood sugar. There are drugs for that, but if she's lucky, they'll try a strict diet and exercise first. She's got a long road to travel, Kate. For a kid, it's hard. She has to learn how to self-monitor her blood sugar, regulate her diet and meds if there are any. This is not an easy condition to live with. It takes major self-discipline and control, which teenagers are not noted for."

"So you knew she wasn't well," Kate said.

"Suspected it." He spoke without looking at her.

"How?"

"There were some symptoms, nothing definitive. The extra weight and skin problems are associated with this condition, but they're common to any teenager, too."

"Did you talk to her about it?"

"She wasn't ready to talk about it." He turned to her, his face shadowed by beard stubble, his eyes tired. "I could have told her to see a doctor, but I have no authority over her. Even dragging her to a checkup against her will wouldn't have done any good. She was at high risk for running away. She still is, maybe more than ever."

"She's not running anywhere," Kate said, her pulse speeding up. "I won't let her go." She saw the way he was looking at her. "What?"

"Have you checked to see whether or not that's up to you?"

"I'm sure it's not, but I'm involved. I can't help myself."

"Do you do this often?" he asked.

"What, get involved in a stranger's life?" She shook her head. "It should be obvious that I'm new to it."

"Why should it be obvious?"

"Look at what happened with Callie. I failed her, and last night she nearly died. I'm terrible at getting involved."

"Kate. You're beautiful at it."

His words made her melt. She didn't dare speak for a moment, certain she'd say too much. The sun crept higher, casting faint fronds of light across the linoleum floor. "That's what's weird about this situation. It's crazy," she went on. "I usually just go about my business, staying focused on things close to home. But Callie . . . She means the world to me. And now that I know what lies ahead of her, I want to jump in and take control. I love that girl, JD. I have no idea how it happened or why, but I love her like she's my own. If anything happens to her, I won't be able to forgive myself."

"Damn it, Kate, listen to yourself. You can help her manage the disease, but it's not up to you to control her."

"Don't yell at me."

"I'm not yelling." He finished off his coffee and tossed the cup in the trash. "I hate to see you get hurt."

She leaned back against the wall. "I don't think there's any doubt in my mind that I'm going to get hurt, but why should that stop me from letting Callie into my heart?"

Unexpectedly, he sat back down beside her. To her

amazement, he reached out and grabbed her hand, bringing her around to face him. She was startled when he cupped her cheek in his hand, the gesture so kind and affectionate that she forgot to breathe. She felt herself drowning in those warm, kind eyes. "Say something," she whispered.

"What do you want me to say?"

She let her shoulders slump. "You always do this."

"Do what?" He kept his hand where it was, tracing his thumb along the rise of her cheekbone.

"See, you're doing it again." Though she could have stayed there forever, looking into his eyes, she took his hand away and scooted back from him on the bench. "There's, um, something that's been at the back of my mind ever since our conversation last night." She fumbled for the words. "You know, what you were saying right before Callie collapsed." Kate lost her nerve and faltered. "You probably don't even remember the conversation."

"You mean when I said I was crazy about you and you asked me if I was talking about lust or love."

She sighed with relief. At least she hadn't imagined it. "Yes, that. I'm wondering . . . if you really meant what you said."

He took her measure with a long, unreadable look. She braced herself for a denial. She had given him the perfect escape hatch. He could say no, he didn't mean it, he'd been caught up in the heat of the moment, and now that he'd had a chance to think it through, he realized he'd spoken in haste.

"I'm sorry," she said, overwhelmed by doubts. "I shouldn't put you on the spot like this. You don't have to answer me."

"I don't mind," he said, very serious. Somewhere in the hospital, a voice crackled over the PA system. She ignored it, focusing on JD. With a slow, deliberate movement, he took off his glasses. He moved closer to her and put both arms around her. Finally, he leaned over and kissed her, first with a tender touch of his lips, teasing and exploring, and finally deepening with a passionate hunger.

Her heart leaped and her body heated in helpless response. She was putty in this man's hands. She would become anything for him, do all that he asked of her. She didn't even care about his answer to her question now.

Even so, she was startled when, after what seemed like a long time, he pulled back, letting go of the kiss by degrees. She nearly moaned aloud with yearning, but forced herself to keep it in. They each pulled back. She saw his Adam's apple go up and down as he swallowed, but other than that, he showed little reaction.

A faint, cryptic smile, that was all. Then he put his glasses back on and regarded her placidly. She was dying inside, regretting that she'd even brought up the topic. Then, before she could think of something to say, his smile widened. "Yes," he told her, raising his voice above the crackling sound on the intercom. "I really meant what I said."

Twenty-Two

As romantic declarations went, Kate reflected the next morning at home, this one was a bit diffuse. Maybe even ambiguous. Which was dangerously close to a lie.

"Come on, Kate," she muttered to the blank screen of her laptop, "snap out of it. You found someone to date over the summer. What more do you want?"

She knew. The very thought brought an ironic smile to her lips. Idiotic as it was, she wanted the fairy tale. Even now, even after all the disappointments and reality checks, she still harbored that secret inner yearning. She wanted the moon on a satin pillow, the declaration on bended knee, maybe even the small royal blue velvet box with the glitter of a diamond inside.

"Focus," she said, trying to concentrate on her writing. That was what this summer was supposed to be about. Reinventing herself, forging a new career path. Following a dream she'd had forever. And she was so close. Opportunity dangled in front of her. This was her shot.

Yet try as she might, she couldn't get the conversation with JD out of her mind. She replayed it over and over, parsing the words as though they were some cryptic verse from an ancient oracle.

It doesn't do Aaron a bit of harm to see that someone's crazy about his mother.

He had said that. She remembered the exact words;

they were imprinted on her brain. Was it significant that he had included Aaron in the statement? Could it mean something in and of itself?

"Morning," said Callie, ambling into the kitchen in her robe and flip-flops.

"How are you?" Kate asked.

"I guess we'll find out, won't we?" Callie set up her glucose kit for her morning test. Although she had just started the regimen, she already exhibited a certain weary cynicism about the process. It was painful and tedious. She was going to have to plan every meal and adhere to the testing schedule. She promised she would be diligent about it, but Kate sensed her frustration.

"I'm already sick of being sick," Callie said, setting up the instruction card that came with the kit. "This got old real fast. Like right away."

"Do you want some help with that?"

Callie shook her head. "Might as well figure out how to do this on my own."

"I'm sure you'll get a lot of pointers in class. According to the pamphlet I read at the hospital, you're going to learn to achieve glycemic control through exercise and healthy eating."

"Yeah, great. I'm just dying to get started with that."

Kate knew the glum attitude was to be expected. "We'll be leaving in about an hour," she added. "I've got some errands to do while you're in class."

Callie glared hatefully at her glucometer. "What errands?"

"Research at the library, for starters. See, here's what

I'm thinking," Kate said. "I haven't sold my editor on this idea, but I have a feeling she'll like it. For my next article, I want to tell your story."

For a second, surprise and delight lit her face, but she quickly suppressed it and let out a short laugh. "My story. The tale of a fat loser who winds up with an incurable disease. Like someone would want to read about that. It's the feel-good story of the year."

"Are you kidding? You're amazing, Callie, and you've got it wrong. You're not a loser, you're a survivor. And you're going to take control and get better. You promised," Kate reminded her.

Callie nodded glumly. "Yeah, but that's still not much of a magazine article."

"That's my job."

Callie kept her head down and idly folded the glucometer instructions. "So, would you, like, tell everything?"

"I absolutely won't write a word if you don't want me to. And since you're a minor, I can use an alias for you."

"Like a fake name."

"Anything you want. I believe there will be pictures with the article," she added. "I won't have anything to do with that, but a magazine of this caliber works with only the best. Would that bother you, being photographed?"

"Hello? By a photographer for *Vanity Fair*? Move over, Bush twins." Animation danced in her eyes; then she remembered to act nonchalant again. "I guess I wouldn't mind."

"I have one rule, though," Kate said. "You absolutely, positively, have to tell the truth. That's what makes your story so compelling, the fact that it's so real."

Callie took in a deep breath. "After this, I've got nothing to hide."

"For real?"

"Sure."

"Can you explain why you lied about your age?" Kate asked gently.

"Why do you think?" Callie tossed her head, narrowed her eyes, the familiar toughness hardening her mouth. "In case you haven't noticed, I'm not the ideal foster child. I figure the sooner I get out of the system, the better."

"Better for whom?"

"For me. Jeez." She narrowed her eyes at Kate. "Does it bother you when someone lies?"

"Well, of course. No one likes being lied to."

"No, I mean *really* bothers you, like it makes you hate the person who's lying."

"Callie, I could never hate you."

A frustrated sigh burst from her. "I'm not talking just about me. I just want to know, is lying unforgivable in your book?"

"Clearly not, since you explained why you lied. It was the wrong thing to do, but we're going to work on making it right."

"God, I give up."

Kate studied her for a moment. She had a weird feeling they were talking about different things. "All right, listen. If we're really going to do this project together, you'll have to get used to me asking a lot of questions. Maybe it's not such a good idea."

"I said I wanted to do this."

"Just make sure it's because you want to. You don't owe me anything, Callie."

"I owe you everything, but that's not why I said okay. I think it'd be cool to have you write about me."

"I'll do a good job," Kate said. "I give you my word."

"Deal." Callie nodded. Then she checked the glucometer and then the printed chart. Kate could tell from the expression on her face that the number wasn't good. "I need to get ready," Callie said, and headed for her room.

A few minutes later, Aaron came wandering in, trolling the kitchen for food. "Do I have to go into town with you guys today?"

"No," said Kate. "I'll just leave you alone here all day."

"Cool."

She rolled her eyes. "Of course you're coming. We're leaving in an hour, and no lollygagging. I don't want Callie to be late for her first class."

"I don't see why she needs a class," he said. "She's sick, not stupid."

"The class is going to help her learn to take care of herself so she doesn't get sick." She handed him a Flintstones vitamin with a glass of water. "The class is important, and she's not going to miss it."

"Right."

So far, Aaron knew the basics: Callie had collapsed because she was insulin resistant, and in order to prevent that from developing into a more serious condition, she had to learn to monitor her blood sugar and change her diet. He had accepted all that just fine, but Kate could sense his fear and uncertainty. "All right, buddy," she said. "I bet you have bunches of questions."

"Not bunches, but . . . some."

"You should ask me," she suggested. "I don't have all the answers but I'll take a shot at it."

"How come Callie didn't tell us she was sick?"

Strike one, thought Kate. No way could she answer that. "Maybe we'll ask Callie. I suppose it's because we're getting to know one another gradually. When you first meet someone, you don't tell them everything all at once."

"Like I haven't told her about me being ambidextrous."

"Right. It's no secret. You just haven't gotten around to it yet."

"When is she going to get better?" he asked.

Kate smiled. "She's already better. Our job is to help her stay that way."

"Why doesn't she stay with us for good?"

Strike two. The question cut to the heart of Kate's fears. So long as Callie was under their roof, she could help the girl, but she had no idea how long this would last, given that Callie was still very much a minor. "I don't know. I just don't know how that would work."

"Simple. She should stay with us," Aaron said. Just like that, no equivocation. And just like that, the suggestion made perfect sense to Kate. "Why did she say she was eighteen when she's really fifteen?" he asked.

Strike three. "Women always lie about their age," Kate said lightly, setting a dish of oatmeal in front of him. "I was thinking you'd have different questions about this situation, ones I can actually answer."

"Like how come she's not with her own parents and stuff like that." Aaron rolled his eyes.

"Well, yes. Aren't you wondering?"

"Nope." He squirted maple syrup on the oatmeal. "I already know. Her mother's in jail. She told me that last night when you guys got back from the hospital. Creeps me out. And I'm not wondering where the dad is, so don't even ask." He scooped up a bite of cereal.

Kate smiled; he knew exactly how her mind worked. "No?"

He shook his head. "Dads are overrated."

"Aw, Aaron." She went over to the table, bent down and kissed his head. She knew he still wished for one, dreamed and fantasized about a father who would take him fishing, teach him to pass a football, give him that one-of-a-kind feeling of security she used to have with her own father. But Aaron would never hurt her feelings by saying so.

What her boy could never know was that his yearning hurt her anyway, every day. There was no sharper pain than the knowledge that she couldn't give her child the one thing he wished for.

"Hey, Livingston family." JD knocked on the screen door. Bandit howled a greeting.

"JD." Aaron shot up from his chair and rushed to let him in.

Kate felt like jumping up to greet him, too, but forced herself to stand still. Even after that moment at the hospital—perhaps especially after that moment—she and JD were still trying to figure out what was going on between them. Now that they'd slept together, they were supposed to be taking their relationship . . . somewhere. Instead, Callie's emergency had eclipsed everything.

"You're just in time to save me," Aaron said.

JD strode inside. "Save you from what?"

"Diabetes class." Aaron clutched at his throat and made gagging noises as he reeled sideways.

"Oh, man," JD held his head and sank into a chair. "Don't tell me they're sending you to class. That's too freaky."

Aaron nodded with delight. His sense of humor meshed perfectly with JD's. "Tell me about it."

"I can't," JD said. "Too freaky. Get your sunscreen and water bottle. We're out of here."

"Yes!" Aaron punched the air and pounded up the stairs.

Kate tried to look stern. "In some states, this is known as kidnapping."

"In my book, it's known as diabetes-class avoidance."

"So where are you snatching him away to?"

"Mount Storm King. We're hiking all the way to the top to take pictures."

There was a sound of running feet overhead as Aaron raced to get ready. She glanced out the window at the gleaming peak. "Think he can make it?"

"He's got what it takes," JD said.

Kate turned to him. "This is really nice of you."

"Don't look so surprised. I don't mind hanging out with Aaron."

Kate knew that taking pictures from the summit of Mount Storm King was not the point of the exercise. It was only an excuse. JD seemed to like Aaron, even apart from Kate. The idea filled her with a warmth so intense that it startled her. "He can be a handful, you know that, right?" She felt compelled to warn him.

"I can handle him."

I know.

"Kate, I don't get it," he said, stepping close to her. His hands came up to cup her shoulders.

She wanted to sink against him, to let him surround her. But that urge only reminded her of how tired she sometimes got of standing on her own. "I'm not used to guys who understand Aaron, who like him, flaws and all."

"Get used to it," he murmured, his gaze holding hers. "To a boy like Aaron, the world is always new."

Kate's throat ached, and for a moment, she couldn't speak. He got it. Finally, here was someone who understood and regarded her son with compassionate eyes. Kate was floored by the idea. The whole world saw

Aaron as a challenge, a problem. But not JD. She couldn't believe what a relief it was, to meet someone who saw what she saw in her boy. Finally, she said exactly what was on her mind. "Thank you."

His hand slipped down her back, a sweet echo of the way he'd touched her when they made love. "You're still looking at me funny."

She smiled, knowing her heart was in her eyes. "Guys like you don't come along every day."

"That's good. I wouldn't want the competition."

He leaned closer, and she wanted his kiss more than she wanted the next breath of air. The sound of a door slamming somewhere else in the house broke them apart. Kate stepped back, nervously smoothing her hands down her skirt.

Callie came out, still in her bathrobe. "Morning," she said, helping herself to a glass of water.

"I hear you're headed to town today," JD said.

Kate wouldn't look at him, though she held that moment between them inside her. This was supposed to be Callie's day, she reminded herself. "You seem a little nervous, honey," she said to the girl.

"I'm scared," she admitted, picking at her breakfast of buttered toast. "I've never been good at school. I make terrible grades."

Kate tried not to panic about Callie's lack of confidence. There were no grades at stake now. Just her life. "You won't be graded, but you need to learn some important things," Kate said. "You might even make a few friends."

"Sure, that'd be great. A class full of fat losers." She shook her head in disgust. "Like me."

Kate went and put her arm around her. "You want some cheese with that whine?"

Callie stiffened. "I changed my mind. Let's not go. I'll just read the brochures they gave me."

"We're going."

She backed away. "You can't make me."

Kate felt a beat of panic. "Why are you balking? This is to save your life, Callie."

"It's bullshit," she burst out. "I'm not going."

"You can't ignore this."

"Watch me."

"Callie." JD's voice broke in, calm but deeply commanding.

"God, not you, too." She glared at him. "You can't make me, either."

"Wouldn't dream of it."

Kate was about to object but he silenced her with a slight shake of his head.

"Fine," Callie's voice was soft now, tremulous. "I'll just read that book they sent home with me."

"You do that," JD said easily.

Kate gritted her teeth. He of all people ought to understand how critical this was.

"I will," Callie said, setting her chin at a stubborn angle.

"You're s'posed to go to the class," Aaron pointed out. "The doctor said."

"What do you care?" Callie asked him. "This is my

problem, not yours or Kate's or anybody else's."

"He cares," Kate snapped, unable to stay silent any longer. "And I care, and so does JD. We all care, and you're being selfish by refusing to follow doctor's orders."

Callie's face drained to white. She looked as though Kate had slapped her. "*I'm* being selfish? You think I asked for this? You think I like being a freak?"

"You're not a freak," Kate said, inches from losing her temper. "You're going to this class."

"I'm not."

"Come with us, then," JD suggested. "Aaron and I are going to climb a mountain today. So what'll it be? The class, or the mountain?"

Callie glared out the window at the sheer mountains that seemed to rear up from the depths of the lake. "I'm sick, remember? I'd keel over."

"I was going to stop at the Rite-Aid to buy makeup after class today," Kate said. Then she held out the bright plastic gift cards Callie had received for her birthday. "And don't you have some shopping to do?"

Callie turned her glare on Kate. "I'll go to the stupid class, then. I'm going to take a shower." She stomped from the room.

Kate sent Aaron off to grab the digital camera. "Not even nine o'clock and I'm exhausted," she said to JD.

He hooked an arm around her. "Let's go outside. It's a beautiful morning."

She marveled at how soothing it was simply to have somebody to lean on. They went out and sat on the dock, facing the gleaming blue-green mountains and their own reflections in the glassy surface of the water. Each time she was around him, she was filled with a shivery sense of destiny, as though they were meant to be together. But how much of that was wishful thinking? How much of that was sheer gratitude on her part, that she'd finally met someone who was happy to form a bond with her son as well as her?

Rather than putting her at ease with him, the fact that she was falling so hard for him simply intensified the tension. She wondered if he felt that, too, but realized she still didn't know him well enough to ask.

"You're quiet," he commented.

Well, maybe it was time to ask, she decided. "So are you."

"I have to go away for a while."

Oh. Now, here was something new. She stayed quiet, expecting him to offer to fill in the blanks. He said nothing, though; simply braced his hands behind him on the dock and leaned back. All right, she thought. You're a reporter, Kate. Get the guy talking.

"Where are you going?"

"To L.A."

She felt a beat of excitement, even though he seemed blasé about it. "You must be going for an admissions interview."

He blinked as though startled, then flashed a smile. "That's right."

"Well, I think they'll be so impressed with you, they'll want to sign you up right away."

"I don't think it works like that, Kate. But thanks for the vote of confidence."

"It's not just me. You've very good. Seeing you with Callie," she said, "you were like a different person, working on her."

"What's that supposed to mean?"

"It's just . . . I saw a different side of you, one I've never seen before. When you helped Callie, I saw you as the person you are in your real life."

"I'm just a guy doing my job. Fortunately for Callie, her emergency wasn't a huge challenge."

"You're being modest," she observed. "Why is that?"

"I'm not being modest and what's with all the questions?"

"It's time," she said. "We've put off this conversation long enough."

"God, Kate. What conversation?"

"The one where we get to know each other on a deeper level."

He offered a wicked smile. "That doesn't have to involve talking."

"This morning it does." She hugged her knees up to her chest. "I'm not kidding. Here at the lake, we're all out of our element. After seeing you with Callie . . . well, now I'm curious about who you are in your real life."

"So this isn't real?" he asked her, a bemused smile on his lips.

"This is the lake," she said. "When you're not here, what's your life like? Who's in it? I want to know what's important to you."

"You're important to me," he said. "So what are you when you go back to civilization? An amped-up city slicker in stiletto heels?"

She laughed, then bit her lip. "An unemployed city slicker, though I do love my stiletto heels."

"Sorry," he said. "Didn't mean to put you on the spot."

"It's all right," she said. "I'll be okay. I wasn't exactly a happy camper at the paper, anyway."

The warmth seemed to leave his eyes. "The paper," he said.

She nodded. "*Seattle News*. Not exactly the *New York Times*, but . . . it was who I am—a writer. A reporter." He didn't reply, and his silence unsettled her. "So I'm not exactly Brenda Starr," she said. "Don't look so disappointed. They didn't want me to be Brenda Starr at the paper, either."

"I thought you said you were a nature writer, doing something for *National Geographic*."

"You should listen better. I told you I did a piece for *Smithsonian*," she said. "I'm working on a freelance basis."

"How come you never told me you were a newspaper reporter?"

She was taken aback by his tone. "Because I'm not. I used to be." She took a deep breath. "All right, I have nothing to hide from you. I worked at the paper for five years, and at the beginning of the summer I was fired." No point in equivocating. "My boss was the mother of two, divorced. She had no trouble juggling work and family. She was the working-mother poster girl. I, on the other hand, looked like the ultimate screwup. There were a bunch of warnings and citations when I missed deadlines." She saw the question in his eyes. "Call me crazy, but I tended to drop everything when Aaron needed me. Each time a babysitter or his aunt or the school called, I'd stop what I was doing and focus on him. It's a wonder this didn't happen years ago, actually."

"Do you miss your job?" he asked.

"Of course. But when I had to choose between focusing on my son or on work, I chose Aaron. I don't regret it, either, but my priorities did get me fired."

He let out a breath. "So you're not a reporter."

"Not anymore."

He nodded, and she saw his posture relax a little. "I'll be all right," she explained. She wondered briefly if he'd be put off by the prospect of an unemployed girlfriend. "This is a chance for me to try my hand at freelance journalism. I studied it in school but never had the nerve to actually do it. I suppose getting fired is the universe's way of taking all my excuses away from me." She felt a subtle warmth growing inside her, a sense of intimacy at sharing her dream with him. "The *Smithsonian* piece will be published next year, and I've had a stroke of luck with my editor. She got her dream job at *Vanity Fair*, and she's interested in my next project."

"Which is . . . ?"

"Callie's story. The idea's still in the formative stages,

and after last night, I realize I have a lot more work to do. But if it goes, the magazine will send a photographer from Seattle to take pictures."

"Does Callie know about that?"

"Of course. I can't very well tell her story without her cooperation."

"And she's okay with this?"

"She's more than okay. She seems completely intrigued. I have the feeling she wants to tell her story. Maybe to get rid of the burden, maybe to boost her self-esteem. She has a lot of healing to do."

"In the national press?" he asked.

"Why are you being so weird about this?"

His reaction was subtle. Perhaps again she was imagining it, but she sensed him stiffening, pulling away, though he didn't move at all. "I'm not being weird. Just wondering if it's the best idea for Callie."

"It's fine. She's all excited. Why wouldn't it be all right?"

"Some people don't want their lives smeared all over the papers."

"This is not going to be a smear job." She bristled, mystified and disturbed by his disapproval. "It might even do some good." She eyed him sideways. "You sound like a skeptic."

"I *am* a skeptic."

"Why?"

"Because she might be flattered by all the attention, but what good will it do her, really?"

"It's going to validate her." Kate's voice sharpened.

"It's going to make her believe she matters. How can that be a bad thing?"

"She doesn't need to get her picture in a stupid magazine to do that," he said.

She felt both admiration and annoyance. Admiration, because he had so skillfully turned a question about him into an indictment of her, and annoyance because she'd allowed it to happen. "So what are you saying? That I should back off?"

"Yeah, you should back off," he said.

"She doesn't need protecting from me, for heaven's sake." Kate couldn't believe her ears. "This is the way I make my living. I have a son to support. Who are you to criticize—"

"I'm ready," Callie said, coming out of the house, her hair freshly washed and her purse slung over her shoulder.

Kate shot JD a look. "We have to go," she said. "Listen, I'd planned on bringing Aaron with us, so if you'd rather not—"

"I want to spend the day with him," he said. "That's why I'm here."

"All right." Kate got up and brushed herself off. No point in ruining Aaron's day just because JD was being an ass to her. And perhaps, she thought, it was fortunate he was going away for a while. He'd just given her plenty to think about in his absence.

Twenty-Three

JD hated what he had learned about Kate. Based on what she'd told him before today, he'd pictured her as a dreamy nature writer, doing puff pieces about long-dead tribal elders or the nesting habits of sandhill cranes. Now he realized how wrong he was. She was a goddamn journalist. A reporter. Someone who stripped people naked in public, with or without their permission. She was a member of the same club as the guy who had hidden behind a Dumpster at JD's apartment, or the woman who had called 911 with a phony complaint and then, when his crew showed up, proceeded to ask him to pose for a picture with her.

He had been contacted by publications from the *National Review* to *Rolling Stone*, from *Atlantic Monthly* to *The Star*, and he understood what reporters were like. They pretended to be your best friend, your advocate, a sympathetic ally, and then they made you or people you care about bleed in public, not even staying to watch as they moved on to their next victim.

Was that Kate?

"Hey, JD, check this out." On the trail ahead of him, Aaron and Bandit scrambled atop a rock overhang shaped like an anvil. "Hurry up, come on."

"Why do I need to hurry?"

"Because. Jeez, JD."

Since it was a weekday, the trail to the summit was

deserted. It was a relatively easy climb, the steep stretches and switchbacks interspersed with long, sloping traverses and rock formations.

Aaron was a champ at climbing, as JD had suspected he'd be. Even laden with two canteens and a digital camera, the kid marched purposefully, like a member of a stealth mountain commando. He didn't get winded, either, JD observed, but kept up a steady stream of chatter.

Their progress startled chipmunks and a dozen kinds of birds. They passed trees so tall that Aaron insisted on taking a picture, and through the foliage the lake was visible, sinuous and sapphire blue, so far below that it looked utterly uninhabited.

"If we get lost here," Aaron observed, "they'd never find us."

JD didn't tell the boy how deeply that notion appealed to him. "According to this map, we're at the highest point of elevation around the lake." He showed Aaron the topographical hiking map from the ranger station.

"Nope," Aaron said, racing a few yards away. "That's right here, at the marker."

Sure enough, there was a chiseled marker with the elevation in a small plaque. Neither of them was interested in the marker or the plaque, though. They sat together on a huge boulder and looked around at the majestic, breath-stealing scenery. JD took it all in with a sense of awe and privilege. Back East, people didn't think about the fact that there were forests and lakes so remote, that there was air this clear.

Aaron didn't sit still for long, but found a stick to toss for the dog. Watching them, JD wondered how much the place a person grew up mattered in forming his character. If he'd been raised in a small wilderness town rather than a Baltimore tenement, would he have become a different person?

Maybe not. Drug addicts were everywhere, and his mother would have been just as troubled out here as in the inner city. The thought of Janet brought a scowl to his face. She was the reason for his trip to L.A., not a medical school admissions interview as Kate had guessed. Part of Janet's therapy was a family visit and he was her only family. He just hoped he wouldn't be recognized when he visited her.

He wondered what it would be like, telling Kate the truth. "I have a meeting with my mother's drug-addiction recovery team" just didn't sound like the kind of thing that would win a girl's heart. And what was the point, anyway? If she wanted to think he was interviewing for med school, that was her prerogative. And of course, after the things he'd said to her this morning, it was her prerogative to tell him to take a hike for good.

"Smile!" Aaron's voice caught him off guard, and the digital camera recorded his startled expression.

JD fought a sense of paranoia. This was a kid, he told himself. A kid taking a snapshot.

The kid whose mother was a hungry freelance journalist.

"Hand me the camera and I'll get a shot of you," he

suggested, "right here at the mountaintop."

Aaron handed it over. It was a high-end digital model, not at all the child's toy. JD wondered if he could find a Delete button.

Aaron posed like a conqueror, one foot propped on the stone marker, his walking stick planted in the ground, Bandit prancing at his feet. The breeze plucked at his carroty hair and sunlight danced in his eyes, and suddenly the most extraordinary emotion came over JD. It was an unexpected mixture of pride and affectionate amusement, deepened and sharpened by something else, something he'd never felt before and scarcely recognized.

JD had never been a father, but now he realized he knew what a father could feel for his son. It was a deep tenderness that touched him when he watched Aaron do the simplest things—drink a glassful of milk, play with a dog, run and jump off the dock. It was devastating and overwhelming, yet at the same time tinged with quiet joy. He thought about Kate, loving this boy with all that she was, and wondered how the guy who had fathered him managed to stay out of the picture.

"Let's see it," Aaron said. "Set the dial on Back and press the arrow."

The shot of Aaron materialized in the LCD screen. JD wasn't a professional photographer but he had captured perfectly the expression of boyish bravado, the shining innocence and innate sense of pride.

Curious, he hit the Back button again. There he was

in living color. He looked at several more and discovered a series of shots of him climbing the mountain. He looked relaxed and content, unaware that his picture was being taken.

"Hey," he said to Aaron, "what are you, a secret agent?"

Aaron grinned. "Yeah, that's me."

"Where's the Delete button?"

"No way. You're not deleting anything."

"You don't need all these pictures of me. They're just taking up space."

He grabbed the camera from JD. "I do, too." His ears and cheeks turned an ominous shade of red.

Great, thought JD. He was probably winding up for one of his tantrums. Kate had warned him about Aaron's temper, but she hadn't really said what to do about it. "Hey, take it easy," he said, keeping his voice calm and even. "We're buddies."

Aaron backed up, unraveling by inches. "After this summer, I'll never see you again."

So that was what was bothering him. JD didn't tell him otherwise. "I'm not going to lie to you. At the end of the summer, I have to leave the lake, just like you and your mom."

"And Callie," Aaron said.

"Her, too. So why are you letting this bother you now?"

"Because I hate it." With that, he wound up and hurled the camera with all his might.

There was no forethought; JD lunged and caught the

thing in both hands. The power was still on; he flipped it off.

"Call your dog, kid," he said. "We're going back down."

"No, not yet." Aaron's rage dissolved into acute distress. "Come on, JD, I didn't mean to throw the camera, I swear I didn't."

"Right. Looked like a complete accident to me." JD reconnoitered the area, anticipating all the ways Aaron could harm himself. There were sharp sticks and rocks, a steep mountain girded by cliffs, rocky ravines and fallen trees . . . the possibilities were endless. He knew what he was risking here.

"Look, I'm not going to put up with your tantrums," he said. "You're old enough to know better. So let's hit the trail."

"I won't go." His face was almost purple now.

"Fine. I'll go." He put two fingers to his lips and whistled for Bandit. Shit, he thought, now I'm committed. I have to walk away from the kid or look like a pushover.

The dog came running, and JD headed down the mountain. He didn't look back to see if Aaron followed. He just kept walking deliberately, the dog scampering ahead. This could be a bad move, JD reflected. He knew that. Aaron could run off, disappear, get lost in the vast wilderness.

JD made as much noise as he could, hoping the kid would surrender and join him. He had no idea if this ploy would work, though. His experience with kids was so limited. Generally he met them at the worst times of their lives, when they'd injured themselves or swallowed poison or spiked a fever scary enough to warrant a call to 911. Even healthy kids were a mystery to him, their minds operating on a different wavelength. He didn't get them. He didn't know how to be a parent. For all his special training, for all his experience in the field, JD was lost when it came to understanding a child. The one thing he would not do was give up on Aaron or give in to his temper. That was all he knew.

A kid was the ultimate challenge, and this was proof. Forget dodging bullets and saving lives. Compared to raising a child, everything else was a cakewalk.

And yet people did it every day, he reminded himself. They gave their whole heart to a child in an act of faith.

It took all JD's willpower to resist rushing back to where he had ditched the kid and make sure he was okay. If he did that, Aaron would learn that throwing a tantrum was a good way to bring people to your beck and call.

He went around a curve in the trail. Still no Aaron. His stomach clenched. He was ditching Kate's boy. Abandoning a child in the wilderness.

This was a bad idea, and it was getting worse by the minute.

The dog picked up speed, scampering around the next curve of the steep pathway. For a hound, he wasn't very focused on sniffing out his kid.

Come on, Aaron, JD thought. Quit being a little shit.

He decided to pause by the anvil-shaped rock and

take a break. Have a drink of water from the canteen. Did Aaron have enough water? The boy was so little; in the heat of a summer day, dehydration could set in fast.

He tried to act casual as he opened the canteen and put it to his lips. Tipping back his head, he allowed himself to scan the area.

No Aaron.

JD took his time putting the canteen away. Bandit was rooting around somewhere below, but there was no sign of the boy. JD calculated that he'd come just a few hundred yards. Only a short time had passed.

He heaved a sigh and kept going, noisily, hoping the kid would track his progress. But with every step he took, his doubts intensified. This wasn't working. Aaron was just a little kid.

The path split off into two branches, and JD hesitated. Seconds later, he made up his mind. He had to go back the way he came. He couldn't risk losing Aaron just to make a point. All right, kid, he thought. You win. I'll come running back to you.

Defeated by a willful kid who had thrown a camera at him.

He didn't know what else to do. He'd taken a huge risk and it had been a mistake. He whistled for the dog. Then he turned and started back up the mountain. Running. Once the decision was made, he gave in to the sick, pounding urgency of full-blown worry. With the dog now following him, he came around the first switchback. He'd managed to work himself nearly into a panic now. He gathered breath in his lungs to call out for Aaron.

A second later, he was hit by a whirlwind. The boy ran straight to him, nearly knocking the wind out of him.

"Whoa, there," JD said. "Take it easy."

Aaron's face was sweaty and deep red, but when JD looked into his eyes, there was no rage. No fear or distress, either.

"I'm sorry," Aaron said with a curious sober dignity. "I threw the camera on purpose, and I shouldn't have. I'm sorry about the stuff I said to you, too. I don't hate you, not one bit, and I never have."

Judging by the tremor in the boy's voice, JD suspected that this speech was exceedingly difficult for him. He knew his reply mattered a lot and hoped he'd get it right. "I'm impressed by your honesty."

"Do you accept my apology?"

There was a lot to talk about here. JD knew this was something Kate would call a teachable moment, a time to discuss the incident in depth. He ought to talk with Aaron about recognizing anger coming on and discuss ways to deal with his temper before it got away from him. He ought to discuss alternatives and options for managing this strange inner force that took over.

He studied the small face, now soft and vulnerable with remorse, and he thought, *Some other time.*

"Yeah," he said, and held out his right hand. "I accept."

Aaron solemnly shook on it, his hand lingering for a

few beats. "Were you really going to take off and leave me behind?" he asked.

"No way," JD said. "I'd never leave you."

Twenty-Four

Kate consulted the pedometer hooked to the waistband of her shorts. "How're you doing?" she asked Callie, who was walking briskly beside her along the road.

"Just peachy."

"This is mile three," Kate told her. "Do you need a rest?"

"Heck, no. Let's keep going."

They were both sweating profusely in the afternoon sun, but Callie's attitude was good today. They'd been on an emotional roller coaster as Callie came to terms with her condition. Or railed against the injustice of it, or gave in to despondency. From moment to moment, her outlook seemed to change. She veered from rebellion and despair to commitment and determination, all normal reactions, according to the crash course in diabetes control Kate had taken. She was determined to learn as much about the disease as possible. Without so much as a second thought, she'd assumed a parental role with Callie. Lord knew, the girl needed mothering.

And Kate had an undeniable need to mother her. She applied herself to the problem like a military strategist, arming herself with knowledge of insulin resistance and type 2 diabetes, then mapping out a battle plan to vanquish the enemy. She created menus designed to maximize glucose metabolism and laid out an exercise regimen worthy of professional triathletes. She stood over Callie while the girl recorded her glucose readings, her weight and progress in a pocket-size journal Kate had bought for her. They walked at least five miles a day, went kayaking and swimming and rewarded themselves with trips to the movies or excursions that always involved more exercise.

Sometimes they locked horns over working Callie's program, but now, despite the ups and downs, Kate saw glimmers of determination and tangible progress. Callie was already losing weight. It was a blessing of youth that her body responded so quickly to a better diet and exercise. Even after a short time, the loss of fifteen pounds was apparent. Her skin was clearing up, too, thanks to the pills and topical medications the doctor had prescribed. The biggest change of all was in Callie's attitude. She had been devastated by the diagnosis, but in a strange way, it turned out to be a source of motivation.

Dealing with this filled Kate's days. And kept her from falling to pieces over JD. Since they'd clashed over her article about Callie, he had left for L.A. and come back, but she hadn't seen him. It was up to him to make the first move.

Ahead of them, Aaron explored the dunes, glancing back from time to time to see where they were. To vary the daily exercise routine, they had driven to Dungeness Spit, a low, sandy finger jutting out into the Strait of Juan de Fuca. It was spectacularly scenic, a wild and windswept sanctuary for eighty species of birds, with a historic lighthouse at the very tip.

"I'd like to get a copy of your birth certificate," Kate said. "That way, we can take the ferry over to Victoria, do some shopping and sightseeing."

For a moment, yearning shone in Callie's eyes, but she spoke up quickly. "No way. The last thing I want to do is draw attention to myself. Next thing I know, I'll get shoved back into foster care."

The issue had been troubling Kate. For the short term, Callie had a secure living situation. Still, knowing how very young the girl was, Kate would have to take up the matter with officials before long.

"You can't fly below the radar forever," she told her. "At some point—sooner rather than later—the ER report to social services is going to be assigned to a caseworker, who'll show up on our doorstep. She won't have to dig too deep to find that you're classified as a runaway."

"I didn't run. I was chased."

Kate walked along in silence for a few minutes. This was exactly the sort of material she needed for her article, but she was having second thoughts about that, too. She'd been so sure of what she was doing before JD had undermined her confidence.

"You weren't ragging on me about this before," Callie pointed out.

"I thought you were nearly eighteen before. The fact

that you've got three years until you're a legal adult changes everything."

On the drive home, Aaron fell asleep in the back seat of the car. Callie felt agreeably fatigued and distinctly pleased with herself. Some days, the hard work paid off. If she scheduled her eating and exercise right, she had loads of energy, and could feel herself getting stronger. Today was a good day. She had them every so often, which was pretty amazing, considering everything that had happened since her birthday. She'd revealed the lie about her age, and the world hadn't come to an end. She'd been diagnosed with a really bad condition, yet life went on. Not only that, she was doing all right dealing with the situation. It gave her something to control, at least.

Today. Her attitude, it seemed, was a pendulum on a long, long chain. Some days, she hated everything— her disease, herself, her life, her situation. Others, like now, ranged from not half-bad to pretty okay.

"Another reason to get hold of your birth certificate," Kate said, picking up the conversation from a couple of hours ago, "is so you can take driver's ed next year. You want to learn to drive, don't you?"

"Oh, I know how to drive." When she and her mother had come north to Washington, Callie used to take her mother's car, just to see if she could get away with it. The idea, of course, was for her mother to catch her and tell her she was grounded, but of course, that never happened. It was dumb, anyway, a ploy for attention that never worked.

"Legally," Kate said.

"Mmm." Callie looked out the window as they drove through the little tourist town of Sequim, a sunny place surrounded by acres of lavender fields. The silence between them was pleasant, comfortable. She had made use of her driving skills again when she was living with a family whose driveway resembled a crowded parking lot. The father was always asking the kids to move the cars around to let this one or that one in or out. Callie had become the go-to girl for valet parking. Then one day, while moving a rusty Chevy Malibu from the driveway to the street, she'd simply kept going. She'd driven down the residential street and onto the highway, going so slow that passing trucks had blasted their horns at her. She got to the next town before the highway patrol and local police surrounded her and made her pull over. The impulsive move marked her last day with *that* family.

Pulling her mind away from the past, she turned to Kate. "So when are you and JD going to get over your fight?"

Kate's hands tightened on the steering wheel, a dead giveaway. "What fight?"

"Good one," Callie said, "but I'm not buying it." She didn't want to bug Kate or anything, but she was genuinely curious. JD had stopped coming over. He let Aaron visit his place to mess around and help with the boat building, but there were no more suppers together, stories and board games in the evening. No more hearing Kate and JD trying to sneak around, like Callie hadn't figured out exactly what they were up to. She was dying to know if he'd maybe explained to Kate about his real identity, and if Kate had a problem with that. "So what was the fight about?" she persisted.

"Nothing." Her knuckles were still white, her face red.

"You wouldn't take that answer from me or Aaron," Callie said. "Come on, tell me."

Kate sighed and looked in the rearview mirror, adjusting it to check on Aaron.

"Out cold," Callie informed her. "Spill."

"We didn't have a fight. It was a . . . disagreement."

"How is that not a fight?"

"Things didn't get ugly or anything. We simply . . . found a deep difference of opinion about something."

"About what?"

Kate hesitated, bit her lip as she concentrated on the road ahead.

"About me," Callie said. It wasn't a question. All it took was that slight hesitation, and she knew. *Damn it.* "Kate, that's so stupid. I shouldn't even matter—"

"Of course you matter."

"I mean when it comes to you and JD."

"We're not a match, and that became apparent. It's best not to waste time and energy trying to make something work that'll only last the summer no matter what. And that's my decision, and mine alone."

One thing about Kate, she could be totally stubborn. Maybe that's what came of being a single mother all her adult life. She was used to calling the shots.

"What do you mean, you're not a match? That's such bullshit."

"I don't like your language."

"I don't like you shutting me out. I thought we were friends, Kate. Friends tell each other stuff. Jeez, you know my weight and my glucose level and everything."

Kate pursed her lips as if she didn't want to say anything. Then she spoke up. "We quarreled about me making you the subject of an article."

Classic, thought Callie. Of course JD would object to that, and she knew exactly why. Kate didn't, though, and Callie wasn't about to tell her. Or should she? If she let the cat out of the bag, Kate would understand. Or she might get pissed that JD had put one over on her, and blow him off completely. All right, Callie decided. She'd keep her mouth shut. His real identity wasn't her secret to tell, and besides, she'd made a promise. You idiot, JD, she thought. You freaking idiot.

"Did you tell him I *want* you to do the article?"

"Certainly. I also told him that since you're a minor, your identity can't be revealed."

"I still want to do it. I'll tell him myself," Callie said.

"You'll do nothing of the sort. This is between JD and me."

"But it's about me."

Kate flipped on the blinker as she headed through downtown Port Angeles. On First Street, they passed the recruiting office and Callie saw it again, the poster of Jordan Donovan Harris, three feet high in living color outside the shop front. She studied it every time they passed by. He was so hot in that picture. It was amazing how dorky glasses and a baseball cap could conceal so much hotness.

"He thinks I might be exploiting you and your situation," Kate said. "I don't want to do that, Callie, I swear."

"You're not. I'm totally cool with it."

"Do you really want your picture in a national magazine?"

Duh. It would only be the coolest thing ever to happen to her. But Callie had learned the truth about wanting. The harder you wished for something, the more impossible it was to get. So she tried not to wish too hard. "We've already been through this," she reminded Kate. "I'm not like some cover model or anything, but if the magazine wants pictures, it's fine with me. God, JD really ticks me off." She hesitated before she said too much, and cut her gaze away.

"Have you talked to him about this?" Kate asked, frowning at the road.

"No," Callie said quickly. "It just seems like the sort of thing that would make him freak. He's like, this really private person and all." She realized that she felt weirdly invested in the idea of Kate and JD together. It wasn't really her business, but there was something between them, some kind of energy in the air. It was sad, actually, to think that she and JD were on the brink of calling it quits. They seemed like a perfect match, Kate the eternal optimist and Harris the dangerous protector. Not to mention that they were so good-looking, their picture ought to be in celebrity magazines. JD would love that, Callie thought.

These days, Kate seemed . . . diminished. Maybe a little lost. Callie could tell Kate missed him. And then it occurred to her that she wasn't completely powerless here. If she could just think up a reason to get them together again. Surely Kate's place had a leaky faucet or something broken JD could fix. He was all about fixing things. Maybe that was the key, Callie decided, mulling it over.

"Anyway," she said, "I can't believe the two of you are breaking up over this. You're making me feel like the bad-karma fairy."

"You're not," Kate said, "and we're not breaking up. Technically, we weren't together in the first place, so there's nothing to break up."

Callie snorted. "Listen to yourself. Technically? What does that mean?" She waited, but Kate didn't answer. Callie said, "He saved my life, remember?"

"You don't need to remind me that he's a good guy."

"Hello? It's not like they grow on trees."

"You know what?" Kate said with a rare flash of that redheaded temper. "We're not talking about this anymore. We've got a project, and that's to get you well, so let's work on that, okay?"

"Only if you promise we'll get back to work on the article."

Kate pulled off to the shoulder of the road. She took a deep breath, turned and faced Callie. "If I do, it's going to involve going to see your mother."

Callie's heart skipped a beat. "Why?"

"Because she's a huge part of your story. It wouldn't be complete without her."

Callie was seized by a painful combination of panic and yearning. Her mother had failed her in every possible way, ultimately flinging her to the world like a seed blown into the wind. Yet for all that, they were mother and daughter, and even though she didn't want it to mean anything to her, it did. It meant everything. "Whatever," she said. "I don't care."

Twenty-Five

"Callie thinks we've broken up," Kate said, getting the words out quickly before she lost her nerve. Last night, pacing the floor at 3:00 a.m., wondering how to end the stalemate and clear the air with him, she found no answer. Only exhaustion.

This morning he'd shown up as if he'd read her mind, but his purpose didn't seem to be to clear the air between them. After a brief greeting, he said, "She told me you have a porch light that needs fixing."

Didn't he get it? Kate wondered. That was a transparent ploy to get him over here. However, he seemed to be taking it at face value.

He looked up from the wicker porch table, where he'd been bent over some project that lay dismantled in front of him. "Did you want this on a toggle switch or rheostat?" he asked.

"Do I . . . what?"

"This light fixture. What kind of switch do you want?"

"Don't pretend you didn't hear what I said."

"I heard." He rummaged through the canvas carpenter's apron slung low around his waist. "Toggle's fine for a porch light," he concluded.

"You're avoiding the issue," she said. Kate was already regretting the conversation. She sounded like a whiny, possessive girlfriend.

"There is no issue." He set the fixture between two clamps and opened a blister pack of new wire. "I had to go away. Now I'm back."

Kate held her tongue and waited. For what, she wasn't sure. Did she want him to say he was sorry, that he had no right to approve or disapprove of anything she chose to do? Or did she want him to say he was wrong, that writing about Callie's life was a worthy endeavor? That she deserved to know all his comings and goings?

Now that she thought about it, she *was* sore. The answer to all of the above was *yes*.

This was getting complicated. Her feelings for him were getting complicated. If she knew where she stood with him, she'd push the issue, talk it out, argue if necessary. That was what people did when they cared about each other. Yet she and JD weren't arguing; they were avoiding and acting as though whatever it was they had between them wasn't worth fighting over.

Maybe she'd read too much into this. Maybe their relationship worked better as a summer romance, one that would simply fade away on its own at the end of the season.

"Hand me that wire stripper, will you?" he asked.

All right, so he didn't want to talk about it. It was better that way. From day one, they'd gotten along so well it was almost scary. She realized it was because they never dealt with issues bigger than whether to have hamburgers or hot dogs for dinner, or which CD to put on. They should have been content to go on like that through the summer, never reaching deep enough to truly take hold of one another.

She passed him the strippers, pretending she wasn't troubled by her thoughts. "The electrician in town said he couldn't get out here for a couple of weeks."

"I'm your love slave, remember?" he said, laying a copper wire bare.

Kate flushed and automatically scanned the yard for Aaron. He was over by the shed with Luke Newman, helping blow up an air mattress, while Callie sat in an Adirondack chair nearby. Kate watched the kids for a minute, laughing and talking together in the yard. Aaron thought it was awesome to hang out with Luke. And Luke, a big kid himself, showed a remarkable tolerance for Aaron.

"Right," Kate said to JD, flashing a smile. "If I believed that, I'd think up harder stuff for you to do."

Though she spoke lightly, she wondered if he did this

on purpose, if he brought up the idea of love without actually going the distance. They had slept together, but instead of clarifying things, she felt more confused than ever. He talked about being crazy about her, but they never had a direct discussion of exactly how they felt about one another.

She wanted to ask him, but held off because Callie and Luke were coming toward them. The teenager's transformation was remarkable, and Kate glanced over at JD to see if he noticed the changes, but his expression was unreadable.

True to her word, Callie was sticking to her program of glucose monitoring, diet and exercise. Kate used to see her as an overweight, fashion-challenged teen. Now the girl looked as fragile and spiritual as a Charlotte Brontë heroine. Context was everything, Kate reflected.

"We're heading to town," Callie said. "Luke's giving me a ride. I've got class and then we're going to rent a video and watch it at the Newmans'."

"I'll be careful," Luke said, correctly anticipating her next remark. "We'll be home by ten o'clock."

After they left, she said, "It's hard letting them go off on their own like this."

"His car has air bags, and I know where he lives," JD said, as if that explained everything.

She went back to her confused thoughts, and he went back to work. She wondered if he sensed the turbulence in the air between them. They were so new together that she didn't know how to categorize this . . . discussion. They weren't fighting. No one had spoken in a raised voice and they hadn't even broken their rhythm as she handed him tools and he worked on the light.

"We never really talk about how we feel about each other," she blurted out.

He tinkered with the neck of the fixture. "Sure we do." He held out his hand without looking at her. "Clamp."

She gritted her teeth and passed him a clamp. "When?" she asked. "When have we told each other how we feel?"

He held out his hand again. "Phillips-head screwdriver."

She handed it over. "I said, when—"

"I know what you said. You asked me when we ever told each other how we feel. If you need hearts and flowers and deathless soliloquies, you're barking up the wrong tree."

"How romantic," she retorted, feeling a flash of temper. It was stupid to expect anything from this man. From any man. She knew that.

"You want romance," he said, "read a fairy tale."

"I just don't see why it's such a huge problem to talk. I believe in talking. I'm a very verbal person."

"Yeah, I gathered that." He put the cover on the light fixture. "And I don't know about you, Kate, but I tell you how I feel every time I touch you. If you don't realize that, maybe you need to listen better."

Was there any possible response to that besides sitting there with her mouth hanging open? You don't do that anymore, she wanted to say. You don't touch me.

He fitted the fixture in place on the wall and held out a hand for the screws.

She handed them over, wondering at his attitude. He put everything back together with almost surgical precision. When he flipped the breaker and tested the light, she wasn't at all surprised to find it working perfectly.

"I guess that's got it," he said, closing the breaker box.

"Thanks to you, we won't be stumbling around in the dark anymore." She was trying to be civil, but everything felt awry between them. Weird and off kilter.

"No problem." While taking off the carpenter's apron, he studied her. "What's that look?"

"What look?" She pretended not to understand, even though the feeling that something was not right hung between them, a palpable entity, making her feel defensive.

"You're pissed off about something."

"That wouldn't be very neighborly of me, to get mad at the person fixing my porch light."

"You're pissed off," he repeated.

"Don't tell me how I feel." She sat down on the steps, and he sat beside her.

She was torn by the desire to lean against him and the urge to push him away, and her heart sank. So it began, the beginning of the end. This always happened with a guy she liked. Always. She was nuts to think JD would be any different.

Ah, but she had wanted him to be. Like a schoolgirl with a crush, she had yearned for it.

She should have known better. Should have recognized the pattern, which had become such a familiar rhythm in her life. Whenever she liked a guy, things went well for a time. Then something—anything—occurred.

It might be a comment. Maybe just a look. She was always amazed at how little it took for something to undo a fragile bond.

She felt JD's stare and the weight of his expectations. This was it, then. The relationship talk. And so far, it wasn't going well.

She took a deep breath. "Ever find a broken thread on a sweater," she asked him, "and when you pull it, the entire garment unravels?"

He nodded. "I usually quit pulling once I realize it's unraveling."

"Sometimes it unravels on its own," she said, "whether you pull on it or not."

"I don't get your point."

"I do have one. I'm not mad. It's just . . . we're unraveling." Her face heated, and she looked away from him. Spoken aloud, her words sounded silly. And it was stupid of her to feel disappointed. This was the normal course of a relationship for her. She ought to be used to it. "So anyway," she said, "that's my observation, based on my experience."

"What's the broken thread?" he asked.

"You really don't know?"

He didn't answer but simply looked at her, waiting.

This was what men did, she reminded herself. They

let the woman do all the emotional work, and they got to walk away intact. "I told you I was writing about Callie," she reminded him, "and your reaction was to question my choice."

He didn't deny it. Instead, he said, "I just wonder if exposing other people's lives on paper is going to bring you happiness."

Ouch. "This is not about my happiness. And I am not going to defend myself to you. This is something I want, something I intend to work for and you have no right to question me."

"Then we should change the subject."

"It's not that simple. I can't be with someone who doesn't support my dreams and ambitions. That's one of the most basic, unbreakable rules of relationships."

Oh, God, she thought, she had just drawn a line in the sand.

He was quiet. She didn't know what he was thinking.

"Kate—"

"JD—"

They both spoke at once.

"Hey!" Aaron yelled to get their attention. "Watch this!" He was perched on his bike at the top of a steep slope leading down into the yard. As soon as they looked up at him, he leaned down over the handlebars and pushed off. The bike sped downhill, out of control in seconds.

She was on her feet in an instant. JD ran, but they were too far away to intercept him. Even as they yelled at him to stop, he headed flat out down the bumpy hill toward the dock.

Helpless, terrified, she watched her son ride along the dock and off the end, shouting with glee as he launched into the air, then separated from the bike and jumped in with a splash.

The moment he bobbed to the surface and gave a triumphant war whoop, Kate's terror crystallized into fury. Rushing past JD, she went to the end of the dock. The bike floated up, buoyed by a pair of life vests Aaron had strapped to it. He swam over to the ladder, pulling the floating contraption behind him.

"What on earth are you doing?" demanded Kate.

"Nothing."

It was the age-old exchange of angry mothers and naughty sons everywhere.

Aaron focused on JD, who now stood at the edge of the dock, hands on hips, looking down into the water.

"Did you see, JD?" Aaron asked. "Did you? Did you see?"

"I saw. How do you plan on getting that bike out of the water?"

"I got a system all figured out. But did you see how awesome that was?" Grinning even as he shivered with cold, Aaron pulled the bike over to the boat ramp.

Kate glared at JD. She hated that he and Aaron had sided together against her. "You shouldn't have told him it was awesome."

"But it was."

The residue of their quarrel still hung between them. "It's a bad idea to encourage dangerous behavior."

"He doesn't need any encouragement," JD pointed out. "He thought that up on his own."

They walked to the boat ramp and stood waiting while Aaron dragged the bike into the shallows, set it upright, then wheeled it up the ramp.

"You are so grounded," said Kate.

"It was so worth it," replied Aaron.

Twenty-Six

JD attacked the wooden skiff with a vengeance, using the air compressor to clear the field for the next step. The wood had to be as particle-free as he could make it, so when he applied each layer of sealer it would be smooth and flawless. The entire hull needed to be airtight and prepared for multiple coats of marine epoxy and varnish.

He had a hard time keeping his mind on the job, though. Now what? he wondered as he worked, viewing the world through the distorted shield of his safety goggles. What the hell was he supposed to do next?

Like a fool, he'd started something with Kate Livingston. And like an even bigger fool, he'd destroyed it.

It was a freak accident, falling for her. An unplanned event beyond his control. It was not supposed to happen.

He cleaned every particle from the hull of the skiff, as

meticulous as a surgeon sterilizing the field for an operation. He knew plenty about accidents. He'd been in the business of mopping up after them for years.

"It was an accident" was something people said to him on a daily basis when he was on the job. "It wasn't my fault" was another favorite. "No one is to blame." "I didn't mean to." Hearing victims and families utter those words used to frustrate him. Now he realized that all those phrases applied to his tangled affair with Kate. He had come here this summer to disappear and lie low, not to discover a dream he'd never let himself have.

As he changed a plane blade, his hand slipped. He looked down at the deep gash in his finger, watching the blood well up and trickle down. A few seconds passed before he felt the sting. "Idiot," he muttered. He went to the outdoor spigot and flushed the wound, made a field dressing of a clean cloth, then went right back to work. It wasn't like him to be so clumsy. He needed to be more careful.

He was ticked off at himself for letting things go so far. Looking back, he couldn't quite tell how it had happened. He was new to the whole business of giving his heart, and one of the first things he'd discovered was that he couldn't control love. It controlled him. And it wasn't just Kate he loved, but Aaron, too. Even Callie, with her secrets and her hurts, was part of the picture. They made a tight unit that was infinitely larger than each individual. JD wasn't sure how he knew what being a family felt like, either, yet somehow he understood in a deep and hidden place that he'd found the essence of that this summer. It was a closeness and sense of security and contentment that pervaded every moment they were together, even when they were at odds with one another.

There were so many reasons that this wouldn't work, yet he couldn't help wishing he could find a way to be with them, not just for the summer but for good. Clearly Kate had other ideas. After their argument about Callie, there wasn't much more for them to say. Kate had informed him that she couldn't be with him if he didn't support her ambitions, and he couldn't force himself to change his mind about her project with Callie.

That should have been the end of it. Instead, it was more like the onset of an illness he couldn't shake. He thought about her constantly, with the kind of yearning that kept him up at night, took away his need for solitude, distracted him from all but the simplest tasks. Even the manual labor of restoring the boat was almost too much to manage.

He felt sick that he'd blown it with her, yet at the same time, a curious relief took hold. Being alone was part of the plan. He was supposed to lose himself this summer, not lose his heart.

"Congratulations," Callie called out, coming down the driveway toward the workshop. She looked good, with a spring in her step and her bucket of cleaning things, ready to get to work.

"For what?" he asked, checking the bandage on his hand.

"You've been upgraded to *complete* idiot."

"Yeah?"

"Don't pretend you don't know what I mean."

"All right," he said. "I won't pretend. I really don't know what you mean."

"Kate, that's what," Callie said. "It's so stupid for you to get all mad because of the article. And no, she didn't send me to say that, so don't even ask me."

"I'm not mad. I just think it's a bad idea. You ought to reconsider, Callie."

"It's just one article."

"As far as you know," he warned her. "These things can take on a life of their own—"

"I don't care, okay? I'm not like you, JD, all freaked out because you don't like publicity."

"You don't, either," he assured her. "Listen, when all this started happening to me, I systematically lost every element of my private life, and there wasn't a damn thing I could do about it. And when all that was taken away, I had nothing. Then when the thing with my mother happened, I had less than nothing. Trust me, you don't want the attention."

"Then let me find that out for myself."

"By the time you find out, it'll be too late. Suppose someone digs up things about your mother."

"She deserves it."

"Nobody deserves it."

"You know what?" she said in a huff. "I don't want to talk about this anymore. No, wait. I have one more thing to tell you. You're crazy for making this some kind of deal breaker with Kate."

"You already said that."

"Then I'm done talking about it. The ball's in your court."

JD was more than willing to drop the subject. He liked Callie, and she brought out a strong protective instinct in him. He felt a grudging respect for her moxie in bringing up the topic. He didn't want to discuss Kate with her further, though. His differences with Kate ran deeper than the fact that he thought she was making a mistake by turning Callie into the subject for an article. He and Kate had a fundamental difference in their values. When she finished with Callie, she'd move on to new topics, and that was her right. His reservations would always hang between them. She was a reporter in search of a story. He was sick and tired of being the story.

"Your doc say you're well enough to work?" he asked Callie.

She nodded vigorously. He had to admit, the improvement in her health had improved everything about her. This was what he loved about medicine. Sometimes it truly did have the power to heal, to turn a life around, to transform tragedy into a second chance.

"I'm glad you're back," he said.

"Thanks. And, uh, I never said thank-you for what you did for me that night. The night of my birthday. Without you, I would have been a goner."

JD worked all day, scarcely pausing except to pay Callie and tell her goodbye. The sweat and dust all but coated him and the bandage on his hand unraveled in tatters. Then, hot and aching, he peeled off his shirt and dived into the frigid lake. The soft, clear water flowed over him in gentle, cleansing waves even as its brutal chill took his breath away. By swimming out a few hundred feet, he could see Kate's place with its emerald green yard, the house as commanding as a ship under sail. He wondered what she was doing right now. Was she working on her story? Was she messing around with Aaron, chatting with Callie? Maybe she'd gone to town. Maybe she had already met someone else, someone who wasn't paranoid about reporters and didn't sit in judgment of her.

Someone who wasn't keeping a colossal secret from her.

If he hadn't finished off their relationship with their last conversation, the fact that he'd been lying to her all summer would certainly do the trick.

In his imagination, he'd rehearsed the conversation dozens of times:

"Kate, I'm not who you think I am. Wait, I am who you think I am, but there's something you should know about me . . ." Then, as simply as possible, he would explain about the incident at Walter Reed. And Kate, who had once told him he seemed too good to be true, would discover that she'd been right.

Perhaps she'd be understanding. She might even be intrigued by the idea, the novelty of knowing someone who had inadvertently been catapulted into notoriety. But ultimately, he knew, she would discover the destructive side of fame just as Janet had. It was like a monster with a life of its own, out of control. Here at the lake in summer, his identity didn't matter. This wasn't the real world.

The real world was stalking paparazzi, articles crammed with lies, TV-news reporters dogging his footsteps, constantly ringing phones, agents and publicists making wild claims, people who were down on their luck begging for favors. The human psyche just wasn't made to withstand the constant pressure. God knew, JD was proof of that. In time, Kate would grow to hate the attention, particularly when it focused on Aaron. Eventually, she would come to resent JD for bringing on all the unwanted intrusions. Worse, his notoriety could endanger her and Aaron in ways he couldn't even predict. If anything happened to them because of him, he'd never forgive himself.

Sam and Penny assured him that the furor would die down, his mother would get better and one day he'd have his life back. Maybe then. . . .

With strong, smooth strokes, he swam back to shore and let the water stream off his shoulders, down his back and legs. The lake had cleansed him even as it chilled him to the bone. Shaking off water, he went in search of a towel.

Time to deal with other things, he told himself.

He dried himself off and changed clothes, put a fresh dressing on his cut. Then he went to his desk, circling around the neat stacks of paperwork before forcing himself to take a seat. This was not rocket science, he told himself, but he kept hesitating to get the process rolling. In his mind's eye, he pictured the admissions committee going over his application file. With his training and experience as a Green Beret medic, he'd be regarded as a promising candidate. Still, he had no idea how a venerable institution of higher learning might react to his being a celebrity, however reluctant. He'd heard plenty about starlets who interrupted their movie careers to attend Princeton or Stanford, but the difference was, a starlet didn't share his aversion to the limelight.

Another reason for his hesitation was that he wanted to be accepted on his merits as an applicant, not as a guy whose face was once on the cover of *Time* magazine.

Pretending the incident hadn't happened was stupid, Sam always said. The Christmas Eve rescue was part of JD now; he couldn't separate himself from it. Besides, Sam pointed out, in order to get into med school, you used any means at your disposal, even if that meant letting on you were the lead story on the evening news. JD knew damn well he was qualified. He just needed a break.

He massaged his temples, picturing life as a student. Monklike, he would study late into the night and rise early each morning. Becoming a doctor was going to consume him. He'd seen this in other Special Forces medics, many of whom went on to med school. Once they decided to go for it, their studies took as much time and concentration as training for the Green Berets. JD reminded himself that there would be no room in his life for anything but study and practice.

Enough, he thought, flicking the point of a pen in and out, in and out. He had plenty of reasons to stay the hell away from Kate, and only one to keep her close.

And even though he told himself not to, he wondered what she was doing right now.

Twenty-Seven

Kate looked more nervous than Callie actually felt about this photo shoot for *Vanity Fair.* "Don't freak out on me," Callie told her. "Then I'll start freaking, too."

"Okay. I'll work on it." Kate flexed her hands on the steering wheel as she pulled into the strip-center parking lot and headed for the Curl & Twirl, where Callie was supposed to go to get her hair and makeup done.

It was intimidating as hell, Callie thought, and Kate wasn't helping the situation.

"I'm not freaking out," Aaron said from the back seat. He kept fogging the window with his breath and drawing faces with his finger. Jeez, give the kid a Game Boy, Callie wanted to tell Kate. "What's the big deal?" he asked.

"I don't like getting my picture taken."

"Why not?"

"Because I hate the way I look, okay?"

"It's not okay," Kate said, navigating around potholes and speed bumps. "And you don't mean that."

"Fine." Callie didn't want to get into some big discussion with Aaron as audience. Besides, Kate was maybe a little bit right. Since starting the whole diabetes-prevention thing, she'd lost weight and her skin was better—no dark patches and zits. She had learned with some relief that the acanthosis nigricans and acne were not some sort of cosmic punishment but symptoms of diabetes. Once she got that under control, the skin troubles subsided, thank God. "I don't mean it. I love the way I look, and the pictures are going to be gorgeous."

"Now you're being facetious."

"What's facetious?" Aaron asked.

They both ignored him. "I can't help the way I feel," Callie said.

"*I* like the way you look," Aaron piped up.

They kept ignoring him. "Of course you can," Kate replied.

"I *said*," Aaron bellowed, too loudly to ignore, "*I* like the way you look. I like your whole stupid face, so there."

"You crack me up," Callie said.

"You crack me down."

"You're a nut," she added.

"You're the one who's going to get your hair ironed and face painted on," he replied. "Who's the nut now?"

Kate found a parking spot near the salon. "All set?" she asked brightly.

316

"Um, listen," Callie said, "would you mind maybe dropping me off? I mean, that way Aaron wouldn't get bored waiting around—"

"I don't mind watching," he said.

Callie met Kate's eyes and they shared a silent accord. "I'll be back in an hour," Kate said.

"Thanks."

Callie stood on the curb and watched them drive away. They headed down the hill toward the ferry landing, where there was a tall lookout tower Aaron could climb and see clear to Vancouver Island in Canada. She checked her watch, fifteen minutes to kill until the appointment. One thing being homeless had taught her was how to kill time. She was some kind of expert at it. She walked a little ways down the street, catching a glimpse of herself in a shop window, a girl walking by herself, hands in her pockets. Even with Kate and Aaron, she sometimes felt so alone. They were great, but it had been so long since she'd had a friend her age that it felt like a physical ache. Often, she fantasized about being surrounded by a group of friends, laughing together like . . .

She studied the group of kids at the far end of the block, standing around outside the recruiting office. *Luke.* She was sure it was him. Her heart sped up in her chest. She hadn't seen him in a while. A couple of weeks ago, he'd said he couldn't hang out with her as much as he used to. He was busy, because the parks department had increased his hours.

He wasn't busy now. In a group with two other guys

and three girls, he looked happy and animated, his lanky posture relaxed. Callie had asked him if it was weird that she wasn't quite as old as she'd said she was, and he'd said no. She'd asked him if it was weird that she had this medical condition, and he'd said no.

But something was definitely weird.

She hung back and contemplated the situation. He hadn't spotted her yet. She could just slip back around the corner and forget about the whole thing. She knew she wouldn't forget, though. She'd stew about it. All summer long, he'd told her he didn't have any friends up here in the Peninsula, and she'd believed him. He was pretty damn friendly with the kids he was with now.

Finally, he'd made some friends. This could work out really well, Callie told herself. It would be fun to spend the last few weeks of the summer hanging out with a group of kids. The girls wore miniskirts and crop tops that showed their midriffs. They probably had belly-button rings, something Callie had promised herself she'd get once she reached her target weight. One of the girls, who had perfectly straight, blue-black hair, was flirting with Luke, leaning in to him when he spoke, laughing and putting her hand on his arm.

All right, thought Callie. Enough's enough. She squared her shoulders and headed toward him. It was funny how he was standing near the recruiting office with the JD poster, now faded from the sun. Sometimes Callie burned to tell Luke. It was the coolest secret ever. Maybe he'd hang around with her more if she told him who JD really was.

As she neared the group, she put a smile in place. The other kids didn't recognize her, of course, but she could tell Luke did. He acted as if he were seeing a ghost.

This is bad, thought Callie, instantly regretting her decision. This is really, really bad. "Hey, Luke," she said, hoping her friendliness didn't seem forced.

He leaned back against the building. "Hey."

She waited for him to introduce her to the others. She felt them taking her apart with their stares. "So what're you up to?" she asked.

"Staying busy," he said in a bored voice. His gaze was flat, his eyes narrow.

"I can see that." Callie wanted to die. She prayed for the earth to open up right then and there and swallow her whole. She knew it was chickenshit to back down when she ought to get in his face right now. Still, she chose the chickenshit route. He wasn't even worth it, she told herself. He wasn't worth sticking around and fighting for. "Well, I need to be somewhere," she said. "See you."

"Yeah."

She pivoted and headed back the way she had come. Although she tried not to hear, her ears were perfectly tuned in and she overheard Luke giving a short, nervous laugh.

". . . nobody," he said. "Just some kid who cleans houses for my grandmother."

Callie kept walking and didn't stop until she reached the lookout tower at the landing. She spotted Kate's Jeep parked at the base of the tower, and high above, Kate and Aaron tossing oyster crackers to seagulls, who caught them in midair. Just the sight of them seemed to ease her despair, if only a little. They were so cute together, the two of them, a matched set of redheads. Watching them, she felt a funny lightness in her chest. A sense of . . . ownership.

She waved at them and they hurried down, their footsteps bonging on the open steel stairs. "That was quick," Kate said a little breathlessly. Her face changed when she got closer. "What happened?" she asked.

"I've changed my mind. I'm not going," Callie said.

"But the photographer—"

"I'll still get my picture taken. He'll just have to take me like this."

As it turned out, he did just that. They met at Kate's house—Mr. Saloutos and two assistants—and he worked fast, with great confidence. At first, Callie was nervous and self-conscious, but being outside, with the lake spreading out behind her, she started to feel as vast and expansive as the scenery itself. To hell with Luke, she thought, looking right into the camera. This was her time to shine.

Twenty-Eight

Kate sat on the porch steps with her notebook, formulating questions to ask Callie's mother in the interview. Aaron was playing with the dog in the yard, and Callie had taken the county bus to town for her morning class and support group. Meanwhile, Kate was supposed to be getting some work done, but now she was starting to wonder if she was cut out to be a hard-nosed freelance journalist after all. Even thinking up the questions gave her a stomachache. She couldn't imagine asking them, nor could she realistically expect honest answers.

Ms. Evans, what possessed you to live at a commune run by a pedophile?

Were you prepared for him to come after your daughter when she hit puberty?

Later, when you abandoned her in Tacoma, did you suppose there was any way that could be construed as responsible parenting?

In journalism school, she had learned sound principles for extracting information, even from the most reluctant of subjects. However, she couldn't recall what to do if the interviewer herself was reluctant. On the other hand, there was the age-old multifarious method. Just let the subject talk, take it all down and write the truth.

How does it help Callie to have her life smeared all over the press? JD's disapproving voice intruded on her thoughts, undermining her conviction. Shut up, she wanted to tell him. Go away. His opinion didn't have to matter to her, not anymore. She was her own person, she always had been, and for a few crazy weeks, she'd let herself forget that. Now sanity had returned, and she was determined to get over him, the sooner the better.

"Mom," Aaron called from the yard. "Hey, Mom, watch."

Grateful for the distraction, she set aside the notebook, laced her fingers around her knees and leaned back to watch. "Go ahead, buddy," she called to him.

He coaxed Bandit through a trick they'd been working on all summer long. Every once in a while, the dog succeeded, seemingly by accident. Yet today he got it.

"Let us pray," Aaron said, holding his palms up and looking at the sky.

Immediately, the dog sat with paws forward and head bowed, staying that way until Aaron yelled, "A-men!" Then Bandit jumped up and scampered away.

Kate was amazed. Although undeniably lovable, Bandit was not the brightest example of canine intellect. His ability to perform had, thus far, been limited to a few one-word commands.

Or so she thought. Thanks to Aaron's persistence, the beagle had finally caught on to a new trick. And Kate learned something, too. Don't write somebody off just because you think they lack ability.

"You're incredible, both of you," she said. "I'm proud of you, Aaron."

He stood up a little straighter, grinned a little broader. "Proud enough to end my groundation?"

"You wish. One thing has nothing to do with the other."

"Mom—"

"One more peep out of you, and I'll add an extra day of no bike or swimming."

His shoulders hunched forward.

Kate felt terrible, but she knew she had to stick to her guns. Taking away bike and swimming privileges was especially cruel now that summer was running out. Every day counted.

"You did the crime," she said, "you have to do the time."

He looked so miserable. And Lord knew, he deserved a reward for his persistence in teaching Bandit.

"Tell you what," she said, "let's take the kayak out."

"Yeah!" He was already running for the life vests and paddles. In just a few minutes, the two of them were paddling toward the middle of the lake, the sun sparkling in the droplets of water that rained from the oars.

Strictly speaking, she probably should have forbidden him to go out on the lake at all. Then again, she rationalized, grounding him from riding his bike and going swimming made her point. Besides, kayaking was a relatively safe way to enjoy the water, and therefore should be encouraged.

Behind him in the low, sleek craft, she noticed how strong his arms had grown over the summer, how the sunlight streaked his hair. Despite liberal use of sunscreen, freckles dotted his skin. Over the summer, he'd gotten taller, more sure of himself, less angry. My boy is growing up, she thought.

They paddled in silence for a while, the kayak's shadow haunting the intensely blue depths beneath them. She felt a wave of nostalgia. No matter how many times she traveled these waters, the lake always felt new to her, its splendor undiminished by familiarity.

Keeping the rhythm of the oars steady, Aaron said, "I miss JD."

Me, too, thought Kate.

"Why doesn't he come over anymore? Is it because I rode my bike off the dock?"

She sighed. Aaron always blamed himself when men dumped her. "Absolutely not," she said. "Don't be silly."

"I thought you guys were, like, boyfriend and girlfriend."

Kate gritted her teeth. She was an idiot. She knew better than to look twice at a guy. The moment she did, Aaron got his hopes up. Falling for someone put more than her own heart at risk; it risked Aaron's, too. She knew that. How could she have been so careless with her own son? It didn't matter that, right from the start, she'd taken pains to explain to Aaron that JD wasn't a permanent fixture in their lives. Aaron's father fantasies always took flight no matter what she said.

Hearing the sadness in her son's voice, she wanted to

cry, too. "We weren't really . . . meant for each other," she said. "I think we both realized that and went our separate ways."

He still didn't break his rhythm with the paddles. "That's dumb."

"Why do you say that?"

"Because JD likes you. He even likes me."

"Don't be silly. Everyone likes you."

"Yeah, right. I realize I'm supposed to be stupid and all—"

"Aaron—"

"But I know more than you think I know."

"I think you know a lot."

"Like he's perfect for us," Aaron said, "and it stinks that you ran him off."

"I didn't run him off. He left of his own accord, and there's no point expecting him to come back. Even if that's what I wanted, it's not going to happen. It's better this way, Aaron, better that it happened sooner rather than later. The two of us realized we're better off keeping our distance."

"Why?"

"It's complicated."

"It is not. It's simple. He liked us, Mom. He wanted to be with us. I bet he was starting to love us, even. It's not like that happens every day."

Kate nearly dropped her paddle. Who was this person, sounding so grown up and sure of himself?

"Nobody was starting anything," she said. What a liar I am, she realized. No wonder Aaron was so skeptical of everything she said. Taking a deep breath, she tried again. "There are lots of kinds of love, buddy. Some kinds are made to last a lifetime, like the way I love you. And some last just one summer, and then you let go and move on. Trust me, we're better off like this. Just the two of us."

"Right, Mom."

They paddled along in quiet contemplation. By working the foot pedals, she steered them in the opposite direction from JD's place. She tried to keep herself from looking over there, but she was helpless to resist. Don't look, she told herself. Whatever you do, don't look.

She looked.

Although they were some distance away, she could see JD in the yard, cutting the grass with a push mower. He'd taken off his shirt and tucked it into the waistband of his jeans so that it hung down behind him. Sunlight flickered over his sinewy brown arms, strong legs, big shoulders. She couldn't help remembering what it felt like to have those arms around her, or hearing his voice whispering in her ear, or seeing his face lose its usual guarded look when he smiled at her. It hit her then that Aaron was right. She did miss JD and something had been starting between them, something good and real that she should have nurtured and cherished rather than distrusted, questioned and then dismissed. It was too late now, though. Wasn't it?

"Anyway," Aaron continued, "it's not just the two of us. Callie makes three."

"For the summer, anyway," she said.

"She could stay with us longer," Aaron stated.

Kate had been thinking about that very idea. "That's possible. Something to discuss, anyway."

"Who needs to discuss it? We adopted Bandit. We could adopt Callie, too."

Kate knew she should never be startled by anything Aaron said, but he always managed to surprise her. "I've been thinking about the end of summer," Kate told him. "Not about adopting her—that's not possible yet. But if Child Protective Services approves, we could be her foster family. It's just an idea, though. We—all three of us—need to talk about whether or not it's the right choice for Callie and how it would work."

"It would work, no problem."

She had to smile at his simple logic. "Teenagers are a lot of work."

"So was Bandit. So am I."

Kate frowned. "What do you mean by that?"

"C'mon, Mom. You missed so much work trying to keep up with all the school meetings and sports and stuff about me that you finally lost your job, but you didn't care because I'm more important than any job." He sent her a knowing glance over his shoulder. "How am I doing?"

"I'm speechless."

"Are not."

"True. So are you saying that you think you're a lot of trouble?"

"I know I am."

Kate had been so young when she'd been faced with her unplanned pregnancy, yet she still remembered the mingled wonder, horror, joy and terror that had filled her when a home test confirmed her suspicions. After Nathan stepped out of the picture, she had considered both abortion and adoption. Neither option felt right for her. She'd kept Aaron, welcomed him with open arms, and she was grateful for that every day. *Your boy is a blessing,* JD had said. No matter what happened after, she would always remember that he had told her that.

"Do you also know you're a lot of joy?" she asked Aaron.

"Yep. That's why I'm saying it would work to be Callie's family."

"For us. It would work for you and me."

"Right."

"Do you think it would work for Callie?"

"I don't know about that."

Neither did Kate. "That's why nobody's mind is made up," she said to Aaron. "I need to talk to her about it. Then we have to let Callie decide how she feels about this."

"You can do that right now," Aaron said, pointing his paddle toward the house.

She was coming down the driveway as the county transit bus lumbered away. Bandit leaped at the girl in greeting, barking ecstatically. She squatted and petted him, letting him lick her face. Watching them as the kayak glided up to the dock, Kate felt a strong tug of affection. Callie had been a member of this family all summer. This didn't have to end.

After lunch, a FedEx truck arrived with a small, flat package. "This is a tough location to find," the driver said as Kate signed for the parcel.

"That's what we like about it." Kate smiled, though when she saw who the sender was, her stomach clenched with apprehension. She went back into the house to find Callie and Aaron just finishing up the lunch dishes. Aaron dashed outside before she could assign him any more chores.

"Who was that?" asked Callie.

Kate didn't answer right away. She brought her laptop computer to the kitchen table, then handed Callie the package.

"Oh," said Callie, her voice soft and nervous-sounding. Her hand trembled a little as she opened the package, which contained a shiny CD.

Kate put the disk into the drive and almost forgot to breathe while the thing booted up.

"These are going to suck, I just know it," Callie murmured.

Kate didn't say anything. Knowing how fragile Callie was, Kate prayed the photographs wouldn't hurt her more, but the potential was there. In her years at the paper, she'd seen her share of harsh and unflattering shots. But this was *Vanity Fair*, she told herself. The magazine used the best photographers in the business.

The first image flickered onto the screen, and Kate

slowly let out her breath. She glanced over at Callie, who appeared mesmerized.

"Well," said Kate. "I guess the suspense is over, eh?"

As they scrolled through the photos, Kate's heart soared. The pictures had a lyrical quality, which captured the richness of the lakeside setting in all its majesty. Gilded by the light of sunset, the background resembled an idealized painting, something Maxfield Parrish might have done. Yet as captivating as the lake and mountains were, the true star of the photos was Callie herself. Somehow, the talented photographer's lens had found her toughness, but also her vulnerability. The photos showed Callie as her best self. She had not been glamorized by special effects or touching up, but instead, she was depicted with a stark, unsparing honesty that suited her much better.

"I think that's my favorite," Kate said, indicating a shot of Callie looking up slightly into the camera's eye. The picture captured her intelligence and sadness, yet the slight curve of her mouth hinted at a sturdy sense of humor. Kate had an urge to rush over to JD's place, to show him the pictures like a proud mother. She killed the impulse, of course. JD would hate the pictures no matter how beautiful they turned out. His stubborn disapproval was wedged between them, cold and immovable. He was being ridiculous.

Yet he made her question herself constantly. Was this an invasion of Callie's privacy for profit? Or would the piece illuminate a life in a way that would affect people when they read it?

"I'm so excited," Callie said, scrolling through the pictures again. "These are better than I ever thought they could be."

"You're beautiful," Kate told her. "These pictures truly do you justice." Impulsively, she touched the girl's hand, and for once, Callie didn't flinch. "I'm so glad you're getting your health back," she added.

"Every time I start getting ticked off at you for being the diet and exercise Nazi, I remind myself of that."

"Am I a Nazi about it?"

"You're pretty bossy. It's okay, though."

"That's the only way I know how to be a parent." It just slipped out. Kate wondered if Callie had noticed. If she did, she didn't say anything.

They finished oohing and aahing over the photographs, then got ready for their afternoon walk, a four-mile loop to the end of the road and then back to East Beach. Though Aaron groused about not being allowed to ride his bike, he gamely took the lead, holding the dog's leash and darting ahead. At the end of the walk, they stopped for a break at the beach. Callie and Kate sat side by side on a picnic bench, sipping from their water bottles. Unwilling to keep still, Aaron went down by the water to dig trenches and tunnels for his trucks in the sand, whistling tunelessly as he worked.

"He's an awesome kid," Callie said after a while.

Startled, Kate smiled at her. "I think so, too."

"He's always busy. The kids in the foster homes where I lived sat around watching TV all the time."

"Which is one reason I haven't had a TV since he was three years old. He started singing the Clorox-bleach song in the grocery store one day, and that did it for me. I got rid of the set that day, and now I only borrow one every four years to watch the Olympics. Could be a huge mistake, I don't know. Sometimes I think raising a child is like performing some enormous social experiment with no control group."

Callie was quiet again, yet Kate could sense her need to talk. "How are things going? In your group and class?"

"My diabetes counselor says I'm doing a lousy job on my journal," Callie said. "She wants me to work harder on taking notes on all my thoughts and feelings."

"Have you done that yet?"

Callie shrugged. "I bore myself."

"I can't imagine that."

"Hah. I should call the thing 'Diary of a Whining Girl.' Boring, I tell you. Glucose check, eat, work, sleep . . . repeat all over again." She slid a glance at Kate, then looked down. "I wrote something else."

"What's that?"

"It's just stupid." She knotted her hands together. "Sometimes I wish I had the kind of life you and Aaron have. A life that will give me a chance." She dropped her voice even lower. "All that love."

Kate held her breath, kept in the words she wanted so badly to say. Take this slowly, she cautioned herself. "You'll need to make some decisions soon. In the fall, you're going back to school."

"No way. I'm getting a job."

"Your job is to be a good student."

"Like that would help me?"

"Better than working off the books and hiding out," Kate said. "I know it's harsh, Callie, but you have to face facts. By the end of summer, you'll need to figure out what you intend to do about your living situation."

"I don't need to figure anything out. I'll just take it day by day, like I was before I met you guys."

"Sleeping in unheated houses," Kate reminded her. "Starving one day, overeating the next. According to Dr. Randall, that's a major contributing factor to your condition."

"I'm sick of hearing about my freaking condition," Callie snapped. "I'm sick of thinking about the freaking future."

"Are you scared?"

"Screw you, Kate. Just . . . screw you." Callie shot to her feet and stalked away.

Kate refused to let herself feel hurt. Instead, she got up very slowly and approached Callie. She didn't touch her, just asked the question again. "Are you scared?"

Callie's shoulders slumped. "All the time." She turned to face Kate, and her face looked pale and stiff with apprehension. "Listen, I spent a long time with my counselor yesterday," she said. "A really, really long time."

Finally the truth was coming out, Kate realized. This was it.

"We talked about my options for next year. She

333

wants me to consider a group home."

Kate didn't let herself react, though her heart plummeted. She couldn't stand the thought of Callie with a group of other kids, some of them even tougher than she was. "How do you feel about that?" she asked.

"Now you sound like the freaking counselor."

"I'm not trying to counsel you. I just want to know."

Callie paced back and forth on the bank. "I've heard it's not as bad as it sounds. It'll keep me from having to adjust to a new family. That's a plus, because fitting in with a family is something I'm not real good at."

Kate tried to keep herself calm. It was time, she thought. She prayed she could bring up her idea without running Callie off. "I could argue with that," she said.

"Well, thanks, but it's looking like the group home is going to be it, until I can save up for a place of my own. Everyone I've talked to says it's pretty okay."

She sounded as though she was trying as hard as possible not to care one way or another.

"Don't worry about 'everyone,'" Kate said, not quite sure who that included. "That's not what matters," she pointed out. "What matters is making the best decision for you."

"I don't know how to do that." Her voice trembled.

"What is it, Callie?" Kate asked her. "Something's the matter. And it's not just the group home."

Callie studied the ground and mumbled something.

"I'm sorry," Kate said. "I didn't hear what you said."

"Luke dumped me."

Kate made herself stay very still, showing no reaction

as she pondered this development. Only a short time ago, Callie had been crazy about Luke. She thought he was her one shot at a normal life.

"I didn't realize that," Kate said, choosing her words with care. "I'm sorry."

Callie shrugged her shoulders. "It's okay."

"It's not okay," Kate said.

"True."

"Are you all right?"

"I guess. We were just friends. It's not like he was the love of my life or anything. But it sucks that he was the only friend I had and now I don't even have him."

Kate understood. This was a girl who didn't let herself get attached. Life had taught her that emotional ties were tenuous, and not to be trusted. "Oh, honey—"

"It's no big deal." Callie waved off her concern in a gesture so elaborately casual that Kate knew the girl's heart was broken. "I didn't really ever expect him to stick by me." She sat down and drew her knee up to her chest, looped her arms around it. "No one ever does."

"He's an idiot," Kate said. She tried to be light and sarcastic, but she knew what that pain felt like. She'd endured being dumped; she understood how it hurt. "Boys generally are. If you want to talk about—"

"I don't need—" Callie broke off and her eyes filled, and Kate ached for her, knowing how hard she tried to keep it all in. Moments later, she was sobbing, a symphony of great, choking gasps and shudders, her entire body shuddering with sadness. A few people nearby looked at them but Callie was oblivious, and Kate didn't care. She put her arms around the girl, stroked her hair and let her cry it out, and in that moment their connection was so strong that Kate could feel all of Callie's grief, her doubts and her fears.

Callie struggled to talk even as she mopped her face with the edge of her shirt. "I just want to be normal for once in my life. I want to go to the movies with a boy and gab with my best friend on the phone and just . . . just be normal."

"You're better than normal. You're amazing, I swear," said Kate, and she meant it.

"You know what I mean."

Kate did. Though she didn't speak of it, Callie was thinking about the fact that her life had never been her own. She had survived a bizarre childhood, she'd been shuffled through a foster system that had failed her and now she was faced with raising herself alone with no support system, a terrifying disease and uncertain prospects.

"We should go back," Callie said, and got up.

Kate called out for Aaron, who had found a group of kids to play with. He grabbed the dog's leash and sped up the road ahead of them. Kate matched Callie stride for stride. It was time to say something, Kate knew. Past time. Do I want this? she wondered. Could I do this? Would she say yes?

Her throat felt tight. Callie would be like . . . a daughter. A sister for Aaron.

"I've been thinking," Kate said. She glanced sideways at Callie, hoping her next words wouldn't chase the girl off. Enough dancing around this, Kate thought. Just say it. "I applied to be a foster parent. I need to go back to Seattle for an interview with the King County CPS. Once I'm approved, you can live with us."

Callie stumbled on the asphalt road but kept going. Kate studied her shocked, disbelieving expression. The girl didn't say anything.

"That is," Kate went on, "if you want to. I know I'm not old enough to be your actual mother, but I can offer a stable home and my unflagging support, and that's a promise." She tried not to push too hard, but as soon as the words were out, she realized how much she wanted to be there for Callie during the all-important high-school years. The arrangement wouldn't be easy for any of them, but it was the right thing to do. Kate felt it in her bones.

Callie picked up the pace, and Kate hurried to match her strides. "I know my offer seems sudden to you, but not to me. This has been on my mind for quite a while."

"I have no idea what to say."

"You don't have to say anything right away. I hope you'll think about it seriously."

"I'm not going to be able to think of anything else."

"Of course, you're free to consider other options. I'm far from perfect, as you've probably noticed. I don't have a husband—"

"And you're doing just fine," Callie said loyally.

"Thank you. But I'll be honest with you. Not a day goes by that I don't think about the fact that Aaron is growing up without a father."

"Same as the majority of all kids," Callie pointed out.

"I don't have a regular job," Kate said, playing devil's advocate.

"What are you, trying to talk me out of it?"

"I'm telling it like it is so you can make a good decision. I'm single and jobless."

"You work every day. You're making it as a writer. Plus, you said you have real estate in Seattle."

The rental property. To Callie, any home owned free and clear must seem like a gold mine. Kate was humbled. As a single mother, she'd always felt hard done by, as though life hadn't given her enough. In Callie's eyes, she had it all. "You can take time to think about your decision," said Kate. "Just remember, you'll be a member of the family for as long as you need us, and I hope that's forever."

Callie stared straight ahead at the paved trail. "You don't need to do this."

"I *want* to do it." Kate battled the urge to give her a gentle shake. "What's the matter?"

"I don't like getting attached, you know?"

"No, I don't know. What's wrong with getting attached?"

"It sucks when things don't work out."

"Then we'll make sure it works out."

"I don't get you." Callie's pace stayed brisk, but there was a softness in her voice. "You're so, like, Rebecca of Sunnybrook Farm, all cheerful and wholesome and everything."

"Would you rather live with a Goth?"

"What's a Goth?" asked Aaron. He had circled around behind them and was bringing up the rear.

"Someone who wears black all the time and rarely speaks," Kate said. She looked at Callie. "Is that right?"

Callie was fighting laughter. "Yeah, I guess."

Twenty-Nine

"Nervous?" Kate's chirpy voice grated on Callie the next day as they drove over the Hood Canal Bridge, heading to the Kitsap Peninsula and an appointment Callie definitely did not want to keep. Since Aaron was spending the day with Mrs. Newman, the ride was filled with long silences.

God. She could read Callie like a book. "Oh, no," Callie said. "It's always a barrel of laughs to go see my mother." She stared out the window. Vine maples and evergreen forests swished past, and every once in a while she caught a glimpse of the water through the trees. For some reason, the breathtaking scenery made her want to cry, the normal state of affairs for her these days.

She had been drifting around in a dreamlike state, overwhelmed by the decision she had to make. She and Kate talked endlessly about what life would be like as a family in Seattle. Kate described her neighborhood as quiet, with big trees and older homes. What Kate didn't know was that Callie had never lived in an actual neighborhood. Nor had she ever had a place of her own in a private house, except with Kate. In Seattle, Callie would have her own room and a shared bath with Aaron. The high school was less than a mile from Kate's house. It had a thousand students and its own radio station. Kate had promised to enroll Callie in driver's ed, and when the time came, help her apply to college.

College. It was the first time anyone had mentioned it to Callie with any sense of possibility at all. Yet to Kate, going to college seemed perfectly doable, a logical step after high school and a goal within reach. Maybe that was why Callie was so scared to go for it. She'd learned from experience that wanting something too badly was the kiss of death. As soon as she made up her mind that she had to have something, it was ripped away from her. Luke was the perfect example. He'd held out the hand of friendship, maybe even hinted that there could be more, and then he blew her off. Dumped her. Kicked her out to the curb like a load of garbage.

Kate and the life she wanted to give Callie were just as tenuous. Yet Callie, even having been knocked in the dirt so many times, desperately wanted to accept the offer. Ever since Kate had proposed her idea, Callie had walked around with a giant lump in her throat, ready to burst into stupid tears at any moment. She couldn't keep herself from imagining having a permanent place with Kate and Aaron. A clean, orderly house to come home to after school every day, supper around a table, her own bed each night. It was all so freaking Norman

Rockwell, the kind of thing kids in foster homes made fun of. Callie knew exactly why they ridiculed close families. It was to protect themselves from shriveling up from wanting it so badly.

Drawing a shell of sullenness around her, she sank deeper into silence. And Kate, ever understanding, didn't push her to talk. She didn't press for a decision, either. At some point she would, though. Callie knew that. Because later today, they had an appointment with CPS to discuss Kate's proposed arrangement with a caseworker.

First, though, they had a stop to make. Callie tore her gaze away from the passing scenery and glanced down at the official-looking envelope that lay on the seat between them. The outside was stamped Washington State Correction Center for Women and the inside contained their clearance passes to visit Callie's mother.

Callie shifted in her seat, wishing she could scoot away from the documents lying there.

"Sorry," Kate said as if reading her mind. "I know it's rough—"

"You don't know," Callie said. "How could you possibly? You have nice parents and this great family. I've seen the pictures, Kate. I've heard the stories. You had this perfect childhood, so you can't possibly know what this is like."

"You know what I think?" she said. "I think the old saying is true. It's never too late to have a happy childhood."

"Right." Callie studied her fingernails. Frosted peony.

"You can still say no to visiting your mother. Since it was my idea in the first place, I can talk to her by myself."

"I'll do it," Callie said. In spite of everything she had some kind of sick loyalty to her mother, a need to see her and hear her voice. "You probably think it's totally weird that I'm willing to be in the same room with her."

"With your mother?" Kate shook her head. "It's not weird at all."

"Even though she was devoted to that creep, Timothy Stone? And when that fell apart, she dragged me to Washington and ditched me?"

"You didn't choose her, but you've got her."

Callie didn't say anything. She had learned to play her cards close to the chest and old habits died hard.

At the state women's prison in Purdy, Kate acted as if it was no big deal, parking in a Visitor slot, showing their credentials at the gate office. She acted perfectly calm as they descended the granite stairway, going lower with every step. They had to be searched with wands that never touched them but felt like an intrusion anyway. They passed through gate after gate, each one closing before the next opened. She could tell Kate was nervous, going through the security routine of sliding doors, fluorescent hand stamps, sealed rooms.

Callie's first foster home had been close by the prison, so close that she could see the reflection of its too-bright lights at night, blotting out the stars. She knew her way around this place. On the way to the visitors' unit, they passed through a garden that always surprised people when they saw it. It was filled with riotously blooming sweet peas and dahlias, and there was even a pond with rose petals floating on the surface. In the crook of an ornamental plum tree was a nest, and birdsong floated on the breeze. It resembled the perfect oasis if you ignored the miles of cyclone fence and coils of razor wire surrounding the compound.

The inmates they passed averted their eyes. Disengaging, a prison counselor had called it. If you made eye contact, it was a challenge. Yet somehow, the downcast gazes had intimidated the heck out of Callie when she'd first come here. Now she wasn't just immune. She had learned to disengage, too.

She checked to see how Kate was taking it all in. At first glance, you wouldn't think she was tough enough to deal with something like this. She looked like Alice in Wonderland, with her shampoo-ad hair and big eyes. But there was more to her than that. She had a core of steel, and that was evident when an inmate sized her up and she refused to flinch.

They waited in a room furnished with molded-plastic chairs and shiny laminate tables. The linoleum floors were scuffed and it was hot as an oven, with no breeze through the open transom windows. Kate sat down and placed her notepad and pencil on the table in front of her. She lined them up perfectly straight, then sent Callie an ironic smile. "Not that I'm nervous or anything."

Callie smiled back. "Don't worry about it. Everybody is."

A few minutes later, her mom was brought in by a guard. Kate stood up fast, the feet of her chair scraping the floor. Callie stayed seated, her arm over the back of the chair. She felt a storm of emotion in her gut—anger and discomfort, and a terrible explosion of hope and yearning—but she kept it all in and acted nonchalant. "Hey," she said, and finally, reluctantly, got up.

"Hey, yourself." Mom's eyes flickered over her. "You finally lost some weight."

"I collapsed and almost died on my birthday," Callie said, wondering even as she spoke why she bothered. "I've been diagnosed with insulin resistance. That's a precursor of type 2 diabetes."

Her mother's face didn't change. "Shouldn't have let yourself get so heavy."

After that, of course, they didn't hug, didn't smile. They were long past the stage of pretending there was any sort of bond between them. Everyone sat down, and her mom kept a poker face, like Callie knew she would. Callie was more interested in watching Kate's reaction. People were always startled when they saw Callie's mom. They were surprised by how petite she was, how beautiful. Renée Zellweger with a number stenciled on the back of her shirt.

Kate was surprised, all right, Callie could tell, even though she'd already seen Mom's mug shot and sort of knew what to expect. But she covered up her reaction, smiling as she said, "Ms. Evans, I'm Kate Livingston.

I've been looking forward to meeting you."

Callie's mom drummed her fingers on the table. "Why?"

"Curiosity, mostly." Kate sat back down. Sure enough, she was not going to blow smoke up anyone's ass and pretend she was here out of compassion. "And research for an article I'm writing. I was hoping you'd be willing to talk with me about your life with Callie."

Mom's dark eyes narrowed. "What kind of article?"

"For a magazine. It's scheduled to run in *Vanity Fair* next year."

"So you're a reporter?"

"Freelance writer."

"And if I don't feel like telling you anything?"

Kate folded her hands, prim as a lady in church. "I'll use the court records and Callie's own impressions."

"Oh, so you're writing a work of fiction."

"I beg your pardon?" Kate sounded polite, but the question was a clear challenge.

"This interview is over," Mom said, getting up, her mouth a curl of disgust. "I've got nothing to say to either of you."

It hit Callie then that this person had never been a mother to her. Kate was the closest thing she'd ever had to a real mother. All her life, she had been waiting and hoping for her mom to be something Kate had become in just one summer. She knew now that she'd been trying to hang on to nothing, to thin air, to her idea of what a mother should be, and that was so stupid. It was like trying to catch the rain between your fingers. Now, Kate—she was the real thing. But the scary part of that was that she might not last.

Kate was quiet for a moment. Callie was scared she might mention her idea about letting Callie live with her. They'd agreed not to bring it up until Callie made her decision. She hoped Kate would remember that.

Kate offered a tight, controlled smile. Then she carefully picked up the pad of paper and pencil and stood.

The guard stepped forward to escort Callie's mother back to her unit. But Mom had one more thing to say. "She'll screw you over, just you watch. The kid's a born liar and a cheater. She'll screw you like she screwed me, and then we'll see who's so self-righteous."

"Care to explain that further?" Kate asked.

"You'll find out for yourself." The guard walked her to the door. The last thing Callie's mother said was, "Ask her. Ask her how come she ran away from her last home. Ask why they never tried to find her."

Thirty

Summer storms rarely struck at the lake, but occasionally, the mountains would produce a change in the weather. In late August, nature offered a hint of the coming season. The air turned misty as a brooding bank of clouds moved in, followed by gusts of wind howling through the corridor created by the mountains around the lake. Kate found her gaze drawn to the window as the weather intensified, driving curtains of rain across the water. She loved the drama of a good storm, with its dim, strange light, the dense pressure of the air, the sound of the wind tearing at the treetops and the rain beating on the roof. It was true that an idyllic summer day on the lake was a thing of beauty. Yet weather like this had its own peculiar majesty, feeding the melancholy side of her and somehow quieting the restlessness in her soul.

Chilled by the cold wind blowing down from the mountains, she made a fire in the woodstove and all day long worked by the dancing light visible through the amber glass in the stove door. Across the table from her, Aaron alternated between drawing intricate maps of some imaginary place and playing with his army action figures, who were rappelling off the backs of chairs, under enemy fire. From time to time, Kate paused in her work to watch her son thoughtfully, though she said nothing, loath to interrupt the fantasy. Aaron worked his heroes hard. He always had.

Callie had been productive all day. She had cleaned her room and changed the linens, swept the porch and mopped the kitchen floor without being asked. She claimed she was feeling cooped up by the rain, and the activity would keep her from going stir-crazy. In the days since their visit to the corrections center, she hadn't spoken of the visit to her mother, not to deny the things Sonja Evans had said, nor to confirm them, either. But Kate sensed an air of penance or atonement in Callie's actions and heard again the echo of Sonja's words—*Ask her. . . .*

She took a deep breath and caught the girl's eye. "I've been wondering about something your mother said."

Callie's eyes narrowed. "Yeah?"

"About why you had problems at your foster homes."

"That's over," Callie said. "I'm through running away."

"So what's changed?"

She studied the floor, then glanced over at Aaron. He seemed oblivious, lost in his make-believe world. "I never told this to anyone, not even my mother. She's the reason I kept running away, so I could go see her. I missed her so much, it's crazy."

Kate's heart ached for her. "It's not crazy."

"It is. She's not worth it. She never wanted me around. And she was right," Callie added softly. "I tend to ruin things."

Finally, thought Kate. She'd been waiting for Callie to respond to Sonja's comments. "That's not what your mother said. She told me to ask you why you left your last family. I didn't ask, though. I figured it's up to you whether or not you want to tell me."

"I did ruin it," Callie said, her voice matter-of-fact. "The Youngs were a good family, and I ruined things with them. If I hadn't left on my own, they would have sent me packing."

Kate said nothing, hoping her silence would keep the invitation open.

Sure enough, a moment later, Callie said softly, "I

screwed everything up. Me, all by myself. The Youngs wanted to help me. I didn't let them, though. I pushed them away, and when they pushed back, I ran."

Kate could easily picture it. Callie's self-protective instincts were stronger than her trust in people's basic goodness. She had acted out of self-preservation, pure and simple. Kate recognized that.

"You're going to have to change the way you deal with people who love you and want to help you," Kate told her.

"Yeah, right. Whatever you say." She headed for the utility room. "I need to get some clothes out of the dryer."

Kate turned her attention back to revising the lengthy article. Her editor had declared the topic important, the photos remarkable, and the last time Kate was in cell phone range, they had talked for an hour about how the piece would be published. It would have a strong position in features, a shoutline on the front cover and a thumbnail photograph on the contents page. Kate gave all the credit to Callie, whose input had a devastating honesty. Kate herself had merely been the scribe, taking down a story of danger and endurance. Reporting Callie's unflinching narrative without judgment, Kate had known all along, was the only way the piece would be effective.

Kate hoped Callie would be happy with the published article. True, it was unsparing and not always flattering, but no reader would ever lose sympathy for her. Kate had even persuaded the magazine to include a sidebar with information about diabetes. In the past ten years, the number of teens with type 2 diabetes had doubled.

Sometimes when she was writing, Kate still thought about the things JD had said to her. He had wondered at the humanity of profiting from other people's pain, from exposing someone's private life to the world. As much as it bothered her to hear such things, the comments lingered in her mind and actually made her do a better job on the article. She weighed the merits of every word and phrase. If something smacked of exploitation or sensationalism, she struck it. She allowed nothing except the powerful truth, most of which came from the words Callie herself spoke. Kate would not obscure, soft-pedal or romanticize any of the events. Nor would she embellish or dramatize them.

She would simply write the truth from her perspective. Callie had no problem with that. And sometimes when she related events from her past, her flat, matter-of-fact delivery had a certain devastating power. Kate was determined to capture that. Ironically, she had JD to thank for making sure the work had absolute integrity. With his disapproval and skepticism as a constant reminder, she made certain her care, precision and altruism never wavered.

Not that she would thank him for the unsolicited advice. That would be too big a leap. She couldn't imagine the conversation. Could she really say, "You made me a better writer" or "I did a better job on this piece because of what you said"?

He had still undermined her ambition and devalued

her dream. That wasn't how to love someone.

She reflected on her past relationships. Men had always left without really knowing her, without giving her dreams a chance. She thought JD was different, but that was probably wishful thinking.

Anyway, she was moving on. The meeting had gone well with the caseworker, though the application and qualification process was an eye-opener. A foster parent had to commit to any number of possibilities. She had to provide a safe and loving home and promise to give her time, energy and heart to the process. Kate discovered that not only did she feel confident that she could do this, she was looking forward to it.

Her mother had warned her not to tangle herself up, being a foster mother. She'd declared it burdensome and maybe even hazardous, but Kate didn't see it that way. She wanted to do this, to deepen her bond with Callie and make the girl a part of her life. The caseworker promised that, assuming Kate's references and background checked out, Callie would soon be a part of her home. The yearning for this to work out was strong in Kate. She loved and respected Callie and wanted her to have the same chances and options any teenager enjoyed. Sometimes Kate lay awake at night and wondered if she had enough to give this girl. She hoped so. She and Aaron didn't constitute a traditional family, but just because she didn't have a husband didn't mean she had to deprive herself—and Aaron—of another child in the household.

The whole experience made Kate realize that she had

choices. Having Callie, even just for the summer, had opened her mind to possibilities she'd never before considered. She drummed her fingers on the keyboard. Maybe she would chronicle that experience next, the journey of a single mother becoming a foster parent. Her editor wanted to know what her next project was. Perhaps this was it, Kate thought. This was what she was meant to be doing. Telling the stories of ordinary women from a personal perspective.

As the thought crossed her mind, a current of heat shot through her, a keen awareness. She vibrated like a tuning fork. When something felt this right, it rang in her bones, and she sensed that now. She sat up and paid attention. This was not some huge, radical concept. Lord knew, it was hardly original. Yet the idea felt right. It was a good fit, and she knew she could add her own voice to the canon.

"Well," she said. "Good thing I got that figured out."

"What's that?" Callie stepped into the main room, wearing one of her work aprons and rubber gloves. It was startling to see how dramatically she'd changed since her birthday. She had her mother's beauty, though Callie was blond while Sonja was dark. As the pounds came off and her health improved, that beauty shone through more and more each day.

"My direction. My next writing project. I loved writing this article about you, Callie, and when it's done, I want to do more stories about women and choices."

"What women?"

"All kinds. Women who are dealing with loss, like Mrs. Newman. Or those who have aging parents, or are struggling to raise their kids or to make ends meet, or—" She stopped, not wanting to say the next thing that popped into her mind: women who need to move on after a breakup. "Any woman, any age, who's faced with choices," she said to Callie. "How's that sound?"

"Like something in a women's magazine."

"Exactly." Kate saved her work and shut the laptop. "Let's get dinner, then. I think it's perfect weather for chicken soup and grilled-cheese sandwiches."

"Soup from a can?" Aaron asked, looking up from his play.

"'Fraid so, buddy."

"Yes!" he said, punching the air.

Kate and Callie traded a smile. They worked together washing lettuce and chopping carrots for the salad. Kate put the ingredients for the vinaigrette in a jar and gave it to Aaron to shake, the perfect job for him. "I'm going to miss this place," Callie said quietly, looking out the big picture window.

"We come back every year," Aaron said immediately, lining his army men up along the counter. "No problem."

Callie reached over and ruffled his hair. "Right, kid."

Kate watched the worry tugging at Callie. She had been shuffled around so much that she never knew what lay ahead for her.

"We're going to do everything we can to keep you with us through high school," Kate said.

"That's a long time," Callie pointed out.

"Three more years," Aaron said.

"I'll probably ruin things before that," Callie muttered.

Aaron rolled his eyes and took his army men elsewhere. He had little patience with Callie's angst.

"Don't be negative," Kate said, keeping her voice light, though she found Callie's attitude worrisome. "The key to getting things to work out is believing they will."

Callie smiled briefly and sliced into a tomato. "That's the key to fooling yourself."

"You're too young to be cynical," Kate told her.

"I think I damn well earned the right," Callie replied, an edge in her voice.

"That's in the past. From now on, you're with us, and you don't have to be so tough anymore. You also don't have to swear."

"Swear?"

"The D word."

"Oh, for Chri— Pete's sake," Callie said.

Kate glanced over at Aaron. He was soaking all this in like a sponge, loving it. "Listen, both of you," she said. "This summer, you've been our guest, Callie. But from now on, we're going to function like a family. The placement counselor said we'll need to work out clear house rules. One of mine is that we don't use vulgar language. All right?"

"Fine," Callie said. "Whatever."

"It's not asking all that much," Kate pointed out.

"One step at a time, that's what they told us."

"All right."

"Pass me the salad tongs," said Kate.

They fixed the soup and sandwiches, then sat down to eat while watching the rain in the wind on the lake. "I'm bored," Aaron announced, pulling the crust off his grilled cheese.

"How about a game of Parcheesi after dinner?" Kate offered.

"Chairman of the bored," he concluded, then asked Callie, "Is Luke coming over tonight?"

She kept her gaze out the window. "Nope."

"Tomorrow?"

"Not tomorrow, either." She shifted restlessly in her chair. "I'm not . . . Luke and I are not going to be hanging out anymore."

"Bummer." Aaron got up to clear the table. Kate smiled at him, pleased that she hadn't had to ask him to do it. At the beginning of the summer, this might have taken ten minutes of nagging, so this was real progress.

"Are you sure about Luke?" Kate asked her.

"What do you mean?"

"Are you ready to give up on him, or is he worth fighting for? You gave up without a fight."

"Like you did with JD."

The words struck Kate like rocks. She and Callie understood each other all too well.

Callie said no more but went to help Aaron finish the dishes. She seemed agitated, cleaning the kitchen with extra vigor. When Bandit whined to go out, Callie volunteered to take him, grabbing a cobwebbed golf umbrella from the stand on the porch. The dog raced around the yard, searching for the ideal spot to do his business. Aaron insisted on going out as well, wearing galoshes and an ancient army-fatigue poncho.

Good, thought Kate, watching from the porch. Aaron found her heart-to-hearts with Callie completely boring, and he needed to run off all that energy. When he came in, he might even submit to a warm bath. Callie stood under the umbrella, her shoulders hunched against the wind. She looked both alone and resolute, yet far too small to take on the world.

A gust of wind blew across the lake, flattening the water before it. Aaron's poncho billowed out around him and Callie's umbrella was lifted from beneath. The ribs strained, but Callie held on fast with both hands until the gust of wind passed her by.

Like you did with JD?

Kate squinted through the mist but could barely see the Schroeder place. Still, she felt her stomach knotting with tension. She'd been telling herself it was time to quit dreaming and move on. Maybe she was wrong about that.

She clapped her hands to call the dog back in, then went to stoke the fire in the stove.

Thirty-One

JD spotted wispy threads of wood smoke twisting up from the chimney of Kate's house. In the dank gray of twilight, the windows of the house glowed a cheery yellow-gold, little beams through the midst of a rare summer storm.

Everywhere there were signs that summer was sliding to its inevitable end. The days were already getting noticeably shorter, and the lashing storm was a foretaste of gusty autumn. He rolled his shoulders back and rotated his head, feeling the fatigue of the hours he'd put in, working on his med school application. Yes, he was going for it. He had a time line for getting his materials in, including the dreaded "personal statement." He knew he'd be putting that off for a long time. Ultimately, though, he'd do what it took, same as he had all his life. By the time he finished the process, UCLA would know more about him than his own mother.

Bad analogy, he thought. His own mother knew virtually nothing about him. In truth, she had been singularly uninvolved with him throughout his childhood. Controlled by her addiction, she would sometimes stagger home after days of using, and look at him as if she couldn't remember his name.

Those times stayed buried in the past—until he was thrust into the public eye. Her relapse had been swift and brutal, but fortunately he could now afford the best and most discreet treatment available. His visit had gone predictably. She was remorseful and determined to get better. One good thing about the clinic was its experience with high-profile patients. They guarded people's privacy rigorously, and he was grateful for that. A part of him wished he could talk about it with Kate, but that was out of the question now, of course.

He had to go back, too. He'd promised his mother he would, and this time, he really did have an admissions interview scheduled. Summer was coming to an end, anyway. He hated the idea of leaving the lake, but it was time. The Schroeders were coming out for Labor Day, and although Sam had invited him to stay, he had no intention of intruding. It was time to get back to his own life. He hoped that by now he'd be an obscure, barely recognized has-been.

Restless, he decided to go out to the shed and mess with the boat for a while. It was finished, but he wanted the wherry in perfect shape for Sam and his family. He put on the overhead shop light and inspected the restoration job. The mahogany and oak strips, arranged in alternating geometric patterns, were now as smooth as polished stones, glowing with amber depths. The joints were clean and tight, the seams virtually invisible. The interior of the hull had seating for three and there was a tiny storage well in the bow. Once he reattached the rudder with the new hardware he bought, he'd be in business.

Despite the fact that he liked the work, his mood did not improve. As always, he was distracted by thoughts of Kate. He hated the way things were between them—an impasse neither was willing to breach. She was a reporter. The enemy. It was just as well he was leaving.

Maybe he'd been a fool to fall in love with her. But at least he'd been a happy fool.

He fitted the rudder and tiller in place as the last of the light disappeared. Still, the storm didn't let up, beating relentlessly on the roof of the shed. The sense of being utterly alone here was strong as he stood in the cocoon of light cast by the overhead lamp. When he'd first come here, he had reveled in the vast sense of isolation afforded by the secluded lake. After all the attention, it was what he'd craved. He had gratefully sunk into anonymity, wishing he could stay like that forever.

Since he'd met Kate, his isolation felt completely different. It felt like loneliness.

He wiped his hands on a polishing cloth and stepped back to inspect the job. It was then that he finally realized all the work he'd done, turning a wreck into a beautiful, gleaming boat, meant nothing. Doing something well didn't mean a thing. It meant only that he'd spent untold hours on this project. Now that it was finished, what next?

He was haunted by a sense of things left undone, unsaid. Finishing a project wasn't enough, even though he'd wanted it to be. A relationship, he reminded himself, was not a project.

Kate, he thought. He needed to see her before he left. Aaron, too, and Callie.

The decision felt good. He closed up the shed and made a dash for the cabin. The rain descended in a thick curtain, soaking him to the skin and fogging his glasses. He ducked inside and stood shivering for a minute. Kate had the right idea, building a fire. There was no other way to keep the place warm except with the woodstove.

The trouble was, the woodpile was outside, a good twenty yards from the house. He was already drenched. Might as well go for it. Grabbing a flashlight, he splashed across the yard toward the woodpile, gathering an armload of logs from under the blue plastic tarp. When he got back inside, he was not only wet but muddy and sprinkled with wood chips and sawdust. A brown wolf spider picked its way delicately down his arm.

JD figured maybe he should get cleaned up before going to see Kate. He opened the door and shook off the spider, then went back inside. As he stood dripping on the floor and wiping off his glasses, the stark gleam of headlights washed across the room.

He frowned. It was too dark to see who had come calling. Company? A lost traveler? Had he gotten Sam's arrival date wrong?

He heard the faint thud of a car door slamming, then the stomp of feet on the porch steps. Putting on his glasses, he opened the door. There stood Kate, huddled in an oversize jacket and holding a faded golf umbrella. She shook it out, closed it and leaned it on the stoop by the door.

It was all he could do not to grab her, hold her against his chest, tell her every crazy thought in his head. "Kate—"

"JD, I—"

"Come inside." He shut the door against the aggressive gusts. She looked windblown and bedraggled and beautiful to him. Yet her eyes were troubled. "What's the matter?" he asked.

"What do you mean?"

"Are the kids all right? How's Callie?"

"Oh . . ." She smiled very briefly. "Callie's great."

"And Aaron . . . ?"

"Fine, too." She must have recognized the way he was studying her, with the probing, assessing look of a paramedic. "Honest."

"So this is where I examine you all over and say, 'Where does it hurt, ma'am?'"

"You don't want to do that," she said. "I might tell you the truth."

"I can handle it," he said.

"The truth is, I am hurt. What happened between us—that hurt me. And not seeing you, well, that hurts, too."

"I know. God, Kate, I'm sorry."

She folded her arms across her chest, a protective gesture. He didn't blame her. She said, "You're a mess."

"I went out to get wood for a fire," he explained. "Chilly tonight."

"Uh-huh." She shivered, glanced nervously around the place. "JD—"

"Kate—" He stopped himself. They were both so

361

damn nervous that normal conversation wasn't going to work, so he pulled her against him. "I've missed you," he said. Then he kissed her, not gently but with a heated urgency that drew a startled gasp from her.

She pushed her hands against his chest and simultaneously pulled back. He wondered what he was seeing in her eyes—protest? Pain? Conflict? He refused to look away, silently daring her to object. Instead, she curled her fists into his wet shirtfront and went up on tiptoe, kissing him as fiercely as he had just kissed her.

When they came up for air, he admitted, "I was going to come and see you."

"You were?" Her smile seized at his heart.

"I was going to shower first."

Her smile changed into a look that was softer. Darker. "Why don't we take care of that right now?"

It turned into a shower of record length, lasting until the hot water ran out. Then they moved to a heap of blankets in front of the woodstove by the light of the dancing flames through the glass. Kate's lovemaking made JD wonder how he'd managed to stay away at all. She made love with a combination of passion and delight and a genuine affection he'd never felt from a woman before, and when he held her in his arms, he knew, for the first time in his life, the true meaning of happiness.

Much later, they lay tangled in the soft blankets and listened to the rain on the roof. He held her against him even closer than before, and the unfamiliar joy welled up in him. He shuddered slightly, unprepared for its strange power.

"Are you cold?" she asked, snuggling against him.

"No," he said. He gathered her closer still and drew a quilt around them both. "I wish I'd been the one to come to you," he said.

She shifted, turning so that her face nearly touched his. The firelight softly flickered over her skin. "It wasn't a contest to see who blinked first."

"I know," he said. "I'm an idiot."

She smiled and kissed him. "I suppose that's part of your charm."

"Yeah?"

"Uh-huh. Irresistible."

"I've missed you, Kate," he told her again. Then he thought: *I love you.* He needed to tell her that, too.

"I'm no genius, either," she said. "I guess . . . I went into this expecting the worst. I guess I kept looking for a way for us to fall apart, and it became a self-fulfilling prophecy. I thought . . . you had to be too good to be true. So I decided you couldn't possibly be for real. Dumb, huh?"

"Kate—"

"I shouldn't have been so defensive," she said. "You were just being protective of Callie and open with me. I love that so much about you. Your openness. Your honesty." She kissed him again as his heart sank like a rock. She propped her arms on his chest and held his gaze with hers. "I love you, JD," she told him.

Damn. Now what? What could he say to that? He told

her the most honest saying he could think of. "Me too, Kate. I love you, too."

She smiled sweetly, maybe a little smugly. "Just remember, I was the first to say it."

"Does that matter?"

"Not to me. I'm teasing."

There was so much more he needed to say to her, to explain, but it was late, and still raining, and he didn't feel like talking at all. He didn't want to ruin the look of wonder he saw in her eyes. There would be time enough for talking later.

They slept. JD couldn't tell what time it was when something awakened him, though it was still dark. The rain continued its patter on the roof and the fire burned low, a core of glowing embers that cast a faint orange light over the face of the woman beside him. The unguarded beauty of her stirred him. *I love you.* Telling her had been the easiest thing in the world because it was the truest thing he knew. And to hear her say it to him . . . that was a miracle, plain and simple. The last thing he'd ever expected, the last thing he deserved and the only thing he wanted. For now, he decided, for tonight, he would be happy. He wouldn't worry about the difficulties that lay ahead.

He gently kissed her temple and lay still for a while, listening to the rain and the rhythm of his pulse in his ears. She shifted in her sleep, snuggled closer to him. It pierced him, the love and trust she gave so openly. He didn't quite know what to make of it.

She woke up slowly and smiled the instant she saw him. Propping herself up on one elbow, she squinted out the window. "It's getting light out."

He saw the first gray threads of dawn creasing the sky above the mountains. "Still dark," he insisted. "Go back to sleep."

"The sun is coming up," she said. "I have to go."

"Why? Do you turn to stone by light of day?"

"No, worse. An irresponsible mother. I don't want my son to catch me sleeping around."

"You're not sleeping around." He tugged at the blanket, baring her shoulder. "You're sleeping with me."

"You're going to get me in trouble."

"This is trouble?" He couldn't help himself. He had to touch her, glide his hands over the warm pale velvet of her skin. "Freckles are sexy," he whispered in her ear. She shuddered and gave a little moan.

"That's it," she said, making a visible effort to climb to her feet. "I'm out of here." She started pulling on her clothes. She had this crazy red bra that made him want her all over again, but he could tell she was agitated now, eager to get home.

He got up and felt her eyes on him. "It's that underwear of yours," he said. "Can't help myself."

"Get dressed," she ordered, blushing. "Hurry."

He reluctantly pulled on a pair of jeans and hastily zipped them. Then he bent to add a log to the fire. It flared up, gilding everything in its path.

She was still watching him as she pulled on her thick

wool socks and combed her hair with her fingers. "We need to work on your conversation skills. You hate talking about yourself, don't you?"

She had no idea. "I'll tell you anything you need to know," he said. It was time, past time, to come clean with her.

"Good. I'll hold you to that." She finger-combed her hair, which only made it messier. Sexier.

"You're beautiful, Kate," he told her.

"Uh-huh." She stuck her feet into rubber garden clogs.

"I mean it. Just like this, in a sweat suit that doesn't fit and plastic shoes."

"It must be true love, then. You're crazy." At the door, she stopped and turned back to him. "Maybe I can steal away again tonight. We'll work on those conversation skills of yours."

He hesitated. Of all the lousy timing. "I won't be here tonight."

Her eyes showed a flash of Irish temper. "Already change your mind about me?"

He stepped closer, caught her in his arms. "Nothing like that. I'm going back to L.A., and Sam is bringing his family out here for Labor Day. I'm heading for Seattle tonight. Flying out early tomorrow morning."

Her face fell. "Tomorrow? But we've only just—"

He pressed his finger to her lips. "I know. I'm sorry." He wanted to tell her that he'd be back, that they could sort things out and he'd explain everything to her, but he wasn't used to making promises, not to anyone.

"So you're just leaving?"

"Yes. This was never supposed to be permanent."

"I see. And were you planning on coming back?"

"No."

She flinched.

He gathered her against him. "It's true, Kate. I wasn't going to come back. But now . . ." He stopped to kiss her softly. "Now I know I have a reason to."

She sighed with contentment. "You're a bit slow on the uptake."

He kissed her again, this time his mouth pressing deep with suggestion. He could feel her reluctance to pull away.

"I really need to get back before the kids wake up," she said. Then a smile lit her face. "We can all go to Seattle together."

"Kate—"

"Really, it's no trouble. I have things to do in the city, too." She looked as though she might burst. "I have news. Ask me." Her smile was infectious, curling around his heart.

"I'm asking."

"I'm submitting the final paperwork to Child Protective Services. Aaron and I are going to be Callie's foster family. I'm so excited, JD. It's going to be wonderful for us all."

She made it sound so simple. For Kate, it was simple. Callie needed a home, and Kate had one to offer. JD finally got it, finally figured out why she'd taken it so hard when he'd criticized her work. When you loved someone, their approval meant everything. He cupped her cheek in his hand. "You're amazing."

"Yeah, that's me," she said. "Amazing."

Thirty-Two

The last time Kate told a man she loved him, he had left her pregnant and alone. No wonder it had taken her ten years to get up the nerve to do it again. She was a different person now—a grown woman, a single mother—yet she felt as giddy as a teenager after her first date. She floated through the morning with an idiotic grin on her face. JD had promised to come to breakfast, and later, they were all going to Seattle together. She showered, then rinsed the blackberries they had picked the day before. She even sang along with the radio—"Dancing in the Street" by Martha and the Vandellas—loud enough to wake Callie, whom Kate immediately drafted into an impromptu dance.

By the end of the song, they were both flushed and laughing.

Callie's smile lingered as she got out her glucose kit, now an unchangeable part of her routine each morning. Thus far, every reading had been in the acceptable range, staving off the need for medication. Kate tried not to be too inquisitive. Soon enough, Callie would be an adult, living on her own, and she would have to manage the disease on her own.

"Dock of the Bay" came on the radio and they hummed it together while fixing breakfast. As she whisked the eggs in a bowl, Kate yelled for Aaron to come to breakfast.

Callie flashed her a smile. "He can't hear you. He's out on the lake."

Kate dropped her whisk in the sink and dashed outside. Sure enough, Bandit was running up and down the dock, keeping a worried eye on a boat out on the lake.

"I'll kill them both," she said, though just the sight of JD raised a ripple of happiness inside her. "They both know they're supposed to ask permission."

"He showed up while you were in the shower," Callie explained. "I said it would be all right."

Kate took a deep breath. The whole world looked brand new. The storm had washed everything clean, leaving the sky a deep, clear blue, the green of the forest renewed, the lake as pristine and transparent as a mirror. The air smelled sweet, almost dizzyingly so, and was bright with birdsong.

"So you and JD made up, right?" asked Callie.

Kate felt a rush of color in her cheeks. "What makes you say that?"

"You went over to his place last night." She shook her head. "Sneaking out after hours. That's supposed to be my specialty."

"I wasn't sneaking."

"No, just leaving really quietly without telling anyone."

"But—"

"God, Kate, chill." Callie laughed. "I think it's totally fly that you're with him." She waved at the boat in the distance, gesturing for them to return. "He came looking for you, but then Aaron spotted him and wouldn't leave him alone until JD offered him a ride."

As the sleek wooden rowboat glided toward them, Kate felt Callie watching her. "So it's all good between you, right?" the girl asked.

Last night was perfect, Kate thought. She had never felt so cherished, so consumed with passion, so certain she was in the right place. With Callie, she was more noncommittal. "We'll see." She surprised herself with her own uncertainty. Everything had seemed perfectly clear this morning in his arms. This was too new. She wasn't used to it.

"So did he tell you—" Callie broke off, pushed her hands into her pockets.

"Tell me what?" *That he loves me?* Kate couldn't keep the grin from her face. He said it. He said it. He said it.

Callie kept her eyes down. Kate studied her, sensing that she had something on her mind. "Callie?" she prompted.

"I just wondered if he told you how he feels."

"I think maybe we fell in love." Kate couldn't help herself. It was way too early to be spreading this around, but she had to say it aloud.

"Maybe?" Callie snorted. "I'd say definitely."

"How can you be more sure than I am?" Kate asked.

"I have twenty-twenty vision. And I know what I see."

The boat approached the end of the dock. Bandit whined and pranced.

"Mom!" Aaron yelled, scrambling out and unbuckling his life vest. "Check out JD's boat, Mom. It's cool, huh?"

Kate was busy checking out JD. "Yeah, buddy. It's cool."

Later that day, they went to pick up JD for the trip to Seattle. He had locked up the cabin and was waiting for them. Wearing lovingly faded jeans, a golf shirt and aviator shades, he looked more like a professional athlete than like Paul Bunyan.

For a moment, Kate was taken aback. Out here at the lake, it was easy to forget they had other lives, filled with other people. It was something to talk about, she decided. She wanted to know who was important to him, who was missing him this summer. She wanted to meet his parents, wanted to introduce him to her mother.

"You're looking at me funny," he remarked, closing the back of the Jeep.

He wouldn't think she was so funny if he knew what was on her mind. "It's going to get awkward tonight, in Seattle," she said. "Since before Aaron was born, I haven't . . . No one's ever stayed the night."

He bent down and kissed her forehead, easing the frown away. "Aaron can handle it."

Can I? she wondered. That was the thing about being a single mom. She was used to being in charge of every aspect of their lives. Now, seemingly overnight, there were two more people in her life. And though she adored both Callie and JD, she knew her world was about to change.

"That's all you're taking?" she asked. "The duffel bag?"

"I travel light."

She took it as a good sign; he would definitely come back for the rest of his things. Then it occurred to her that she was already having doubts about them. Stop it, Kate, she thought. She got back in the Jeep and snapped on the radio.

Although it was just over a hundred miles to Seattle, it felt as though they were crossing continents and time zones. The towering, dense forests of the Olympic Peninsula gave way to the weekend cottages of the Hood Canal and then Bainbridge Island, where they drove onto the massive white-and-green car ferry for the final leg of the trip. Callie and Aaron went to the passenger deck to play video games. Kate and JD climbed the stairs to the top deck outside to look at the scenery. The deck was crowded with vacationers soaking up the last of the August sun, tourists snapping pictures of Mount Rainier or the Space Needle, restless kids chasing each other, and smokers gathered at the aft railing, the only place on the boat that permitted smoking. Kate studied a cluster of kids about Callie's age, pierced and tattooed and clad in leather, sucking on menthol cigarettes. Just the sight of them made her nervous about raising Callie. But nervous or not, it was what she'd signed up for.

She watched a portly man in a business suit talking on a cell phone as he paced in agitation. His face was beet red, nearly purple, and a contrail of cigarette smoke followed him. Welcome back to the city, reflected Kate. Even here on the ferryboat, she could feel the pace speed up.

They strolled toward the bow, passing a clown in full regalia making balloon animals. A couple of rowdy boys played with a set of military action figures. Stopping to watch for a moment, she leaned against a green enamel–painted railing and looked at the familiar scenery. Having lived here all her life, Kate always had to remind herself of how magical the place was for tourists and newcomers. It was like no other place on earth, especially in summer, when the rain was a distant memory. With JD at her side, she saw the sights with new eyes—the white-crested mountains rising out of the Sound, ferries and barges steaming back and forth, pleasure crafts and fishing boats exploring the forested islands and inlets. The same water that reflected the glass and steel spires of Seattle was home to whales, seals, eagles and salmon.

"Some of my earliest memories are of racing for the ferry on the way to the lake," she said. "One time, I made us miss the boat because I had to hunt down my pet hamster. My brother shunned me the whole first week of summer to punish me for making us late. Back then, there were only a few ferry crossings each day, so missing the boat could be really tragic."

He took her hand and kissed it. "There's always another boat, Kate."

"So I'm told." She loved it that he'd kissed her hand and then kept hold of it. She felt like a high-school girl going public to show off her new boyfriend. The thought made her laugh and fling her arms around his neck.

People passing by glanced at them and some smiled indulgently. Kate realized she and JD looked exactly like the young lovers she used to regard with a pang of empty yearning.

A harried young couple, watching over a pack of small children, including a little girl and rowdy boys playing with action figures, gathered nearby. The father was trying to take their picture while the mother pushed a fussy toddler in a wobbly stroller.

Somehow, the father managed to corral the boys at the railing for a group shot. His wife handed the toddler a cookie to get her to stop whining.

"We should offer to take their picture," Kate said, waving at the man to get his attention.

JD balked. "Somebody else can do that."

Lord, she thought, was he really that shy? She went over to the man with the camera. "Let me take that shot so you can be in it, too."

"Hey, thanks. It's a digital, point-and-shoot. The shutter's right here."

"Got it. I'll take a couple."

The man hurried to join his family. They stood together with Mount Rainier floating like a pale confection in the background. He picked up the baby and turned her toward the camera.

The boys behaved horribly, teasing and cuffing each other, fighting over their Green Beret action figures.

"Everybody smile," Kate called out, snapping one, two, three pictures. She reviewed them on the small screen and gave a thumbs-up. Years from now, she thought as she handed back the camera, the mother wouldn't remember how ill behaved the kids were or how tired she felt. She would only remember how young they all were, and what a beautiful day it was, out on the Sound.

"You have a lovely family," she told the woman.

"Thanks. It's our first summer vacation together. We just got married." She gestured at the boys. "Blended family—his, mine and ours."

Love was hard work, Kate thought. And it was so worth it, as Aaron would say.

"How about a picture of the two of you?" the woman asked. "You're such a cute couple."

A couple, thought Kate. We're a couple. A cute couple. "I don't have a camera with me," she said.

"I'll e-mail you." The woman held out the camera. "Come on, smile!"

Kate could feel JD stiffen and pull back. She felt suddenly awkward, like a fraud. She didn't belong with this man, had no claim on him. Still, the woman seemed so eager that Kate went along with it. She tucked her arm around his and then impulsively rose on tiptoe, took off his dark glasses and placed a shy kiss on his cheek.

She was struck by his tense and frowning face. "Pretend you like me," she whispered in his ear.

He cracked a smile then, chuckled a little. Kate hoped the camera caught that.

Afterward, she gave the woman her e-mail address. As the young mother put away the camera, she looked at JD, did a double take. "Have we met? You look familiar."

"No, ma'am," he said. "Thanks again." With a politely dismissive smile, he turned away to look at the scenery. The toddler started whining again, and the woman wheeled the stroller away. Kate wondered how JD felt about kids, if he wanted a family of his own. And that led her to wonder about the family he'd come from. Who were they and what were they like? Did he miss them? Had he told them about her?

"What are you looking at?" he asked, and she realized he'd caught her staring, with all her dreams in her eyes.

Slipping her arm around his waist, she smiled up at him. "You. I can't believe I found you," she said, her heart spilling over with happiness.

"I didn't know you were looking."

"Very funny. You know what I mean."

"Yeah," he said, "I do."

Ask him, she urged herself. It's time. She took a deep breath, felt the summer breeze lift her hair. "What's going to happen?" she asked him. "I mean, once summer's over," she added, cringing inside at how pathetic she sounded. She wasn't needy, she reminded herself. She had been without JD for twenty-nine years and she had a wonderful life. She could do without him again.

"What's funny?" he asked her, and she realized she had laughed aloud.

"In the time it's taking you to think up an answer to that question, I've already had an entire love affair and breakup with you."

"Yeah? How'd we do?"

"We were fabulous together. The breakup was horrible, but we survived, a little worse for wear."

"Good to know."

"You still haven't answered my question."

"I was hoping you wouldn't notice that."

"Why don't you want to talk about this?"

He took a deep breath, linked his arms loosely about her waist. His gaze darted around the deck, taking in the seagulls flying alongside the boat like a military escort, the dozens of cameras snapping away. "I do want to talk about it, Kate. There are things I need to explain—"

"What things?" A host of possibilities rafted through her mind—he was married, he had a disease, he'd changed his mind about her . . .

"It's kind of a long story," he said. "Let me take you to dinner tonight. Pick your favorite restaurant in all of Seattle, and I'll take you there."

Now possibilities blossomed in her head—an evening

of romance, a confession of undying love, a proposal on bended knee . . .

"Mom!" Aaron burst from the stairwell. "Hey, Mom, guess what?"

They separated quickly and Kate offered a rueful smile. "Hazards of the dating parent," she said, slipping into her mom persona as she turned to Aaron. "What is it, buddy?"

"You won't believe who's on the boat," he said. "You totally won't believe it."

Callie joined them, a little breathless. "It's no big deal, kid."

"Is too." Aaron grabbed Kate's hand, pulled her along the deck. "You come, too, JD. Come and see." He led them past the boat's huge painted steam vents and offered a grand gesture. *"Eyewitness News!"* he declared.

A small knot of people gathered at a safe distance from the reporter, cameramen and crew. It was not unusual to encounter a local or even a national news crew on the ferry. It was one of those settings that defined Seattle. The ferries had been in the news lately, too. Considered potential targets of terror attacks, they were now patrolled by Homeland Security agents and bomb-sniffing dogs. She recognized Melinda Procter of the local news, microphone in hand, taping some broadcast while an assistant kept trying to lacquer her hair in place with a coating of heavy-duty spray.

She glanced at JD and was completely taken aback by the expression on his face. Instead of being impressed by the sight, he looked . . . guilty.

I'm the world's worst journalist, she thought.

The news crew seemed to be doing another take on their taping, this time with the reporter talking into the camera as she strolled along the railing. Aaron and Callie, along with a trail of other passengers, found it all fascinating.

Then, as she tried to figure out a way to ask JD some hard questions, someone screamed. At first, Kate thought it was the cry of a seagull, but then she recognized a woman's frightened voice.

The news crew was drawn to a commotion at the rear. Kate grabbed JD's arm. "What's going on?"

"I don't know. We'll be getting to the dock any minute. Let's go back to the car."

"Don't you want to check it out?"

"Couldn't be less interested." He headed for the stairway that led down to the car deck.

"Well," said Kate under her breath, "speak for yourself." She broke away and joined the crowd, grabbing Aaron by the hand. "Hold on there," she said. "Where's Callie?"

"I dunno." Aaron climbed up on a green-painted bench to get a better look. "Check it out, Mom. This guy's sick or something."

She stepped up next to Aaron. The portly businessman she'd noticed earlier lay on the deck, his face ashen. He didn't appear to be breathing.

Kate yelled to JD at the same moment as an announcement over the ferry's PA system, requesting the assistance of a doctor. JD was already at the stairway when she called to him. He didn't hesitate to return, but the look on his face was one of pure reluctance.

It was Callie who carved a path for him through the crowd. "Move," she ordered in a voice that unexpectedly rang with authority. "This guy's a paramedic."

That proved to be the magic word. The crowd, with the exception of an aggressive cameraman, melted away, leaving a circle around the fallen man.

"What happened?" JD asked, breaking into action. "Did anybody see what happened?" As he spoke, he took off his dark glasses and dropped to his knees. It was a persona Kate had glimpsed before, the night of Callie's emergency—confident, sure of himself and in control of the situation. She found it both thrilling and comforting at once.

"Is there a defibrillator on this boat?" he asked. Without waiting for an answer, he undid the man's tie and shirt, baring a barrel-shaped chest sprinkled with salt-and-pepper hair.

"He just collapsed," said one of the tattooed teenagers. "He was on his phone, and then he keeled over."

"What's his name?"

"I don't know. I think he's by himself."

Aaron stood on tiptoe and craned his neck. Kate grabbed his hand but didn't take her eyes off JD. No one did. The whole boat, including the TV news crew, was spellbound. She had never seen skin quite that shade before. It was the color of cold ash.

"Is the guy dead?" Aaron asked.

"JD's working on him," she said.

The answer on the defibrillator came back negative. JD had probably expected that. He was already at work administering CPR. A crew member showed up with a big red box. JD pulled a stethoscope from it and went back to work.

A peculiar energy zipped through the crowd as the emergency unfolded. There was a sense of breath-held tension and a collective spirit that seemed to be willing JD to save the man. Several dozen cell phones were already out as bystanders called 911. The *Eyewitness News* cameras kept rolling. JD didn't look up, didn't break his concentration as he kept working.

Kate heard the ferry's engines kick in as the boat sped up. Even before it reached the dock, she could see the lights of emergency vehicles flashing onshore. Fortunately for the victim, there was a fully equipped fire station located right at Colman dock, where the ferry would pull in.

JD didn't let up, not for a single second. Kate noticed something peculiar about the observers gathered around. Incredibly, some of the onlookers took pictures. She couldn't believe her eyes. It was in unbelievably poor taste. What was wrong with these people?

She kept hold of Aaron's hand. She didn't see where Callie had gone, though she doubted the girl would stray far from the action. As the ferry arrived, announcements blared over the PA system. Drivers and passengers were requested to keep all stairways and exits clear. Docking the boat seemed to take forever.

By the time a team of EMTs arrived, mass hysteria had taken hold. Covered in sweat, his chest heaving, JD stepped back to let the EMTs take over while he filled them in on what had happened. There was too much noise to hear the words exchanged. But the outcome was clear when two of the rescue workers got to work strapping the man to a backboard.

The third rescue worker exchanged a few more words with JD, then shook his hand. With the paddles ready, the emergency crew whisked the man to the waiting freight elevator.

One of the news-crew cameras went along with them. Kate expected the crowd and the rest of the crew to follow. Instead, the strangest thing happened.

JD got mobbed.

That was the only way she could think of it. People pressed in on him, clamoring for attention; cameras were aimed at him from all directions. Shouts of "Sergeant Harris" filled the air. He seemed to be drowning in a sea of people.

"What's going on?" Aaron tugged at her hand.

She didn't reply, but stepped down from the bench and tried to get to JD. The crush of the crowd was intimidating. She was not the type to go crashing through a mob. She circled the mass of people, looking for a way in. She nearly tripped over the news crew's power cords. She could hear the reporter saying: ". . . live breaking news from the MV

Wenatchee. Just moments ago, Sergeant Jordan Donovan Harris stepped in to save yet another life . . ."

Thoroughly confused, Kate called out to JD but she doubted he could hear her. She passed the woman with the stroller and all the kids, who said, "You know, I thought I recognized him. He looks totally different as a civilian."

Kate felt as though she was losing her mind. Why was everyone calling him Sergeant Harris, as if he was— She froze, still clutching Aaron's hand.

Sergeant Harris. Sergeant Jordan Donovan Harris.

Kate felt herself go numb, as if someone had given her a shot of Novocain.

What if he wasn't the person she thought he was? She had accepted without question that he was a friend of the Schroeders. That he was on hiatus from his job as EMT on the East Coast and that he intended to go to medical school. She had not doubted any of his claims, not for a single moment.

"Mom, are we going back to the car or what?" Aaron asked.

Callie showed up from somewhere. In one glance, Kate understood that the girl knew exactly what was going on.

Finally, after what seemed like hours, he somehow managed to break free. The reporter trotted along beside him, peppering him with questions. Onlookers thrust pens and scraps of paper at him, begging for autographs. He ignored the requests, shaking them off. The man who walked toward Kate, his eyes dark with determination and anger, looked exactly like JD. But everything was different now. He wasn't JD. He had never been JD.

What do you know? she thought, still insulated by the numbness of shock. *I've been sleeping with America's hero.* She'd been with him all summer long as he hid in plain sight. She'd never questioned his skills, not just as a paramedic, but his knowledge of orienteering, engineering, his ability to speak perfect French. All top-level Special Forces medics had to have those skills, but she had simply accepted him at face value.

Now she found herself in a surreal situation. The man walking toward her was Sergeant Jordan Donovan Harris, hero to a nation, complete stranger to Kate.

Thirty-Three

Of all the luck, JD thought in disgust as he headed down to the car deck, an unwilling Pied Piper followed by an instant fan club. Short of diving over the side, there was no way to elude the crowd or the probing lens of the camera. They followed him en masse to Kate's Jeep. A barrage of shouted questions rained down on him. Even after the four of them reached the Jeep and got in, people wouldn't leave them alone.

"Lock the doors," he ordered Kate.

"What—"

"Just lock the damn doors," he repeated.

She wasn't quick enough. Somebody opened the rear door beside Aaron.

"Sergeant Harris," someone yelled.

He twisted around and slammed the door shut. This time, Kate hit the lock button. The dog was in a frenzy, barking his head off at the curiosity seekers. It was excruciating, sitting there trapped like a fish in a bowl, waiting for the ferry to empty out while people swarmed the vehicle.

When the line of cars finally started to move, Kate glared straight ahead at the exit ramp and said, "Why didn't you tell me?"

Even the ferry workers, who were supposed to be directing traffic, waved wildly at the Jeep as it passed.

"That's why," he said grimly.

"It's so cool that you're him," Aaron said. "We read an article about him—about you—in *Weekly Reader*." He bounced up and down in his seat.

Callie rested a hand on his shoulder. "Chill, kid, okay? Put on your seat belt."

Aaron stopped bouncing. "Yeah, whatever," he said, imitating Callie's bored tone.

"Someone will probably try to follow you," he said to Kate. "You might want to take an indirect route."

"This is crazy."

He didn't reply.

"These people are crazy," she added. "I'm not going to be intimidated by them."

Great, he thought. Early on, he used to feel that

way—defiant, unwilling to compromise his personal liberty. It hadn't taken long to discover the reality, though. Defiance never worked with a mob.

As they left the ferry and headed up an elevated ramp, a black SUV closed in on them.

"Oh, Lord," Kate said, checking the rearview mirror, "I take that back. I *am* intimidated."

"I'm sorry about this, Kate."

"I'll just bet you are," she murmured.

He understood her anger, her sense of betrayal. He would do his best to explain, but his situation was so bizarre, he wasn't sure he could make her understand.

"Hey, JD," Aaron said. "Do I still call you JD?"

"Sure," he said. "That's what my friends have always called me."

"So that guy tried to blow up the President, right?" Aaron said. "I can't believe you were there. What happened to the guy, huh? Was he a terrorist? Did you blow him away?"

"He wasn't . . . no. He was a confused, stupid guy who wanted attention."

"And instead, you stopped him," Aaron said. "That's cool."

Inevitably, Kate noticed Callie's uncharacteristic silence. She flicked a glance in the rearview mirror. "Did you know about this?"

"Yes," Callie said in a quiet, confessional voice. She was obviously relieved to get it off her chest.

Kate's hands tightened on the steering wheel. "You told her and not me?" she asked JD.

"I figured it out on my own," Callie said in exasperation. "Jeez."

"It would have been totally cool if I'd known," Aaron said. "You should have told us."

JD felt a familiar creeping exhaustion, the dull surrender that had driven him underground and made him want to lose himself in anonymity. He thought of a dozen things to say, none of them adequate, so he said nothing. The dispute stayed open, hanging over them like a thundercloud as Kate drove across the twisted arch of the West Seattle Bridge and down into a neighborhood of cozy, pastel-painted houses and streets lined with too many parked cars.

He checked the side-view mirror out the window. He was fairly sure they hadn't been tailed, but that hardly mattered. Kate's address could be traced in a matter of minutes by anyone who had jotted down the tag number of the Jeep.

Everything had shifted by the time Kate turned down a quiet, bluff-top cul-de-sac lined with big-leaf maples. This was Callie's homecoming, JD reminded himself. Regardless of what had happened on the ferry, they had to shift gears and put Callie first. He hated that his notoriety had taken the focus off of her, but fame had a nasty way of doing that. Kate seemed as determined as he to regroup. Without even having to discuss the matter, they put aside the drama on the ferry and shared a common goal—to make Callie feel good about her new foster home.

As soon as he saw Kate's house, JD knew he needn't have worried. Just like the lakeside cottage, this house resembled something out of a storybook, a neat clapboard bungalow with a white picket fence and latticework up the sides entwined with roses. It was one of four houses on the cul-de-sac. The others were equally charming, and across the way, a neighbor came out and waved, welcoming Kate home.

Callie took it all in with shining eyes, this new world that was to be hers. There was such needy hunger in her gaze that JD wanted to caution her not to get too caught up in all this. He knew something about the unattainable, the futility of hope and the way it hardened into disappointment. But he knew his life experience would fall on deaf ears when Aaron grabbed Callie's hand and ran to the house, eager to show Callie his world.

"Hurry up, Mom," he said. The dog jumped up and scratched at the door.

Kate unlocked the house and let Aaron burst inside, bringing Callie along with him. Filled with nervous energy, Kate went around opening windows to let in the late-summer breeze, passing through rooms filled with framed family pictures, books, all the comforts of a well-kept house. "Do you think Callie will like it here?" She caught the look on his face. "What?"

"You live in a Disney movie, Kate. What's not to like?"

"He's right," Callie said, coming into the room.

JD winced, wishing she hadn't overheard.

She didn't seem offended, though. At the moment,

she simply looked wide-eyed and full of hope. He felt a wave of admiration for this kid. Even after all she'd been through, she held on to hope.

"It's great," Callie said. "Totally fly."

"Really? It's fly?" asked Kate. Her face lit up, and JD felt a physical pang of love.

"Totally." Callie shuffled her feet. Suddenly she looked her age, young and awkward. "Um, I've been meaning to tell you guys something. Now that you're here together, I feel like I should speak up."

Kate's smile faded to worry. "Is everything all right?"

"Yeah, sure. That's the thing. See, what happened this summer, my getting sick and all, well, at first it was like the disaster of the century. I figured my life was pretty much over, that everything was going to basically suck from here on out."

"Callie—" Kate stepped forward but then stopped as though afraid of what would come next. JD wanted to reassure her, but he knew Callie's next words would do that.

"Anyway," she said, "it didn't turn out that way at all. I won't kid you and say I'm glad I got sick. The truth is, I hate having this disease. I hate having to monitor myself, and eat on a stupid schedule. I hate not having sugar and not being able to eat like a regular kid. I hate aerobic exercise and lifting." She paused, because her voice cracked. A pained expression shadowed her face as she swallowed. "But here's the thing. If all that hadn't happened, I wouldn't have you."

JD knew how hard it was for her to say these things. And how necessary. He suspected Kate and Aaron had given her the same things they'd given him—the sense of what it was like to be a member of a family and a vision that life could be better.

Callie took a deep, unsteady breath. "Anyway, that's what I wanted to say. That, and . . . thank you. And don't get all teary-eyed on me, or it'll just be weird."

"Deal with it, then," Kate said, teary-eyed as she pulled her into a hug. "Ah, Callie. Remember what we talked about? It's never too late to have a happy child-hood."

Though meant for the girl, the words struck JD hard. Yes, he thought. *Yes.*

Aaron, who had been watching from the doorway, looked a little queasy. "Can we go outside?" he asked.

"I'll go with you in a sec." Callie stood back and dried her face. She hugged JD, though they both felt a little ill at ease. "My medical bills were paid by your foundation, weren't they?"

"That's what it's for." He expected nothing in return from her, but she gave it anyway. A look of gratitude came from her heart, springing up like a flower, lighting her face.

"It doesn't matter to me, all that stuff about you being America's hero. You're my hero." She went up on tiptoe to kiss his cheek, then stepped back. "And now I'd better go hang out with Aaron before someone else goes into a diabetic coma from all this sweetness."

Kate burst into soggy laughter and reached for a

Kleenex. After Callie and Aaron were gone, she said, "You have a foundation."

"Yes."

"Darn it, JD, don't you understand that I won't tolerate this anymore? I don't want any more evasive one-word replies from you."

"That wasn't evasive. It was straightforward. I said yes, I have a foundation."

"Now you're being a jerk, willfully."

"What do you want from me?" he demanded.

"Answers," she said. "Explanations. Oh, here's a concept. How about the truth? Or don't I deserve that?"

"What you deserve, Kate, is so much more than I can give you." The admission had the bitter taste of truth. There was a cost to the way he had grown up, raising himself without a safety net, and this was it. He simply did not know how to be what a woman like Kate needed, what she deserved.

"Why on earth would you say something like that?"

"Because it's true. I don't know how to be anything but a medic. If you're looking for husband material, you won't find it here." The words came out on a wave of panic and uncertainty. He could see the truth hit her like a blow. God, she didn't get it. How could he explain that he had no idea how a man turned himself into a husband, a father? That he would rather walk away now than hurt her and Aaron? "What happened today on the ferry . . . it means I need to go away for a while longer. I don't know what else to do. I just know I can't live like that."

She wrapped her arms around her midsection and stepped back. "That's why you were so horrible to me about Callie's article." Hurt drained her face of color. "You thought I would go public with you. You didn't trust me. That's why you didn't tell me."

"I didn't tell anyone. I was sick of myself. Sick of being this media creation."

"You could've trusted me."

"I didn't trust anybody."

"But you had no trouble sleeping with me," she said.

A terrible silence stretched out between them. He had the sensation of watching a wreck in slow motion, with the sound turned down. He had damaged them beyond repair, destroyed them. What lay between them was unsalvageable. And it was, he realized bleakly, just as well for her, though she didn't realize that yet. "Kate," he said, trying to offer the explanation she deserved, "I can't be what you need me to be."

"How do you know what I need?"

He gestured at the perfect house, the *Pleasantville* neighborhood visible through the picture window in the front. "My life is crazy. I have no idea where I'll end up."

"You act like there's no way to deal with fame," she said. "People do it every day. Look at Tiger Woods or John McCain—"

"There's a big difference between them and me," he said. "They asked for their fame and recognition. They worked for it and strove for it. I never wanted any of this, and I promise you, Kate, you don't want it, either."

"There is only one reason you're saying these things," she said. "You're scared."

He felt her anger dart into him. He hated this, and he hated the old pain and shame of what his mother was. He needed to get out of here before the media figured out where he'd gone. Maybe there was still a chance Kate could stay anonymous. "I'll call for a taxi. I can catch a flight to L.A. today rather than waiting until morning."

"Just like that?" she asked in a low, pained voice.

"I'll go standby," he said, then realized what she was asking. Didn't he want to stay and fight for her? Hell, yes, he did. But what he wanted mattered less than doing the right thing. "I need to talk to Aaron and Callie, and then it'll be time to go."

They stood on opposite sides of an unbridgeable gap. He found himself thinking about the day she'd ripped a fishhook out of his thumb. Be quick and I'll survive, he'd said. She wore the same expression now. A few seconds ticked by. Then he went to find the kids.

"You said you'd never leave me." Aaron threw the baseball hard. Lacking a glove, JD caught it bare-handed. The leather stung his palm to the bone.

"I meant in the woods that day," he said, tossing the ball back. Playing a game of catch in the front yard was the only way he could get Aaron to listen. The taxi would be here any minute to take him to the airport and he was running out of time. "I'd never leave you alone in the woods."

"Big deal. That's no kind of promise. Anybody would say that to a kid." He drilled the ball back at JD. Bandit watched with bright-eyed intensity, ready to pounce if the ball came his way.

"Poor choice of words," JD admitted, making the catch and then flexing his fingers. The kid had some arm. He knew he'd carry the ache of this game of catch around for days. "I should have explained that."

"It's dumb that you're just taking off."

Probably, thought JD as he threw the ball back. Aaron missed the catch, and the baseball went bouncing along the edge of the fence, both the boy and the dog in hot pursuit.

A green-and-white taxi pulled up to the curb. Aaron straightened up and the beagle trotted off with the baseball. Aaron turned to JD, keeping his eyes steady as he called out, "Mom, he's leaving."

Kate and Callie came outside, and JD found himself wishing he knew of a way to stay.

"Take this," Callie said, handing him a thick envelope. "Some reading for the plane."

Kate looked at her and frowned, but said nothing. Finally, she told JD, "Have a safe trip."

They were beautiful to him, all three of them. They were his family this summer, as close as he'd had to the real thing. At the lake they'd been safe from harm, but here in the world he couldn't protect them from the paparazzi and prying questions they'd face if he stuck around.

"When are you coming back?" Aaron asked.

"I don't know." He briefly hugged each one of them, encountering stiff resistance. It felt awkward. Hell, it was awkward. And even though he said he didn't know, he did.

Thirty-Four

"You shouldn't have let him go," Callie said, coming into Kate's study in her nightgown.

It was late, and Aaron was asleep, but apparently Callie was as sleepless as Kate. "It wasn't up to me. He left," she said.

"You could have stopped him."

"And then what?"

"Then you'd be together."

"I can't see that happening."

"Why not?"

"I could make you a list of reasons, but only one really matters. He doesn't want to be with me. Maybe he doesn't want to be with anyone, I don't know."

"That's bull. He is so in love with you, he can't even see straight."

Kate felt a twist of yearning but covered it up. "Very funny, Miss Know-it-all."

"I know more than you do about his life."

Kate imagined him telling Callie the truth about himself. They'd undoubtedly had long, searching talks, leaving Kate out of the loop. At the thought of that, she felt something ugly—envy. He'd shared things with Callie and kept the wool pulled over Kate's eyes.

"Well?" Callie asked, sitting in a swivel chair by the desk, "Aren't you curious?"

"I suppose if he wanted me to have that information, he would have told me."

"Get off it, Kate. These things are not secrets." She leaned forward conspiratorially, drew her knee up to her chest. "I bet you don't know why he went into the service."

"I don't." Of course she didn't. It was one of the million things he hadn't bothered to tell her.

"See, he had this horrible mother—worse than mine, even—and all his life he worked just to survive. He took every odd job he could get his hands on. That's why he's so good at fixing things. He saved up as much as he could, and he was going to use it for college. Then his loser mom had to go into rehab, and that used up every penny he'd saved. So he went into the service instead."

Callie had known all this while Kate had been in the dark. Here she was, sleeping with the guy, and he couldn't even level with her. Yet he'd told Callie his life story.

Despite the deep resentment she felt, Kate couldn't help imagining the sort of life Callie described. Before meeting Callie and writing her story, she couldn't have done it, could not have conceived of a mother putting her child aside for a selfish purpose, and the effect that had on the child. Now she was starting to get it. Starting to understand. With a background like that, JD didn't know how a family worked. Like Callie, he didn't think he knew how to get it right. But he wasn't stupid, she thought. He could learn these things.

"You're mad," Callie observed, studying Kate's face.

"Not at you. He should've told me this himself," Kate said.

Callie scowled. "Yeah, right. You think it's fun to admit this stuff? The only reason he told me is that I was going off the deep end. I needed to hear that a person can survive a rotten mother. You didn't."

Kate managed a thin smile. Deep down, though, she felt shattered. He'd given up on them so easily, she thought. And then it hit her—so had she.

Callie looked over Kate's shoulder at the computer screen. "Is that an Internet connection?" Callie said.

Kate touched the keyboard to light up the screen. Several browser windows were open. "I was reading up on Jordan Donovan Harris. Check this out." She clicked on a photo to enlarge it.

Callie found a chair and scooted closer. "God, he was so . . ."

Hot, thought Kate. That would be the word for it. Her wonder grew as she gazed at picture after picture on the Internet. They even found and watched a video clip of the event that had skyrocketed him to fame.

"So when did you figure it out?" she asked Callie. They gazed at a shot of him in fatigues, a much younger JD with his arm slung around Sam Schroeder. In the background, a place identified as Konar Province loomed like an inhospitable moonscape.

"The first time I went over to work at his place. I came across some celebrity magazine and made the connection. He didn't even try to deny it. Told me everything right away."

"Why didn't you tell me?"

"I promised I wouldn't. I gave him my word."

And, of course, it wasn't up to Callie to inform Kate that the man she loved was hiding his identity from her. That was JD's job, and he hadn't done it.

She clenched her teeth and continued browsing through the information. Last Christmas Eve, a shocked nation had been informed that the Terror Alert had shot up to red, the highest possible category. The video loop was all over the nightly news, of course, and still photos were blazoned across the front pages of national newspapers. The incident had been meticulously analyzed, frame by frame, by various experts.

Eventually, when the motive behind the attack was discovered, the national sense of terror changed to a peculiar queasy sadness. The attacker was no foreign threat but one of their own. Terence Lee Muldoon was a football all-American in high school. He came from an impoverished family. Assured of a generous enlistment bonus, he had joined the military and received the U.S. Army's most rigorous, extensive training to turn him into a member of a super-elite top-secret commando.

He should have had a long and distinguished career, defending the defenseless around the world. Instead, he fell victim to one of the Pentagon's most cruel loopholes.

Just a few months shy of his thirty-six-month obligation, Muldoon had been wounded while on assignment in the Middle East, losing a kidney in a vehicle accident, which rendered him permanently disabled. Even as he lay recovering from surgery, he had been informed that, because he'd failed to fulfill the terms of his enlistment, he would have to repay his bonus. His name had already been submitted to a collection agency.

Anyone could understand his fury. But no one could have predicted what he would do about it.

With spectacularly convoluted logic, Muldoon decided that his predicament was the fault of the President of the United States. A top-level operative, Muldoon planned his attack, intending to annihilate the Commander-in-Chief, a wing of the hospital and himself in a matter of seconds.

According to a special report in the *Washington Post*, he had no trouble getting the deadly plastic explosives by using falsified ordnance procurement papers.

"Narcissistic personality disorder" was what the expert analysts said of his utter confidence in arranging his own transport to Walter Reed on Christmas Eve. His timing was perfect, because, it was later discovered, he had gained access to the schedule and route of the President of the United States. Muldoon had made just one single miscalculation. There was something he had chosen to overlook about Walter Reed Army Medical Center. And that was that people like Jordan Donovan Harris worked there, military personnel as highly trained and dangerous as Muldoon himself.

As she and Callie browsed through the media reports and Web logs, it became clear to Kate why this incident had so captivated the nation. There were no ambiguities here, no mistakes or cover-ups, just a rogue soldier, a medic doing his job and a good outcome. Ultimately, the only blood spilled came from Muldoon and JD, and both men survived their wounds.

People loved it. They loved the pure drama of good triumphing over evil. And when the facts became known, they loved JD even more. His was the rags-to-riches story of American success. Raised in the Baltimore projects by a hardworking single mother—a detail that made Callie grumble with skepticism—he had a distinguished career in the U.S. Army as a medic for the Green Berets. This meant he had all the skills of a Green Beret with something more, something that meant the difference between success and failure for his unit—the ability to save lives.

Overnight, the breathless media dubbed him the perfect American hero. Skilled, strong, smart, self-sacrificing and modest. And above all, in the right place at the right time. Across the nation, people subdued their Christmas celebrations, some even observing a moment of silence to pray for the recovery of Sergeant Harris. Some to this day believed the power of prayer had saved him, enabling him to wake from a coma and rise from his hospital bed. Others credited the Herculean efforts of a peerless surgical staff.

"If you're going to throw yourself on top of a suicide bomber," a hospital spokesman said in an interview, "you could pick no better place to do that than Walter Reed."

"Where do these people come from?" Kate murmured.

"Keep reading," Callie said. While Harris lay in a medically induced coma, the nation sat vigil. Churches and temples across the nation posted words of support and encouragement on their marquees: "God Bless Jordan Donovan." Yellow ribbons took the place of Christmas ornaments and New Year's spangles. Kate recalled reading a feature in the paper and feeling profoundly thankful that there were men like this in the world.

She was still thankful. Privileged, even, that she knew him. Yet at the same time filled with an ache of sadness. The very fact that he was a hero had become the wedge that drove them apart.

"It's weird, seeing all this stuff," Callie said. "It's about him, but it's not him."

"In the press, you get an impression of the person. Not the person himself." Kate knew then that it didn't matter what she had written about Callie. Readers of the article would never know this girl, not really. Maybe that was what JD had been trying to tell her.

"I'm tired," said Callie. "I'm going to bed. You should keep reading, though. Read about what happened to his mother. Then you'll see why he didn't want anyone to know who he was."

Callie went to bed, but Kate was still restless, reading a seemingly endless variety of material about him. Jealousy burned in her gut as she read that he'd had a girlfriend named Tina, a congressional aide who disclosed everything from his affinity for blue crab to his sexual appetites, and whose dating book became a hot seller. I hope he dropped you fast and hard, Kate thought. And sure enough, just like Callie said, she learned that he'd survived a nightmare childhood with a woman who hadn't been any sort of mother at all. Janet Harris had embraced the spoils of her son's fame, but then it had been her downfall. She'd slid back into her old habits and, according to more than one recent report, she had checked into a clinic in Southern California.

Kate's e-mail flag popped up. The message was from an unfamiliar sender, yet as soon as she saw the photo, she remembered. It felt like a lifetime ago that she and JD had ridden the ferry like any young lovers, posing while a stranger had snapped their picture. Now that she understood what he'd been hiding, she recognized the tension in his face, his discomfort in front of the camera.

"It was a privilege to meet you and Jordan," the woman had written.

True, thought Kate. It was. Before she met JD, she thought she knew what loneliness felt like. Now she realized she hadn't a clue.

Thirty-Five

At 5:45 a.m., the phone began to shrill in Kate's ear. Spoiled by the low-tech solitude of the lake, she practically fell out of bed as she reached for the receiver, bidding goodbye to a perfectly good dream.

"Sorry to wake you," said her sister-in-law, Barbara, calling from the East Coast. "I thought you might want to know that you're on *Good Morning America*."

Kate sat straight up in bed, the last vestiges of sleep doused by mortification. "What?"

"*GMA*. I'm sure it'll air out there, too. Go find a TV and check it out."

"What on earth—"

"So is he there now?"

"Is who . . ." Finally Kate's head cleared. "You mean JD."

"Is that what you call him? God, Kate, how long have you been together?"

Not long enough. "Tell me what you saw."

"First, it was all about the guy—Sergeant Harris. There was a clip from Seattle showing him doing CPR. Then some stuff about how he disappeared from the public eye for a few months. Tabloids said he was taping a reality show. That he's the next 'Bachelor' and you're the one he picked."

The thought of a TV bachelor show made Kate shudder. "He was at the lake," she explained. "He was using the Schroeders' cabin."

"Incredible. Kate, I can't believe you didn't tell us."

I can't believe he didn't tell me. She couldn't bring herself to admit that she'd been duped by him. It was no family secret that she was unlucky in love, but this went beyond unlucky. This just made her look . . . dense.

In the background, sounds of Barbara's family could be heard—running feet, children's voices, laughter. Barbara covered the receiver to tell them to pipe down. With four kids, an uninterrupted phone conversation simply didn't happen.

"So on the news, they showed him getting in the car with you," Barbara said. "How cool is that?"

"Must be a slow news day." Kate shoved her feet into a pair of scuffs and put on her terry-cloth robe, which had seen better days but was still comfortable. She gave Barb the briefest, simplest version of events she could summon before having her first cup of coffee. As she spoke, she shuffled downstairs and put on the pot.

"So what's he like?"

Gone, Kate thought. That's what he's like. She knew she wouldn't be able to get that out without falling apart. "Quiet," she said, sifting through memories of him. From the first moment she laid eyes on him, he had shown her exactly who he was. She just hadn't picked up on it. He was a rescuer, whether that meant bailing a stranger out at the grocery store, befriending a troubled little boy, making love to a lonely woman or saving someone's life. At least he hadn't been able to hide his authentic self completely. But he'd hidden enough to fool her.

That, of course, was the operative word—fool. He'd made a fool of her.

And oh, she had loved every minute of it.

"Nitwit," she muttered.

"What's that?" Barb asked.

"Nothing," said Kate. She'd practically forgotten she

404

was still on the phone. "Just thinking aloud."

"Well, I can't wait to meet him," Barb declared. "He just seems too good to be true."

"Oh, he is that." It was too early in the morning to explain the whole summer. She felt raw and confused, far from ready to discuss this with anyone. "Listen, do you suppose I could call you back later?"

After they said goodbye, Kate busied herself with mundane things—putting away the dishes, filling the dog's bowl with fresh water, taking out last night's trash. She tried to focus on getting things done today—making the final arrangements for Callie, getting her registered for school and driver's ed. The end of summer was closing in fast. After that, all that remained was to return to the lakeside cottage and close it up for the season.

Later, Aaron and Bandit came downstairs to troll for breakfast. "Morning," he mumbled. He seemed pale to her, and subdued. He looked like the shy, unhappy boy he'd been at the beginning of summer.

"Hey, kiddo," she said, holding the bag of trash. "Get that door for me, will you?"

Aaron pushed open the back door. Bandit shot out first. Though not usually a noisy dog, the beagle immediately started barking.

"Hush, Bandit, you'll wake the neighbors," Kate said, stepping out to the driveway, where the trash cans were kept.

A flash went off in her face. Something—a microphone—jabbed at her and a chorus of questions filled the air, the words running together like a chant in a foreign language. *Miss Livingston or is it Mrs. are you married is that Sergeant Harris's love child how long have you known him did he really leave the service we just have a few questions. . . .*

Kate dropped the sack of garbage. Wet coffee grinds and eggshells sprayed across the asphalt. She clutched Aaron's hand and they froze, pinned by terror like Bambi and his mom in the crosshairs. In a blur of panic, she called desperately for the dog. The flashing cameras recorded her open mouth, her uncombed hair, the frayed bathrobe.

A reporter with big shoulders and a tape recorder broke free of the pack. "Give us a break, hon. This is our living here," he said.

"You've made a big mistake," she managed to say. "There's no story here. There's nothing at all."

"Bullshit," the guy said. "Everybody's got a story."

She winced at his language, moved closer to Aaron. "Maybe. But mine's not anything people would want to read. Go away. Go hunt down an actual celebrity and let me get back to my life." Fortunately, Bandit returned on command. She ducked inside, yanking Aaron along with her. After she slammed the door shut, she leaned against it, breathing hard.

"Are you all right?" she asked Aaron.

"Are you kidding?" He grinned and went to peer out the window. "That was awesome."

Kate looked at the phone on the table and contemplated calling 911. Ultimately, though, she simply closed all the drapes and made Aaron stay inside until it was time for their meeting at CPS to submit the final papers for Callie and register her at school. Kate was jumpy, taking a circuitous route on their errands and glancing in the rearview mirror every few seconds to see if they were being followed.

The early-morning ambush in front of her house had been but a taste of what JD had endured for months, she realized. It explained why he had left his life in Washington, D.C., fleeing to escape the public eye. However, it did not explain why he had left her.

"Mom, where's wedlock?" Aaron asked.

"Why do you ask?" She felt distracted. It had been a long week. JD hadn't called. Her heart was on the floor and her life was in turmoil.

"Well, it says in *Star Tracks* that you had me out of there." He turned the paper toward her. "Right here. It says, 'Katherine Livingston had a baby out of wedlock . . .' Does that mean you were locked out of a wedding or something?"

"Give me that." She snatched the paper from him and put it in the trash. "Don't pay attention to any of that stuff," she said.

She was sick to her stomach. This had gotten out of hand and she had no control over it. What a terrible, terrible object lesson, she thought. She had always imagined what it was like to be the reporter chasing the story—exhilarating, sometimes even important. As a fashion writer for a minor paper, she had dreamed of it, aspired to it. Now she knew the vile feeling of seeing herself in a ratty bathrobe in the newspaper's gossip section, clutching the hand of her bewildered-looking son.

Strangers contacted her by phone, by e-mail, by showing up at her house. Most were harmless curiosity seekers, but a few genuinely creeped her out, like the guy asking her to give him a pair of panties. Reporters dug up dirt on her—she'd had a baby out of wedlock. Her grandfather was a sixties radical and she'd been fired from her last job.

Perhaps worst of all was the phone call from Callie's caseworker. An Internet blog speculated that Callie was on drugs, just like Harris's mother. Kate was outraged, but worse than that, powerless. She realized that if she engaged in the debate, people would assume she took the charges seriously. If she ignored them, some would say it was because the charges were true. There were e-mails from her editor, wanting the inside scoop. Kate was ready to tear out her hair. One day, a call came in from Callie's caseworker. She had concerns about placing Callie in Kate's care. She wasn't sure all this media attention would be good for Callie.

"It's not good for anyone," Kate agreed. JD's words came back to haunt her: *I never wanted any of this, and I promise you, Kate, you don't want it, either.*

And in the end, she did exactly what he had done. Chased by a notoriety she did not want, she fled to the lake.

PART FIVE

"The secret of health for both mind and body is not to mourn for the past, worry about the future, or anticipate troubles but to live in the present moment wisely and earnestly."

—Buddha

Thirty-Six

"Last chance to go for a swim," Callie told Aaron. Their final chores at the lakeside cottage were done, pretty much. Kate had gone to town to reroute the mail and do some errands. It meant the world to Callie that Kate trusted her to watch Aaron. At the beginning of summer, she hadn't wanted them to go near the water without her watching. Now that Aaron could swim and Callie was part of the family, Kate had relaxed her vigilance. She treated Callie like . . . a daughter.

Callie and Aaron had worked hard all afternoon. They had hosed down the kayak and stowed it in the boathouse along with the lawn furniture and picnic set. After a championship round of croquet—Callie won, hands down—they put away the equipment for next year. They brought in the flag and folded it like a holy relic, putting it in an ancient department-store box. It was so cool that Kate and Aaron belonged to a family that came back here year after year, Callie thought. The flag was so old, it had only forty-eight stars.

They cleared out every scrap of food so the local raccoons and field mice would not be tempted to break in. Now there was nothing left to do except wait for Kate to bring home their farewell dinner in disposable containers. In the morning, they'd turn off the water to drain the pipes so they wouldn't freeze in winter, and then they were out of here.

Callie couldn't help smiling at Aaron's tragic expression. "Hey, it's not the end of the world, kid. Just the end of summer." She didn't try to explain further, and honestly, felt none of his despondency. She was not one of those to get all sentimental over the passing of the season. In fact, she was looking forward to the start of school. Not that she would ever be dorky enough to admit it. It just felt so good to be doing things a normal kid would do—cleaning her room, listening to music, getting ready for the first day of school. When Kate promised to take her school shopping once they got to the city, Callie felt such a thrill that she had to hide her reaction.

"I'm staying up all night," Aaron vowed.

"Whatever floats your boat." She knew he would never be able to do it. After swimming, supper and a few rounds of cards, he'd be falling asleep on his feet. That was something she loved about Aaron. He was totally predictable, like a little machine—eat, play, talk, sleep in a never-ending cycle.

"Race you to the water!" Still tying the drawstring of his trunks, Aaron ran across the yard to the dock.

Callie took off after him, reveling in her newfound feeling of agility. Thirty pounds ago, she barely had enough energy to walk, let alone run. She wore a black tankini and she looked . . . okay. Kelly Osbourne–okay, maybe.

She caught up with Aaron and grabbed his hand just as they both went off the end of the dock. Together, they made a huge splash and came up laughing. As always, the water was numbingly cold, yet at the same time, gloriously clean. She felt weightless and sleek, darting around with Aaron, occasionally diving deep to see if she could reach the bottom. She never could, of course. The lake's dark, endless depth was part of its mystery.

Popping to the surface, she kept an eye on Aaron, even though he needed supervision less and less each time he swam. Once he got over being afraid of the water, he grew stronger every day.

"What are you looking at?" he asked her.

"A kid who swims like an otter." Treading water, she relished the expression on his face. Then she told him something she had never said before, though she had thought it. "I'm proud of you."

"Hey, me, too," he said. "I'm proud of you."

They grinned at each other for a few seconds and then it got all awkward, so she splashed water in his face and he dived for cover. Inevitably, they were overcome by the cold and had to get out. Bandit greeted them like long-lost friends while they toweled off and then lay around on the weathered planks of the dock, letting the sun dry their hair.

After a while, Aaron said, "I feel bad for Mom. She's sad about JD."

"Seems that way," Callie said. "She'll be all right."

"I guess I'm kind of sad, too."

"Well, you wouldn't be human if you weren't sad sometimes, so welcome to the human race."

She enjoyed the feel of the sunlight on her face. What a summer it had been. Begun in despair, it was ending on a note of hope. She had a foster family, a plan for the future. The painful past would always be there, like her insulin resistance would always be there. She could deal with both now, she was sure of it.

A few minutes later, she was startled by the creak of a footfall on the dock and the coolness of a shadow falling over her. She sat up to look, and blinked at the light. Like a bulky, man-shaped eclipse, Luke Newman blotted out the sun as he stood there surrounded by a halo of dazzling light.

"Luke." Aaron scrambled to his feet. "Hey, Luke. Where've you been?"

"Keeping busy."

Instantly self-conscious, Callie got up, too. She was tempted to wrap herself in a towel, but resisted the urge. She was who she was, and didn't intend to hide that from him ever again. "Hey," she said, her voice perfectly neutral.

"Hey, yourself."

"I'm starving," Aaron said with startling diplomacy.

"I'll be inside. C'mon, Bandit."

After he left, a strained silence stretched out between Luke and Callie. Finally, he said, "You look good."

She knew that she did. His eyes were a mirror, reflecting an image that was quite different from the girl he'd first met this summer. "I feel good."

More silence, but the question screamed inside her. What do you want from me? What are you doing back here now?

"That's good," he said. "Listen, Callie . . ." He paused and looked at her as if expecting her to rescue him.

Let him wait, she thought. She was not going to step in and make this easy for him. "Yeah?"

"I want you to know I'm sorry I treated you the way I did. Okay?"

Even though her heart soared, she made herself hold back. "No. It's not okay. You acted as though we were friends—*good* friends—but you kept that a secret from everybody but me." She still cringed when she thought about that day at the shopping center. She'd been so happy to see him, so excited about meeting his friends. She could still feel the icy derision of the other kids, the terrible twist of sarcasm when he'd dismissed her. Finding out he'd kept their friendship a secret had knocked her for a loop. He was ashamed to be seen with a fat weirdo.

"That's my loss," he said now, "and I've got no excuse except I was an ass. You're special, and you always have been. I feel like an asshole for treating you the way I did."

"You were an asshole." She picked up her towel, started to turn away.

"Just hear me out." He put his hand on hers, brought her back around to face him. "I miss you."

His words wrapped around her heart the same way his hand wrapped around hers. "You really mean it?"

"I came to ask you if you want to go bowling tonight. Some of us are meeting at Bowl Me Over later. Can you come?"

Finally, after a whole summer of waiting, he was offering to introduce her to a group of friends. But when she spoke, she said, "I'm going to stick around here tonight. We're leaving in the morning."

He paused, digested the news. She saw a flicker of disappointment in his face. "You sure?"

"I'm sure." She couldn't keep from smiling when she added, "I'm going to live with Kate in Seattle."

"You look happy about that."

"I *am* happy." It felt so weird to be saying that. It felt so weird that, for the first time in forever, it was true.

"I've got news, too," Luke said. "I signed up for the Coast Guard."

She couldn't picture him all shaved and buff and in uniform, but he looked really proud and excited. "Luke, that's so great."

"Yeah, I'm pumped. Anyway, I just wanted to see you, see if you can forgive me."

A light breeze lifted her hair off her shoulders. "Thanks."

"Anyway, basic training starts after Labor Day, and

after that, who knows where I'll end up. I was thinking maybe we could keep in touch by e-mail."

"All right. Yes, we could do that."

"I want you to know I feel bad about what happened. It was all my fault. I was completely stupid about it, so I hope . . ." His voice trailed off and he looked supremely uncomfortable.

"No hard feelings." As the words left her mouth, Callie knew it was true. They were just a couple of kids. They both had a lot to learn.

Thirty-Seven

Kate stopped at the post office to change her delivery back to Seattle. While waiting in line, she watched a couple together, teasing each other with an easy familiarity that brought an unexpected ache to her heart. Love could be so simple one moment and so complicated the next and, too often for Kate, impossible. The couple in line ahead of her magnified her loneliness, and she was horrified to feel the pressure of tears in her throat and eyes.

Get a grip, she warned herself. Hurry. Then the man turned and caught her staring at him. She glanced down at a nonexistent watch, pretending she hadn't been watching him at all. For some reason, the threat of tears wouldn't go away. She slid her change-of-address form across the counter, then headed for the door.

"Kate? Kate Livingston—it's me, Sam Schroeder." The couple now stood at the door as though waiting for her.

From somewhere deep inside, she summoned a smile. Despite the passage of years, he hadn't changed that much. He'd always been a sunny, uncomplicated person and he still looked that way. "My Lord. Sam Schroeder. It's been ages."

He held the door for her and they went outside, standing in front of the post office's garden of prizewinning roses. "I'd like you to meet my wife, Penny. We came out to the lake for Labor Day weekend. It's the first chance I've had to bring her and the kids."

"It's nice to meet you," Kate said, though she had never felt less like meeting someone and making small talk. "You picked the perfect time of year to come."

"Thanks. We love it here already. The boys are never going to get over having to go back and start school. And speaking of the kids," she added, "I'd better go check on them. We'll wait in the car." She hurried across the parking lot, leaving Kate and Sam standing there.

It should have been awkward, knowing that Sam would surely remember their bumbling summer embraces back when they were kids, but it wasn't. So much time had passed that it might have happened to different people, people she didn't know anymore. Rather than feeling awkward, she felt . . . empty. "You have a family," she said.

"I do. And a job and a mortgage, like a real grownup.

Listen, you should come over to our place. Bring your boy—"

"Whoa. Bring my boy?"

"To meet mine. I have two kids."

"How do you know I have a son?" she asked him, feeling suspicion prickle across her skin.

"JD told me," he said easily. "I swear, sometimes it's like pulling teeth to get him to talk, but not when it comes to you and . . . Adam, is it? Aaron?"

Kate's cheeks felt as if they were on fire. "So you and JD . . . you talked about me." It felt weird to be having such a personal conversation with him after such a long time. Or maybe not. Maybe after *Us* magazine published your bra size, nothing was off-limits.

"He's my best friend," Sam told her. "I'll say what I have to say. You mean a lot to him, Kate, and the feeling's mutual, right?"

"Did he tell you that?"

"Nope. The look on your face did."

She remembered something about Sam. Growing up with three older sisters, he had a rare understanding of women and an almost magical ability to read their thoughts. Apparently, that hadn't changed. She clutched her purse securely against her. "We're not . . . we never—" She stopped, horrified to feel a fresh sting of tears.

"I'm sorry," he said. "I can see this is upsetting you."

"It's so stupid to be upset," she said.

"No, it isn't. So did you fall in love with him?"

"I'm leaving now," she said, heading for her car.

417

He walked along with her, refusing to be put off. "Then be in love with him. Quit mooning around."

"I'm not mooning. Does this look like mooning? You don't even know me anymore, Sam. Certainly not well enough to give me advice. It's none of your business, anyway."

"He's my best friend. That makes it my business. Listen, every woman he's ever known has either screwed him over or given up on him. He doesn't really think anything else is possible."

"Maybe it's not."

"You know it is."

Kate rolled her eyes. "Like I'm some expert."

"You are." He smiled at her, and she glimpsed the boy she had known so long ago. "You always have been."

She smiled, hoping he didn't notice how close she was to shattering. Sam, with his adorable wife and kids, seemed to find it easy to give out advice. "Goodbye, Sam," she said quietly.

That night, Kate brought home pizza and salad for dinner. They toasted one another with sparkling water and played one last game of gin rummy, which lasted until Aaron nearly nodded off at the table. She sent him to bed with a promise that she'd be up to tuck him in. Callie headed to her room and was soon engrossed in the pages of a novel.

"It was a great summer, wasn't it?" Kate said to Aaron, sitting on the edge of his bed.

"Sure."

"You learned to swim, buddy."

"Yep."

"And you got bigger and stronger and you weren't even lonely for your cousins." She felt a need to remind him of all the good things that had happened so he wouldn't dwell on JD's absence.

"Maybe a little." He was struggling to keep his eyes open.

"And Callie is coming to stay with us." She had managed to convince the caseworker that the media would go away now that JD was gone.

"Uh-huh." He gave up the battle and snuggled under the covers.

Kate rubbed his back for a few minutes, then slipped out of the room and went back downstairs. She wasn't the least bit tired. The encounter with Sam today had left her feeling unsettled, maybe a little jumpy.

Straightening the kitchen cupboards for the last time of the summer, she came across a half-full bottle of red wine. It was probably spoiled by now. She held it poised over the sink, ready to dump it out, then stopped herself.

What the heck, she thought, taking out a wineglass. She'd never tried drinking alone before. She'd never tried wallowing. In the past, she always made herself face the world with a positive attitude, come what may. Yet this was different, impossible to push aside or deny. A deep ache of melancholy tugged at her, and just for tonight, she decided to let it. Why not? This was supposed to be the summer of her independence, her reaffirmation that she was perfectly content being exactly who she was—a single mother, a writer, a daughter, a sister. Back in June, she had come here determined to recover from the blow of being fired and to emerge better and stronger for her efforts.

Instead, the impossible had happened. She had met a man and fallen from the dizzying height of a precipice, plunging heart and soul in love.

She smiled at the memory, even as she flinched from the hurt.

The bottle was left over from a night she recalled with painful clarity. It was the Merlot she and JD had shared one night. She remembered sitting on the porch swing with him and watching a family of ducks as the sun went down. She remembered thinking that everything had fit together so perfectly that night. Most especially her and JD. She let her mind drift through the summer, remembering the talk and laughter they'd shared, and every intimate touch, every romantic whisper.

Her hand trembled and the bottle neck clinked against the wineglass as she poured. Then she took both the glass and the bottle and headed outside. Two-fisted-drinking alone, she thought, walking down to the water's edge. That had to be a first for her.

A mysterious summer moon was up. Riding the jagged shoulders of the mountains around the lake, it appeared huge, and close enough to touch.

"Here's to you," Kate said, sitting on the dock and raising her glass to the moon. "And to . . . whatever." She couldn't think of a single uplifting thing to say. She drank deeply, noting that one thing had gone right today—the wine wasn't spoiled. The water lapped in gentle whispers at the shore. Across the way, she could see a few lights. There were a couple of boats out in the distance; she could see a bow lantern moving along the water.

She knocked back more wine and decided she was doing a terrible job of wallowing. She kept trying to be rational, to tell herself to snap out of it. What had happened to her was depressingly common, something that befell women every day. She had fallen in love and it hadn't worked out. Simple enough. But there was nothing easy about the way she was hurting.

The boat with the lantern seemed to be drawing closer. She swirled the wine in her glass and stared at the lone figure silhouetted against the moon, powerful arms moving in long, smooth strokes as he rowed.

Kate's heart shifted into overdrive. She sat glued to the spot, her legs dangling off the end of the dock. And finally, at the worst possible moment, the tears she had been fighting all day slipped down her cheeks. She tried wiping them away with the tail of her shirt, but the tears kept coming, an unending stream of relief and joy and fear and anticipation.

JD rowed the wherry alongside the dock and tied onto a mooring cleat. "I've heard it's rude to drink alone."

"I wasn't alone." She sniffed and brushed at her face again. "I was raising a toast to the moon."

"You're crazy, you know that?"

"I do," she said, and quit trying to stop the tears. Her

emotions were part of who she was. No more hiding or pretending. "What are you doing here?"

"I came by seaplane from Seattle. It's the quickest way."

"I meant, what are you doing?"

"Callie gave me a copy of your article to read," he said. "It's a fine piece and you deserve to be proud of it."

"And that's what you came here to tell me?"

"I've got a lot more to say. I'm just getting started." He stood and straddled the boat and dock, gallantly holding out his hand, palm up. "Get in. I'll take you for a ride."

She set aside the wine and the goblet, climbed to her feet and took his hand.

"Hello, gorgeous," he said, leaning down to kiss her. His kiss shattered her. Not that it was particularly sexy or passionate. It was just that the feel and taste of him were so dear to her that she nearly came apart from the sheer joy of kissing him, when only a moment ago she thought she'd never see him again.

She sat down in the boat, bracing her arms on either side. He pushed off and rowed easily out onto the dark, mysterious water. The wherry was a work of art. The light and dark planks, in their distinctive herringbone pattern, dazzled the eye. She knew the perfectly smooth finish had to be the result of hours—days—of patient sanding and restoring. Every joint and curve flowed seamlessly, inviting her hands to glide along the edges.

"I need to know why," she told him.

"Why I left, or why I came back?"

"Both. Why would you hide away, pretending it never happened?" she asked.

"Because it nearly ruined someone I care about."

She understood now. After the flurry of attention in Seattle, she got it. "I hate that you hid the truth from me."

"I hid it from everybody."

"I'm not 'everybody.'"

"That's true," he said quietly. "You became so much more, Kate."

It seemed a painful admission. "You did a wonderful thing, not just by saving the President, but by giving people hope. Watching you, knowing you did that, makes people feel safe again and know there's good in the world."

"I don't want to be anybody's great white hope," he said. "I just want to live my life."

"And is that what you were doing? Or were you just letting the days go by?"

He rowed for a few minutes without speaking. Then he said, "I stayed because you made me feel like I was living for the first time. And then I left because I don't want to put you in the spotlight. But . . . this is who I am." He spread his hands, palms up. "Someone who loves you even though you deserve better. Someone who'll be your best friend, your lover, for as long as you'll have me." He set the oars in the oarlocks and let the boat drift. "That's the answer to the second part of your question. It's why I came back, to do whatever it takes to be with you. I love you, Kate. I love everything about you."

She smiled through her tears. He claimed he'd never give her hearts and flowers and fairy tales. He didn't know that was exactly what he was doing now. "See?" she whispered. "That wasn't so hard."

"You're right. It's the easiest thing I've ever done."

"So . . . now what?" she asked.

He hesitated, and she feared he might have come back for the wrong reasons—a long-distance relationship, or one that was part-time. "JD—"

"I realized something when I was away. I don't want to be in L.A. if you're here. I want to do this, make a life with you, live with you and Aaron and Callie . . . I could forget L.A. and apply to UW. That is, if there's a reason for me to do that."

"Yes," she said, gripping the sides of the boat. "There is every reason to do that."

"You have to understand. All this—eventually, it'll die down, but not right away. There's a film in the works, and I can't stop it. My only hope is that it gets hung up in development limbo. Who knows how long the nosy reporters and photographers will be hanging around."

"Your mother couldn't handle it. I can," Kate said. "Callie and Aaron can, too. We'll do it together."

He smiled, and the moonlight was kind to his face, making him look young and idealistic and filled with hope. "Listen, if I go down on bended knee right now, this thing will capsize. So you'll have to use your imagination."

She was too full of everything to speak, so she nodded.

"You don't have to imagine this." He took out a small box and placed it in her hand. She felt the warm fur of velvet. In the moonlight, it looked royal blue. She opened it and saw the moon on a satin pillow, its beautiful white clarity reflected in every facet of the diamond solitaire.

"This is exactly. . . . How did you know?"

"Come on, Kate. What a question."

Oh, he knew her. He knew every dream that lived in her heart. He knew she wanted the fairy tale, and he was determined to give it to her. To have someone love her like this . . . she was overwhelmed.

"So will you?" he asked her. "Forever?"

She caught her breath and thought, this is it. The idea was startling and exhilarating and life-changing, not just for her, but for Aaron and maybe even Callie. And she wanted it so badly that she scared herself, but being scared was nothing new to her.

"Yes," she said, "yes, yes, yes." She pressed forward into his arms and the boat rocked but stayed upright, stirring the moonlight on the water into a pool of brightness.

Recipes for Summer Living

ROCKIN' CRAB DIP
courtesy of
www.AmericanFireFighter.com

Serve this with crackers—preferably on a Saturday, since that's apparatus cleaning day and the cook can help clean.

½ lb Maryland crabmeat, picked clean
1 8-oz package cream cheese
½ cup sour cream
2 tbsp mayonnaise
1 tbsp lemon juice
1 tsp Worcestershire sauce
½ tsp dry mustard
1 tbsp milk
¼ cup grated cheddar cheese
pinch garlic salt
a sprinkle of paprika, for garnish

Mix cream cheese, sour cream, mayo, lemon juice, Worcestershire sauce, mustard and garlic salt. Add enough milk to make a creamy consistency, then stir in half the grated cheese and all the crabmeat. Pour into greased 1-quart casserole. Top with remaining cheese. Bake for about 30 minutes at 325° F until mixture is bubbly and browned on top.

PORCH SWING FRENCH TOAST

Courtesy of Carole Eppler of Porch Swing Bed & Breakfast, Cheyenne, Wyoming.
This recipe won first place in the State of Wyoming Bed & Breakfast Recipe Contest. The award was presented by Wyoming's First Lady, Sheri Geringer.

Ingredients:
2 tbsp butter
4 eggs
½ cup orange juice
½ cup cream
1 8-oz can crushed pineapple
¼ cup sugar
1 tbsp grated orange zest
½ tsp vanilla
¼ tsp nutmeg
1 loaf French bread, cut into 1-inch slices
½ cup chopped pecans

Topping:
¼ cup butter, softened
½ cup firmly packed brown sugar
1 tbsp light corn syrup
½ cup chopped pecans

Method:

The night before, melt butter in a 9 x 13–inch pan and place bread in pan. Combine all ingredients and pour over bread. Combine topping ingredients, except for nuts. Spread topping over bread and sprinkle with nuts. Cover and refrigerate. The next morning, preheat oven to 350° F and bake 40 minutes or until golden. Serves 6.

CAMPFIRE TROUT

This seems like a lot of work, especially if you have to catch and clean the fish. Turn it into pure fun by getting a child to help.

small lake or rainbow trout; larger brookies
  work, too
corn on the cob
onion
tomato
lemon
butter
herbs
salt and pepper to taste

Husk corn carefully, keeping the husks intact while removing the silk. Sauté the onion in butter. Add the chopped tomatoes. Toss in herbs and seasonings.

Stuff the fish with this mixture and layer slices of lemon on the sides. Wrap individual fish in the corn husks, using twine or kitchen string to fasten the husks around the fish. Lay the bundles on the grill or the coals and cook about 10 minutes per side, until the fish flakes with a fork. Brush the corn with seasoned butter and grill alongside the fish.

CROWN OF ARTICHOKE HEART SALAD WITH GOAT CHEESE

Courtesy of C'est Si Bon restaurant, Port Angeles, Washington (*www.cestsibon-frenchcuisine.com*).

2 large artichokes
⅓ lb goat cheese
½ tsp Worcestershire sauce
salt, pepper, green peppercorn to taste
parsley, chives to taste
1 15 ½ oz can whole tomatoes
1-2 tbsp balsamic vinegar
1 mint leaf

Boil the artichokes and remove and save the leaves. Cut off the fuzzy part of the artichoke heart. Cut the artichoke heart into six wedges. In a food processor, add goat cheese, pinch of cayenne pepper, Worcestershire sauce, salt, pepper and green peppercorn. Grind up mixture, then place it in the middle of a salad plate. Surround the cheese with artichoke pieces, place chopped parsley and chives on top of the cheese. In a blender, mix tomato with mint, pepper, salt, vinegar, then strain, dribble it over the cheese and artichoke bottoms. Use the rest to dip the artichoke leaves.

ALL-SHOOK-UP ICE CREAM
Designed to keep restless children busy.

1 tbsp sugar or equivalent sugar substitute
½ cup half & half or cream
¼ tsp vanilla
6 tbsp rock salt
1 pint-size Ziploc plastic bag
1 gallon-size Ziploc plastic bag
ice cubes

1. Fill the gallon size plastic bag half-full of ice and add rock salt.
2. Put cream, vanilla and sugar into the small bag and seal it completely.
3. Place the small bag inside the large one and seal it, too.
4. Shake until mixture has turned into ice cream, about 6–8 minutes.
5. Rinse off the small bag, then open carefully and enjoy.
Optional: Add fresh fruit or nuts.

S'MORES FOR DUMMIES

This is the perfect remedy for burnt marshmallows. Toast a marshmallow, slip off the skin and roll the gooey marshmallow in miniature M&Ms. Sandwich between graham crackers and eat.

Center Point Publishing
600 Brooks Road ● PO Box 1
Thorndike ME 04986-0001 USA

(207) 568-3717

US & Canada:
1 800 929-9108

DOGGIE STARZ
PET PHOTOGRAPHY
Priceless memories at a low, low price

PHOTO SHOOT
CALL SHEET

ON SET: 9:00 am

STAR #1: Pig (Pug)

STAR #2: ~~Trevor (Dachshund)~~

PIG PIG
PIG PIG.

For that lovely cast back in '99.
I'm just so sorry . . .

Scholastic Canada Ltd.
604 King Street West, Toronto, Ontario M5V 1E1, Canada

Scholastic Inc.
557 Broadway, New York, NY 10012, USA

Scholastic Australia Pty Limited
PO Box 579, Gosford, NSW 2250, Australia

Scholastic New Zealand Limited
Private Bag 94407, Botany, Manukau 2163, New Zealand

Scholastic Children's Books
Euston House, 24 Eversholt Street, London NW1 1DB, UK

www.scholastic.ca

The artwork in this book is acrylic (with pens and pencils) on watercolour paper.
Typeset in Adobe Caslon.

Library and Archives Canada Cataloguing in Publication

Blabey, Aaron, author, illustrator

Pig the star / Aaron Blabey.

ISBN 978-1-4431-6337-8 (hardcover).--ISBN 978-1-4431-6338-5 (softcover)

I. Title.

PZ10.3.B519Ps 2018   j823'.92   C2017-906429-0

First published by Scholastic Australia in 2017.

This edition published by Scholastic Canada in 2018.

Text and illustrations copyright © 2017 by Aaron Blabey.

6 5 4 3 2 1   Printed in China   LFA   18 19 20 21 22 23

PIG the STAR

Aaron Blabey

Scholastic Canada Ltd.
Toronto New York London Auckland Sydney
Mexico City New Delhi Hong Kong Buenos Aires

Pig was a Pug
and I'm sorry to say,
he just LOVED attention.
He'd show off all day.

He'd shout, "LOOK AT ME!
I'm the BEST!
I'm a STAR!"

But then came the day
that he took it too far . . .

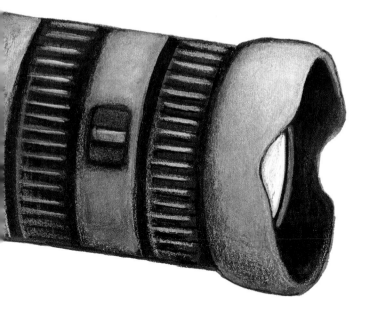

Yes, Trevor and Pig
had a big photo shoot.

They wore little costumes.

They looked really cute.

"Isn't this fun?" giggled Trevor with glee.

KING OF ROCK & ROLL

But Pig pushed right past him
and yelled,

"LOOK
AT
ME!"

"Aren't I just fabulous?

Aren't I divine?

Now back off, *Salami*!
These costumes are

MINE!"

Yes, Pig ruled the photos.

He hogged every shot.

He whispered to Trevor,
"I'm HOT and you're not."

And under the lights
as the camera went SNAP,
Pig felt like a rock star . . .

. . . and started to RAP—

"YO!

I'm a star, y'all!

Yeah, dog— I'm the BEST!

Now, get me a donut,
you sausage-shaped pest!"

But then something happened
that changed the whole shoot.
The man with the camera said . . .

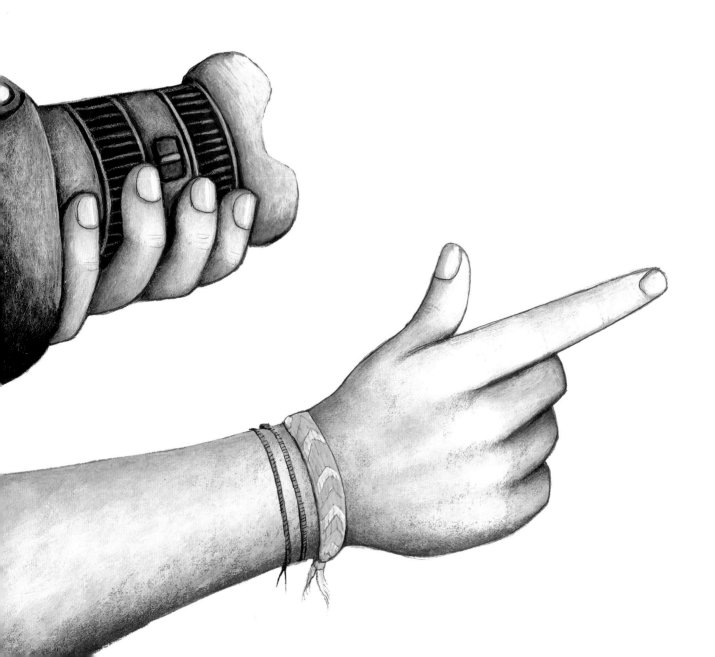

"*That* dog is CUTE!"

"Wow, Trevor's a STAR!"
the photographer said.

Pig couldn't believe it!

And then he saw RED.

He shrieked,

"I'M THE STAR!"

and he knocked Trevor flat!

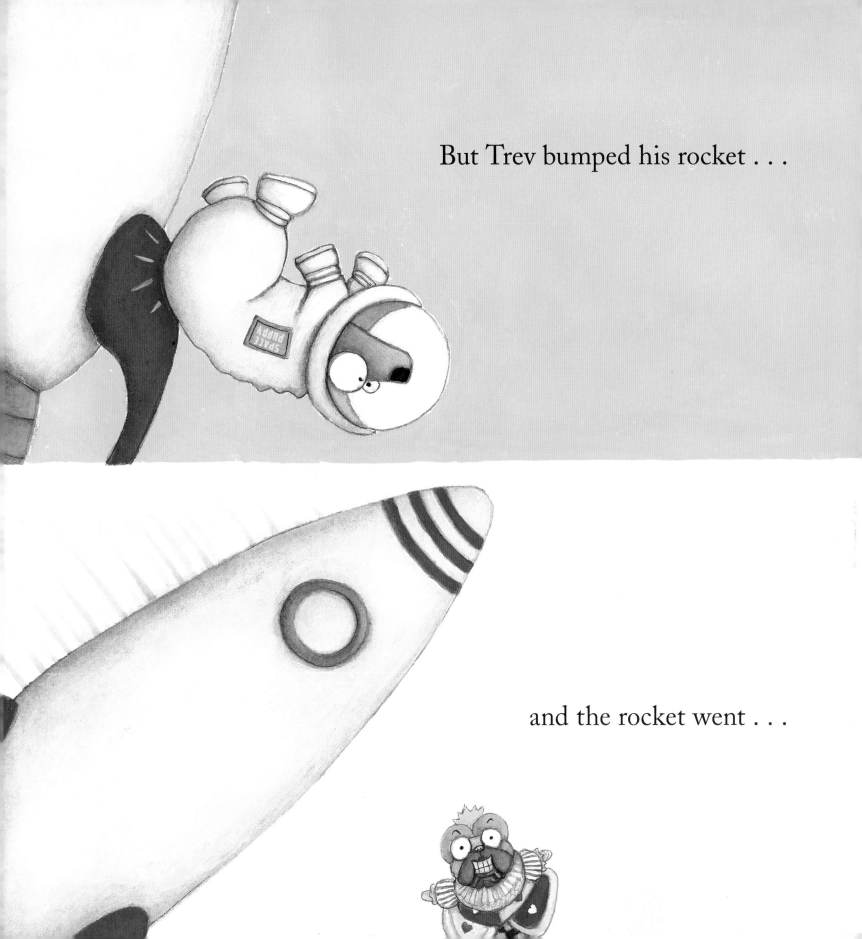

But Trev bumped his rocket . . .

and the rocket went . . .

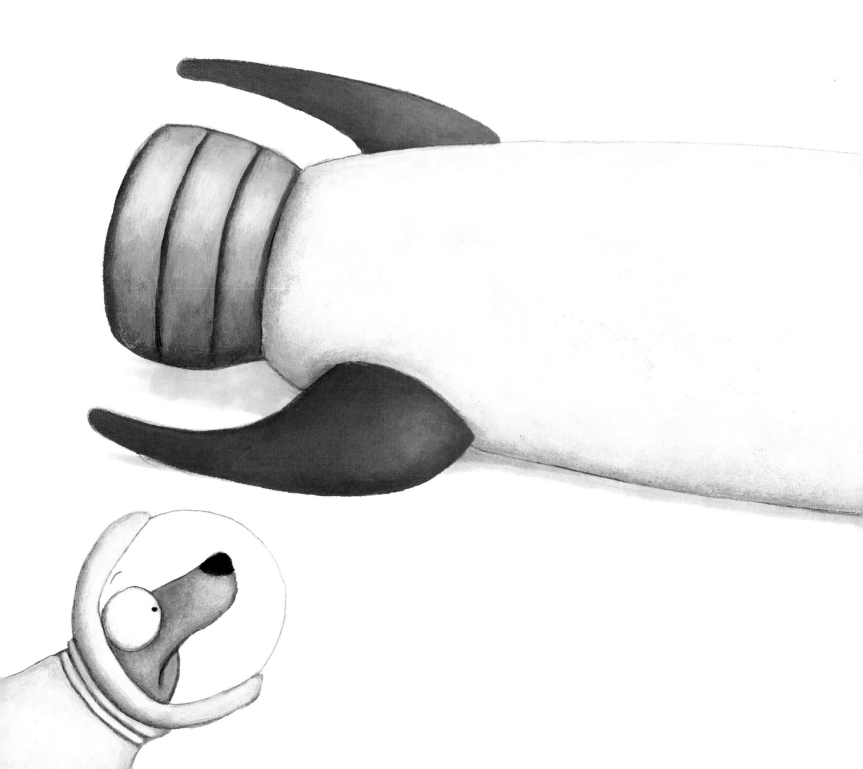

. . . SPLAT!

These days it's different,
I'm happy to say.
Pig's dreadful antics
have all gone away.

He's not such a show-off.
He's not such a swine.
And although it annoys him . . .

He lets Trevor shine.